Identity Theft

AND OTHER STORIES

NO LONGER PROPERTY OF
SEATTLE PUBLIC LIBRARY

Books by Robert J. Sawyer

NOVELS
Golden Fleece
End of an Era
The Terminal Experiment
Starplex
Frameshift
Illegal Alien
Factoring Humanity
Flashforward
Calculating God
Mindscan
Rollback

 The Neanderthal Parallax
Hominids
Humans
Hybrids

The Quintaglio Ascension
Far-Seer
Fossil Hunter
Foreigner

COLLECTIONS
Iterations (introduction by James Alan Gardner)
Relativity (introduction by Mike Resnick)
Identity Theft (introduction by Robert Charles Wilson)

ANTHOLOGIES
Tesseracts 6 (with Carolyn Clink)
Crossing the Line (with David Skene-Melvin)
Over the Edge (with Peter Sellers)
Boarding the Enterprise (with David Gerrold)

Identity Theft

AND OTHER STORIES

Robert J. Sawyer

Introduction by Robert Charles Wilson

Red Deer PRESS

Copyright © 2008 Robert J. Sawyer
Introduction © 2008 Robert Charles Wilson
Copyright for individual stories featured on page 286

5 4 3 2 1

All rights reserved. No part of this publication may be reproduced, stored in a retrieval system or transmitted, in any form or by any means, without the prior written permission of Red Deer Press or, in case of photocopying or other reprographic copying, a licence from Access Copyright (Canadian Copyright Licensing Agency), 1 Yonge Street, Suite 1900, Toronto, ON M5E 1E5, fax (416) 868-1621.

Published by Red Deer Press
A Fitzhenry & Whiteside Company
1512, 1800–4 Street S.W., Calgary, Alberta, Canada t2s 2s5
www.reddeerpress.com

Copyedited by Fiona Kelleghan
Cover and text design by Karen Thomas, Intuitive Design International Ltd.
Cover image courtesy NASA, EAS, D. Bennett (University of Notre Dame),
    and J. Anderson (Rice University)
Printed and bound in Canada by Friesens for Red Deer Press

Financial support provided by the Canada Council, and the Government of Canada through the Book Publishing Industry Development Program (BPIDP).

Canada Council   Conseil des Arts
for the Arts   du Canada

Library and Archives Canada Cataloguing in Publication
Sawyer, Robert J
    Identity theft and other stories / Robert J. Sawyer ; introduction by
Robert Charles Wilson.
ISBN 978-0-88995-411-3 (bound).—ISBN 978-0-88995-412-0 (pbk.)
    I. Title.
PS8587.A389835I34 2008   C813'.54   C2007-905117-0

United States Cataloguing-in-Publication Data
Sawyer, Robert J.
    Identity theft and other stories / introduction by Robert Charles Wilson ; Robert J.
Sawyer.
[240] p. : cm.
ISBN: 9780889954120 (pbk.)
1. Short stories, Canadian – 20th century. I. Wilson, Robert Charles. II. Title.
813.0108971 dc22   PR9199.3S248Id   2008

DEDICATION

For

Kirstin Morrell

A C K N O W L E D G M E N T S

Sincere thanks to the editors who originally published these stories: Lou Anders, Gregory Benford, Kristen Pederson Chew, Douglas Cudmore, Julie E. Czerneda, Martin H. Greenberg, John Helfers, Janis Ian, Mike Resnick, Stanley Schmidt, Larry Segriff, Mark Tier, Carol Toller, and Edo van Belkom. Thanks, too, to Bob Hilderley and Dennis Johnson for introducing me to the wonders of working with Canadian publishers; to Fitzhenry & Whiteside for buying this collection; and to Amy Hingston and Karen Petherick Thomas for shepherding it through production and publication.

Many thanks, also, to my agent, Ralph Vicinanza; to Robert Charles Wilson for the wonderful introduction; and to the friends who stood by me while I was writing these pieces, especially Carolyn Clink, David Livingstone Clink, Marcel Gagné, Terence M. Green, Kirstin Morrell, Sally Tomasevic, and Andrew Weiner.

Finally, thanks to the 1,200 members of my online discussion group. Feel free to join us at:

www.groups.yahoo.com/group/robertjsawyer/

C O N T E N T S

Rob Sawyer: Ignore Him

BY ROBERT CHARLES WILSON

Let me explain.

I was asked to introduce Robert J. Sawyer to readers of this collection of his stories—but biographical information about Rob is easy to come by. See, for instance, the About the Author at the end of this book (but don't skip the intervening stuff: you won't be disappointed). Or check out his website, sfwriter.com. Rob has even been the subject of an hour-long Canadian TV profile, *Inside the Mind of Robert J. Sawyer*. You can fairly readily discover that he's won any number of awards—the Hugo, the Nebula, the John W. Campbell Memorial Award, the *Science Fiction Chronicle* Reader Award, Canada's Aurora, Japan's *Seiun*, China's Galaxy Award, France's *Le Grand Prix de l'Imaginaire*, Spain's *Premio UPC de Ciencia Ficción*, some of these more than once. All this is well-known.

And his literary career is easy enough to chart, from his first novel in 1990, *Golden Fleece*, through the Neanderthal Parallax trilogy (*Hominids, Humans,* and *Hybrids*), to his latest, *Rollback*, with stops for short fiction and nonfiction along the way.

But I want you to ignore all that.

Ignore it, because the avalanche of honors and achievements can begin to seem intimidating. And that is precisely what Rob is not: intimidating. In fact he's one of the most approachable SF writers around.

Like many readers who came to SF at an impressionable age, I once believed that a published author must be an Olympian being—a wise or at least worldly philosopher-god who rises at noon, feeds his muse a diet of scotch/rocks, and debauches his soul into the keys of a rusty Underwood Noiseless while the rest of the world sleeps. Great, but how would you actually *talk* to such a creature?

Rob exists to defy these misconceptions. Wise he may be; but he's more earthy than Olympian, prefers chocolate milk to scotch, and writes from the comfort of a La-Z-Boy recliner. (I don't know what time he gets out of bed.) He'll talk to you about paleoanthropology, if you like, but he's equally at home reminiscing about *Thunderbirds* or *Josie and the Pussycats*. (He probably has a favorite Pussycat.) He possesses a well-developed sense of humor, but it's more generous than cutting. He enjoys meeting people and will usually give you the benefit of the doubt in a conflict; you can get on the wrong side of Robert J. Sawyer, but it takes work.

He's also conspicuously Canadian, in a way those of us who wander the tenebrous nightland between nationalities (I'm an expat American, myself) can never be. I think this makes some Americans uneasy—the unspoken belief that Canada really is, as the beer ads say, the best part of North America. It's hard to miss it in his work. But Rob also practices that most Canadian of virtues, Looking at Both Sides of the Question, which means that his love for his native country never comes off as jingoistic or anti-American. And for those of us who *do* know Canada there's a pleasing resonance in Rob's writing—he's privy to the secret handshakes; he can tell the difference between Wendy Mesley and Peter Mansbridge, Uncle Bobby and Jerome the Giraffe, Jean Chrétien and the Honourable Member from Kicking Horse Pass.

But again I have to emphasize, don't let any of this intimidate you. Rob grew up in suburban Toronto, went to school there, picked up some public-appearance skills at Ryerson University (which is why he's more at home at a podium than some of us reclusive schlubs and stammering poets), dabbled in journalism before turning to fiction full-time, married a wonderful woman named Carolyn Clink, and currently lives with her, his books, and a collection of hominid skulls in a penthouse condo in Mississauga.

Want to know more? Ask Rob, if you see him at a science-fiction convention or writer's conference (he goes to lots of them). As I said, he's approachable. And so is his fiction—it's among the most accessible SF being produced today, enjoyed with equal pleasure by hard-core fans and those who normally disdain the genre. Ignore his laurels and plaudits, which is what I meant by the smartass title of this introduction. But please don't ignore this collection of his recent short stories: the work of one of the most interesting, outgoing, and thoughtful SF writers walking the earth today.

Identity Theft

Doubleday's venerable Science Fiction Book Club, which normally only publishes reprint editions of books, recently experimented with doing its own original anthologies—special collections of brand-new stories that would only be available through them. One of the first such collections was an anthology edited by Mike Resnick called Down These Dark Spaceways. *It contains six SF hard-boiled detective novellas by award-winning authors (Mike, me, Catherine Asaro, David Gerrold, Jack McDevitt, and Robert Reed).*

Why did Mike ask me to contribute? Well, my science fiction often has crime or mystery overtones; indeed, I won the Crime Writers of Canada's Arthur Ellis Award for Best Short Story of 1993 for my time-travel tale "Just Like Old Times," and The Globe and Mail: Canada's National Newspaper *called my SF courtroom drama* Illegal Alien *"the best Canadian mystery of 1997." My other SF/crime crossovers include the novels* Golden Fleece, Fossil Hunter, The Terminal Experiment, Frameshift, Flashforward, Hominids, *and* Mindscan.

My story for Down These Dark Spaceways *follows. At 25,000 words, it's by far the longest piece in this collection, so I'm leading off with it—but I'll note up front that the last story in this book, "Biding Time," is a sequel to it.*

To my delight, "Identity Theft" won Spain's Premio UPC de Ciencia Ficción, which, at 6,000 euros, is the world's largest cash prize for science-fiction writing. It was also a finalist for the Canadian Science Fiction and Fantasy Award ("the Aurora"), as well as for the top two awards in the science-fiction field: the World Science Fiction Society's Hugo Award (SF's "People's Choice" Award) and the Science Fiction and Fantasy Writers of America's Nebula Award (SF's "Academy Award")—making "Identity Theft" the first (and so far only) original publication of the SFBC to ever be nominated for those awards.

The door to my office slid open. "Hello," I said, rising from my chair. "You must be my nine o'clock." I said it as if I had a ten o'clock and an eleven o'clock, but I didn't. The whole Martian economy was in a slump, and, even though I was the only private detective on Mars, this was the first new case I'd had in weeks.

"Yes," said a high, feminine voice. "I'm Cassandra Wilkins."

I let my eyes rove up and down her body. It was very good work; I wondered if she'd had quite so perfect a figure before transferring. People usually ordered replacement bodies that, at least in broad strokes, resembled their originals, but few could resist improving them. Men got buffer, women got curvier, and everyone modified their faces, removing asymmetries, wrinkles, and imperfections. If and when I transferred myself, I'd eliminate the gray in my blond hair and get a new nose that would look like my current one had before it'd been broken a couple of times.

"A pleasure to meet you, Ms. Wilkins," I said. "I'm Alexander Lomax. Please have a seat."

She was a little thing, no more than a hundred and fifty centimeters, and she was wearing a stylish silver-gray blouse and skirt, but no makeup or jewelry. I'd expected her to sit down with a catlike, fluid movement, given her delicate features, but she just sort of plunked herself into the chair. "Thanks," she said. "I do hope you can help me, Mr. Lomax. I really do."

Rather than immediately sitting down myself, I went to the coffee maker. I filled my own mug, then opened my mouth to offer Cassandra a cup, but closed it before doing so; transfers, of course, didn't drink. "What seems to be the problem?" I said, returning to my chair.

It's hard reading a transfer's expression: the facial sculpting was usually very good, but the movements were somewhat restrained. "My husband— oh, my goodness, Mr. Lomax, I hate to even say this!" She looked down at her hands. "My husband ... he's disappeared."

I raised my eyebrows; it was pretty damned difficult for someone to disappear here. New Klondike was only three kilometers in diameter, all of it locked under the dome. "When did you last see him?"

"Three days ago."

My office was small, but it did have a window. Through it, I could see one of the supporting arches that helped to hold up the transparent dome over New Klondike. Outside the dome, a sandstorm was raging, orange clouds obscuring the sun. Auxiliary lights on the arch compensated for that, but Martian daylight was never very bright. That's a reason why even those who had a choice were reluctant to return to Earth: after years of only dim illumination, apparently the sun as seen from there was excruciating. "Is your husband, um, like you?" I asked.

She nodded. "Oh, yes. We both came here looking to make our fortune, just like everyone else."

I shook my head. "I mean is he also a transfer?"

"Oh, sorry. Yes, he is. In fact, we both just transferred."

"It's an expensive procedure," I said. "Could he have been skipping out on paying for it?"

Cassandra shook her head. "No, no. Joshua found one or two nice specimens early on. He used the money from selling those pieces to buy the NewYou franchise here. That's where we met—after I threw in the towel on sifting dirt, I got a job in sales there. Anyway, of course, we both got to transfer at cost." She was actually wringing her synthetic hands. "Oh, Mr. Lomax, please help me! I don't know what I'm going to do without my Joshua!"

"You must love him a lot," I said, watching her pretty face for more than just the pleasure of looking at it; I wanted to gauge her sincerity as she replied. After all, people often disappeared because things were bad at home, but spouses are rarely forthcoming about that.

"Oh, I do!" said Cassandra. "I love him more than I can say. Joshua is a wonderful, wonderful man." She looked at me with pleading eyes. "You have to help me get him back. You just have to!"

I looked down at my coffee mug; steam was rising from it. "Have you tried the police?"

Cassandra made a sound that I guessed was supposed to be a snort: it had the right roughness, but was dry as Martian sand. "Yes. They—oh, I hate to speak ill of anyone, Mr. Lomax! Believe me, it's not my way, but—

well, there's no ducking it, is there? They were useless. Just totally useless."

I nodded slightly; it's a story I heard often enough—I owed most of what little livelihood I had to the local cops' incompetence and indifference. "Who did you speak to?"

"A—a detective, I guess he was; he didn't wear a uniform. I've forgotten his name."

"What did he look like?"

"Red hair, and—"

"That's Mac," I said. She looked puzzled, so I said his full name. "Dougal McCrae."

"McCrae, yes," said Cassandra. She shuddered a bit, and she must have noticed my surprised reaction to that. "Sorry," she said. "I just didn't like the way he looked at me."

I resisted running my eyes over her body just then; I'd already done so, and I could remember what I'd seen. I guess her original figure hadn't been like this one; if it had, she'd certainly be used to admiring looks from men by now.

"I'll have a word with McCrae," I said. "See what's already been done. Then I'll pick up where the cops left off."

"Would you?" Her green eyes seemed to dance. "Oh, thank you, Mr. Lomax! You're a good man—I can tell!"

I shrugged a little. "I can show you two ex-wives and a half-dozen bankers who'd disagree."

"Oh, no," she said. "Don't say things like that! You *are* a good man, I'm sure of it. Believe me, I have a sense about these things. You're a good man, and I know you won't let me down."

Naïve woman; she'd probably thought the same thing about her husband—until he'd run off. "Now, what can you tell me about your husband? Joshua, is it?"

"Yes, that's right. His full name is Joshua Connor Wilkins—and it's Joshua, never just Josh, thank you very much." I nodded. Guys who were anal about being called by their full first names never bought a round, in my experience. Maybe it was a good thing that this clown was gone.

"Yes," I said. "Go on." I didn't have to take notes, of course. My office computer was recording everything, and would extract whatever was useful into a summary file for me.

Cassandra ran her synthetic lower lip back and forth beneath her artificial upper teeth, thinking for a moment. Then: "Well, he was born in Calgary, Alberta, and he's thirty-eight years old. He moved to Mars seven mears ago." Mears were Mars-years; about double the length of those on Earth.

"Do you have a picture?"

"I can access one," she said. She pointed at my desk terminal. "May I?"

I nodded, and Cassandra reached over to grab the keyboard. In doing so, she managed to knock over my coffee mug, spilling hot joe all over her dainty hand. She let out a small yelp of pain. I got up, grabbed a towel, and began wiping up the mess. "I'm surprised that hurt," I said. "I mean, I *do* like my coffee hot, but ..."

"Transfers feel pain, Mr. Lomax," she said, "for the same reason that biologicals do. When you're flesh-and-blood, you need a signaling system to warn you when your parts are being damaged; same is true for those of us who have transferred. Admittedly, artificial bodies are much more durable, of course."

"Ah," I said.

"Sorry," she replied. "I've explained this so many times now—you know, at work. Anyway, please forgive me about your desk."

I made a dismissive gesture. "Thank God for the paperless office, eh? Don't worry about it." I gestured at the keyboard; fortunately, none of the coffee had gone down between the keys. "You were going to show me a picture?"

"Oh, right." She spoke some commands, and the terminal responded— making me wonder what she'd wanted the keyboard for. But then she used it to type in a long passphrase; presumably she didn't want to say hers aloud in front of me. She frowned as she was typing it in, and backspaced to make a correction; multiword passphrases were easy to say, but hard to type if you weren't adept with a keyboard—and the more security conscious you were, the longer the passphrase you used.

Anyway, she accessed some repository of her personal files, and brought up a photo of Joshua-never-Josh Wilkins. Given how attractive Mrs. Wilkins was, he wasn't what I expected. He had cold, gray eyes, hair buzzed so short as to be nonexistent, and a thin, almost lipless mouth; the overall effect was reptilian. "That's before," I said. "What about after? What's he look like now that he's transferred?"

"Umm, pretty much the same," she said.

"Really?" If I'd had that kisser, I'd have modified it for sure. "Do you have pictures taken since he moved his mind?"

"No actual pictures," said Cassandra. "After all, he and I only just transferred. But I can go into the NewYou database, and show you the plans from which his new face was manufactured." She spoke to the terminal some more, and then typed in another lengthy passphrase. Soon enough, she had a computer-graphics rendition of Joshua's head on my screen.

"You're right," I said, surprised. "He didn't change a thing. Can I get copies of all this?"

She nodded, and spoke some more commands, transferring various documents into local storage.

"All right," I said. "My fee is two hundred solars an hour."

"That's fine, that's fine, of course! I don't care about the money, Mr. Lomax—not at all. I just want Joshua back. Please tell me you'll find him."

"I will," I said, smiling my most reassuring smile. "Don't you worry about that. He can't have gone far."

▌▐ ▌▐ ▌▐

Actually, of course, Joshua Wilkins *could* perhaps have gone quite far—so my first order of business was to eliminate that possibility.

No spaceships had left Mars in the last ten days, so he couldn't be off-planet. There was a giant airlock in the south through which large spaceships could be brought inside for dry-dock work, but it hadn't been cracked open in weeks. And, although a transfer could exist freely on the Martian surface, there were only four personnel airlocks leading out of the dome, and they all had security guards. I visited each of those airlocks and checked, just to be sure, but the only people who had gone out in the last three days were the usual crowds of hapless fossil hunters, and every one of them had returned when the dust storm began.

I remember when this town had started up: "The Great Fossil Rush," they called it. Weingarten and O'Reilly, two early private explorers who had come here at their own expense, had found the first fossils on Mars and had made a fortune selling them back on Earth. More valuable than any precious metal; rarer than anything else in the solar system—actual evidence of extraterrestrial life! Good fist-sized specimens went for millions in online auctions; excellent football-sized ones for billions. There was no greater status symbol than to own the petrified remains of a Martian pentaped or rhizomorph.

Of course, Weingarten and O'Reilly wouldn't say precisely where they'd found their specimens, but it had been easy enough to prove that their spaceship had landed here, in the Isidis Planitia basin. Other treasure hunters started coming, and New Klondike—the one and only town on Mars—was born.

Native life was never widely dispersed on Mars; the single ecosystem that had ever existed here seemed to have been confined to an area not much bigger than Rhode Island. Some of the prospectors—excuse me, fossil hunters—who came shortly after W&O's first expedition found a few nice specimens, although most had been badly blasted by blowing sand.

Somewhere, though, was the mother lode: a bed that produced fossils more finely preserved than even those from Earth's famed Burgess Shale. Weingarten and O'Reilly had known where it was—they'd stumbled on it by pure dumb luck, apparently. But they'd both been killed when their heat shield separated from their lander when re-entering Earth's atmosphere after their third expedition here—and, in the twenty mears since, no one had yet rediscovered it.

People were still looking, of course. There'd always been a market for transferring consciousness; the potentially infinite lifespan was hugely appealing. But here on Mars, the demand was particularly brisk, since artificial bodies could spend days or even weeks on the surface, searching for paleontological gold, without worrying about running out of air. Of course, a serious sandstorm could blast the synthetic flesh from metal bones and scour those bones until they were whittled to nothing; that's why no one was outside right now.

Anyway, Joshua-never-Josh Wilkins was clearly not outside the dome, and he hadn't taken off in a spaceship. Wherever he was hiding, it was somewhere in New Klondike. I can't say he was breathing the same air I was, because he wasn't breathing at all. But he was *here*, somewhere. All I had to do was find him.

I didn't want to duplicate the efforts of the police, although "efforts" was usually too generous a term to apply to the work of the local constabulary; "cursory attempts" probably was closer to the truth, if I knew Mac.

New Klondike had twelve radial roadways, cutting across the nine concentric rings of buildings under the dome. My office was at dome's edge; I could have taken a hovertram into the center, but I preferred to walk. A good detective knew what was happening on the streets, and the hovertrams, dilapidated though they were, sped by too fast for that.

I didn't make any bones about staring at the transfers I saw along the way. They ranged in style from really sophisticated models, like Cassandra Wilkins, to things only a step up from the Tin Woodman of Oz. Of course, those who'd contented themselves with second-rate synthetic forms doubtless believed they'd trade up when they eventually happened upon some decent specimens. Poor saps; no one had found truly spectacular remains for mears, and lots of people were giving up and going back to Earth, if they could afford the passage, or were settling in to lives of, as Thoreau would have it, quiet desperation, their dreams as dead as the fossils they'd never found.

I continued walking easily along; Mars gravity is about a third of Earth's. Some people were stuck here because they'd let their muscles atrophy; they'd never be able to hack a full gee again. Me, I was stuck here for other reasons, but I worked out more than most—Gully's Gym, over by the shipyards— and so still had reasonably strong legs; I could walk comfortably all day if I had to.

The cop shop was a five-story building—it could be that tall, this near the center of the dome—with walls that had once been white, but were now a grimy grayish pink. The front doors were clear alloquartz, same as the overhead dome, and they slid aside as I walked up to them. At the side of the lobby was a long red desk—as if we don't see enough red on Mars—with a map showing the Isidis Planitia basin; New Klondike was a big circle off to one side.

The desk sergeant was a flabby lowbrow named Huxley, whose uniform always seemed a size too small for him. "Hey, Hux," I said, walking over. "Is Mac in?"

Huxley consulted a monitor, then nodded. "Yeah, he's in, but he don't see just anyone."

"I'm not just anyone, Hux. I'm the guy who picks up the pieces after you clowns bungle things."

Huxley frowned, trying to think of a rejoinder. "Yeah, well ..." he said, at last.

"Oooh," I said. "Good one, Hux! Way to put me in my place."

He narrowed his eyes. "You ain't as funny as you think you are, Lomax," he said.

"Of course I'm not," I said. "Nobody could be *that* funny." I nodded at the secured inner door. "Going to buzz me through?"

"Only to be rid of you," said Huxley. So pleased was he with the wit of this remark that he repeated it: "Only to be rid of you."

Huxley reached below the counter, and the inner door—an unmarked black panel—slid aside. I pantomimed tipping a nonexistent hat at Hux, and headed into the station proper. I then walked down the corridor to McCrae's office; the door was open, so I rapped my knuckles against the plastic jamb.

"Lomax!" he said, looking up. "Decided to turn yourself in?"

"Very funny, Mac," I said. "You and Hux should go on the road together."

He snorted. "What can I do for you, Alex?"

Mac was a skinny biological, with shaggy orange eyebrows shielding his blue eyes. "I'm looking for a guy named Joshua Wilkins."

Mac had a strong Scottish brogue—so strong, I figured it must be an affectation. "Ah, yes," he said. "Who's your client? The wife?"

I nodded.

"A bonnie lass," he said.

"That she is," I said. "Anyway, you tried to find her husband, this Wilkins ..."

"We looked around, yeah," said Mac. "He's a transfer, you knew that?" I nodded.

"Well," Mac said, "she gave us the plans for his new face—precise measurements, and all that. We've been feeding all the video made by public security cameras through facial-recognition software. So far, no luck."

I smiled. That's about as far as Mac's detective work normally went: things he could do without hauling his bony ass out from behind his desk. "How much of New Klondike do they cover now?" I asked.

"It's down to sixty percent of the public areas," said Mac. People kept smashing the cameras, and the city didn't have the time or money to replace them.

"You'll let me know if you find anything?"

Mac drew his shaggy eyebrows together. "You know the privacy laws, Alex. I can't divulge what the security cameras see."

I reached into my pocket, pulled out a fifty-solar coin, and flipped it. It went up rapidly, but came down in what still seemed like slow motion to me, even after all these years on Mars; Mac didn't require any special reflexes to catch it in midair. "Of course," he said, "I suppose we could make an exception ..."

"Thanks. You're a credit to law-enforcement officials everywhere."

He snorted again, then: "Say, what kind of heat you packing these days? You still carrying that old Smith & Wesson?"

"I've got a license," I said, narrowing my eyes.

"Oh, I know, I know. But be careful, eh? The times, they are a-changin'. Bullets aren't much use against a transfer, and there are getting to be more of those each day."

I nodded. "So I've heard. How do you guys handle them?"

"Until recently, as little as possible," said Mac. "Turning a blind eye, and all that."

"Saves getting up," I said.

Mac didn't take offense. "Exactly. But let me show you something." We left his office, went further down the corridor and entered another room.

He pointed to a device on the table. "Just arrived from Earth," he said. "The latest thing."

It was a wide, flat disk, maybe half a meter in diameter, and five centimeters thick. There were a pair of U-shaped handgrips attached to the edge, opposite each other. "What is it?" I asked.

"A broadband disrupter," he said. He picked it up and held it in front of himself, like a gladiator's shield. "It discharges an oscillating multi-frequency electromagnetic pulse. From a distance of four meters or less, it will completely fry the artificial brain of a transfer—killing it as effectively as a bullet kills a human."

"I don't plan on killing anyone," I said.

"That's what you said the last time."

Ouch. Still, maybe he had a point. "I don't suppose you have a spare one I can borrow?"

Mac laughed. "Are you kidding? This is the only one we've got so far."

"Well, then," I said, heading for the door, "I guess I'd better be careful."

▋▊ ▋▊ ▋▊

My next stop was the NewYou building. I took Third Avenue, one of the radial streets of the city, out the five blocks to it. The building was two stories tall and was made, like most structures here, of red laser-fused Martian sand bricks. Flanking the main doors were a pair of wide allo-quartz display windows, showing dusty artificial bodies dressed in fashions from about two mears ago; it was high time somebody updated things.

Inside, the store was part showroom and part workshop, with spare components scattered about: here, a white-skinned artificial hand; there, a black lower leg; on shelves, synthetic eyes and spools of colored monofilament that I guessed were used to simulate hair. There were also all sorts of internal parts on worktables: motors and hydraulic pumps and joint hinges. A half-dozen technicians were milling around, assembling new bodies or repairing old ones.

Across the room, I spotted Cassandra Wilkins, wearing a beige suit today. She was talking with a man and a woman, who were biological;

potential customers, presumably. "Hello, Cassandra," I said, after I'd closed the distance between us.

"Mr. Lomax!" she said, excusing herself from the couple. "I'm so glad you're here—so very glad! What news do you have?"

"Not much," I said. "I've been to visit the cops, and I thought I should start my investigation here. After all, your husband owned this franchise, right?"

Cassandra nodded enthusiastically. "I knew I was doing the right thing hiring you," she said. "I just knew it! Why, do you know that lazy detective McCrae never stopped by here—not even once!"

I smiled. "Mac's not the outdoorsy type," I said. "And, well, you get what you pay for."

"Isn't that the truth?" said Cassandra. "Isn't that just the God's honest truth!"

"You said your husband moved his mind recently?"

She nodded her head. "Yes. All of that goes on upstairs, though. This is just sales and service down here."

"Can you show me?" I asked.

She nodded again. "Of course—anything you want to see, Mr. Lomax!" What I wanted to see was under that beige suit—nothing beat the perfection of a transfer's body—but I kept that thought to myself. Cassandra looked around the room, then motioned for another staff member—also female, also a transfer, also gorgeous, and this one did wear tasteful makeup and jewelry—to come over. "I'm sorry," Cassandra said to the two customers she'd abandoned a few moments ago. "Miss Takahashi here will look after you." She then turned to me. "This way."

We went through a curtained doorway and up a set of stairs. "Here's our scanning room," said Cassandra, indicating the left-hand one of a pair of doors; both doors had little windows in them. She stood on tiptoe to look in the scanning-room window, and nodded, apparently satisfied by what she saw, then opened the door. Two people were inside: a balding man of about forty, who was seated, and a standing woman who looked twenty-five; the woman was a transfer herself, though, so there was no way of knowing her real age. "So sorry to interrupt," Cassandra said. She looked at the man in the chair, while gesturing at me. "This is Alexander Lomax. He's providing some, ah, consulting services for us."

The man looked at me, surprised, then said, "Klaus Hansen," by way of introduction.

"Would you mind ever so much if Mr. Lomax watched while the scan was being done?" asked Cassandra.

Hansen considered this for a moment, frowning his long, thin face. But then he nodded. "Sure. Why not?"

"Thanks," I said. "I'll just stand over here." I moved to the far wall and leaned back against it.

The chair Hansen was sitting in looked a lot like a barber's chair. The female transfer who wasn't Cassandra reached up above the chair and pulled down a translucent hemisphere that was attached by an articulated arm to the ceiling. She kept lowering it until all of Hansen's head was covered, and then she turned to a control console.

The hemisphere shimmered slightly, as though a film of oil was washing over its surface; the scanning field, I supposed.

Cassandra was standing next to me, arms crossed in front of her chest. It was an unnatural-looking pose, given her large bosom. "How long does the scanning take?" I asked.

"It's a quantum-mechanical process," she replied. "So the scanning is rapid. But it'll take about ten minutes to move the data into the artificial brain. And then ..."

"And then?" I said.

She lifted her shoulders, as if the rest didn't need to be spelled out. "Why, and then Mr. Hansen will be able to live forever."

"Ah," I said.

"Come along," said Cassandra. "Let's go see the other side." We left that room, closing its door behind us, and entered the one next door. This room was a mirror image of the previous one, which I guess was appropriate. Standing erect in the middle of the room, supported by a metal armature, was Hansen's new body, dressed in a fashionable blue suit; its eyes were closed. Also in the room was a male NewYou technician, who was biological.

I walked around, looking at the artificial body from all angles. The replacement Hansen still had a bald spot, although its diameter had been reduced by half. And, interestingly, Hansen had opted for a sort of permanent designer-stubble look; the biological him was clean-shaven at the moment.

Suddenly the simulacrum's eyes opened. "Wow," said a voice that was the same as the one I'd heard from the man next door. "That's incredible."

"How do you feel, Mr. Hansen?" asked the male technician.

"Fine," he said. "Just fine."

"Good," the technician said. "There'll be some settling-in adjustments, of course. Let's just check to make sure all your parts are working ..."

"And there it is," said Cassandra, to me. "Simple as that." She led me out of the room, back into the corridor.

"Fascinating," I said. I pointed at the left-hand door. "When do you take care of the original?"

"That's already been done. We do it in the chair."

I stared at the closed door, and I like to think I suppressed my shudder enough so that Cassandra was unaware of it. "All right," I said. "I guess I've seen enough."

Cassandra looked disappointed. "Are you sure don't want to look around some more?"

"Why?" I said. "Is there anything else worth seeing?"

"Oh, I don't know," said Cassandra. "It's a big place. Everything on this floor, everything downstairs ... everything in the basement."

I blinked. "You've got a basement?" Almost no Martian buildings had basements; the permafrost layer was very hard to dig through.

"Yes," she said. "Oh, yes." She paused, then looked away. "Of course, no one ever goes down there; it's just storage."

"I'll have a look," I said.

And that's where I found him.

He was lying behind some large storage crates, face down, a sticky pool of machine oil surrounding his head. Next to him was a fusion-powered jackhammer, the kind many of the fossil hunters had for removing surface rocks. And next to the jackhammer was a piece of good old-fashioned paper. On it, in block letters, was written, "I'm so sorry, Cassie. It's just not the same."

It's hard to commit suicide, I guess, when you're a transfer. Slitting your wrists does nothing significant. Poison doesn't work, and neither does drowning.

But Joshua-never-anything-else-at-all-anymore Wilkins had apparently found a way. From the looks of it, he'd leaned back against the rough cement wall, and, with his strong artificial arms, had held up the jackhammer, placing its bit against the center of his forehead. And then he'd held down on the jackhammer's twin triggers, letting the unit run until it had managed to pierce through his titanium skull and scramble the soft material of his artificial brain. When his brain died, his thumbs let up on the triggers, and he dropped the jackhammer, then tumbled over himself. His head had twisted sideways when it hit the concrete floor. Everything below his eyebrows was intact; it was clearly the same face Cassandra Wilkins had shown me.

I headed up the stairs and found Cassandra, who was chatting in her animated style with another customer.

"Cassandra," I said, pulling her aside. "Cassandra, I'm very sorry, but ..."

She looked at me, her green eyes wide. "What?"

"I've found your husband. And he's dead."

She opened her pretty mouth, closed it, then opened it again. She looked like she might fall over, even with gyroscopes stabilizing her. I put an arm around her shoulders, but she didn't seem comfortable with it, so I let her go. "My ... God," she said at last. "Are you ... are you positive?"

"Sure looks like him," I said.

"My God," she said again. "What ... what happened?"

No nice way to say it. "Looks like he killed himself."

A couple of Cassandra's coworkers had come over, wondering what all the commotion was about. "What's wrong?" asked one of them—the same Miss Takahashi I'd seen earlier.

"Oh, Reiko," said Cassandra. "Joshua is dead!"

Customers were noticing what was going on, too. A burly flesh-and-blood man, with arms as thick around as most men's legs, came across the room; he seemed to be the boss here. Reiko Takahashi had already drawn Cassandra into her arms—or vice-versa; I'd been looking away when it had happened—and was stroking Cassandra's artificial hair. I let the boss do what he could to calm the crowd, while I used my commlink to call Mac and inform him of Joshua Wilkins's suicide.

■ ■ ■

Detective Dougal McCrae of New Klondike's finest arrived about twenty minutes later, accompanied by two uniforms. "How's it look, Alex?" Mac asked.

"Not as messy as some of the biological suicides I've seen," I said. "But it's still not a pretty sight."

"Show me."

I led Mac downstairs. He read the note without picking it up.

The burly man soon came down, too, followed by Cassandra Wilkins, who was holding her artificial hand to her artificial mouth.

"Hello, again, Mrs. Wilkins," said Mac, moving to interpose his body between her and the prone form on the floor. "I'm terribly sorry, but I'll need you to make an official identification."

I lifted my eyebrows at the irony of requiring the next of kin to actually look at the body to be sure of who it was, but that's what we'd gone back to with transfers. Privacy laws prevented any sort of ID chip or tracking device being put into artificial bodies. In fact, that was one of the many incentives to transfer; you no longer left fingerprints or a trail of identifying DNA everywhere you went.

Cassandra nodded bravely; she was willing to accede to Mac's request. He stepped aside, a living curtain, revealing the artificial body with the gaping head wound. She looked down at it. I'd expected her to quickly avert her eyes, but she didn't; she just kept staring.

Finally, Mac said, very gently, "Is that your husband, Mrs. Wilkins?"

She nodded slowly. Her voice was soft. "Yes. Oh, my poor, poor Joshua ..."

Mac stepped over to talk to the two uniforms, and I joined them. "What do you do with a dead transfer?" I asked. "Seems pointless to call in the medical examiner."

By way of answer, Mac motioned to the burly man. The man touched his own chest and raised his eyebrows in the classic "Who, me?" expression. Mac nodded again. The man looked left and right, like he was crossing some imaginary road, and then came over. "Yeah?"

"You seem to be the senior employee here," said Mac. "Am I right?"

The man nodded. "Horatio Fernandez. Joshua was the boss, but, yeah, I guess I'm in charge until head office sends somebody new out from Earth."

"Well," said Mac, "you're probably better equipped than we are to figure out the exact cause of death."

Fernandez gestured theatrically at the synthetic corpse, as if it were— well, not *bleedingly* obvious, but certainly apparent.

Mac nodded. "It's just a bit too pat," he said, his voice lowered conspiratorially. "Implement at hand, suicide note." He lifted his shaggy orange eyebrows. "I just want to be sure."

Cassandra had drifted over without Mac noticing, although of course I had. She was listening in.

"Yeah," said Fernandez. "Sure. We can disassemble him, check for anything else that might be amiss."

"No," said Cassandra. "You can't."

"I'm afraid it's necessary," said Mac, looking at her. His Scottish brogue always put an edge on his words, but I knew he was trying to sound gentle.

"No," said Cassandra, her voice quavering. "I forbid it."

Mac's voice got a little firmer. "You can't. I'm legally required to order an autopsy in every suspicious case."

Cassandra wheeled on Fernandez. "Horatio, I order you not to do this."

Fernandez blinked a few times. "Order?"

Cassandra opened her mouth to say something more, then apparently thought better of it. Horatio moved closer to her, and put a hulking arm around her small shoulders. "Don't worry," he said. "We'll be gentle." And then his face brightened a bit. "In fact, we'll see what parts we can salvage— give them to somebody else; somebody who couldn't afford such good stuff if it was new." He smiled beatifically. "It's what Joshua would have wanted."

The next day, I was siting in my office, looking out the small window. The dust storm had ended. Out on the surface, rocks were strewn everywhere, like toys on a kid's bedroom floor. My wrist commlink buzzed, and I looked at it in anticipation, hoping for a new case; I could use the solars. But the ID line said NKPD. I told the device to accept the call, and a little picture of Mac's red-headed face appeared on my wrist. "Hey, Lomax," he said. "Come on by the station, would you?"

"What's up?"

The micro-Mac frowned. "Nothing I want to say over open airwaves."

I nodded. Now that the Wilkins case was over, I didn't have anything better to do anyway. I'd only managed about seven billable hours, damnitall, and even that had taken some padding.

I walked into the center along Ninth Avenue, entered the lobby of the police station, traded quips with the ineluctable Huxley, and was admitted to the back.

"Hey, Mac," I said. "What's up?"

"'Morning, Alex," Mac said, rolling the R in "Morning." "Come in; sit down." He spoke to his desk terminal, and turned its monitor around so I could see it. "Have a look at this."

I glanced at the screen. "The report on Joshua Wilkins?" I said.

Mac nodded. "Look at the section on the artificial brain."

I skimmed the text, until I found that part. "Yeah?" I said, still not getting it.

"Do you know what 'baseline synaptic web' means?" Mac asked.

"No, I don't. And you didn't either, smart-ass, until someone told you."

Mac smiled a bit, conceding that. "Well, there were lots of bits of the artificial brain left behind. And that big guy at NewYou—Fernandez, remember?—he really got into this forensic stuff, and decided to run it through some kind of instrument they've got there. And you know what he found?"

"What?"

"The brain stuff—the raw material inside the artificial skull—was pristine. It had never been imprinted."

"You mean no scanned mind had ever been transferred into that brain?"

Mac folded his arms across his chest and leaned back in his chair. "Bingo."

I frowned. "But that's not possible. I mean, if there was no mind in that head, who wrote the suicide note?"

Mac lifted those shaggy eyebrows of his. "Who indeed?" he said. "And what happened to Joshua Wilkins's scanned consciousness?"

"Does anyone at NewYou but Fernandez know about this?" I asked.

Mac shook his head. "No, and he's agreed to keep his mouth shut while we continue to investigate. But I thought I'd clue you in, since apparently the case you were on isn't really closed—and, after all, if you don't make money now and again, you can't afford to bribe me for favors."

I nodded. "That's what I like about you, Mac. Always looking out for my best interests."

▌▌ ▐▌ ▐▌

Perhaps I should have gone straight to see Cassandra Wilkins, and made sure that we both agreed that I was back on the clock, but I had some questions I wanted answered first. And I knew just who to turn to. Raoul Santos was the city's top computer expert. I'd met him during a previous case, and we'd recently struck up a small-f friendship—we both shared the same taste in bootleg Earth booze, and he wasn't above joining me at some of New Klondike's sleazier saloons to get it. I used my commlink to call him, and we arranged to meet at the Bent Chisel.

The Bent Chisel was a little hellhole off of Fourth Avenue, in the sixth concentric ring of buildings. I made sure I had my revolver, and that it was loaded, before I entered. The bartender was a surly man named Buttrick, a biological who had more than his fair share of flesh, and blood as cold as ice. He wore a sleeveless black shirt, and had a three-day growth of salt-and-pepper beard. "Lomax," he said, acknowledging my entrance. "No broken furniture this time, right?"

I held up three fingers. "Scout's honor."

Buttrick held up one finger.

"Hey," I said. "Is that any way to treat one of your best customers?"

"My best customers," said Buttrick, polishing a glass with a ratty towel, "pay their tabs."

"Yeah," I said, stealing a page from Sgt. Huxley's *Guide to Witty Repartee*. "Well." I headed on in, making my way to the back of the bar, where my favorite booth was located. The waitresses here were topless, and soon enough one came over to see me. I couldn't remember her name off-hand, although we'd slept together a couple of times. I ordered a scotch on the rocks; they normally did that with carbon-dioxide ice here, which was much cheaper than water ice on Mars. A few minutes later, Raoul Santos arrived. "Hey," he said, taking a seat opposite me. "How's tricks?"

"Fine," I said. "She sends her love."

Raoul made a puzzled face, then smiled. "Ah, right. Cute. Listen, don't quit your day job."

"Hey," I said, placing a hand over my heart, "you wound me. Down deep, I'm a stand-up comic."

"Well," said Raoul, "I always say people should be true to their inner-most selves, but ..."

"Yeah?" I said. "What's your innermost self?"

"Me?" Raoul raised his eyebrows. "I'm pure genius, right to the very core."

I snorted, and the waitress reappeared. She gave me my glass. It was just a little less full than it should have been: either Buttrick was trying to curb his losses on me, or the waitress was miffed that I hadn't acknowledged our former intimacy. Raoul placed his order, talking directly into the woman's breasts. Boobs did well in Mars gravity; hers were still perky even though she had to be almost forty.

"So," said Raoul, looking over steepled fingers at me. "What's up?" His face consisted of a wide forehead, long nose, and receding chin; it made him look like he was leaning forward even when he wasn't.

I took a swig of my drink. "Tell me about this transferring game."

"Ah, yes," said Raoul. "Fascinating stuff. Thinking of doing it?"

"Maybe someday," I said.

"You know, it's supposed to pay for itself within three mears," he said, "'cause you no longer have to pay life-support tax after you've transferred."

I was in arrears on that, and didn't like to think about what would happen if I fell much further behind. "That'd be a plus," I said. "What about you? You going to do it?"

"Sure. I want to live forever; who doesn't? 'Course, my dad won't like it."

"Your dad? What's he got against it?"

Raoul snorted. "He's a minister."

"In whose government?" I asked.

"No, no. A *minister*. Clergy."

"I didn't know there were any of those left, even on Earth," I said.

"He *is* on Earth, but, yeah, you're right. Poor old guy still believes in souls."

I raised my eyebrows. "Really?"

"Yup. And because he believes in souls, he has a hard time with this idea of transferring consciousness. He would say the new version isn't the same person."

I thought about what the supposed suicide note said. "Well, is it?"

Raoul rolled his eyes. "You, too? Of course it is! The mind is just software—and since the dawn of computing, software has been moved from one computing platform to another by copying it over, then erasing the original."

I frowned, but decided to let that go for the moment. "So, if you do transfer, what would you have fixed in your new body?"

Raoul spread his arms. "Hey, man, you don't tamper with perfection."

"Yeah," I said. "Sure. Still, how much could you change things? I mean, say you're a midget; could you choose to have a normal-sized body?"

"Sure, of course."

I frowned. "But wouldn't the copied mind have trouble with your new size?"

"Nah," said Raoul. The waitress returned. She bent over far enough while placing Raoul's drink on the table that her breast touched his bare forearm; she gave me a look that said, "See what you're missing, tiger?" When she was gone, Raoul continued. "See, when we first started copying consciousness, we let the old software from the old mind actually try to directly control the new body. It took months to learn how to walk again, and so on."

"Yeah, I read something about that, years ago," I said.

Raoul nodded. "Right. But now we don't let the copied mind do anything but give orders. The thoughts are intercepted by the new body's main computer. *That* unit runs the body. All the transferred mind has to do is *think* that it wants to pick up this glass, say." He acted out his example, and took a sip, then winced in response to the booze's kick. "The computer takes care of working out which pulleys to contract, how far to reach, and so on."

"So you could indeed order up a body radically different from your original?" I said.

"Absolutely," said Raoul. He looked at me through hooded eyes. "Which, in your case, is probably the route to go."

"Damn," I said.

"Hey, don't take it seriously," he said, taking another sip, and allowing himself another pleased wince. "Just a joke."

"I know," I said. "It's just that I was hoping it wasn't that way. See, this case I'm on: the guy I'm supposed to find owns the NewYou franchise here."

"Yeah?" said Raoul.

"Yeah, and I think he deliberately transferred his scanned mind into some body other than the one that he'd ordered up for himself."

"Why would he do that?"

"He faked the death of the body that looked like him—and, I think he'd planned to do that all along, because he never bothered to order up any improvements to his face. I think he wanted to get away, but make it look like he was dead, so no one would be looking for him anymore."

"And why would he do that?"

I frowned, then drank some more. "I'm not sure."

"Maybe he wanted to escape his spouse."

"Maybe—but she's a hot little number."

"Hmm," said Raoul. "Whose body do you think he took?"

"I don't know that, either. I was hoping the new body would have to be at least roughly similar to his old one; that would cut down on the possible suspects. But I guess that's not the case."

"It isn't, no."

I nodded, and looked down at my drink. The dry-ice cubes were sublimating into white vapor that filled the top part of the glass.

"Something else is bothering you," said Raoul. I lifted my head, and saw him taking a swig of his drink. A little bit of amber liquid spilled out of his mouth and formed a shiny bead on his recessed chin. "What is it?"

I shifted a bit. "I visited NewYou yesterday. You know what happens to your original body after they move your mind?"

"Sure," said Raoul. "Like I said, there's no such thing as moving software. You copy it, then delete the original. They euthanize the biological version, once the transfer is made, by frying the original brain."

I nodded. "And if the guy I'm looking for put his mind into the body intended for somebody else's mind, and that person's mind wasn't copied anywhere, then ..." I took another swig of my drink. "Then it's murder, isn't it? Souls or no souls—it doesn't matter. If you shut down the one and only copy of someone's mind, you've murdered that person, right?"

"Oh, yes," said Raoul. "Deader than Mars itself is now."

I glanced down at the swirling fog in my glass. "So I'm not just looking for a husband who's skipped out on his wife," I said. "I'm looking for a cold-blooded killer."

▓ ▓ ▓

I went by NewYou again. Cassandra wasn't in—but that didn't surprise me; she was a grieving widow now. But Horatio Fernandez—he of the massive arms—was on duty.

"I'd like a list of all the people who were transferred the same day as Joshua Wilkins," I said.

He frowned. "That's confidential information."

There were several potential customers milling about. I raised my voice so they could hear. "Interesting suicide note, wasn't it?"

Fernandez grabbed my arm and led me quickly to the side of the room. "What the hell are you doing?" he whispered angrily.

"Just sharing the news," I said, still speaking loudly, although not quite loud enough now, I thought, for the customers to hear. "People thinking of uploading should know that it's not the same—at least, that's what Joshua Wilkins said in that note."

Fernandez knew when he was beaten. The claim in the putative suicide note was exactly the opposite of NewYou's corporate position: transferring was supposed to be flawless, conferring nothing but benefits. "All right, all right," he hissed. "I'll pull the list for you."

"Now that's service," I said. "They should name you employee of the month."

He led me into the back room and spoke to a computer. I happened to overhear the passphrase for accessing the customer database; it was just six words—hardly any security at all.

Eleven people had moved their consciousnesses into artificial bodies that day. I had him transfer the files on each of the eleven into my wrist commlink. "Thanks," I said, doing that tip-of-the-nonexistent-hat thing I do. Even when you've forced a man to do something, there's no harm in being polite.

███ ███ ███

If I was right that Joshua Wilkins had appropriated the body of some-body else who had been scheduled to transfer the same day, it shouldn't be too hard to figure out whose body he'd taken; all I had to do, I figured, was interview each of the eleven.

My first stop, purely because it happened to be the nearest, was the home of a guy named Stuart Berling, a full-time fossil hunter. He must have had some recent success, if he could afford to transfer.

Berling's home was part of a row of townhouses off Fifth Avenue, in the fifth ring. I pushed his door buzzer, and waited impatiently for a response. At last he appeared. If I wasn't so famous for my poker face, I'd have done a double take. The man who greeted me was a dead ringer for Krikor Ajemian, the holovid star—the same gaunt features and intense eyes, the same mane of dark hair, the same tightly trimmed beard and mustache. I guess not everyone wanted to keep even a semblance of their original appearance.

"Hello," I said. "My name is Alexander Lomax. Are you Stuart Berling?"

The artificial face in front of me surely was capable of smiling, but chose not to. "Yes. What do you want?"

"I understand you only recently transferred your consciousness into this body."

A nod. "So?"

"So, I work for the NewYou—the head office on Earth. I'm here to check up on the quality of the work done by our franchise here on Mars." Normally, this was a good technique. If Berling was who he said he was, the question wouldn't faze him. But if he were really Joshua Wilkins, he'd know I was lying, and his expression might betray this. But transfers didn't have faces that were as malleable; if this person was startled or suspicious, nothing in his plastic features indicated it.

"So?" Berling said again.

"So I'm wondering if you were satisfied by the work done for you?"

"It cost a lot," said Berling.

I smiled. "Yes, it does. May I come in?"

He considered this for a few moments, then shrugged. "Sure, why not?" He stepped aside.

His living room was full of work tables, covered with reddish rocks from outside the dome. A giant lens on an articulated arm was attached to one of the work tables, and various geologist's tools were scattered about.

"Finding anything interesting?" I asked, gesturing at the rocks.

"If I was, I certainly wouldn't tell you," said Berling, looking at me sideways in the typical paranoid-prospector's way.

"Right," I said. "Of course. So, *are* you satisfied with the NewYou process?"

"Sure, yeah. It's everything they said it would be. All the parts work."

"Thanks for your help," I said, pulling out my PDA to make a few notes, and then frowning at its blank screen. "Oh, damn," I said. "The silly thing has a loose fusion pack. I've got to open it up and reseat it." I showed him the back of the unit's case. "Do you have a little screwdriver that will fit that?"

Everybody owned some screwdrivers, even though most people rarely needed them, and they were the sort of thing that had no standard storage location. Some people kept them in kitchen drawers, others kept them in tool chests, still others kept them under the bathroom sink. Only a person who had lived in this home for a while would know where they were.

Berling peered at the little slot-headed screw, then nodded. "Sure," he said. "Hang on."

He made an unerring beeline for the far-side of the living room, going to a cabinet that had glass doors on its top half, but solid metal ones on its bottom. He bent over, opened one of the metal doors, reached in, rummaged for a bit, and emerged with the appropriate screwdriver.

"Thanks," I said, opening the case in such a way that he couldn't see inside. I then surreptitiously removed the little bit of plastic I'd used to insulate the fusion battery from the contact it was supposed to touch. Meanwhile, without looking up, I said, "Are you married, Mr. Berling?" Of course, I already knew the answer was yes; that fact was in his NewYou file.

He nodded.

"Is your wife home?"

His artificial eyelids closed a bit. "Why?"

I told him the honest truth, since it fit well with my cover story: "I'd like to ask her whether she can perceive any differences between the new you and the old."

Again, I watched his expression, but it didn't change. "Sure, I guess that'd be okay." He turned and called over his shoulder, "Lacie!"

A few moments later, a homely flesh-and-blood woman of about fifty appeared. "This person is from the head office of NewYou," said Berling, indicating me with a pointed finger. "He'd like to speak to you."

"About what?" asked Lacie. She had a deep, not-unpleasant voice.

"Might we speak in private?" I said.

Berling's gaze shifted from Lacie to me, then back to Lacie. "Hrmpph," he said, but then, a moment later, added, "I guess that'd be all right." He turned around and walked away.

I looked at Lacie. "I'm just doing a routine follow-up," I said. "Making sure people are happy with the work we do. Have you noticed any changes in your husband since he transferred?"

"Not really."

"Oh?" I said. "If there's anything at all ..." I smiled reassuringly. "We want to make the process as perfect as possible. Has he said anything that's surprised you, say?"

Lacie crinkled her face. "How do you mean?"

"I mean, has he used any expressions or turns of phrase you're not used to hearing from him?"

A shake of the head. "No."

"Sometimes the process plays tricks with memory. Has he failed to know something he should know?"

"Not that I noticed," said Lacie.

"What about the reverse? Has he known anything that you wouldn't expect him to know?"

She lifted her eyebrows. "No. He's just Stuart."

I frowned. "No changes at all?"

"No, none ... well, almost none."

I waited for her to go on, but she didn't, so I prodded her. "What is it? We really would like to know about any difference, any flaw in our transference process."

"Oh, it's not a flaw," said Lacie, not meeting my eyes.

"No? Then what?"

"It's just that ..."

"Yes?"

"Well, just that he's a demon in the sack now. He stays hard forever."

I frowned, disappointed not to have found what I was looking for on the first try. But I decided to end the masquerade on a positive note. "We aim to please, ma'am. We aim to please."

▌▌ ▌▌ ▌▌

I spent the next several hours interviewing four other people; none of them seemed to be anyone other than who they claimed to be.

Next on my list was Dr. Rory Pickover, whose home was an apartment in the innermost circle of buildings, beneath the highest point of the dome.

He lived alone, so there was no spouse or child to question about any changes in him. That made me suspicious right off the bat: if one were going to choose an identity to appropriate, it ideally would be someone without close companions. He also refused to meet me at his home, meaning I couldn't try the screwdriver trick on him.

I thought we might meet at a coffee shop or a restaurant—there were lots in New Klondike, although none were doing good business these days. But he insisted we go outside the dome—out onto the Martian surface. That was easy for him; he was a transfer now. But it was a pain in the ass for me; I had to rent a surface suit.

We met at the south airlock just as the sun was going down. I suited up—surface suits came in three stretchy sizes; I took the largest. The fish-bowl helmet I rented was somewhat frosted on one side; sandstorm-scouring, no doubt. The air tanks, slung on my back, were good for about four hours. I felt heavy in the suit, even though in it I still weighed only about half of what I had back on Earth.

Rory Pickover was a paleontologist—an actual scientist, not a treasure-seeking fossil hunter. His pre-transfer appearance had been almost stereotypically academic: a round, soft face, with a fringe of graying hair. His new body was lean and muscular, and he had a full head of dark brown hair, but the face was still recognizably his. He was carrying a geologist's hammer, with a wide, flat blade; I rather suspected it would nicely smash my helmet. I had surreptitiously transferred the Smith & Wesson from the holster I wore under my jacket to an exterior pocket on the rented surface suit, just in case I needed it while we were outside.

We signed the security logs, and then let the technician cycle us through the airlock.

Off in the distance, I could see the highland plateau, dark streaks marking its side. Nearby, there were two large craters and a cluster of smaller ones. There were few footprints in the rusty sand; the recent storm had obliterated the thousands that had doubtless been there earlier. We walked out about five hundred meters. I turned around briefly to look back at the transparent dome and the buildings within.

"Sorry for dragging you out here," said Pickover. He had a cultured

British accent. "I don't want any witnesses." Even the cheapest artificial body had built-in radio equipment, and I had a transceiver inside my helmet.

"Ah," I said, by way of reply. I slipped my gloved hand into the pocket containing the Smith & Wesson, and wrapped my fingers around its reassuring solidity.

"I know you aren't just in from Earth," said Pickover, continuing to walk. "And I know you don't work for NewYou."

We were casting long shadows; the sun, so much tinier than it appeared from Earth, was sitting on the horizon; the sky was already purpling, and Earth itself was visible, a bright blue-white evening star.

"Who do you think I am?" I asked.

His answer surprised me, although I didn't let it show. "You're Alexander Lomax, the private detective."

Well, it didn't seem to make any sense to deny it. "Yeah. How'd you know?"

"I've been checking you out over the last few days," said Pickover. "I'd been thinking of, ah, engaging your services."

We continued to walk along, little clouds of dust rising each time our feet touched the ground. "What for?" I said.

"You first, if you don't mind," said Pickover. "Why did you come to see me?"

He already knew who I was, and I had a very good idea who he was, so I decided to put my cards on the table. "I'm working for your wife."

Pickover's artificial face looked perplexed. "My ... wife?"

"That's right."

"I don't have a wife."

"Sure you do. You're Joshua Wilkins, and your wife's name is Cassandra."

"What? No, I'm Rory Pickover. You know that. You called me."

"Come off it, Wilkins. The jig is up. You transferred your consciousness into the body intended for the real Rory Pickover, and then you took off."

"I—oh. Oh, Christ."

"So, you see, I know. Too bad, Wilkins. You'll hang—or whatever the hell they do with transfers—for murdering Pickover."

"No." He said it softly.

"Yes," I replied, and now I pulled out my revolver. It really wouldn't be much use against an artificial body, but until quite recently Wilkins had been biological; hopefully, he was still intimidated by guns. "Let's go."

"Where?"

"Back under the dome, to the police station. I'll have Cassandra meet us there, just to confirm your identity."

The sun had slipped below the horizon now. He spread his arms, a supplicant against the backdrop of the gathering night. "Okay, sure, if you like. Call up this Cassandra, by all means. Let her talk to me. She'll tell you after questioning me for two seconds that I'm not her husband. But— Christ, damn, Christ."

"What?"

"I want to find him, too."

"Who? Joshua Wilkins?"

He nodded, then, perhaps thinking I couldn't see his nod in the growing darkness, said, "Yes."

"Why?"

He tipped his head up, as if thinking. I followed his gaze. Phobos was visible, a dark form overhead. At last, he spoke again. "Because *I'm* the reason he's disappeared."

"What?" I said. "Why?"

"That's why I was thinking of hiring you myself. I didn't know where else to turn."

"Turn for what?"

Pickover looked at me. "I did go to NewYou, Mr. Lomax. I knew I was going to have an enormous amount of work to do out here on the surface now, and I wanted to be able to spend days—weeks!—in the field, without worrying about running out of air, or water, or food."

I frowned. "But you've been here on Mars for six mears; I read that in your file. What's changed?"

"*Everything,* Mr. Lomax." He looked off in the distance. "Everything!" But he didn't elaborate on that. Instead, he said. "I certainly know this Wilkins chap you're looking for; I went to his store, and had him transfer my consciousness from my old biological body into this one. But he also kept a copy of my mind—I'm sure of that."

I raised my eyebrows. "How do you know?"

"Because my computer accounts have been compromised. There's no way anyone but me can get in; I'm the only one who knows the passphrase. But someone *has* been inside, looking around; I use quantum encryption, so you can tell whenever someone has even *looked* at a file." He shook his head. "I don't know how he did it—there must be some technique I'm unaware of—but somehow Wilkins has been extracting information from the copy of my mind. That's the only way I can think of that anyone might have learned my passphrase."

"You think Wilkins did all this to access your bank accounts? Is there really enough money in them to make it worth starting a new life in somebody else's body? It's too dark to see your clothes right now, but, if I recall correctly, they looked a bit ... shabby."

"You're right. I'm just a poor scientist. But there's something I know that could make the wrong people rich beyond their wildest dreams."

"And what's that?" I said.

He continued to walk along, trying to decide, I suppose, whether to trust me. I let him think about that, and at last, Dr. Rory Pickover, who was now just a starless silhouette against a starry sky, said, in a soft, quiet voice, "I know where it is."

"Where what is?"

"The alpha deposit."

"The what?"

"Sorry," he said. "Paleontologist's jargon. What I mean is, I've found it: I've found the mother lode. I've found the place where Weingarten and O'Reilly had been excavating. I've found the source of the best preserved, most-complete Martian fossils."

"My God," I said. "You'll be *rolling* in it."

Perhaps he shook his head; it was now too dark to tell. "No, sir," he said, in that cultured English voice. "No, I won't. I don't want to *sell* these fossils. I want to preserve them; I want to protect them from these plunderers, these ... these *thieves*. I want to make sure they're collected properly, scientifically. I want to make sure they end up in the best museums, where they can be studied. There's so much to be learned, so much to discover!"

"Does Wilkins know now where this ... what did you call it? This alpha deposit is?"

"No—at least, not from accessing my computer files. I didn't record the location anywhere but up here." Presumably he was tapping the side of his head.

"But you think Wilkins extracted the passphrase from a copy of your mind?"

"He must have."

"And now he's presumably trying to extract the location of the alpha deposit from that copy of your mind."

"Yes, yes! And if he succeeds, all will be lost! The best specimens will be sold off into private collections—trophies for some trillionaire's estate, hidden forever from science."

I shook my head. "But this doesn't make any sense. I mean, how would Wilkins even know that you had discovered the alpha deposit?"

Suddenly Pickover's voice was very small. "I'd gone in to NewYou— you have to go in weeks in advance of transferring, of course, so you can tell them what you want in a new body; it takes time to custom-build one to your specifications."

"Yes. So?"

"So, I wanted a body ideally suited to paleontological work on the surface of Mars; I wanted some special modifications—the kinds of the things only the most successful prospectors could afford. Reinforced knees; extra arm strength for moving rocks; extended spectral response in the eyes, so that fossils will stand out better; night vision so that I could continue digging after dark; but ..."

I nodded. "But you didn't have enough money."

"That's right. I could barely afford to transfer at all, even into the cheapest off-the-shelf body, and so ..."

He trailed off, too angry at himself, I guess, to give voice to what was in his mind. "And so you hinted that you were about to come into some wealth," I said, "and suggested that maybe he could give you what you needed now, and you'd make it up to him later."

Pickover sounded sad. "That's the trouble with being a scientist; sharing information is our natural mode."

"Did you tell him precisely what you'd found?" I asked.

"No. No, but he must have guessed. I'm a paleontologist, I've been studying Weingarten and O'Reilly for years—all of that is a matter of public record. He must have figured out that I knew where their fossil beds are. After all, where else would a guy like me get money?" He sighed. "I'm an idiot, aren't I?"

"Well, Mensa isn't going to be calling you any time soon."

"Please don't rub it in, Mr. Lomax. I feel bad enough as it is, and—" His voice cracked; I'd never heard a transfer's do that before. "And now I've put all those lovely, lovely fossils in jeopardy! Will you help me, Mr. Lomax? Please say you'll help me!"

I nodded. "All right. I'm on the case."

▓ ▓ ▓

We went back into the dome, and I called Raoul Santos on my commlink, getting him to meet me at Rory Pickover's little apartment at the center of town. It was four floors up, and consisted of three small rooms—an interior unit, with no windows.

When Raoul arrived, I made introductions. "Raoul Santos, this is Rory Pickover. Raoul here is the best computer expert we've got in New Klondike. And Dr. Pickover is a paleontologist."

Raoul tipped his broad forehead at Pickover. "Good to meet you."

"Thank you," said Pickover. "Forgive the mess, Mr. Santos. I live alone. A lifelong bachelor gets into bad habits, I'm afraid." He'd already cleared debris off of one chair for me; he now busied himself doing the same with another chair, this one right in front of his home computer.

"What's up, Alex?" asked Raoul, indicating Pickover with a movement of his head. "New client?"

"Yeah," I said. "Dr. Pickover's computer files have been looked at by some unauthorized individual. We're wondering if you could tell us from where the access attempt was made."

"You'll owe me a nice round of drinks at the Bent Chisel," said Raoul.

"No problem," I said. "I'll put it on my tab."

Raoul smiled, and stretched his arms out, fingers interlocked, until his knuckles cracked. Then he took the now-clean seat in front of Pickover's computer and began to type. "How do you lock you files?" he asked, without taking his eyes off the monitor.

"A verbal passphrase," said Pickover.

"Anybody besides you know it?"

Pickover shook his artificial head. "No."

"And it's not written down anywhere?"

"No, well ... not as such."

Raoul turned his head, looking up at Pickover. "What do you mean?"

"It's a line from a book. If I ever forgot the exact wording, I could always look it up."

Raoul shook his head in disgust. "You should always use random passphrases." He typed keys.

"Oh, I'm sure it's totally secure," said Pickover. "No one would guess—"

Raoul interrupted. "Your passphrase being, 'Those privileged to be present ...'"

I saw Pickover's jaw drop. "My God. How did you know that?"

Raoul pointed to some data on the screen. "It's the first thing that was inputted by the only outside access your system has had in weeks."

"I thought passphrases were hidden from view when entered," said Pickover.

"Sure they are," said Raoul. "But the comm program has a buffer; it's in there. Look."

Raoul shifted in the chair so that Pickover could see the screen clearly over his shoulder. "That's ... well, that's very strange," said Pickover.

"What?"

"Well, sure that's my passphrase, but it's not quite right."

I loomed in to have a peek at the screen, too. "How do you mean?" I said.

"Well," said Pickover, "see, my passphrase is 'Those privileged to be present at a family festival of the Forsytes'—it's from the opening of *The Man of Property*, the first book of the Forsyte Saga by John Galsworthy.

I love that phrase because of the alliteration—'privileged to be present,' 'family festival of the Forsytes.' Makes it easy to remember."

Raoul shook his head in you-can't-teach-people-anything disgust. Pickover went on. "But, see, whoever it was typed in even more."

I looked at the glowing string of letters. In full it said: *Those privileged to be present at a family festival of the Forsytes have seen them dine at half past eight, enjoying seven courses.*

"It's too much?" I said.

"That's right," said Pickover, nodding. "My passphrase ends with the word 'Forsytes.'"

Raoul was stroking his receding chin. "Doesn't matter," he said. "The files would unlock the moment the phrase was complete; the rest would just be discarded—systems that principally work with spoken commands don't require you to press the enter key."

"Yes, yes, yes," said Pickover. "But the rest of it isn't what Galsworthy wrote. It's not even close. *The Man of Property* is my favorite book; I know it well. The full opening line is 'Those privileged to be present at a family festival of the Forsytes have seen that charming and instructive sight—an upper middle-class family in full plumage.' Nothing about the time they ate, or how many courses they had."

Raoul pointed at the text on screen, as if it had to be the correct version. "Are you sure?" he said.

"Of course!" said Pickover. "Galsworthy's public domain; you can do a search online and see for yourself."

I frowned. "No one but you knows your passphrase, right?"

Pickover nodded vigorously. "I live alone, and I don't have many friends; I'm a quiet sort. There's no one I've ever told, and no one who could have ever overheard me saying it, or seen me typing it in."

"Somebody found it out," said Raoul.

Pickover looked at me, then down at Raoul. "I think ..." he said, beginning slowly, giving me a chance to stop him, I guess, before he said too much. But I let him go on. "I think that the information was extracted from a scan of my mind made by NewYou."

Raoul crossed his arms in front of his chest. "Impossible."

"What?" said Pickover, and "Why?" said I.

"Can't be done," said Raoul. "We know how to copy the vast array of interconnections that make up a human mind, and we know how to reinstantiate those connections in an artificial substrate. But we don't know how to decode them; nobody does. There's simply no way to sift through a digital copy of a mind and extract specific data."

Damn! If Raoul was right—and he always was in computing matters—then all this business with Pickover was a red herring. There probably was no bootleg scan of his mind; despite his protestations of being careful, someone likely had just overheard his passphrase, and decided to go spelunking through his files. While I was wasting time on this, Joshua Wilkins was doubtless slipping further out of my grasp.

Still, it was worth continuing this line of investigation for a few minutes more. "Any sign of where the access attempt was made?" I asked Raoul.

He shook his head. "No. Whoever did it knew what they were doing; they covered their tracks well. The attempt came over an outside line—that's all I can tell for sure."

I nodded. "Okay. Thanks, Raoul. Appreciate your help."

Raoul got up. "My pleasure. Now, how 'bout that drink."

I opened my mouth to say yes, but then it hit me—what Wilkins must be doing. "Umm, later, okay? I've—I've got some more things to take care of here."

Raoul frowned; he'd clearly hoped to collect his booze immediately. But I started maneuvering him toward the door. "Thanks for your help, Raoul. I really appreciate it."

"Um, sure, Alex," he said. He was obviously aware he was being given the bum's rush, but he wasn't fighting it too much. "Anytime."

"Yes, thank you awfully, Mr. Santos," said Pickover.

"No problem. If—"

"See you later, Raoul," I said, opening the door for him. "Thanks so much." I tipped my nonexistent hat at him.

Raoul shrugged, clearly aware that something was up, but not motivated sufficiently to find out what. He went through the door, and I hit the button that caused it to slide shut behind him. As soon as it was closed, I put an arm around Pickover's shoulders, and propelled him back to the computer. I pointed at the line Raoul had highlighted on the screen, and read the ending of it aloud: "'... dine at half past eight, enjoying seven courses.'"

Pickover nodded. "Yes. So?"

"Numbers are often coded info," I said. "'Half past eight; seven courses.' What's that mean to you?"

"To me?" said Pickover. "Nothing. I like to eat much earlier than that, and I never have more than one course."

"But it could be a message," I said.

"From who?"

There was no easy way to tell him this. "From you to you."

He drew his artificial eyebrows together in puzzlement. "What?"

"Look," I said, motioning for him to sit down in front of the computer, "Raoul is doubtless right. You can't sift a digital scan of a human mind for information."

"But that must be what Wilkins is doing."

I shook my head. "No," I said. "The only way to find out what's in a mind is to ask it interactively."

"But ... but no one's asked me my passphrase."

"No one has asked *this* you. But Joshua Wilkins must have transferred the extra copy of your mind into a body, so that he could deal with it directly. And that extra copy must be the one that's revealed your codes to him."

"You mean ... you mean there's another me? Another *conscious* me?"

"Looks that way."

"But ... no, no. That's ... why, that's *illegal*. Bootleg copies of human beings—my God, Lomax, it's obscene!"

"I'm going to go see if I can find him," I said.

"*It*," said Pickover, forcefully.

"What?"

"*It*. Not him. I'm the only 'him'—the only real Rory Pickover."

"So what do you want me to do when I find it?"

"Erase it, of course. Shut it down." He shuddered. "My God, Lomax, I feel so ... so violated! A stolen copy of my mind! It's the ultimate invasion of privacy ..."

"That may be," I said. "But the bootleg is trying to tell you something. He—*it*—gave Wilkins the passphrase, and then tacked some extra words onto it, in order to get a message to you."

"But I don't recognize those extra words," said Pickover, sounding exasperated.

"Do they *mean* anything to you? Do they suggest anything?"

Pickover re-read what was on the screen. "I can't imagine what," he said, "unless ... no, no, I'd never think up a code like that."

"You obviously just *did* think of it. What's the code?"

Pickover was quiet for a moment, as if deciding if the thought was worth giving voice. Then: "Well, New Klondike is circular in layout, right? And it consists of concentric rings of buildings. Half past eight—that would be between Eighth and Ninth Avenue, no? And seven courses—in the seventh circle out from the center? Maybe the damned bootleg is trying to draw our attention to a location, a specific place here in town."

"Between Eighth and Ninth, eh? That's a rough area. I go to a gym near there."

"The old shipyards," said Pickover. "Aren't they there?"

"Yeah." I started walking toward the door. "I'm going to investigate."

"I'll go with you," said Pickover.

I looked at him and shook my head. He would doubtless be more of a hindrance than a help. "It's too dangerous," I said. "I should go alone."

Pickover looked for a few moments like he was going to protest, but then he nodded. "All right. I hope you find Wilkins. But if you find another me ..."

"Yes?" I said. "What would you like me to do?"

Pickover gazed at me with pleading eyes. "Erase it. Destroy it." He shuddered again. "I never want to see the damned thing."

∎ ∎ ∎

I had to get some sleep—damn, but sometimes I do wish I were a transfer. I took the hovertram out to my apartment, and let myself have five hours—Mars hours, admittedly, which were slightly longer than Earth ones—and then headed out to the old shipyards. The sun was just coming up as I arrived there. The sky through the dome was pink in the east and purple in the west.

Some active maintenance and repair work was done on spaceships here, but most of these ships were no longer spaceworthy and had been abandoned. Any one of them would make a good hideout, I thought; spaceships were shielded against radiation, making it hard to scan through their hulls to see what was going on inside.

The shipyards were large fields holding vessels of various sizes and shapes. Most were streamlined—even Mars's tenuous atmosphere required that. Some were squatting on tail fins; some were lying on their bellies; some were supported by articulated legs. I tried every hatch I could see on these craft, but, so far, they all had their airlocks sealed tightly shut.

Finally, I came to a monstrous abandoned spaceliner—a great hull, some three hundred meters long, fifty meters wide, and a dozen meters high. The name *Mayflower II* was still visible in chipped paint near the bow—which is the part I came across first—and the slogan "Mars or Bust!" was also visible.

I walked a little farther alongside the hull, looking for a hatch, until—

Yes! I finally understood what a fossil hunter felt like when he at last turned up a perfectly preserved rhizomorph. There was an outer airlock door here, and it was open. The other door, inside, was open, too. I stepped through the chamber, entering the ship proper. There were stands for holding space suits, but the suits themselves were long gone.

I walked over to the far end of the room, and found another door—one of those submarine-style ones with a locking wheel in the center. This one was closed, and I figured it would probably have been sealed shut at some point, but I tried to turn the wheel anyway, just to be sure, and damned if it didn't spin freely, disengaging the locking bolts. I pulled the door open, and stepped through it, into a corridor. The door was on spring-loaded hinges; as soon as I let go of it, it closed behind me, plunging me into darkness.

Of course, I'd brought a flashlight. I pulled it off my belt and thumbed it on.

The air was dry and had a faint odor of decay to it. I headed down the corridor, the pool of illumination from my flashlight going in front of me, and—

A squealing noise. I swung around, and the beam from my flashlight caught the source before it scurried away: a large brown rat, its eyes two tiny red coals in the light. People had been trying to get rid of the rats—and cockroaches and silverfish and other vermin that had somehow made it here from Earth—for mears.

I turned back around and headed deeper into the ship. The floor wasn't quite level: it dipped a bit to—to starboard, they'd call it—and I also felt that I was gaining elevation as I walked along. The ship's floor had no carpeting; it was just bare, smooth metal. Oily water pooled along the starboard side; a pipe must have ruptured at some point. Another rat scurried by up ahead; I wondered what they ate here, aboard the dead hulk of the ship.

I thought I should check in with Pickover—let him know where I was. I activated my commlink, but the display said it was unable to connect. Of course: the radiation shielding in the spaceship's hull kept signals from getting out.

It was getting awfully cold. I held my flashlight straight up in front of my face, and saw that my breath was now coming out in visible clouds. I paused and listened. There was a steady dripping sound: condensation, or another leak. I continued along, sweeping the flashlight beam left and right in good detective fashion as I did so.

There were doors at intervals along the corridor—the automatic sliding kind you usually find aboard spaceships. Most of these panels had been pried open, and I shone my flashlight into each of the revealed rooms. Some were tiny passenger quarters, some were storage, one was a medical facility—all the equipment had been removed, but the examining beds betrayed the room's function.

I checked yet another set of quarters, then came to a closed door, the first one I'd seen along this hallway.

I pushed the open button, but nothing happened; the ship's electrical system was dead. Of course, there was an emergency handle, recessed into the door's thickness. I could have used three hands just then: one to hold my flashlight, one to hold my revolver, and one to pull on the handle. I tucked the flashlight into my right armpit, held my gun with my right hand, and yanked on the recessed handle with my left.

The door hardly budged. I tried again, pulling harder—and almost popped my arm out of its socket. Could the door's tension control have been adjusted to require a transfer's strength to open it? Perhaps.

I tried another pull, and to my astonishment, light began to spill out from the room. I'd hoped to just yank the door open, taking advantage of the element of surprise, but the damned thing was only moving a small increment with each pull of the handle. If there was someone on the other side, and he or she had a gun, it was no doubt now leveled directly at the door.

I stopped for a second, shoved the flashlight into my pocket, and— damn, I hated having to do this—holstered my revolver so that I could free up my other hand to help me pull the door open. With both hands now gripping the recessed handle, I pulled with all my strength, letting out an audible grunt as I did so.

The light from within stung my eyes; they'd grown accustomed to the soft beam from the flashlight. Another pull, and the door panel had now slid far enough into the wall for me to slip into the room by turning side-ways. I took out my gun, and let myself in.

A voice, harsh and mechanical, but no less pitiful for that: *"Please ..."*

My eyes swung to the source of the sound. There was a worktable, with a black top, attached to the far wall. And strapped to that table—

Strapped to that table was a transfer's synthetic body. But this wasn't like the fancy, almost-perfect simulacrum that my client Cassandra inhab-ited. This was a crude, simple humanoid form, with a boxy torso and limbs made up of cylindrical metal segments. And the face—

The face was devoid of any sort of artificial skin. The eyes, blue in color and looking startlingly human, were wide, and the teeth looked like dentures loose in the head. The rest of the face was a mess of pulleys and fiber optics, of metal and plastic.

"Please ..." said the voice again. I looked around the rest of the room.

There was a fusion battery, about the size of a softball, with several cables snaking out of it, including some that led to portable lights. There was also a closet, with a simple door. I pulled it open—this one slid easily—to make sure no one else had hidden in there while I was coming in. An emaciated rat that had been trapped there at some point scooted out of the closet, and through the still partially open corridor door.

I turned my attention to the transfer. The body was clothed in simple denim pants and a T-shirt.

"Are you okay?" I said, looking at the skinless face.

The metal skull moved slightly left and right. The plastic lids for the glass eyeballs retracted, making the non-face into a caricature of imploring. *"Please ..."* he said for a third time.

I looked at the metal restraints holding the artificial body in place: thin nylon bands, pulled taut, that were attached to the tabletop. I couldn't see any release mechanism. "Who are you?" I said.

I was half-prepared for the answer, of course. "Rory Pickover." But it didn't sound anything like the Rory Pickover I'd met: the cultured British accent was absent, and this synthesized voice was much higher pitched.

Still, I shouldn't take this sad thing's statement at face value—especially since it had hardly any face. "Prove it," I said. "Prove you're Rory Pickover."

The glass eyes looked away. Perhaps the transfer was thinking of how to satisfy my demand—or perhaps he was just avoiding my eyes. "My citizenship number is 48394432."

I shook my head. "No good," I said. "It's got to be something *only* Rory Pickover would know."

The eyes looked back at me, the plastic lids lowered, perhaps in suspicion. "It doesn't matter who I am," he said. "Just get me out of here."

That sounded reasonable on the surface of it, but if this *was* another Rory Pickover ...

"Not until you prove your identity to me," I said. "Tell me where the alpha deposit is."

"Damn you," said the transfer. "The other way didn't work, so now you're trying this." The mechanical head looked away. "But this won't work, either."

"Tell me where the alpha deposit is," I said, "and I'll free you."

"I'd rather die," he said. And then, a moment later, he added wistfully, "Except ..."

I finished the thought for him. "Except you can't."

He looked away again. It was hard to feel for something that looked so robotic; that's my excuse, and I'm sticking to it. "Tell me where O'Reilly and Weingarten were digging. Your secret is safe with me."

He said nothing. The gun in my hand was now aimed at the robotic head. "Tell me!" I said. "Tell me before—"

Off in the distance, out in the corridor: the squeal of a rat, and—

Footfalls.

The transfer heard them, too. Its eyes darted left and right in what looked like panic.

"Please," he said, lowering his volume. As soon as he started speaking, I put a vertical index finger to my lips, indicating that he should be quiet, but he continued: "Please, for the love of God, get me out of here. I can't take any more."

I made a beeline for the closet, stepping quickly in and pulling that door most of the way shut behind me. I positioned myself so that I could see—and, if necessary, shoot—through the gap. The footfalls were growing louder. The closet smelled of rat. I waited.

I heard a voice, richer, more human, than the supposed Pickover's. "What the—?"

And I saw a person—a transfer—slipping sideways into the room, just as I had earlier. I couldn't yet see the face from this angle, but it wasn't Joshua. The body was female, and I could see that she was a brunette. I took in air, held it, and—

And she turned, showing her face now. My heart pounded. The delicate features. The wide-spaced green eyes.

Cassandra Wilkins.

My client.

She'd been carrying a flashlight, which she set now on another, smaller table. "Who's been here, Rory?" Her voice was cold.

"No one," he said.

"The door was open."

"You left it that way. I was surprised, but ..." He stopped, perhaps realizing to say any more would be a giveaway that he was lying.

She tilted her head slightly. Even with a transfer's strength, that door must be hard to close. Hopefully she'd find it plausible that she'd given the handle a final tug, and had only assumed that the door had closed completely when she'd last left. Of course, I immediately saw the flaw with that story: you might miss the door not clicking into place, but you wouldn't fail to notice that light was still spilling out into the corridor. But most people don't consider things in such detail; I'd hoped she'd buy Pickover's suggestion.

And, after a moment more's reflection, she seemed to do just that, nodding her head, apparently to herself, then moving closer to the table onto which the synthetic body was strapped. "We don't have to do this again," said Cassandra. "If you just tell me ..."

She let the words hang in the air for a moment, but Pickover made no response. Her shoulders moved up and down a bit in a philosophical shrug. "It's your choice," she said. And then, to my astonishment, she hauled back her right arm and slapped Pickover hard across the robotic face, and—

And Pickover screamed.

It was a long, low, warbling sound, like sheet-metal being warped, a haunted sound, an inhuman sound.

"Please ..." he hissed again, the same plaintive word he'd said to me, the word I, too, had ignored.

Cassandra slapped him again, and again he screamed. Now, I've been slapped by lots of women over the years: it stings, but I've never screamed. And surely an artificial body was made of sterner stuff than me.

Cassandra went for a third slap. Pickover's screams echoed in the dead hulk of the ship.

"Tell me," she said.

I couldn't see his face; her body was obscuring it. Maybe he shook his head. Maybe he just glared defiantly. But he said nothing.

She shrugged again; they'd obviously been down this road before. She moved to one side of the bed and stood by his right arm, which was pinned to his body by the nylon strap. "You really don't want me to do this," she said. "And I don't have to, if..." She let the uncompleted offer hang there for a few seconds, then: "Ah, well." She reached down with her beige, realistic-looking hand, and wrapped three of her fingers around his right index finger. And then she started bending it backward.

I could see Pickover's face now. Pulleys along his jawline were working; he was struggling to keep his mouth shut. His glass eyes were rolling up, back into his head, and his left leg was shaking in spasms. It was a bizarre display, and I alternated moment by moment between feeling sympathy for the being lying there, and feeling cool detachment because of the clearly artificial nature of the body.

Cassandra let go of Pickover's index finger, and, for a second, I thought she was showing some mercy. But then she grabbed it as well as the adjacent finger, and began bending them both back. This time, despite his best efforts, guttural, robotic sounds did escape from Pickover.

"Talk!" Cassandra said. *"Talk!"*

I'd recently learned—from Cassandra herself—that artificial bodies had to have pain sensors; otherwise, a robotic hand might end up resting on a heating element, or too much pressure might be put on a joint. But I hadn't expected such sensors to be so sensitive, and—

And then it hit me, just as another of Pickover's warbling screams was torn from him. Cassandra knew all about artificial bodies; she sold them, after all. If she wanted to adjust the mind-body interface of one so that pain would register particularly acutely, doubtless she could. I'd seen a lot of evil things in my time, but this was perhaps the worst. Scan a mind, put it in a body wired for hypersensitivity to pain, and torture it until it gave up its secrets. Then, of course, you just wipe the mind, and—

"You *will* crack eventually, you know," she said, almost conversationally, as she looked at Pickover's fleshless face. "Given that it's inevitable, you might as well just tell me what I want to know."

The elastic bands that served as some of Pickover's facial muscles contracted, his teeth parted, and his head moved forward slightly but rapidly. I thought for half a second that he was incongruously blowing her a kiss, but then I realized what he was really trying to do: spit at her. Of course, his dry mouth and plastic throat were incapable of generating moisture, but his mind—a human mind, a mind accustomed to a biological body—had summoned and focused all its hate into that most primal of gestures.

"Very well," said Cassandra. She gave his fingers one more nasty yank backwards, holding them at an excruciating angle. Pickover alternated screams and whimpers. Finally, she let his fingers go. "Let's try something different," she said. She leaned over him. With her left hand, she pried his right eyelid open, and then she jabbed her right thumb into that eye. The glass sphere depressed into the metal skull, and Pickover screamed again. The artificial eye was presumably much tougher than a natural one, but, then again, the thumb pressing into it was also tougher. I felt my own eyes watering in a sympathetic response.

Pickover's artificial spine arched up slightly, as he convulsed against the two restraining bands. From time to time, I got clear glimpses of Cassandra's face, and the perfectly symmetrical artificial smile of glee on it was almost as sickening.

At last, she stopped grinding her thumb into his eye. "Had enough?" she said. "Because if you haven't ..."

Pickover was indeed still wearing clothing; it was equally gauche to walk the streets nude whether you were biological or artificial. But now, Cassandra's hands moved to his waist. I watched as she undid his belt, unsnapped and unzipped his jeans, and then pulled the pants as far down his metallic thighs as they would go before she reached the restraining strap that held his legs to the table. Transfers had no need for underwear, and Pickover wasn't wearing any. His artificial penis and testicles now lay exposed. I felt my own scrotum tightening in dread.

And then Cassandra did the most astonishing thing. She'd had no compunctions about bending back his fingers with her bare hands. And she hadn't hesitated when it came to plunging her naked thumb into his eye. But now that she was going to hurt him down there, she seemed to want no direct contact. She started looking around the room; for a second, she was looking directly at the closet door. I scrunched back against the far wall, hoping she wouldn't see me. My heart was pounding.

Finally, she found what she was looking for: a wrench, sitting on the floor. She picked it up, raised the wrench above her head and, and looked directly into Pickover's one good eye—the other had closed as soon as she'd removed her thumb, and had never reopened as far as I could tell. "I'm going to smash your ball bearings into iron filings, unless ..."

He closed his other eye now, the plastic lid scrunching.

"Count of three," she said. "One."

"I can't," he said in that low volume that served as his whisper. "You'd ruin them, sell them off—"

"Two."

"Please! They belong to science! To all humanity!"

"Three!"

Her arm slammed down, a great arc slicing through the air, the silver wrench smashing into the plastic pouch that was Pickover's scrotum. He let out a scream greater than any I'd yet heard, so loud, indeed, that it hurt my ears despite the muffling of the partially closed closet door.

She hauled her arm up again, but waited for the scream to devolve into a series of whimpers. "One more chance," she said. "Count of three." His whole body was shaking. I felt nauseous.

"One."

He turned his head to the side, as if by looking away he could make the torture stop.

"Two."

A whimper escaped his artificial throat.

"Three!"

I found myself looking away, too, unable to watch as—

"All right!"

It was Pickover's voice, shrill and mechanical, shouting.

"All right!" he shouted again. I turned back to face the tableau: the human-looking woman with a wrench held up above her head, and the terrified mechanical-looking man strapped to the table. "All right," he repeated once more, softly now. "I'll tell you what you want to know."

"You'll tell me where the alpha deposit is?" asked Cassandra, lowering her arm.

"Yes," he said. "Yes."

"Where?"

Pickover was quiet.

"Where?"

"God forgive me ..." he said softly.

She began to raise her arm again. *"Where?"*

"Sixteen-point-four kilometers south-southwest of Nili Patera," he said. "The precise coordinates are ..." and he spoke a string of numbers.

"You better be telling the truth," Cassandra said.

"I am." His voice was tiny. "To my infinite shame, I am."

Cassandra nodded. "Maybe. But I'll leave you tied up here until I'm sure."

"But I told you the truth! I told you everything you need to know."

"Sure you did," said Cassandra. "But I'll just confirm that."

I stepped out the closet, my gun aimed directly at Cassandra's back. "Freeze," I said.

Cassandra spun around. "Lomax!"

"Mrs. Wilkins," I said, nodding. "I guess you don't need me to find your husband for you anymore, eh? Now that you've got the information he stole."

"What? No, no. I still want you to find Joshua. Of course I do!"

"So you can share the wealth with him?"

"Wealth?" She looked over at the hapless Pickover. "Oh. Well, yes, there's a lot of money at stake." She smiled. "So much so that I'd be happy to cut you in, Mr. Lomax—oh, you're a good man. I know you wouldn't hurt me!"

I shook my head. "You'd betray me the first chance you got."

"No, I wouldn't. I'll need protection; I understand that—what with all the money the fossils will bring. Having someone like you on my side only makes sense."

I looked over at Pickover and shook my head. "You tortured that man."

"That 'man,' as you call him, wouldn't have existed at all without me. And the real Pickover isn't inconvenienced in the slightest."

"But ... *torture*," I said. "It's inhuman."

She jerked a contemptuous thumb at Pickover. "He's not human. Just some software running on some hardware."

"That's what you are, too."

"That's *part* of what I am," Cassandra said. "But I'm also *authorized.* He's bootleg—and bootlegs have no rights."

"I'm not going to argue philosophy with you."

"Fine. But remember who works for whom, Mr. Lomax. I'm the client—and I'm going to be on my way now."

I held my gun rock-steady. "No, you're not."

She looked at me. "An interesting situation," she said, her tone even. "I'm unarmed, and you've got a gun. Normally, that would put you in charge, wouldn't it? But your gun probably won't stop me. Shoot me in the head, and the bullet will just bounce off my metal skull. Shoot me in the chest, and at worst you might damage some components that I'll eventually have to get replaced—which I can, and at a discount, to boot.

"Meanwhile," she continued, "I have the strength of ten men; I could literally pull your limbs from their sockets, or crush your head between my hands, squeezing it until it pops like a melon and your brains, such as they are, squirt out. So, what's it going to be, Mr. Lomax? Are you going to let me walk out that door and be about my business? Or are you going to pull that trigger, and start something that's going to end with you dead?"

I was used to a gun in my hand giving me a sense of power, of security. But just then, the Smith & Wesson felt like a lead weight. She was right: shooting her with it was likely to be no more useful than just throwing it at her. Of course, there were crucial components in an artificial body's makeup; I just didn't happen to know what they were, and, anyway, they probably varied from model to model. If I could be sure to drop her with one shot, I'd do it. I'd killed before in self-defense, but ...

But this wasn't self-defense. Not really. If I didn't start something, she was just going to walk out. Could I kill in cold ... well, not cold *blood.* But she *was* right: she was a person, even if Pickover wasn't. She was the one and only legal instantiation of Cassandra Wilkins. The cops might be corrupt here, and they might be lazy. But even they wouldn't turn a blind eye on attempted murder. If I shot her, and somehow got away, they'd hunt me down. And if I didn't get away, she *would* be attacking me in self-defense.

"So," she said, at last. "What's it going to be?"

"You make a persuasive argument, Mrs. Wilkins," I said in the most reasonable tone I could muster under the circumstances.

And then, without changing my facial expression in the slightest, I pulled the trigger.

I wondered if a transfer's time sense ever slows down, or if it is always perfectly quartz-crystal timed. Certainly, time seemed to attenuate for me then. I swear I could actually see the bullet as it followed its trajectory from my gun, covering the three meters between the barrel and—

And not, of course, Cassandra's torso.

Nor her head.

She was right; I probably couldn't harm her that way.

No, instead, I'd aimed past her, at the table on which the *faux* Pickover was lying on his back. Specifically, I'd aimed at the place where the thick nylon band that crossed over his torso, pinning his arms, was anchored on the right-hand side—the point where it made a taut diagonal line between where it was attached to the side of the table and the top of Pickover's arm.

The bullet sliced through the band, cutting it in two. The long portion, freed of tension, flew up and over his torso like a snake that had just had forty thousand volts pumped through it.

Cassandra's eyes went wide in astonishment that I'd missed her, and her head swung around. The report of the bullet was still ringing in my ears, of course, but I swear I could also hear the *zzzzinnnng!* of the restraining band snapping free. To be hypersensitive to pain, I figured you'd have to have decent reaction times, and I hoped that Pickover had been smart enough to note in advance my slight deviation of aim before I fired it.

And, indeed, no sooner were his arms free than he sat bolt upright—his legs were still restrained—and grabbed one of Cassandra's arms, pulling her toward him. I leapt in the meager Martian gravity. Most of Cassandra's body was made of lightweight composites and synthetic materials, but I was still good old flesh and blood: I outmassed her by at least thirty kilos. My impact propelled her backwards, and she slammed against the table's side. Pickover shot out his other arm, grabbing Cassandra's second arm, pinning her backside against the edge of the table. I struggled to regain a sure footing, then brought my gun up to her right temple.

"All right, sweetheart," I said. "Do you really want to test how strong your artificial skull is?"

Cassandra's mouth was open; had she still been biological, she'd probably have been gasping for breath. But her heartless chest was perfectly still. "You can't just shoot me," she said.

"Why not? Pickover here will doubtless back me up when I say it was self-defense, won't you, Pickover?"

He nodded. "Absolutely."

"In fact," I said, "you, me, this Pickover, and the other Pickover are the only ones who know where the alpha deposit is. I think the three of us would be better off without you on the scene anymore."

"You won't get away with it," said Cassandra. "You can't."

"I've gotten away with plenty over the years," I said. "I don't see an end to that in sight." I cocked the hammer, just for fun.

"Look," she said, "there's no need for this. We can all share in the wealth. There's plenty to go around."

"Except you don't have any rightful claim to it," said Pickover. "You stole a copy of my mind, and tortured me. And you want to be rewarded for that?"

"Pickover's right," I said. "It's his treasure, not yours."

"It's *humanity's* treasure," corrected Pickover. "It belongs to all mankind."

"But I'm your client," Cassandra said to me.

"So's he. At least, the legal version of him is."

Cassandra sounded desperate. "But—but that's a conflict of interest!"

"So sue me," I said.

She shook her head in disgust. "You're just in this for yourself!"

I shrugged amiably, and then pressed the barrel even tighter against her artificial head. "Aren't we all?"

"Shoot her," said Pickover. I looked at him. He was still holding her upper arms, pressing them in close to her torso. If he'd been biological, the twisting of his torso to accommodate doing that probably would have been quite uncomfortable. Actually, now that I thought of it, given his heightened sensitivity to pain, even this artificial version was probably hurting from twisting that way. But apparently this was a pain he was happy to endure.

"Do you really want me to do that?" I said. "I mean, I can understand, after what she did to you, but ..." I didn't finish the thought; I just left it in the air for him to take or leave.

"She *tortured* me," he said. "She deserves to die."

I frowned, unable to dispute his logic—but, at the same time, wondering if Pickover knew that he was as much on trial here as she was.

"Can't say I blame you," I said again, and then added another "but," and once more left the thought incomplete.

At last, Pickover nodded. "But maybe you're right. I can't offer her any compassion, but I don't need to see her dead."

A look of plastic relief rippled over Cassandra's face. I nodded. "Good man," I said. I'd killed before, but I never enjoyed it.

"But, still," said Pickover, "I would like *some* revenge."

Cassandra's upper arms were still pinned by Pickover, but her lower arms were free. To my astonishment, they both moved. The movement startled me, and I looked down, just in time to see them jerking toward her groin, almost as if to protect ...

I found myself staggering backward; it took a second for me to regain my balance. *"Oh, my God ..."*

Cassandra had quickly moved her arms back to a neutral, hanging-down position—but it was too late. The damage had been done.

"You ..." I said. I normally was never at a loss for words, but I was just then. "You're ..."

Pickover had seen it, too; his torso had been twisted just enough to allow him to do so.

"No woman ..." he began slowly.

Cassandra hadn't wanted to touch Pickover's groin—even though it was artificial—with her bare hands. And when Pickover had suggested exacting revenge for what had been done to him, Cassandra's hands had moved instinctively to protect—

Jesus, why hadn't I see it before? The way she plunked herself down in a chair, the fact that she couldn't bring herself to wear makeup or jewelry in her new body; her discomfort at intimately touching or being intimately touched by men: it was obvious in retrospect.

Cassandra's hands had moved instinctively to protect *her own testicles*.

"You're not Cassandra Wilkins," I said.

"Of course I am," said the female voice.

"Not on the inside, you're not," I said. "You're a man. Whatever mind has been transferred into that body is male."

Cassandra twisted violently. Goddamned Pickover, perhaps stunned by the revelation, had obviously loosened his grip, because she got free. I fired my gun again and the bullet went straight into her chest; a streamer of machine oil, like from a punctured can, shot out, but there was no sign that the bullet had slowed her down.

"Don't let her get away!" shouted Pickover, in his rough mechanical voice. I swung my gun on him, and for a second I could see terror in his eyes, as if he thought I meant to off him for letting her twist away. But I aimed at the nylon strap restraining his legs and fired. This time, the bullet only partially severed the strap. I reach down and yanked at the remaining filaments, and so did Pickover. They finally broke and this strap, like the first, snapped free. Pickover swung his legs off the table, and immediately stood up. An artificial body had many advantages, among them not being woozy or dizzy after lying down for God-only-knew how many days.

In the handful of seconds it had taken to free Pickover, Cassandra had made it out the door that I'd pried partway open, and was now running down the corridor in the darkness. I could hear splashing sounds, meaning she'd veered far enough off the corridor's centerline to end up in the water pooling along the starboard side, and I heard her actually bump into the wall at one point, although she immediately continued on. She didn't have her flashlight, and the only illumination in the corridor would have been what was spilling out of the room I was now in—a fading glow to her rear as she ran along, whatever shadow she herself was casting adding to the difficulty of seeing ahead.

I squeezed out into the corridor. I still had my flashlight in my pocket; I fished it out and aimed it just in front of me; Cassandra wouldn't benefit much from the light it was giving off. Pickover, who, I noted, had now done his pants back up, had made his way through the half-open door and was now standing beside me. I started running, and he fell in next to me.

Our footfalls now drowned out the sound of Cassandra's; I guessed she must be some thirty or forty meters ahead. Although it was almost pitch black, she presumably had the advantage of having come down this corridor several times before; neither Pickover nor I had ever gone in this direction.

A rat scampered out of our way, squealing as it did so. My breathing was already ragged, but I managed to say, "How well can you guys see in the dark?"

Pickover's voice, of course, showed no signs of exertion. "Only slightly better than biologicals can."

I nodded, although he'd have to have had better vision than he'd just laid claim to in order to see it. My legs were a lot longer than Cassandra's, but I suspected she could pump them more rapidly. I swung the flashlight beam up, letting it lance out ahead of us for a moment. There she was, off in the distance. I dropped the beam back to the floor in front of me.

More splashing from up ahead; she'd veered off once more. I thought about firing a shot—more for the drama of it, than any serious hope of bringing her down—when I suddenly became aware that Pickover was passing me. His robotic legs were as long as my natural ones, and he could piston them up and down at least as quickly as Cassandra could.

I tried to match his speed, but wasn't able to. Even in Martian gravity, running fast is hard work. I swung my flashlight up again, but Pickover's body, now in front of me, was obscuring everything further down the corridor; I had no idea how far ahead Cassandra was now—and the intervening form of Pickover prevented me from acting out my idle fantasy of squeezing off a shot.

Pickover continued to pull ahead. I was passing open door after open door, black mouths gaping at me in the darkness. I heard more rats, and Pickover's footfalls, and—

Suddenly, something jumped on my back from behind me. A hard arm was around my neck, pressing sharply down on my Adam's apple. I tried to call out to Pickover, but couldn't get enough breath out ... or in. I craned my neck as much as I could, and shone the flashlight beam up on the ceiling, so that some light reflected down onto my back from above.

It was Cassandra! She'd ducked into one of the other rooms, and lain in wait for me. Pickover was no detective; he had completely missed the signs of his quarry no longer being in front of him—and I'd had Pickover's body blocking my vision, plus the echoing bangs of his footfalls to obscure my hearing. I could see my own chilled breath, but, of course, not hers.

I tried again to call out to Pickover, but all I managed was a hoarse croak, doubtless lost on him amongst the noise of his own running. I was already oxygen-deprived from exertion, and the constricting of my throat was making things worse; despite the darkness I was now seeing white flashes in front of my eyes, a sure sign of asphyxiation. I only had a few seconds to act—

And act I did. I crouched down as low as I could, Cassandra still on my back, her head sticking up above mine, and I leapt with all the strength I could muster. Even weakened, I managed a powerful kick, and in this low Martian gravity, I shot up like a bullet. Cassandra's metal skull smashed into the roof of the corridor. There happened to be a lighting fixture directly above me, and I heard the sounds of shattering glass and plastic.

I was descending now in maddeningly slow motion, but as soon as I was down, Cassandra still clinging hard to me, I surged forward a couple of paces then leapt up again. This time, there was nothing but unrelenting bulkhead overhead, and Cassandra's metal skull slammed hard into it.

Again the slow-motion fall. I felt something thick and wet oozing through my shirt. For a second, I'd thought Cassandra had stabbed me—but no, it was probably the machine oil leaking from the bullet hole I'd put in her earlier. By the time we had touched down again, Cassandra had loosened her grip on my neck as she tried to scramble off me. I spun around and fell forward, pushing her backward onto the corridor floor, me tumbling on top of her. Despite my best efforts, the flashlight was knocked from my grip by the impact, and it spun around, doing a few complete circles before it ended up with its beam facing away from us.

I still had my revolver in my other hand, though. I brought it up, and, by touch, found Cassandra's face, probing the barrel roughly over it. Once, in my early days, I'd rammed a gun barrel into a thug's mouth; this time, I had other ideas. I got the barrel positioned directly over her left eye, and pressed down hard with it—a little poetic justice.

I said, "I bet if I shoot through your glass eye, aiming up a bit, I'll tear your artificial brain apart. You want to find out?"

She said nothing. I called back over my shoulder, *"Pickover!"* The name echoed down the corridor, but I had no idea whether he heard me. I turned my attention back to Cassandra—or whoever the hell this really was. I cocked the trigger. "As far as I'm concerned, Cassandra Wilkins is my client—but you're not her. Who are you?"

"I *am* Cassandra Wilkins," said the voice.

"No, you're not," I said. "You're a man—or, at least, you've got a man's mind."

"I can *prove* I'm Cassandra Wilkins," said the supine form. "My name is Cassandra Pauline Wilkins; my birth name is Collier. I was born in Sioux City, Iowa, on 30 October 2079. I immigrated to New Klondike in July 2102. My citizenship number is—"

"Facts. Figures." I shook my head. "Anyone could find those things out."

"But I know stuff no one else could possibly know. I know the name of my childhood pets; I know what I did to get thrown out of school when I was fifteen; I know precisely where the original me had a tattoo; I ..."

She went on, but I stopped listening.

Jesus Christ, it was almost the perfect crime. No one could really get away with stealing somebody else's identity—not for long. The lack of intimate knowledge of how the original spoke, of private things the original knew, would soon enough give you away, unless—

Unless you were the *spouse* of the person whose identity you'd appropriated.

"You're not Cassandra Wilkins," I said. "You're Joshua Wilkins. You took her body; you transferred into it, and she transferred—" I felt my stomach tighten; it really was a nearly perfect crime. "And she transferred *nowhere*; when the original was euthanized, she died. And that makes you guilty of murder."

"You can't prove that," said the female voice. "No biometrics, no DNA, no fingerprints. I'm whoever I say I am."

"You and Cassandra hatched this scheme together," I said. "You both figured Pickover had to know where the alpha deposit was. But then you decided that you didn't want to share the wealth with anyone—not even your wife. And so you got rid of her, and made good your escape at the same time."

"That's crazy," the female voice said. "I *hired* you. Why on—on *Mars*—would I do that, then?"

"You expected to the police to come out to investigate your missing-person report; they were supposed to find the body in the basement of NewYou. But they didn't, and you knew suspicion would fall on you—the supposed spouse!—if you were the one who found it. So you hired me—the dutiful wife, worried about her poor, missing hubby! All you wanted was for me to find the body."

"Words," said Joshua. "Just words."

"Maybe so," I said. "I don't have to satisfy anyone else. Just me. I will give you one chance, though. See, I want to get out of here alive—and I don't see any way to do that if I leave you alive, too. Do you? If you've got an answer, tell me—otherwise, I've got no choice but to pull this trigger."

"I promise I'll let you go," said Joshua.

I laughed, and the sound echoed in the corridor. "You promise? Well, I'm sure I can take that to the bank."

"No, seriously," said Joshua. "I won't tell anyone. I—"

"Are you Joshua Wilkins?" I asked.

Silence.

"Are you?"

I felt the face moving up and down a bit, the barrel of my gun shifting slightly in the eye socket as it did so. "Yes."

"Well, rest in peace," I said, and then, with relish, added, *"Josh."*

I pulled the trigger.

The flash from the gun barrel briefly lit up the female, freckled face, which was showing almost human horror. The revolver snapped back in my hand, then everything was dark again. I had no idea how much damage the bullet would do to the brain. Of course, the artificial chest wasn't rising and falling, but it never had been. And there was nowhere to check for a pulse. I decided I'd better try another shot, just to be sure. I shifted slightly, thinking I'd put this one through the other eye, and—

And Joshua's arms burst up, pushing me off him. I felt myself go airborne, and was aware of Joshua scrambling to his feet. He scooped up the flashlight, and as he swung it and himself around, it briefly illuminated his face. There was a deep pit where one eye used to be.

I started to bring the gun up and—

And Joshua thumbed off the flashlight. The only illumination was a tiny bit of light, far, far down the corridor, spilling out from the torture room; it wasn't enough to let me see Joshua clearly. But I squeezed the trigger, and heard a bullet ricochet—either off some part of Joshua's metal internal skeleton, or off the corridor wall.

I was the kind of guy who always knew *exactly* how many bullets he had left: two. I wasn't sure I wanted to fire them both off blindly, but—

I could hear Joshua moving closer. I fired again. This time, the feminine voice box made a sound between an *oomph* and the word "ouch," so I knew I'd hit him.

One bullet to go.

I started walking backward—which was no worse than walking forward; I was just as likely to trip either way in this near-total darkness. The body in the shape of Cassandra Wilkins was much smaller than mine—but also, although it shamed the macho me to admit it, much stronger. It could probably grab me by the shoulders and pound my head up into the ceiling, just as I'd pounded hers—and I rather suspect mine wouldn't survive. And if I let it get hold of my arm, it could probably wrench the gun from me; five bullets hadn't been enough to stop the artificial body, but one was all it would take to ice me for good.

And so I decided it was better to have an empty gun than a gun that could potentially be turned on me. I held the weapon out in front, took my best guess, and squeezed the trigger one last time.

The revolver barked, and the flare from the muzzle lit the scene, stinging my eyes. The artificial form cried out—I'd hit a spot its sensors felt was worth protecting with a major pain response, I guess. But the being kept moving forward. Part of me thought about turning tail and running—I still had the longer legs, even if I couldn't move them as fast—but another part of me couldn't bring myself to do that. The gun was of no more use, so I threw it aside. It hit the corridor wall, making a banging sound, then fell to the deck plates, producing more clanging as it bounced against them.

Of course, as soon as I'd thrown the gun away, I realized I'd made a mistake. *I* knew how many bullets I'd shot, and how many the gun held, but Joshua probably didn't; even an empty gun could be a deterrent if the other person thought it was loaded.

We were facing each other—but that was all that was certain. Precisely how much distance there was between us I couldn't say. Although running produced loud, echoing footfalls, either of us could have moved a step or two forward or back—or left or right—without the other being aware of it. I was trying not to make any noise, and a transfer could stand perfectly still, and be absolutely quiet, for hours on end.

I had no idea how badly I'd hurt him. In fact, given that he'd played possum once before, it was possible the sounds of pain were faked, just to make me think he was damaged. My great grandfather said clocks used to make a ticking sound with the passing of each second; I'd never heard such a thing, but I was certainly conscious of time passing in increments as we stood there, each waiting for the other to make a move.

Suddenly, light exploded in my face. He'd thumbed the flashlight back on, aiming it at what turned out to be a very good guess as to where my eyes were. I was temporarily blinded, but his one remaining mechanical eye responded more efficiently, I guess, because now that he knew exactly where I was, he leapt, propelling himself through the air and knocking me down.

This time, both hands closed around my neck. I still outmassed Joshua and managed to roll us over, so he was on his back and I was on top. I arched my back and slammed my knee into his balls, hoping he'd release me ...

... except, of course, he didn't have any balls; he only thought he did. *Damn!*

The hands were still closing around my gullet; despite the chill air, I felt myself sweating. But with his hands occupied, mine were free: I pushed my right hand onto his chest—startled by the feeling of artificial breasts there—and probed around until I found the slick, wet hole my first bullet had made. I hooked my right thumb into that hole, pulled sideways, and brought in my left thumb, as well, squeezing it down into the opening, ripping it wider and wider. I thought if I could get at the internal components, I might be able to rip out something crucial. The artificial flesh was soft, and there was a layer of what felt like foam rubber beneath it—and beneath that, I could feel hard metal parts. I tried to get my whole hand in, tried to yank out whatever I could, but I was fading fast. My pulse was thundering so loudly in my ears I couldn't hear anything else, just a *thump-thump-thumping*, over and over again, the *thump-thump-thumping* of ...

Of footfalls! Someone was running this way, and—

And the scene lit up as flashlights came to bear on us.

"There they are!" said a harsh, mechanical voice that I recognized as belonging to Pickover. "There they are!"

"NKPD!" shouted another voice I also recognized—a deep, Scottish brogue. "Let Lomax go!"

Joshua looked up. "Back off!" he shouted—in that female voice. "If you don't, I'll finish him."

Through blurring vision, I thought I could see Mac hesitating. But then he spoke again. "If you kill him, you'll go down for murder. You don't want that."

Joshua relaxed his grip a bit—not enough to let me escape, but enough to keep me alive as a hostage, at least a little while longer. I sucked in cold air, but my lungs still felt like they were on fire. In the illumination from the flashlights I could see the improved copy of Cassandra Wilkins's face craning now to look at McCrae. Transfers didn't show as much emotion as biologicals did, but it was clear that Joshua was panicking.

I was still on top. I thought if I waited until Joshua was distracted, I could yank free of his grip without him snapping my neck. "Let go of him," Mac said firmly. It was hard to see him; he was the one holding the light source, after all, but I suddenly became aware that he was also holding a large disk. "Release his neck, or I'll deactivate you for sure."

Joshua practically had to roll his green eyes up into his head to see Mac, standing behind him. "You ever use one of those before?" he said, presumably referring to the disrupter disk. "No, I know you haven't—no transfer has been killed on Mars in weeks, and that technology only just came out. Well, I work in the transference business. I know the disruption isn't instantaneous. Yes, you can kill me—but not before I kill Lomax."

"You're lying," said McCrae. He handed his flashlight to Pickover, and brought the disk up in front of him, holding it vertically by its two U-shaped handles. "I've read the specs."

"Are you willing to take that chance?" asked Joshua.

I could only arch my neck a bit; it was very hard for me to look up and see Mac, but he seemed to be frowning, and, after a second, he turned partially away. Pickover was standing behind him, and—

And suddenly an electric whine split the air, and Joshua was convulsing beneath me, and his hands were squeezing my throat even more tightly than before. The whine—a high keening sound—must have been coming from the disrupter. I still had my hands inside Joshua's chest and could feel his whole interior vibrating as his body racked. I yanked my hands out and grabbed onto his arms, pulling with all my might. His hands popped free from my throat, and his whole luscious female form was shaking rapidly. I rolled off him; the artificial body kept convulsing as the keening continued. I gasped for breath and all I could think about for several moments was getting air into me.

After my head cleared a bit, I looked again at Joshua, who was still convulsing, and then I looked up at Mac, who was banging on the side of the disrupter disk. I realized that, now that he'd activated it, he had no idea how to deactivate it. As I watched, he started to turn it over, presumably hoping there was some control he'd missed on the side he couldn't see—and I realized that if he completed his move, the disk would be aimed backward, in the direction of Pickover. Pickover clearly saw this, too: he was throwing his robot-like arms up, as if to shield his face—not that that could possibly do any good.

I tried to shout "No!," but my voice was too raw, and all that came out was a hoarse exhalation of breath, the sound of which was lost beneath the keening. In my peripheral vision, I could see Joshua lying facedown. His vicious spasms stopped as the beam from the disrupter was no longer aimed at him.

But even though I didn't have any voice left, Pickover did, and his shout of *"Don't!"* was loud enough to be heard over the electric whine of the disrupter. Mac continued to rotate the disk a few more degrees before he realized what Pickover was referring to. He flipped the disk back around, then continued turning it until the emitter surface was facing straight down. And then he dropped it, and it fell in Martian slo-mo, at last clanking against the deck plates, a counterpoint to the now-muffled electric whine. I hauled myself to my feet and moved over to check on Joshua, while Pickover and Mac hovered over the disk, presumably looking for the off switch.

There were probably more scientific ways to see if the transferred Joshua was dead, but this one felt right just then: I balanced on one foot, hauled back the other leg, and kicked the son of a bitch in the side of that gorgeous head. The impact was strong enough to spin the whole body through a quarter-turn, but there was no reaction at all from Joshua.

Suddenly, the keening died, and I heard a self-satisfied *"There!"* from Mac. I looked over at him, and he looked back at me, caught in the beam from the flashlight Pickover was holding. Mac's bushy orange eyebrows were raised and there was a sheepish grin on his face. "Who'd have thought the off switch had to be pulled out instead of pushed in?"

I tried to speak, and found that I did have a little voice now. "Thanks for coming by, Mac. I know how you hate to leave the station."

Mac nodded in Pickover's direction. "Yeah, well, you can thank this guy for putting in the call," he said. He turned, and faced Pickover full-on. "Just who the hell are you, anyway?"

I saw Pickover's mouth begin to open in his mechanical head, and a thought rushed through my mind. This Pickover was bootleg. Both the other Pickover and Joshua Wilkins had been correct: such a being shouldn't exist, and had no rights. Indeed, the legal Pickover would doubtless continue to demand that this version be destroyed; no one wanted an unauthorized copy of himself wandering around.

Mac was looking away from me, and toward the duplicate of Pickover. And so I made a wide sweeping of my head, left to right, then back again. Pickover apparently saw it, because he closed his mouth before sounds came out, and I spoke, as loudly and clearly as I could in my current condition. "Let me do the introductions," I said, and I waited for Mac to turn back toward me.

When he had, I pointed at Mac. "Detective Dougal McCrae," I said, then I took a deep breath, let it out slowly, and pointed at Pickover, "I'd like you to meet Joshua Wilkins."

Mac nodded, accepting this. "So you found your man? Congratulations, Alex." He then looked down at the motionless female body. "Too bad about your wife, Mr. Wilkins."

Pickover turned to face me, clearly seeking guidance. "It's so sad," I said quickly. "She was insane, Mac—had been threatening to kill her poor husband Joshua here for weeks. He decided to fake his own death to escape her, but she got wise to it somehow, and hunted him down. I had no choice but to try to stop her."

As if on cue, Pickover walked over to the dead artificial body, and crouched beside it. "My poor dear wife," he said, somehow managing to make his mechanical voice sound tender. He lifted his skinless face toward Mac. "This planet does that to people, you know. Makes them go crazy." He shook his head. "So many dreams dashed."

Mac looked at me, then at Pickover, then at the artificial body lying on the deck plating, then back at me. "All right, Alex," he said, nodding slowly. "Good work."

I tipped my nonexistent hat at him. "Glad to be of help."

■ ■ ■

I walked into the dark interior of the Bent Chisel, whistling.

Buttrick was behind the bar, as usual. "You again, Lomax?"

"The one and only," I replied cheerfully. That topless waitress I'd slept with a couple of times was standing next to the bar, loading up her tray. I looked at her, and suddenly her name came to me. "Hey, Diana!" I said.

"When you get off tonight, how 'bout you and me go out and paint the town ..." I trailed off: the town was *already* red; the whole damned planet was.

Diana's face lit up, but Buttrick raised a beefy hand. "Not so fast, lover boy. If you've got the money to take her out, you've got the money to settle your tab."

I slapped two golden hundred-solar coins on the countertop. "That should cover it." Buttrick's eyes went as round as the coins, and he scooped them up immediately, as if he was afraid they'd disappear—which, in this joint, they probably would.

"I'll be in the booth in the back," I said to Diana. "I'm expecting Mr. Santos; when he arrives, could you bring him over?"

Diana smiled. "Sure thing, Alex. Meanwhile, what can I get you? Your usual poison?"

I shook my head. "Nah, none of that rotgut. Bring me the best scotch you've got—and pour it over *water* ice."

Buttrick narrowed his eyes. "That'll cost extra."

"No problem," I said. "Start up a new tab for me."

A few minutes later, Diana came by the booth with my drink, accompanied by Raoul Santos. He took the seat opposite me. "This better be on you, Alex," said Raoul. "You still owe me for the help I gave you at Dr. Pickover's place."

"Indeed it is, old boy. Have whatever you please."

Raoul rested his receding chin on his open palm. "You seem in a good mood."

"Oh, I am," I said. "I got paid this week."

The man the world now accepted as Joshua Wilkins had returned to NewYou, where he'd gotten his face finished and his artificial body upgraded. After that, he told people it was too painful to continue to work there, given what had happened with his wife. So he sold the NewYou franchise to his associate, Horatio Fernandez. The money from the sale gave him plenty to live on, especially now that he didn't need food and didn't have to pay the life-support tax anymore. He gave me all the fees his dear departed wife should have—plus a very healthy bonus.

I'd asked him what he was going to do now. "Well," he said, "even if you're the only one who knows it, I'm still a paleontologist—and now I can spend days on end out on the surface. I'm going to look for new fossil beds."

And what about the other Pickover—the official one? It took some doing, but I managed to convince him that it had actually been the late Cassandra, not Joshua, who had stolen a copy of his mind, and that she was the one who had installed it in an artificial body. I told Dr. Pickover that when Joshua discovered what his wife had done, he destroyed the bootleg and dumped the ruined body that had housed it in the basement of the NewYou building.

Not too shabby, eh? Still, I wanted more. I rented a surface suit and a Mars buggy and headed out to 16.4 kilometers south-southwest of Nili Patera. I figured I'd pick myself up a lovely rhizomorph or a nifty pentaped, and never have to work again.

Well, I looked and looked and looked, but I guess the duplicate Pickover had lied about where the alpha deposit was; even under torture, he hadn't betrayed his beloved fossils. I'm sure Weingarten and O'Reilly's source is out there somewhere, though, and the legal Pickover is doubtless hard at work thinking of ways to protect it from looters.

I hope he succeeds. I really do.

But for now, I'm content just to enjoy this lovely scotch.

"How about a toast?" suggested Raoul, once Diana had brought him his booze.

"I'm game," I said. "To what?"

Raoul frowned, considering. Then his eyebrows climbed his broad forehead, and he said, "To being true to your innermost self."

We clinked glasses. "I'll drink to that."

Come All Ye Faithful

Sometimes, quite unintentionally, a writer develops a schtick: something that identifies himself or herself to the reading public.

*Early in my career, there was no doubt that dinosaurs were my schtick. Four of my first five novels dealt with them: the Quintaglio trilogy (*Far-Seer, Fossil Hunter, *and* Foreigner*), and the standalone* End of an Era. *The great beasts are also all over my first short-story collection,* Iterations, *published in 2002.*

But starting with my fifth novel, The Terminal Experiment *(winner of the 1995 Nebula Award), my schtick, it seems, has been the conflict between faith and rationality. That theme also runs through such later books as* Calculating God *and my Neanderthal Parallax trilogy (the Hugo-winning* Hominids, *plus* Humans *and* Hybrids*).*

And it's here again, in this short story, which was written for my dear friend Julie E. Czerneda's Space Inc., *an anthology about off-Earth jobs.*

❖ ■ ■ ❖

"Damned social engineers," said Boothby, frowning his freckled face. He looked at me, as if expecting an objection to the profanity, and seemed disappointed that I didn't rise to the bait.

"As you said earlier," I replied calmly, "it doesn't make any practical difference."

He tried to get me again: "Damn straight. Whether Jody and I just live together or are legally married shouldn't matter one whit to anyone but us."

I wasn't going to give him the pleasure of telling him it mattered to God; I just let him go on. "Anyway," he said, spreading hands that were also freckled, "since we have to be married before the Company will give us a license to have a baby, Jody's decided she wants the whole shebang: the cake, the fancy reception, the big service."

I nodded. "And that's where I come in."

"That's right, Padre." It seemed to tickle him to call me that. "Only you and Judge Hiromi can perform ceremonies here, and, well ..."

"Her honor's office doesn't have room for a real ceremony, with a lot of attendees," I offered.

"That's it!" crowed Boothby, as if I'd put my finger on a heinous conspiracy. "That's exactly it. So, you see my predicament, Padre."

I nodded. "You're an atheist. You don't hold with any religious mumbo-jumbo. But, to please your bride-to-be, you're willing to have the ceremony here at Saint Teresa's."

"Right. But don't get the wrong idea about Jody. She's not ..."

He trailed off. Anywhere else on Mars, declaring someone wasn't religious, wasn't a practicing Christian or Muslim or Jew, would be perfectly acceptable—indeed, would be the expected thing. Scientists, after all, looked askance at anyone who professed religion; it was as socially unacceptable as farting in an airlock.

But now Boothby was unsure about giving voice to what in all other circumstances would have been an easy disclaimer. He'd stopped in here at Saint Teresa's over his lunch hour to see if I would perform the service, but was afraid now that I'd turn him down if he revealed that I was being asked to unite two nonbelievers in the most holy of institutions.

He didn't understand why I was here—why the Archdiocese of New York had put up the money to bring a priest to Mars, despite the worldwide shortage of Catholic clergy. The Roman Catholic Church would always rather see two people married by clergy than living in sin—and so, since touching down at Utopia Planitia, I'd united putative Protestants, secular Jews, and more. And I'd gladly marry Boothby and his fiancée. "Not to worry," I said. "I'd be honored if you had your ceremony here."

Boothby looked relieved. "Thank you," he replied. "Just, you know, not too many prayers."

I forced a smile. "Only the bare minimum."

Boothby wasn't alone. Almost everyone here thought having me on Mars was a waste of oxygen. But the New York Diocese was rich, and they knew that if the church didn't have a presence early on in Bradbury Colony, room would never be made for it.

There had been several priests who had wanted this job, many with much better theological credentials than I had. But two things were in my favor. First, I had low food requirements, doing fine on just 1200 calories a day. And second, I have a Ph.D. in astronomy, and had spent four years with the Vatican observatory.

The stars had been my first love; it was only later that I'd wondered who put them there. Ironically, taking the priest job here on Mars had meant giving up my celestial research, although being an astronomer meant that I could double for one of the "more important" colonists, if he or she happened to get sick. That fact appeased some of those who had tried to prevent my traveling here.

It had been a no-brainer for me: studying space from the ground, or actually going into space. Still, it seemed as though I was the only person on all of Mars who was really happy that I was here.

Hatch 'em, match 'em, and dispatch 'em—that was the usual lot for clergy. Well, we hadn't had any births yet, although we would soon. And no one had died since I'd arrived. That left marriages.

Of course, I did perform mass every Sunday, and people did come out. But it wasn't like a mass on Earth. Oh, we had a choir—but the people who had joined it all made a point of letting each other know that they weren't religious; they simply liked to sing. And, yes, there were some bodies warming the pews, but they seemed just to be looking for something to do; leisure-time activities were mighty scarce on Mars.

Perhaps that's why there were so few troubled consciences: there was nothing to get into mischief with. Certainly, no one had yet come for confession. And when we did communion, people always took the wine—of which there wasn't much available elsewhere—but I usually had a bunch of wafers left at the end.

Ah, well. I would do a bang-up job for Boothby and Jody on the wedding—so good that maybe they'd let me perform a baptism later.

"Father Bailey?" said a voice.

I turned around. Someone else needing me for something, and on a Thursday? Well, well, well ...

"Yes?" I said, looking at the young woman.

"I'm Loni Sinclair," she said. "From the Communications Center."

"What can I do for you, my child?"

"Nothing," she said. "But a message came in from Earth for you—scrambled." She held out her hand, proffering a thin white wafer. I took it, thanked her, and waited for her to depart. Then I slipped it into my computer, typed my access code, and watched in astonishment as the message played.

"Greetings, Father Bailey," said the voice that had identified itself as Cardinal Pirandello of the Vatican's Congregation for the Causes of Saints. "I hope all is well with you. The Holy Father sends his special apostolic blessing." Pirandello paused, as if perhaps reluctant to go on, then: "I know that Earth news gets little play at Bradbury Colony, so perhaps you haven't seen the reports of the supposed miracle at Cydonia."

My heart jumped. Pirandello was right about us mostly ignoring the mother planet: it was supposed to make living permanently on another world easier. But Cydonia—why, that was here, on Mars ...

The Cardinal went on: "A televangelist based in New Zealand has claimed to have seen the Virgin Mary while viewing Cydonia through a telescope. These new ground-based scopes with their adaptive optics have astonishing resolving power, I'm told—but I guess I don't have to tell you that, after all your time at Castel Gandolfo. Anyway, ordinarily, of course, we'd give no credence to such a claim—putative miracles have a way of working themselves out, after all. But the televangelist in question is Jurgen Emat, who was at seminary fifty years ago with the Holy Father, and is watched by hundreds of millions of Roman Catholics. Emat claims that his vision has relevance to the Third Secret of Fatima. As you know, Fatima is much on the Holy Father's mind these days, since he intends to canonize Lucia dos Santos next month. Both the postulator and the reinstated *advocatus diaboli* feel this needs to be clarified before Leo XIV visits Portugal for this ceremony."

I shifted in my chair, trying to absorb it all.

"It would, of course," continued the recorded voice, "take a minimum of two years for a properly trained cardinal to travel from the Vatican to Mars. We know you have no special expertise in the area of miracles, but, as the highest-ranking Catholic official on Mars, his Holiness requests that you visit Cydonia, and prepare a report. Full details of the putative miracle follow ..."

❚❚❚   ❚❚❚   ❚❚❚

It took some doing—my mere presence was an act of forbearance, I knew—but I managed to finagle the use of one of Bradbury Colony's ground-effect shuttles to go from Utopia Planitia to Cydonia. Of course, I couldn't pilot such a vehicle myself; Elizabeth Chen was at the controls, leaving me most of a day to study.

Rome didn't commit itself easily to miracles, I knew. After all, there were charlatans who faked such things, and there was always the possibility of us getting egg on our collective faces. Also, the dogma was that all revelations required for faith were in the scriptures; there was no need for further miracles.

I looked out the shuttle's windows. The sun—tiny and dim compared with how it appeared from Earth—was touching the western horizon. I watched it set.

The shuttle sped on, into the darkness.

❚❚❚   ❚❚❚   ❚❚❚

"We speak today of the Third Secret of Fatima," said Jurgen Emat, robust and red of face at almost eighty, as he looked out at his flock. I was watching a playback of his broadcast on my datapad. "The Third Secret, and the miracle I myself have observed.

"As all of those who are pure of heart know, on May 13, 1917, and again every month of that year until October, three little peasant children saw visions of our Blessed Lady. The children were Lucia dos Santos, then aged 10, and her cousins Francisco and Jacinta Marto, ages eight and seven.

"Three prophecies were revealed to the children. The third was known only to a succession of Popes until 2000, when, while beatifying the two younger visionaries, who had died in childhood, John Paul II ordered the Congregation for the Doctrine of Faith to make that secret public, accompanied by what he called 'an appropriate commentary.'

"Well, the secret *is* indeed public, and has been for almost seventy years, but that commentary was anything but appropriate, twisting the events in the prophecy to relate to the 1981 attempt on John Paul II's life by Mehmet Ali Agca. No, that interpretation is incorrect—for I myself have had a vision of the true meaning of Fatima."

Puh-leeze, I thought. But I continued to watch.

"Why did I, alone, see this?" asked Emat. "Because unlike modern astronomers, who don't bother with eyepieces anymore, I looked upon Mars directly through a telescope, rather than on a computer monitor. Holy Visions are revealed only to those who gaze directly upon them."

An odd thing for a televangelist to say, I thought, as the recording played on.

"You have to remember, brethren," said Jurgen, "that the 1917 visions at Fatima were witnessed by children, and that the only one who survived childhood spent her life a cloistered nun—the same woman Pope Leo XIV intends to consecrate in a few weeks' time. Although she didn't write down the Third Secret until 1944, she'd seen little of the world in the intervening years. So, everything she says has to be re-interpreted in light of that. As Vatican Secretary of State Cardinal Angelo Sodano said upon on the occasion of the Third Secret's release, 'The text must be interpreted in a symbolic key.'"

Jurgen turned around briefly, and holographic words floated behind him: *We saw an Angel with a flaming sword in his left hand; flashing, it gave out flames that looked as though they would set the world on fire ...*

"Clearly," said Jurgen, indicating the words with his hand, "this is a rocket launch."

I shook my head in wonder. The words changed: *And we saw in an immense light that is God—something similar to how people appear in a mirror when they pass in front of it—a Bishop dressed in white ...*

Jurgen spread his arms now, appealing for common sense. "Well, how do you recognize a bishop? By his miter—his liturgical headdress. And what sort of headdress do we associate with odd reflections? The visors on space helmets! And what color are spacesuits? White—always white, to reflect the heat of the sun! Here, the children doubtless saw an astronaut. But where? Where?"

New words replacing old: ... *passed through a big city ... half in ruins ...*

"And that," said Jurgen, "is our first clue that the vision was specifically of Mars, of the Cydonia region, where, since the days of *Viking*, mystics have thought they could detect the ruins of a city, just west of the so-called Face on Mars."

Gracious Christ, I thought. Surely the Vatican can't have sent me off to investigate that? The so-called "Face" had, when photographed later, turned out to be nothing but a series of buttes with chasms running through them.

Again, the words floating behind Jurgen changed: *Beneath the two arms of the Cross there were two Angels ...*

"Ah!" said Jurgen, as if he himself were surprised by the revealed text, although doubtless he'd studied it minutely, working up this ridiculous story.

"The famed Northern Cross," continued Jurgen, "part of the constellation of Cygnus, is as clearly visible from Mars' surface as it is from Earth's. And Mars' two moons, Phobos and Deimos, depending on their phases, might appear as two angels beneath the cross ..."

Might, I thought. *And monkeys might fly out of my butt.*

But Jurgen's audience was taking it all in. He was an old-fashioned preacher—flamboyant, mesmerizing, long on rhetoric and short on logic, the kind that, regrettably, had become all too common in Catholicism since Vatican III.

The floating words morphed yet again: ... *two Angels each with a crystal aspersorium in his hand ...*

"An aspersorium," said Jurgen, his tone begging indulgence from all those who must already know, "is a vessel for holding holy water. And where, brethren, is water more holy than on desiccated Mars?" He beamed at his flock. I shook my head.

"And what," said Jurgen, "did the angels Phobos and Deimos do with their aspersoria?" More words from the Third Secret appeared behind him in answer: *They gathered up the blood of the Martyrs.*

"Blood?" said Jurgen, raising his bushy white eyebrows in mock surprise. "Ah, but again, we have only blessed Sister Lucia's interpretation. Surely what she saw was simply red liquid—or liquid that *appeared* to be red. And, on Mars, with its oxide soil and butterscotch sky, *everything* appears to be red, even water!"

Well, he had a point there. The people of Mars dressed in fashions those of Earth would find gaudy in the extreme, just to inject some color other than red into their lives.

"And, when I gazed upon Cydonia, my brethren, on the one hundred and fiftieth anniversary of the first appearance of Our Lady of the Rosary at Fatima, I saw her in all her glory: the Blessed Virgin.

"How did I know to look at Cydonia, you might ask? Because the words of Our Lady had come to me, telling me to turn my telescope onto Mars. I heard the words in my head late one night, and I knew at once they were from blessed Mary. I went to my telescope and looked where she had told me to. And nine minutes later, I saw her, pure and white, a dot of perfection moving about Cydonia. Hear me, my children! Nine minutes later! Our Lady's thoughts had come to me instantaneously, but even her most holy radiance had to travel at the speed of light, and Mars that evening was 160 million kilometers from Earth—nine light minutes!"

■ ■ ■

I must have dozed off. Elizabeth Chen was standing over me, speaking softly. "Father Bailey? Father Bailey? Time to get up ..."

I opened my eyes. Liz Chen was plenty fine to look at—hey, I'm celibate; not dead!—but I was unnerved to see her standing here, in the passenger cabin, instead of sitting up front at the controls. It was obvious from the panorama flashing by outside my window that we were still speeding along a few meters above the Martian surface. I'll gladly put my faith in God, but autopilots give me the willies.

"Hmm?" I said.

"We're approaching Cydonia. Rise and shine."

And give God the glory, glory ... "All right," I said. I always slept well on Mars—better than I ever did on Earth. Something to do with the 37% gravity, I suppose.

She went back into the cabin. I looked out the window. There, off in the distance, was a side view of the famous Face. From this angle, I never would have given it a second glance if I hadn't known its history among crackpots.

Well, if we were passing the Face, that meant the so-called cityscape was just 20 kilometers southwest of here. We'd already discussed our travel plans: she'd take us in between the "pyramid" and the "fortress," setting down just outside the "city square."

I started suiting up.

▦ ▦ ▦

The original names had stuck: The pyramid, the fortress, the city square. Of course, up close, they seemed not in the least artificial. I was bent over now, looking out a window.

"Kind of sad, isn't it?" said Liz, standing behind me, still in her coveralls. "People are willing to believe the most outlandish things on the scantest of evidence."

There was just a hint of condescension in her tone. Like almost everyone else on Mars, she thought me a fool—and not just for coming out here to Cydonia, but for the things I'd built my whole life around.

I straightened up, faced her. "You're not coming out?"

She shook her head. "You had your nap on the way here. Now it's my turn. Holler if you need anything." She touched a control, and the inner door of the cylindrical airlock chamber rolled aside, like the stone covering Jesus' sepulcher.

What, I wondered, would the Mother of our Lord be doing here, on this ancient, desolate world? Of course, apparitions of her were famous for occurring in out-of-the-way places: Lourdes, France; La'Vang, Vietnam; Fatima, Portugal; Guadalupe, Mexico. All of them were off the beaten track.

And yet, people did come to these obscure places in their millions after the fact. It had been a century and a half since the apparitions at Fatima, and that village still attracted five million pilgrims annually.

Annually. I mean *Earth* annually, of course. Only the anal retentive worry about the piddling difference between a terrestrial day and a Martian sol, but the Martian year was twice as long as Earth's. So, Fatima, I guess, gets *ten* million visitors per Martian year ...

I felt cold as I looked at the landscape of rusty sand and towering rock faces. It was psychosomatic, I knew: my surface suit—indeed white, as Jurgen Emat had noted—provided perfect temperature control.

The city square was really just an open area, defined by wind-sculpted sandstone mounds. Although in the earliest photos, it had perhaps resembled a piazza, it didn't look special from within it. I walked a few dozen meters then turned around, the lamp from my helmet piercing the darkness.

My footprints stretched out behind me. There were no others. I was hardly the first to visit Cydonia, but, unlike on the Moon, dust storms on Mars made such marks transitory.

I then looked up at the night sky. Earth was easy enough to spot—it was always on the ecliptic, of course, and right now was in ... my goodness, isn't that a coincidence!

It was in Virgo, the constellation of the Virgin, a dazzling blue point, a sapphire outshining even mighty Spica.

Of course, Virgo doesn't depict the Mother of Our Lord; the constellation dates back to ancient times. Most likely, it represents the Assyrian fertility goddess, Ishtar, or the Greek harvest maiden, Persephone.

I found myself smiling. Actually, it doesn't depict anything at all. It's just a random smattering of stars. To see a virgin in it was as much a folly as seeing the ruins of an ancient Martian city in the rocks rising up around me. But I knew the ... well, not the *heavens*, but the night sky ... like the back of my hand. Once you'd learned to see the patterns, it was almost impossible *not* to see them.

And, say, there was Cygnus, and—whaddaya know!—Phobos, and, yes, if I squinted, Deimos too, just beneath it.

But no. Surely the Holy Virgin had not revealed herself to Jurgen Emat. Peasant children, yes; the poor and sick, yes. But a televangelist? A rich broadcast preacher? No, that was ridiculous.

It wasn't explicitly in Cardinal Pirandello's message, but I knew enough of Vatican politics to understand what was going on. As he'd said, Jurgen Emat had been at seminary with Viktorio Lazzari—the man who was now known as Leo XIV. Although both were Catholics, they'd ended up going down widely different paths—and they were anything but friends.

I'd only met the Pontiff once, and then late in his life. It was almost impossible to imagine the poised, wise Bishop of Rome as a young man. But Jurgen had known him as such, and—my thoughts were my own; as long as I never gave them voice, I was entitled to think whatever I wished—and to know a person in his youth is to know him before he has developed the mask of guile. Jurgen Emat perhaps felt that Viktorio Lazzari had not deserved to ascend to the Holy See. And now, with this silly announcement of a Martian Marian vision, he was stealing Leo's thunder as the Pope prepared to visit Fatima.

Martian. Marian. Funny I'd never noticed how similar those words were before. The only difference ...

My God.

The only difference is the lowercase t—the *cross*—in the middle of the word pertaining to Mars.

No. No. I shook my head inside the suit's helmet. Ridiculous. A crazy notion. What had I been thinking about? Oh, yes: Emat trying to undermine the Pope. By the time I got back to Utopia Planitia, it would be late Saturday evening. I hadn't thought of a sermon yet, but perhaps that could be the topic. In matters of faith, by definition, the Holy Father was infallible, and those who called themselves Catholics—even celebrities like

Jurgen Emat—had to accept that, or leave the faith.

It wouldn't mean much to the ... yes, I thought of them as my *congregation*, even sometimes my flock ... but of course the group that only half-filled the pews at Saint Teresa's each Sunday morn were hardly that. Just the bored, the lonely, those with nothing better to do. Ah, well. At least I wouldn't be preaching to the converted ...

I looked around at the barren landscape, and took a drink of pure water through the tube in my helmet. The wind howled, plaintive, attenuated, barely audible inside the suit.

Of course, I knew I was being unfairly cynical. I *did* believe with all my heart in Our Lady of the Rosary. I knew—knew, as I know my own soul!— that she has in the past shown herself to the faithful, and ...

And *I* was one of the faithful. Yes, pride goeth before destruction, and an haughty spirit before a fall—but I was more faithful than Jurgen Emat. It was true that Buzz Aldrin had taken Holy Communion upon landing on the moon, but I was bringing Jesus' teachings farther than anyone else had, here, in humanity's first baby step out toward the stars ...

So, Mary, where are you? If you're here—if you're with us here on Mars, then show yourself! My heart is pure, and I'd love to see you.

Show yourself, Mother of Jesus! Show yourself, Blessed Virgin! Show yourself!

▌ ▌ ▌

Elizabeth Chen's tone had the same mocking undercurrent as before. "Have a nice walk, Father?"

I nodded.

"See anything?"

I handed her my helmet. "Mars is an interesting place," I said. "There are always things to see."

She smiled, a self-satisfied smirk. "Don't worry, Father," she said, as she put the helmet away in the suit locker. "We'll have you back to Bradbury in plenty of time for Sunday morning."

I sat in my office, behind my desk, dressed in cassock and clerical collar, facing the camera eye. I took a deep breath, crossed myself, and told the camera to start recording.

"Cardinal Pirandello," I said, trying to keep my voice from quavering, "as requested, I visited Cydonia. The sands of Mars drifted about me, the invisible hand of the thin wind moving them. I looked and looked and looked. And then, blessed Cardinal, it happened."

I took another deep breath. "I saw *her*, Eminence. I saw the Holy Virgin. She appeared to float in front of me, a meter or more off the ground. And she was surrounded by spectral light, as if a rainbow had been bent to the contours of her venerable form. And she spoke to me, and I heard her voice three times over, and yet with each layer nonetheless clear and easily discernible: one in Aramaic, the language Our Lady spoke in life; a second in Latin, the tongue of our Church; and again in beautiful, cultured English. Her voice was like song, like liquid gold, like pure love, and she said unto me ..."

Simply sending a message to Cardinal Pirandello wouldn't be enough. It might conveniently get lost. Even with the reforms of Vatican III, the Church of Rome was still a bureaucracy, and still protected itself.

I took the recording wafer to the Communications Center myself, handing it to Loni Sinclair, the woman who had brought Pirandello's original message to me.

"How would you like this sent, Father?"

"It is of some import," I said. "What are my options?"

"Well, I can send it now, although I'll have to bill the ... um, the ..."

"The parish, my child."

She nodded, then looked at the wafer. "And you want it to go to both of these addresses? The Vatican, and CNN?"

"Yes."

She pointed to an illuminated globe of the Earth, half embedded in the wall. "CNN headquarters is in Atlanta. I can send it to the Vatican right now, but the United States is currently on the far side of Earth. It'll be hours before I can transmit it there."

Of course. "No," I said. "No, then wait. There are times when both Italy and the U.S. simultaneously face Mars, right?"

"Not all of the U.S.—but Georgia, yes. A brief period."

"Wait till then, and send the message to both places at the same time."

"Whatever you say, Father."

"God bless you, child."

Loni Sinclair couldn't quite mask her amusement at my words. "You're welcome," she replied.

■ ■ ■

Four years have passed. Leo XIV has passed on, and John Paul III is now pontiff. I have no idea if Jurgen Emat approves of him or not—nor do I care. Dwelling on Earthly matters is frowned upon here, after all.

Five million people a year still come to Fatima. Millions visit Lourdes and Guadalupe and La'Vang.

And then they go home—some feeling they've been touched by the Holy Spirit, some saying they've been healed.

Millions of faithful haven't made it to Mars. Not yet; that will take time. But tens of thousands have come, and, unlike those who visited the other shrines, most of them stay. After traveling for years, the last thing they want to do is turn around and go home, especially since, by the time they'd arrived here, the propitious alignment of Earth and Mars that made their journey out take only two years has changed; it would take much longer to get home if they left shortly after arriving.

And so, they stay, and make their home here, and contribute to our community.

And come to my masses. Not out of boredom. Not out of loneliness. But out of belief. Belief that miracles do still occur, and can happen as easily off-Earth as on it.

I am fulfilled, and Mars, I honestly believe, is now a better place. This *is* a congregation, a flock. I beam out at its members from the pulpit, feeling their warmth, their love.

Now I only have one problem left. To lie to Cardinal Pirandello had been a violation of my oath, of the teachings of my faith. But given that I'm the only priest on all of Mars, to whom will I confess my sin?

Immortality

*Janis Ian is a wonderfully popular folk singer, best known for "Society's Child"
and "At Seventeen." Turns out, though, that she's also a big science-fiction fan,
and she began attending World Science Fiction Conventions in 2001. Soon,
she and Mike Resnick hatched the idea of having all of Janis's favorite SF
authors write stories inspired by her song lyrics. The resulting anthology,* Stars,
*turned out to be one of the major SF books of 2003, and I was very honored,
and very proud, to be asked to contribute to it.*

*Still, I found this a difficult story to write, since my point-of-view character
was obviously, and presumptuously, based at least in part on Janis. Although I
had finished a draft of this story on the day I left Toronto for the 2002 World
Science Fiction Convention in San José, I'd actually planned to tell Janis that
I hadn't been able to come up with anything—I just wasn't comfortable with
the story. But Janis greeted me with a big hug and told me how much she was
looking forward to my submission. With great trepidation, I polished it up and
sent it in after the Worldcon, and, to my infinite relief, Janis loved it. Whew!*

⚔ ■ ■ ⚓

*Baby, I'm only society's child
When we're older, things may change
But for now this is the way they must remain*
—Janis Ian

Sixty years.

Sweet Jesus, had it been that long?

But of course it had. The year was now 2023, and then—

Then it had been 1963.

The year of the march on Washington.

The year JFK had been assassinated.

The year I—

No, no, I didn't want to think about that. After all, I'm sure *he* never thinks about it ... or about me.

I'd been seventeen in 1963. And I'd thought of myself as ugly, an unpardonable sin for a young woman.

Now, though ...

Now, I was seventy-seven. And I was no longer homely. Not that I'd had any work done, but there was no such thing as a homely—or a beautiful—woman of seventy-seven, at least not one who had never had treatments. The only adjective people applied to an unmodified woman of seventy-seven was *old*.

My sixtieth high-school reunion.

For some, there would be a seventieth, and an eightieth, a ninetieth, and doubtless a mega-bash for the hundredth. For those who had money—real money, the kind of money I'd once had at the height of my career—there were pharmaceuticals and gene therapies and cloned organs and bodily implants, all granting the gift of synthetic youth, the gift of time.

I'd skipped the previous reunions, and I wasn't fool enough to think I'd be alive for the next one. This would be it, my one, my only, my last. Although I'd once, briefly, been rich, I didn't have the kind of money anymore that could buy literal immortality. I would have to be content knowing that my songs would exist after I was gone.

And yet, today's young people, children of the third millennium, couldn't relate to socially conscious lyrics written so long ago. Still, the recordings would exist, although ...

Although if a tree falls in a forest, and no one is around to hear it, does it make a sound? If a recording—digitized, copied from medium to medium as technologies and standards endlessly change—isn't listened to, does the song still exist? Does the pain it chronicled still continue?

I sighed.

Sixty years since high-school graduation.

Sixty years since all those swirling hormones and clashing emotions.

Sixty years since Devon.

▥ ▥ ▥

It wasn't the high school I remembered. My Cedar Valley High had been a brown-and-red brick structure, two stories tall, with large fields to the east and north, and a tiny staff parking lot.

That building had long since been torn down—asbestos in its walls, poor insulation, no fiber-optic infrastructure. The replacement, larger, beige, thermally efficient, bore the same name but that was its only resemblance. And the field to the east had become a parking lot, since every seventeen-year-old had his or her own car these days.

Things change.

Walls come down.

Time passes.

I went inside.

▥ ▥ ▥

"Hello," I said. "My name is ..." and I spoke it, then spelled the last name—the one I'd had back when I'd been a student here, the one that had been my stage name, the one that pre-dated my ex-husbands.

The man sitting behind the desk was in his late forties; other classes were celebrating their whole-decade anniversaries as well. I suspected he had no trouble guessing to which year each arrival belonged, but I supplied it anyway: "Class of Sixty-Three."

The man consulted a tablet computer. "Ah, yes," he said. "Come a long way, have we? Well, it's good to see you." A badge appeared, printed instantly and silently, bearing my name. He handed it to me, along with two drink tickets. "Your class is meeting in Gymnasium Four. It's down that corridor. Just follow everyone else."

They'd done their best to capture the spirit of the era. There was a US flag with just fifty stars—easy to recognize because of the staggered rows. And there were photos on the walls of Jack and Jackie Kennedy, and Martin Luther King, and a *Mercury* space capsule bobbing in the Pacific, and Sandy Koufax with the Los Angeles Dodgers. Someone had even dug up movie posters for the hits of that year, *Dr. No* and *Cleopatra*. Two video monitors were silently playing *The Beverly Hillbillies* and *Bonanza*. And "Easier Said Than Done" was coming softly out of the detachable speakers belonging to a portable stereo.

I looked around the large room at the dozens of people. I had no idea who most of them were—not at a glance. They were just old folks, like me: wrinkled, with gray or white hair, some noticeably stooped, one using a walker.

But that man, over there ...

There had only been one black person in my class. I hadn't seen Devon Smith in the sixty years since, but this had to be him. Back then, he'd had a full head of curly hair, buzzed short. Now, most of it was gone, and his face was deeply lined.

My heart was pounding harder than it had in years; indeed, I hadn't thought the old thing had that much life left in it.

Devon Smith.

We hadn't talked, not since that hot June evening in '63 when I'd told him I couldn't see him anymore. Our senior prom had only been a week away, but my parents had demanded I break up with him. They'd seen governor George Wallace on the news, personally blocking black students—"coloreds," we called them back then—from enrolling at the University of Alabama. Mom and Dad said their edict was for my own safety, and I went along with it, doing what society wanted.

Truth be told, part of me was relieved. I'd grown tired of the stares, the whispered comments. I'd even overheard two of our teachers making jokes about us, despite all their posturing about the changing times during class.

Of course, those teachers must long since be dead. And as Devon looked my way, for a moment I envied them.

He had a glass of red wine in his hand, and he was wearing a dark gray suit. There was no sign of recognition on his face. Still, he came over. "Hello," he said. "I'm Devon Smith."

I was too flustered to speak, and, after a moment, he went on. "You're not wearing your nametag."

He was right; it was still in my hand, along with the drink chits. I thought about just turning and walking away. But no, no—I couldn't do that. Not to him. Not again.

"Sorry," I said, and that one word embarrassed me further. I lifted my hand, opened my palm, showing the nametag held within.

He stared at it as though I'd shown him a crucifixion wound.

"It's you," he said, and his gaze came up to my face, his brown eyes wide.

"Hello, Devon," I said. I'd been a singer; I still had good breath control. My voice did not crack.

He was silent for a time, and then he lifted his shoulders, a small shrug, as if he'd decided not to make a big thing of it. "Hello," he replied. And then he added, presumably because politeness demanded it, "It's good to see you." But his words were flat.

"How have you been?" I asked.

He shrugged again, this time as if acknowledging the impossibility of my question. How has anyone been for six decades? How does one sum up the bulk of a lifetime in a few words?

"Fine," he said at last. "I've had ..." But whatever it was he'd had remained unsaid. He looked away and took a sip of his wine. Finally, he spoke again. "I used to follow your career."

"It had its ups and downs," I said, trying to keep my tone light.

"That song ..." he began, but didn't finish.

There was no need to specify which song. The one I'd written about him. The one I'd written about what I *did* to him. It was one of my few really big hits, but I'd never intended to grow rich off my—off *our*—pain.

"They still play it from time to time," I said.

Devon nodded. "I heard it on an oldies station last month."

Oldies. I shuddered.

"So, tell me," I said, "do you have kids?"

"Three," said Devon. "Two boys and a girl."

"And grandkids?"

"Eight," said Devon. "Ages two through ten."

"Immortality." I hadn't intended to say it out loud, but there it was, the word floating between us. Devon had his immortality through his genes. And, I suppose, he had a piece of mine, too, for every time someone listened to that song, he or she would wonder if it was autobiographical, and, if so, who the beautiful young black man in my past had been.

"Your wife?" I asked.

"She passed away five years ago." He was holding his wineglass in his left hand; he still wore a ring.

"I'm sorry."

"What about you?" asked Devon. "Any family?"

I shook my head. We were quiet a while. I was wondering what color his wife had been.

"A lot has changed in sixty years," I said, breaking the silence.

He looked over toward the entrance, perhaps hoping somebody else would arrive so he could beg off. "A lot," he agreed. "And yet ..."

I nodded. And yet, there still hadn't been a black president or vice-president.

And yet, the standard of living of African-Americans was still lower than that of whites—not only meaning a shorter natural life expectancy, but also that far fewer of them could afford the array of treatments available to the rich.

And yet, just last week, they'd picked the person who would be the first to set foot on Mars. *Of course it was a man,* I'd thought bitterly when the announcement was made. Perhaps Devon had greeted the news with equal dismay, thinking, *Of course he's white.*

Suddenly I heard my name being called. I turned around, and there was Madeline Green. She was easy to recognize; she'd clearly had all sorts of treatments. Her face was smooth, her hair the same reddish-brown I remembered from her genuine youth. How she'd recognized me, though, I didn't know. Perhaps she'd overheard me talking to Devon, and had identified me by my voice, or perhaps just the fact that I *was* talking to Devon had been clue enough.

"Why, Madeline!" I said, forcing a smile. "How good to see you!" I turned to Devon. "You remember Devon Smith?"

"How could I forget?" said Madeline. He was proffering his hand, and, after a moment, she took it.

"Hello, Madeline," said Devon. "You look fabulous."

It had been what Madeline had wanted to hear, but I'd been too niggardly to offer up.

Niggardly. A perfectly legitimate word—from the Scandinavian for "stingy," if I remembered correctly. But also a word I never normally used, even in my thoughts. And yet it had come to mind just now, recalling, I supposed, what Madeline had called Devon behind his back all those years ago.

Devon lifted his wineglass. "I need a refill," he said.

The last time I'd looked, he'd still had half a glass; I wondered if he'd quickly drained it when he saw Madeline approaching, giving him a way to exit gracefully, although whether it was me or Madeline he wanted to escape, I couldn't say. In any event, Devon was now moving off, heading toward the cafeteria table that had been set up as a makeshift bar.

"I bought your albums," said Madeline, now squeezing my hand. "Of course, they were all on vinyl. I don't have a record player anymore."

"They're available on CD," I said. "And for download."

"Are they now?" replied Madeline, sounding surprised. I guess she thought of my songs as artifacts of the distant past.

And perhaps they were—although, as I looked over at Devon's broad back, it sure didn't feel that way.

▮▮ ▮▮ ▮▮

"Welcome back, class of Nineteen Sixty-Three!"

We were all facing the podium, next to the table with the portable stereo. Behind the podium, of course, was Pinky Spenser—although I doubt anyone had called him "Pinky" for half a century. He'd been student-council president, and editor of the school paper, and valedictorian, and on and on, so he was the natural MC for the evening. Still, I was glad to see that for all his early success, he, too, looked old.

There were now perhaps seventy-five people present, including twenty like Madeline who had been able to afford rejuvenation treatments. I'd had a chance to chat briefly with many of them. They'd all greeted me like an old friend, although I couldn't remember ever being invited to their parties or along on their group outings. But now, because I'd once been famous, they all wanted to say hello. They hadn't had the time of day for me back when we'd been teenagers, but doubtless, years later, had gone around saying to people, "You'll never guess who *I* went to school with!"

"We have a bunch of prizes to give away," said Pinky, leaning into the mike, distorting his own voice; part of me wanted to show him how to use it properly. *"First, for the person who has come the farthest ..."*

Pinky presented a half-dozen little trophies. I'd had awards enough in my life, and didn't expect to get one tonight—nor did I. Neither did Devon.

"And now," said Pinky, *"although it's not from 1963, I think you'll all agree that this is appropriate ..."*

He leaned over and put a new disk in the portable stereo. I could see it from here; it was a CD-ROM that someone had burned at home. Pinky pushed the play button, and ...

And one of my songs started coming from the speakers. I recognized it by the second note, of course, but the others didn't until the recorded version of me started singing, and then Madeline Green clapped her hands together. "Oh, listen!" she said, turning toward me. "It's you!"

And it was—from half a century ago, with my song that had become the anthem for a generation of ugly-ducking girls like me. How could Pinky possibly think I wanted to hear that now, here, at the place where all the heartbreak the song chronicled had been experienced?

Why the hell had I come back, anyway? I'd skipped even the fiftieth reunion; what had driven me to want to attend my sixtieth? Was it loneliness?

No. I had friends enough.

Was it morbid curiosity? Wondering who of the old gang had survived? But, no, that wasn't it, either. That wasn't why I'd come.

The song continued to play. I was doing my guitar solo now. No singing; just me, strumming away. But soon enough the words began again. It was my most famous song, the one I'm sure they'll mention in my obituary.

To my surprise, Madeline was singing along softly. She looked at me, as if expecting me to join in, but I just forced a smile and looked away.

The song played on. The chorus repeated.

This wasn't the same gymnasium, of course—the one where my school dances had been held, the ones where I'd been a wallflower, waiting for even the boys I couldn't stand to ask me to dance. That gym had been bulldozed along with the rest of the old Cedar Valley High.

I looked around. Several people had gone back to their conversations while my music still played. Those who had won the little trophies were showing them off. But Devon, I saw, was listening intently, as if straining to make out the lyrics.

We hadn't dated long—just until my parents found out he was black and insisted I break up with him. This wasn't the song I'd written about us, but, in a way, I suppose it was similar. Both of them, my two biggest hits, were about the pain of being dismissed because of the way you look. In this song, it was me—homely, lonely. And in that other song ...

I had been a white girl, and he'd been the only black—not *boy*, you can't say boy—anywhere near my age at our school. Devon had no choice: if he were going to date anyone from Cedar Valley, she would have had to be white.

Back then, few could tell that Devon was good-looking; all they saw was the color of his skin. But he had been *fine*. Handsome, well muscled, a dazzling smile. And yet he had chosen me.

I had wondered about that back then, and I still wondered about it now. I'd wondered if he'd thought appearances couldn't possibly matter to someone who looked like me.

The song stopped, and—

No.

No.

I had a repertoire of almost a hundred songs. If Pinky was going to pick a second one by me, what were the chances that it would be *that* song?

But it was. Of course it was

Devon didn't recognize it at first, but when he did, I saw him take a half-step backward, as if he'd been pushed by an invisible hand.

After a moment, though, he recovered. He looked around the gym and quickly found me. I turned away, only to see Madeline softly singing this one, too, *la-la-ing* over those lyrics she didn't remember.

A moment later, there was a hand on my shoulder. I turned. Devon was standing there, looking at me, his face a mask. "We have some unfinished business," he said, softly but firmly.

I swallowed. My eyes were stinging. "I am so sorry, Devon," I said. "It was the times. The era." I shrugged. "Society."

He looked at me for a while, then reached out and took my pale hand in his brown one. My heart began to pound. "We never got to do this back in '63," he said. He paused, perhaps wondering whether he wanted to go on. But, after a moment, he did, and there was no reluctance in his voice. "Would you like to dance?"

I looked around. Nobody else was dancing. Nobody had danced all evening. But I let him lead me out into the center of the gym.

And he held me in his arms.

And I held him.

And as we danced, I thought of the future that Devon's grandchildren would grow up in, a world I would never see, and, for the first time, I found myself hoping my songs wouldn't be immortal.

Shed Skin

In the summer of 1982, I worked at Bakka, Toronto's science-fiction specialty bookstore (and now the oldest surviving SF shop in the world). The then-owner, John Rose, encouraged me enormously in my writing, which was just beginning back then, and we remain great friends.

Turns out I wasn't the only one he nurtured. After my stint at Bakka, a bunch of other people who went on to be professional SF or fantasy writers worked there, and all of us were encouraged by John: Tanya Huff, Michelle West, Cory Doctorow, and Nalo Hopkinson among them.

In 2002, to commemorate both John's retirement and the thirtieth anniversary of the store, he asked all his past and present employees who'd gone on to writing careers to each contribute a story to a limited-edition anthology. I wrote this story for that book, and—in a rare turn of events—managed to interest Analog Science Fiction and Fact in reprinting it.

I found the themes and ideas in this story echoing in my head long after I finished writing it. Indeed, I gave a copy of the story to my novel editor at Tor, David G. Hartwell, saying I'd like a contract to revisit the same subject matter at novel length; my agent Ralph Vicinanza, of course, intervened, adding that Rob wanted more money than he'd ever been paid before for a book to do this. Tor said okay, and my novel Mindscan was born. I think it's one of my best books (and it won the John W. Campbell Memorial Award for Best Novel of the Year)—and it has its roots here.

"Shed Skin" was a finalist for the Hugo Award for Best Short Story of the Year, and won Analog magazine's "AnLab" award—the annual Analytical Laboratory readers' choice poll.

◊ ■ ■ ◊

"I'm sorry," said Mr. Shiozaki, as he leaned back in his swivel chair and looked at the middle-aged white man with the graying temples, "but there's nothing I can do for you."

"But I've changed my mind," said the man. He was getting red in the face as the conversation went on. "I want out of this deal."

"You can't change your mind," said Shiozaki. "You've *moved* your mind."

The man's voice had taken on a plaintive tone, although he was clearly trying to suppress it. "I didn't think it would be like this."

Shiozaki sighed. "Our psychological counselors and our lawyers went over the entire procedure and all the ramifications with Mr. Rathburn beforehand. It's what he wanted."

"But I don't want it anymore."

"You don't have any say in the matter."

The white man placed a hand on the table. The hand was flat, the fingers splayed, but it was nonetheless full of tension. "Look," he said, "I demand to see—to see the other me. I'll explain it to him. He'll understand. He'll agree that we should rescind the deal."

Shiozaki shook his head. "We can't do that. You know we can't. That's part of the agreement."

"But—"

"No buts," said Shiozaki. "That's the way it *has* to be. No successor has *ever* come back here. They can't. Your successor has to do everything possible to shut your existence out of his mind, so he can get on with *his* existence, and not worry about yours. Even if he wanted to come see you, we wouldn't allow the visit."

"You can't treat me like this. It's inhuman."

"Get this through your skull," said Shiozaki. "*You* are not human."

"Yes, I am, damn it. If you—"

"If I prick you, do you not bleed?" said Shiozaki.

"Exactly! *I'm* the one who is flesh and blood. I'm the one who grew in my mother's womb. I'm the one who is a descendant of thousands of generations of *Homo sapiens* and thousands of generations of *Homo erectus* and *Homo habilis* before that. This—this other me is just a machine, a robot, an android."

"No, it's not. It is George Rathburn. The one and only George Rathburn."

"Then why do you call him 'it'?"

"I'm not going to play semantic games with you," said Shiozaki. "*He* is George Rathburn. You aren't—not anymore."

The man lifted his hand from the table and clenched his fist. "Yes, I am. I *am* George Rathburn."

"No, you're not. You're just a skin. Just a shed skin."

▌ ▌ ▌

George Rathburn was slowly getting used to his new body. He'd spent six months in counseling preparing for the transference. They'd told him this replacement body wouldn't feel like his old one, and they'd been right. Most people didn't transfer until they were old, until they'd enjoyed as much biological physicality as they could—and until the ever-improving robotic technology was as good as it was going to get during their natural lifetimes.

After all, although the current robot bodies were superior in many ways to the slab-of-flab ones—how soon he'd adopted that term!—they still weren't as physically sensitive.

Sex—the recreational act, if not the procreative one—was possible, but it wasn't quite as good. Synapses were fully reproduced in the nano-gel of the new brain, but hormonal responses were faked by playing back memories of previous events. Oh, an orgasm was still an orgasm, still wonderful—but it wasn't the unique, unpredictable experience of a real sexual climax. There was no need to ask, "Was it good for you?," for it was *always* good, always predictable, always exactly the same.

Still, there were compensations. George could now walk—or run, if he wanted to—for hours on end without feeling the slightest fatigue. And he'd dispensed with sleep. His daily memories were organized and sorted in a six-minute packing session every twenty-four hours; that was his only downtime.

Downtime. Funny that it had been the biological version of him that had been prone to downtime, while the electronic version was mostly free of it.

There were other changes, too. His proprioception—the sense of how his body and limbs were deployed at any given moment—was much sharper than it had previously been.

And his vision was more acute. He couldn't see into the infrared—that was technically possible, but so much of human cognition was based on the idea of darkness and light that to banish them with heat sensing had turned out to be bad psychologically. But his chromatic abilities had been extended in the other direction, and that let him see, among other things, bee purple, the color that often marked distinctive patterns on flower petals that human eyes—the old-fashioned kind of human eyes, that is—were blind to.

Hidden beauty revealed.

And an eternity to enjoy it.

▉ ▉ ▉

"I demand to see a lawyer."

Shiozaki was again facing the flesh-and-blood shell that had once housed George Rathburn, but the Japanese man's eyes seemed to be focused at infinity, as if looking right through him. "And how would you pay for this lawyer's services?" Shiozaki asked at last.

Rathburn—perhaps he couldn't use his name in speech, but no one could keep him from thinking it—opened his mouth to protest. He had money—lots of money. But, no, no, he'd signed all that away. His biometrics were meaningless; his retinal scans were no longer registered. Even if he could get out of this velvet prison and access one, no ATM in the world would dispense cash to him. Oh, there were plenty of stocks and bonds in his name ... but it wasn't *his* name anymore.

"There has to be something you can do to help me," said Rathburn.

"Of course," said Shiozaki. "I can assist you in any number of ways. Anything at all you need to be comfortable here."

"But *only* here, right?"

"Exactly. You knew that—I'm sorry; *Mr. Rathburn* knew that when he chose this path for himself, and for you. You will spend the rest of your life here in Paradise Valley."

Rathburn was silent for a time, then: "What if I agreed to accept your restrictions? What if I agreed *not* to present myself as George Rathburn? Could I leave here then?"

"You *aren't* George Rathburn. Regardless, we can't allow you to have any outside contact." Shiozaki was quiet for a few moments, and then, in a softer tone, he said, "Look, why make things difficult for yourself? Mr. Rathburn provided very generously for you. You will live a life of luxury here. You can access any books you might want, any movies. You've seen our recreation center, and you must admit it's fabulous. And our sex-workers are the best-looking on the planet. Think of this as the longest, most-pleasant vacation you've ever had."

"Except it doesn't end until I die," said Rathburn.

Shiozaki said nothing.

Rathburn exhaled noisily. "You're about to tell me that I'm already dead, aren't you? And so I shouldn't think of this as a prison; I should think of this as heaven."

Shiozaki opened his mouth to speak, but closed it again without saying anything. Rathburn knew that the administrator couldn't even give him that comfort. He wasn't dead—nor would he be, even when this discarded biological container, here, in Paradise Valley, finally ceased to function. No, George Rathburn lived on, a duplicated version of this consciousness in an almost indestructible, virtually immortal robot body, out in the real world.

▥ ▥ ▥

"Hey there, G.R.," said the black man with the long gray beard. "Join me?"

Rathburn—the Rathburn made out of carbon, that is—had entered Paradise Valley's dining hall. The man with the beard had already been served his lunch: a lobster tail, garlic mashed potatoes, a glass of the finest Chardonnay. The food here was exquisite.

"Hi, Dat," Rathburn said, nodding. He envied the bearded man. His name, before he'd transferred his consciousness into a robot, had been Darius Allan Thompson, so his initials, the only version of his birth name allowed to be used here, made a nice little word—almost as good as having a real name. Rathburn took a seat at the same table. One of the ever-solicitous servers—young, female (for this table of straight men), beautiful—was already at hand, and G.R. ordered a glass of champagne. It wasn't a special occasion—nothing was ever special in Paradise Valley—but any pleasure was available to those, like him and Dat, on the Platinum Plus maintenance plan.

"Why so long in the face, G.R.?" asked Dat.

"I don't like it here."

Dat admired the *derrière* of the departing server, and took a sip of his wine. "What's not to like?"

"You used to be a lawyer, didn't you? Back on the outside?"

"I still *am* a lawyer on the outside," said Dat.

G.R. frowned, but decided not to press the point. "Can you answer some questions for me?"

"Sure. What do you want to know?"

▉ ▉ ▉

G.R. entered Paradise Valley's "hospital." He thought of the name as being in quotation marks, since a real hospital was a place you were supposed to go to only temporarily for healing. But most of those who had uploaded their consciousness, who had shed their skins, were elderly. And when their discarded shells checked into the hospital, it was to die. But G.R. was only forty-five. With proper medical treatment, and some good luck, he had a fair chance of seeing one hundred.

G.R. went into the waiting room. He'd watched for two weeks now, and knew the schedule, knew that little Lilly Ng—slight, Vietnamese, fifty—would be the doctor on duty. She, like Shiozaki, was staff—a real person who got to go home, to the real world, at night.

After a short time, the receptionist said the time-honored words: "The doctor will see you now."

G.R. walked into the green-walled examination room. Ng was looking down at a datapad. "GR-7," she said, reading his serial number. Of course, he wasn't the only one with the initials G.R. in Paradise Valley, and so he had to share what faint echo of a name he still possessed with several other people. She looked at him, her gray eyebrows raised, waiting for him to confirm that that was indeed who he was.

"That's me," said G.R., "but you can call me George."

"No," said Ng. "I cannot." She said it in a firm but gentle tone; presumably, she'd been down this road before with others. "What seems to be the problem?"

"I've got a skin tag in my left armpit," he said. "I've had it for years, but it's started to get sensitive. It hurts when I apply roll-on deodorant, and it chafes as I move my arm."

Ng frowned. "Take off your shirt, please."

G.R. began undoing buttons. He actually had several skin tags, as well as a bunch of moles. He also had a hairy back, which he hated. One reason uploading his consciousness had initially seemed appealing was to divest himself of these dermal imperfections. The new golden robot body he'd selected—looking like a cross between the Oscar statuette and C-3PO— had no such cosmetic defects.

As soon as the shirt was off he lifted his left arm and let Ng examine his axilla.

"Hmm," she said, peering at the skin tag. "It does look inflamed."

G.R. had brutally pinched the little knob of skin an hour before, and had twisted it as much as he could in either direction.

Ng was now gently squeezing it between thumb and forefinger. G.R. had been prepared to suggest a treatment, but it would be better if she came up with the idea herself. After a moment, she obliged. "I can remove it for you, if you like."

"If you think that's the right thing to do," said G.R.

"Sure," said Ng. "I'll give you a local anesthetic, clip it off, and cauterize the cut. No need for stitches."

Clip it off? No! No, he needed her to use a scalpel, not surgical scissors. Damn it!

She crossed the room, prepared a syringe, and returned, injecting it directly into the skin tag. The needle going in was excruciating—for a few moments. And then there was no sensation at all.

"How's that?" she asked.

"Fine."

Ng put on surgical gloves, opened a cupboard, and pulled out a small leather case. She placed it on the examination table G.R. was now perched on, and opened it. It contained surgical scissors, forceps, and—

They glinted beautifully under the lights from the ceiling.

A pair of scalpels, one with a short blade, the other with a longer one.

"All right," said Ng, reaching in and extracting the scissors. "Here we go ..."

G.R. shot his right arm out, grabbing the long-bladed scalpel, and quickly swung it around, bringing it up and under Ng's throat. Damn but the thing was sharp! He hadn't meant to hurt her, but a shallow slit two centimeters long now welled crimson across where her Adam's apple would have been had she been a man.

A small scream escaped from Ng, and G.R. quickly clamped his other hand over her mouth. He could feel her shaking.

"Do exactly as I say," he said, "and you'll walk out of this alive. Screw me over, and you're dead."

◼ ◼ ◼

"Don't worry," said Detective Dan Lucerne to Mr. Shiozaki. "I've handled eight hostage situations over the years, and in every case, we've managed a peaceful solution. We'll get your woman back."

Shiozaki nodded then looked away, hiding his eyes from the detective. He should have recognized the signs in GR-7. If only he'd ordered him sedated, this never would have happened.

Lucerne gestured toward the vidphone. "Get the examination room on this thing," he said.

Shiozaki reached over Lucerne's shoulder and tapped out three numbers on the keypad. After a moment, the screen came to life, showing Ng's hand pulling away from the camera at her end. As the hand withdrew, it was clear that G.R. still had the scalpel held to Ng's neck.

"Hello," said Lucerne. "My name is Detective Dan Lucerne. I'm here to help you."

"You're here to save Dr. Ng's life," said GR-7. "And if you do everything I want, you will."

"All right," said Lucerne. "What do you want, sir?"

"For starters, I want you to call me Mr. Rathburn."

"Fine," said Lucerne. "That's fine, Mr. Rathburn."

Lucerne was surprised to see the shed skin tremble in response. "Again," GR-7 said, as if it were the sweetest sound he'd ever heard. "Say it again."

"What can we do for you, Mr. Rathburn?"

"I want to talk to the robot version of me."

Shiozaki reached over Lucerne's shoulder again, pushing the mute button. "We can't allow that."

"Why not?" asked Lucerne.

"Our contract with the uploaded version specifies that there will never be any contact with the shed skin."

"I'm not worried about fine print," said Lucerne. "I'm trying to save a woman's life." He took the mute off. "Sorry about that, Mr. Rathburn."

GR-7 nodded. "I see Mr. Shiozaki standing behind you. I'm sure he told you that what I wanted isn't permitted."

Lucerne didn't look away from the screen, didn't break the eye contact with the skin. "He did say that, yes. But he's not in charge here. *I'm* not in charge here. It's your show, Mr. Rathburn."

Rathburn visibly relaxed. Lucerne could see him back the scalpel off a bit from Ng's neck. "That's more like it," he said. "All right. All right. I don't want to kill Dr. Ng—but I will unless you bring the robot version of me here within three hours." He spoke out of the side of his mouth to Ng. "Break the connection."

A terrified-looking Ng reached her arm forward, her pale hand and simple gold wedding ring filling the field of view.

And the screen went dead.

■ ■ ■

George Rathburn—the silicon version—was sitting in the dark, wood-paneled living room of his large Victorian-style country house. Not that he had to sit; he never grew tired anymore. Nor did he really need his chairs to be padded. But folding his metal body into the seat still felt like the natural thing to do.

Knowing that, barring accidents, he was now going to live virtually forever, Rathburn figured he should tackle something big and ambitious, like *War and Peace* or *Ulysses*. But, well, there would always be time for that later. Instead, he downloaded the latest Buck Doheney mystery novel into his datapad, and began to read.

He'd only gotten halfway through the second screenful of text when the datapad bleeped, signaling an incoming call.

Rathburn thought about just letting the pad record a message. Already, after only a few weeks of immortality, nothing seemed particularly urgent. Still, it might be Kathryn. He'd met her at the training center, while they were both getting used to their robot bodies, and to their immortality. Ironically, she'd been eighty-two before she'd uploaded; in his now-discarded flesh-and-blood shell, George Rathburn would never have had a relationship with a woman so much older than he was. But now that they were both in artificial bodies—his gold, hers a lustrous bronze—they were well on the way to a full-fledged romance.

The pad bleeped again, and Rathburn touched the ANSWER icon— no need to use a stylus anymore; his synthetic fingers didn't secrete oils that would leave a mark on the screen.

Rathburn had that strange feeling he'd experienced once or twice since uploading—the feeling of deep surprise that would have been accompanied by his old heart skipping a beat. "Mr. Shiozaki?" he said. "I didn't expect to ever see you again."

"I'm sorry to have to bother you, George, but we've—well, we've got an emergency. Your old body has taken a hostage here in Paradise Valley."

"What? My God ..."

"He's saying he will kill the woman if we don't let him talk to you."

George wanted to do the right thing, but ...

But he'd spent weeks now trying to forget that another version of him still existed. "I—um—I *guess* it'd be okay if you put him on."

Shiozaki shook his head. "No. He won't take a phone call. He says you have to come here in person."

"But ... but you said ..."

"I know what we told you during counseling, but, dammit, George, a woman's life is at stake. You might be immortal now, but she isn't."

Rathburn thought for another few seconds, then: "All right. All right. I can be there in a couple of hours."

▮ ▮ ▮

The robot-bodied George Rathburn was shocked by what he was seeing on the vidphone in Shiozaki's office. It was him—just as he remembered himself. His soft, fragile body; his graying temples; his receding hairline; his nose that he'd always thought was too large.

But it was him doing something he never could have imagined doing— holding a surgical blade to a woman's throat.

Detective Lucerne spoke toward the phone's pickups. "Okay," he said. "He's here. The other you is here."

On the screen, Rathburn could see his shed skin's eyes go wide as they beheld what he'd become. Of course, that version of him had selected the golden body—but it had only been an empty shell then, with no inner workings. "Well, well, well," said G.R. "Welcome, brother."

Rathburn didn't trust his synthesized voice, so he simply nodded.

"Come on down to the hospital," said G.R. "Go to the observation gallery above the operating theater; I'll go to the operating theater itself. We'll be able to see each other—and we'll be able to talk, man to man."

▮ ▮ ▮

"Hello," said Rathburn. He was standing on his golden legs, staring through the angled sheet of glass that overlooked the operating room.

"Hello," said GR-7, looking up. "Before we go any further, I need you to prove that you are who you say you are. Sorry about this, but, well, it could be *anyone* inside that robot."

"It's me," said Rathburn.

"No. At best it's one of us. But I've got to be sure."

"So ask me a question."

GR-7 was clearly prepared for this. "The first girl to ever give us a blowjob."

"Carrie," said Rathburn, at once. "At the soccer field."

GR-7 smiled. "Good to see you, brother."

Rathburn was silent for a few moments. He swiveled his head on noiseless, frictionless bearings, looking briefly at Lucerne's face, visible on a vidphone out of view of the observation window. Then he turned back to his shed skin. "I, ah, I understand you want to be called George."

"That's right."

But Rathburn shook his head. "We—you and I, when we were one—shared exactly the same opinion about this matter. We wanted to live forever. And that can't be done in a biological body. You *know* that."

"It can't be done *yet* in a biological body. But I'm only 45. Who knows what technology will be available in the rest of our—of *my*—lifetime?"

Rathburn no longer breathed—so he could no longer sigh. But he moved his steel shoulders while feeling the emotion that used to produce a sigh. "You know why we chose to transfer early. You have a genetic predisposition to fatal strokes. But I don't have that—George Rathburn doesn't have that anymore. *You* might check out any day now, and if we hadn't transferred our consciousness into this body, there would have been no immortality for us."

"But we didn't *transfer* consciousness," said GR-7. "We *copied* consciousness—bit for bit, synapse for synapse. You're a copy. *I'm* the original."

"Not as a matter of law," said Rathburn. "You—the biological you—signed the contract that authorized the transfer of personhood. You signed it with the same hand you're using to hold that scalpel to Dr. Ng's throat."

"But I've changed my mind."

"You don't have a mind *to* change. The software we called the mind of

George Rathburn—the only legal version of it—has been transferred from the hardware of your biological brain to the hardware of our new body's nano-gel CPU." The robotic Rathburn paused. "By rights, as in any transfer of software, the original should have been destroyed."

GR-7 frowned. "Except that society wouldn't allow for that, any more than it would allow for physician-assisted suicide. It's illegal to terminate a source body, even after the brain has been transferred."

"Exactly," said Rathburn, nodding his robotic head. "And you have to activate the replacement before the source dies, or else the court will determine that there's been no continuity of personhood and dispose of the assets. Death may not be certain anymore, but taxes certainly are."

Rathburn had hoped GR-7 would laugh at that, hoped that a bridge could be built between them. But GR-7 simply said, "So I'm stuck here."

"I'd hardly call it 'stuck,'" said Rathburn. "Paradise Valley is a little piece of heaven here on Earth. Why not just enjoy it, until you really do go to heaven?"

"I *hate* it here," said GR-7. He paused. "Look, I accept that by the current wording of the law, I have no legal standing. All right, then. I can't make them nullify the transfer—but *you* can. You are a person in the eyes of the law; you can do this."

"But I don't want to do it. I like being immortal."

"But *I* don't like being a prisoner."

"It's not me that's changed," said the android. "It's you. Think about what you're doing. We were never violent. We would never dream of taking a hostage, of holding a knife to someone's throat, of frightening a woman half to death. You're the one who has changed."

But the skin shook his head. "Nonsense. We'd just never been in such desperate circumstances before. Desperate circumstances make one do desperate things. The fact that you can't conceive of us doing this means that you're a *flawed* copy. This—this transfer process isn't ready for prime time yet. You should nullify the copy and let me, the original, go on with your—with our—life."

It was now the robotic Rathburn's turn to shake his head. "Look, you must realize that this can't ever work—that even if I were to sign some paper that transferred our legal status back to you, there are witnesses here to testify that I'd been coerced into signing it. It would have no legal value."

"You think you can outsmart me?" said GR-7. "I *am* you. Of course I know that."

"Good. Then let that woman go."

"You're not thinking," said GR-7. "Or at least you're not thinking hard enough. Come on, this is *me* you're talking to. You must know I'd have a better plan than that."

"I don't see ...."

"You mean you don't want to see. Think, Copy of George. Think."

"I still don't ..." The robotic Rathburn trailed off. "Oh. No, no, you can't expect me to do that."

"Yes, I do," said GR-7.

"But ..."

"But what?" The skin moved his free hand—the one not holding the scalpel—in a sweeping gesture. "It's a simple proposition. Kill yourself, and your rights of personhood will default back to me. You're correct that, right now, I'm not a person under the law—meaning I can't be charged with a crime. So I don't have to worry about going to jail for anything I do now. Oh, they might try—but I'll ultimately get off, because if I don't, the court will have to admit that not just me, but all of us here in Paradise Valley are still human beings, with human rights."

"What you're asking is impossible."

"What I'm asking is the only thing that makes sense. I talked to a friend who used to be a lawyer. The personhood rights *will* revert if the original is still alive, but the uploaded version isn't. I'm sure no one ever intended the law to be used for this purpose; I'm told it was designed to allow product-liability suits if the robot brain failed shortly after transfer. But regardless, if you kill yourself, *I* get to go back to being a free human." GR-7 paused for a moment. "So what's it going to be? Your pseudolife, or the real flesh-and-blood life of this woman?"

"George ..." said the robot mouth. "Please."

But the biological George shook his head. "If you really believe that you, as a copy of me, are more real than the original that still exists—if you really believe that you have a soul, just like this woman does, inside your robotic frame—then there's no particular reason why you should sacrifice yourself for Dr. Ng here. But if, down deep, you're thinking that I'm correct, that she really is alive, and you're not, then you'll do the right thing." He pressed the scalpel's blade in slightly, drawing blood again. "What's it going to be?"

▮ ▮ ▮

George Rathburn had returned to Shiozaki's office, and Detective Lucerne was doing his best to persuade the robot-housed mind to agree to GR-7's terms.

"Not in a million years," said Rathburn, "and, believe me, I intend to be around that long."

"But another copy of you can be made," said Lucerne.

"But it won't be *me*—this me."

"But that woman, Dr. Ng: she's got a husband, three daughters ..."

"I'm not insensitive to that, Detective," said Rathburn, pacing back and forth on his golden mechanical legs. "But let me put it to you another way. Say this is 1875, in the southern US. The Civil War is over, blacks in theory have the same legal status as whites. But a white man is being held hostage, and he'll only be let go if a black man agrees to sacrifice himself in the white man's place. See the parallel? Despite all the courtroom wrangling that was done to make uploaded life able to maintain the legal status, the personhood, of the original, you're asking me to set that aside, and reaffirm what the whites in the South felt they knew all along: that, all legal mumbo-jumbo to the contrary, a black man is worth less than a white man. Well, I won't do that. I wouldn't affirm that racist position, and I'll be damned if I'll affirm the modern equivalent: that a silicon-based person is worth less than a carbon-based person."

"'I'll be damned,'" repeated Lucerne, imitating Rathburn's synthesized voice. He let the comment hang in the air, waiting to see if Rathburn would respond to it.

And Rathburn couldn't resist. "Yes, I know there are those who would say I *can't* be damned—because whatever it is that constitutes the human soul isn't recorded during the transference process. That's the gist of it, isn't it? The argument that I'm not really human comes down to a theological assertion: I can't be human, because I have no soul. But I tell you this, Detective Lucerne: I feel every bit as alive—and every bit as spiritual—as I did before the transfer. I'm convinced that I *do* have a soul, or a divine spark, or an *élan vital*, or whatever you want to call it. My life in this particular packaging of it is *not* worth one iota less than Dr. Ng's, or anyone else's."

Lucerne was quiet for a time, considering. "But what about the other you? You're willing to stand here and tell me that that version—the original, flesh-and-blood version—is *not* human anymore. And you would have that distinction by legal fiat, just as blacks were denied human rights in the old south."

"There's a difference," said Rathburn. "There's a big difference. That version of me—the one holding Dr. Ng hostage—agreed of its own free will, without any coercion whatsoever, to that very proposition. He—*it*—agreed that it would no longer be human, once the transfer into the robot body was completed."

"But he doesn't want it to be that way anymore."

"Tough. It's not the first contract that he—that *I*—signed in my life that I later regretted. But simple regret isn't reason enough to get out of a legally valid transaction." Rathburn shook his robotic head. "No, I'm sorry. I refuse. Believe me, I wish more than anything that you could save Dr. Ng—but you're going to have to find another way to do it. There's too much at stake here for *my* people—for uploaded humans—to let me make any other decision."

▌ ▌ ▌

"All right," Lucerne finally said to the robotic Rathburn, "I give up. If we can't do it the easy way, we're going to have to do it the hard way. It's a good thing the old Rathburn wants to see the new Rathburn directly. Having him in that operating room while you're in the overlooking observation gallery will be perfect for sneaking a sharpshooter in."

Rathburn felt as though his eyes should go wide, but of course they did not. "You're going to shoot him?"

"You've left us no other choice. Standard procedure is to give the hostage-taker everything he wants, get the hostage back, then go after the criminal. But the only thing he wants is for you to be dead—and you're not willing to cooperate. So we're going to take him out."

"You'll use a tranquilizer, won't you?"

Lucerne snorted. "On a man holding a knife to a woman's throat? We need something that will turn him off like a light, before he's got time to react. And the best way to do that is a bullet to the head or chest."

"But ... but I don't want you to kill him."

Lucerne made an even louder snort. "By your logic, he's not alive anyway."

"Yes, but ..."

"But what? You willing to give him what he wants?"

"I can't. Surely you can see that."

Lucerne shrugged. "Too bad. I was looking forward to being able to quip 'Goodbye, Mr. Chips.'"

"Damn you," said Rathburn. "Don't you see that it's because of that sort of attitude that I *can't* allow this precedent?"

Lucerne made no reply, and after a time Rathburn continued. "Can't we fake my death somehow? Just enough for you to get Ng back to safety?"

Lucerne shook his head. "GR-7 demanded proof that it was really you inside that tin can. I don't think he can be easily fooled. But you know him better than anyone else. Could you be fooled?"

Rathburn tipped his mechanical head down. "No. No, I'm sure he'll demand positive proof."

"Then we're back to the sharpshooter."

▮ ▮ ▮

Rathburn walked into the observation gallery, his golden feet making soft metallic clangs as they touched the hard, tiled floor. He looked through the angled glass, down at the operating room below. The slab-of-flab version of himself had Dr. Ng tied up now, her hands and feet bound with surgical tape. She couldn't get away, but he no longer had to constantly hold the scalpel to her throat. GR-7 was standing up, and she was next to him, leaning against the operating table.

The angled window continued down to within a half-meter of the floor. Crouching below its sill was Conrad Burloak, the sharpshooter, in a gray uniform, holding a black rifle. A small transmitter had been inserted in Rathburn's camera hardware, copying everything his glass eyes were seeing onto a datapad Burloak had with him.

In ideal circumstances, Burloak had said, he liked to shoot for the head, but here he was going to have to fire through the plate-glass window, and that might deflect the bullet slightly. So he was going to aim for the center of the torso, a bigger target. As soon as the datapad showed a clean line-of-fire at G.R., Burloak would pop up and blow him away.

"Hello, George," said the robotic Rathburn. There was an open intercom between the observation gallery and the operating theater below.

"All right," said the fleshy one. "Let's get this over with. Open the access panel to your nano-gel braincase, and ..."

But GR-7 trailed off, seeing that the robotic Rathburn was shaking his head. "I'm sorry, George. I'm not going to deactivate myself."

"You prefer to see Dr. Ng die?"

Rathburn could shut off his visual input, the equivalent of closing his eyes. He did that just now for a moment, presumably much to the chagrin of the sharpshooter studying the datapad. "Believe me, George, the last thing I want to do is see anyone die."

He reactivated his eyes. He'd thought he'd been suitably ironic but, of course, the other him had the same mind. GR-7, perhaps suspecting that something was up, had moved Dr. Ng so that she was now standing between himself and the glass,

"Don't try anything funny," said the skin. "I've got nothing to lose."

Rathburn looked down on his former self—but only in the literal sense. He didn't want to see this ... this man, this being, this thing, this entity, this whatever it was, hurt.

After all, even if the shed skin wasn't a person in the cold eyes of the law, he surely still remembered that time he'd—*they'd*—almost drowned swimming at the cottage, and mom pulling him to shore while his arms flailed in panic. And he remembered his first day at junior-high school, when a gang of grade nines had beaten him up as initiation. And he remembered the incredible shock and sadness when he'd come home from his weekend job at the hardware store and found dad slumped over in his easy chair, dead from a stroke.

And that biological him must remember all the good things, too: hitting that home run clear over the fence in grade eight, after all the members of the opposing team had moved in close; his first kiss, at a party, playing spin the bottle; and his first romantic kiss, with Dana, her studded tongue sliding into his mouth; that *perfect* day in the Bahamas, with the most gorgeous sunset he'd ever seen.

Yes, this other him wasn't just a backup, wasn't just a repository of data. He knew all the same things, *felt* all the same things, and—

The sharpshooter had crawled several meters along the floor of the observation gallery, trying to get a clean angle at GR-7. Out of the corner of his robotic vision—which was as sharp at the peripheries as it was in the center—Rathburn saw the sharpshooter tense his muscles, and then—

And then Burloak leaped up, swinging his rifle, and—

And to his astonishment, Rathburn found the words "Look out, George!" emitting from his robotic mouth at a greatly amplified volume.

And just as the words came out, Burloak fired, and the window exploded into a thousand shards, and GR-7 spun around, grabbing Dr. Ng, swinging her in between himself and the sharpshooter, and the bullet hit, drilling a hole through the woman's heart, and through the chest of the man behind her, and they both crumpled to the operating-room floor, and human blood flowed out of them, and the glass shards rained down upon them like robot tears.

▉ ▉ ▉

And so, at last, there was no more ambiguity. There was only one George Rathburn—a single iteration of the consciousness that had first bloomed some forty-five years ago, now executing as code in the nano-gel inside a robotic form.

George suspected that Shiozaki would try to cover up what had occurred back in Paradise Valley—at least the details. He'd have to admit that Dr. Ng had been killed by a skin, but doubtless Shiozaki would want to gloss over Rathburn's warning shout. After all, it would be bad for business if those about to shed got wind of the fact that the new versions still had empathy for the old ones.

But Detective Lucerne and his sharpshooter would want just the opposite: only by citing the robotic Rathburn's interference could they exonerate the sharpshooter from accidentally shooting the hostage.

But nothing could exonerate GR-7 from what he'd done, swinging that poor, frightened woman in front of himself as a shield ...

Rathburn sat down in his country house's living room. Despite his robotic body, he did feel weary—bone-weary—and needed the support of the chair.

He'd done the right thing, even if GR-7 hadn't; he knew that. Any other choice by him would have been devastating not just for himself, but also for Kathryn and every other uploaded consciousness. There really had been no alternative.

Immortality is grand. Immortality is great. As long as you have a clear conscience, that is. As long as you're not tortured by doubt, racked by depression, overcome with guilt.

That poor woman, Dr. Ng. She'd done nothing wrong, nothing at all. And now she was dead.

And he—a version of him—had caused her to be killed.

GR-7's words replayed in Rathburn's memory. *We'd just never been in such desperate circumstances before.*

Perhaps that was true. But he was in desperate circumstances now.

And he'd found himself contemplating actions he never would have considered possible for him before.

That poor woman. That poor dead woman ...

It wasn't just GR-7's fault. It was *his* fault. Her death was a direct consequence of him wanting to live forever.

And he'd have to live with the guilt of that forever.

Unless ...

Desperate circumstances make one do desperate things.

He picked up the magnetic pistol—astonishing what things you could buy online these days. A proximity blast from it would destroy all recordings in nano-gel.

George Rathburn looked at the pistol, at its shiny, hard exterior.

And he placed the emitter against the side of his stainless-steel skull, and, after a few moments of hesitation, his golden robotic finger contracted against the trigger.

What better way, after all, was there to prove that he was still human?

The Stanley Cup Caper

The 2003 World Science Fiction Convention was in Toronto, where I live. The Toronto Star, Canada's largest-circulation newspaper, decided to commemorate that fact—and my then-current Hugo nomination for Hominids *—by commissioning a short story from me predicting the future of Toronto some thirty years down the road (seeing as how it had been thirty years since the last time the Worldcon had been in Toronto).*

I'd just finished reading Dan Brown's runaway bestseller The Da Vinci Code *(which I thoroughly enjoyed), and puzzles and mysteries were very much on my mind. I'm not a hockey fan—sacrilege for a Canadian, I know— but somehow hit on this premise.*

To my delight, the four opening words—a riff on famed Canadian sportscaster Foster Hewitt's trademark "He shoots! He scores!"—are included (along with twenty-two other quotes from me) in The Penguin Dictionary of Popular Canadian Quotations, *edited by John Robert Colombo.*

⚔ ◼ ◼ ✂

"She shoots! She scores! For the first time in sixty-seven years, the Toronto Maple Leafs have won the Stanley Cup! Captain Karen Lopez and her team have skated to victory as the 2031 NHL champions. The hometown crowd here is going wild, and—wait! Wait! Ladies and gentlemen, this is incredible ... we've just received word that the Stanley Cup trophy is missing!"

Detectives Joginder Singh and Trista Chong let their car drive them east along the Gardiner Expressway. At Bathurst, the vehicle headed down into the tunnel. Jo shuddered; he hated the underground portion of the Gardiner. Sadly, his fear of tunnels also kept him from using the subway, even though it now ran all the way from Pearson Airport to the Pickering Solar Power Plant.

Still, the one tolerable thing about going underground here was that he didn't have to lay eyes on the spire of the Quebec Consulate; Trista, fifteen years his junior, didn't really remember a united Canada, but Jo certainly did.

At Yonge, their car resurfaced. South of them was the *Toronto Sun-Star* building. But they were going north: their car let them out across the street from the Hockey Hall of Fame. Of course, there was no place to park; the car would just keep driving around the block until they signaled it to pick them up.

Jo and Trista had spent most of yesterday fruitlessly examining the crime scene at the WestJet Centre. Today, they were going to start by having a look at the duplicate Stanley Cup—the mockup that was on public display at the Hall of Fame—just to get a feel for the dimensions of the stolen object.

Once inside, Jo stood in front of the glass case containing the duplicate, while Trista walked around the case, taking pictures of the duplicate's engraved surface with her pocketbrain. When she was finished, something apparently caught her eye. "Look!" she crowed, pointing to the adjacent glass case. "There it is—taken apart, but there it is!"

Jo glanced at the other case and laughed. "Those are just retired bands."

Trista made a perplexed frown. "Like the Barenaked Ladies?"

"No. Bands from the original trophy. It always consists of the cup on top and five circular bands forming the cylindrical body." He pointed back at the mockup. "See? Each of the five bands has room for listing the members of thirteen winning teams. When they fill the last spot on the bottom band, they retire the top one, slide the other four up, and add a new band. Those bands in that other case are the ones that have already been removed."

Trista took some pictures of the retired bands, then looked back at the mockup, peering at its base. "But the last band on the trophy is already full," she said.

Jo nodded. "That's right. They're going to have to retire the top band this year and start a new one." He paused. "Seen enough?"

Trista nodded. They exited, crossed the street, and waited for their car to come get them. With the Gardiner buried, it was easy to see the Central Nanotechnology Tower on the lakeshore, but there was no point going up to the observation deck anymore. Jo shook his head; he was old enough to remember when the city's nickname had been Hogtown, not Smogtown.

The car took them north on Yonge Street, the toll being debited automatically. It had been ten years since GTA amalgamation, combining Toronto with everything from Mississauga to Oshawa. Still, the stolen trophy had to be somewhere inside the supercity's borders; like every other North American metropolis, T.O. was surrounded by security checkpoints, and something as big as the Stanley Cup couldn't have been smuggled out.

On their left now was the Eaton Centre. Jo's sister had a condominium there, in what had once been a Grand & Toy store; with most people shopping online these days, there was little need for big malls. As they continued up Yonge, the towers of Ryerson—"the Harvard of the North," as CNN-MSNBC had recently dubbed it—were visible off to the right. Jo watched the landscape going by—a succession of Tim Hortons donut shops, pot bars, and licensed bordellos. Trista, meanwhile, had her pocketbrain out and was staring at its screen, studying the pictures she'd taken earlier.

Their car turned right onto Carleton, heading towards Maple Leaf Gardens—a historic site, which perhaps might hold a clue—when suddenly Trista looked up from her screen. "No! Car, turn around—head to University Avenue, and then go south."

Jo looked at his partner. "What's up?"

"I think I know where the Stanley Cup is."

"Where?"

Trista brought up a map of downtown Toronto on her pocketbrain and showed it to him. "Right there," she said, tapping a spot on the screen.

"Oh, come on!" said Jo. "Why would they want it?"

"Did you see what was on that band they're going to retire this year?"

"Thirteen old winning teams," said Jo.

"Yes—but which teams?"

"I have no idea."

She brought up one of the images she'd taken of the duplicate trophy. "The winners from 1953 to 1965."

"So?"

"So I've read what's on all the bands now, including the retired ones. The band they're about to remove lists the only five-wins-in-a-row Stanley Cup champions."

"Really?"

"Yes. See? From 1956 through 1960, Montreal won the Stanley Cup every single year, and—"

Jo got it in a flash. "And there's no way a sovereign Quebec would let the band commemorating that be archived at the Hockey Hall of Fame, which is on Canadian soil. But the Quebec Consulate—"

"Exactly!" said Trista. "The Quebec Consulate is technically Québecois soil."

Jo frowned. "But we don't have any jurisdiction on the consulate grounds."

"I know," said Trista. "It'll take some political wrangling between Ottawa and Quebec."

"Plus ça change, plus c'est la même chose," said Jo.

"What's that mean?" asked Trista. She was young enough that she hadn't had to study French in school.

Jo looked out the car's window as they turned onto University, passing the statue of Mel Lastman. "The more things change," he said, "the more they stay the same."

On The Surface

I'm a huge fan of H.G. Wells. In part, it's because he was the first real practitioner of science fiction as social commentary, the particular brand of the stuff I myself like to write.

But it's also because of Wells's staggering imagination: he invented most of the staples of science fiction, including time travel (The Time Machine), *invisibility* (The Invisible Man), *Martians* (The War of the Worlds), *and antigravity* (The First Men in the Moon). *In fact, I sometimes quip that my 1994 novel* End of an Era *was my attempt to combine all those things into one: it's a time-travel story of invisible Martians who have harnessed antigravity.*

Those who know Wells only from movies might be unaware that the Time Traveler in The Time Machine *doesn't end his journey in the year 802,701 A.D. with the Morlocks and the Eloi. Rather, after escaping from there, he goes much, much further into the future, visiting the waning days of the world, when the sun, bloated and red, hangs low on the horizon. That landscape has haunted me ever since I first read Wells's description of it, and when asked to do a story for an anthology entitled* Future War, *I decided to revisit it.*

❖ ◼ ◼ ❧

For once, at least, I grasped the mental operations of the Morlocks. Suppressing a strong inclination to laugh, I stepped through the bronze frame and up to the Time Machine. I was surprised to find it had been carefully oiled and cleaned. I have suspected since that the Morlocks had even partially taken it to pieces while trying in their dim way to grasp its purpose.

—H.G. Wells, *The Time Machine*, 1895

The Morlock named Grach had heard from others of his kind what the journey through time was like, but those words hadn't prepared him for the reality. As he moved forward, the ghostly world around him flashed, now night, now day, a flapping wing. The strobing light was painful, the darkness a bandage too soon ripped away. But Grach endured it; although he could have thrown his pale-white arm in front of his lidless eyes, the spectacle was too incredible not to watch.

Grach held the left-hand lever steadily, meaning the skimming through tomorrows should have happened at a constant rate. But the apparent time it took for each day-to-night cycle was clearly growing longer. Grach knew what was happening of course; the others had told him. Earth's own day was lengthening as the planet in its senescence settled in to be tidally locked, the same face always toward the sun.

Such perpetual day would have been intolerable for Grach, or any Morlock, except that the sun itself was growing much, much dimmer, even as it grew larger or as Earth spiraled closer to it; debate still raged among the Morlocks about which phenomenon accounted for the solar disk now dominating so much of the sky. The giant red sphere that bobbed about the western horizon—never fully rising, never completely setting—was a dying coal whose wan light was all concentrated in the red end of the spectrum, the one color that did not sting the eyes.

Eventually, as Grach continued his headlong rush into futurity, the bloated sun came to rest, moving not at all in the sky, half its vast bulk below the horizon where the still water of the ocean touched the dark firmament. Grach consulted the gauges on the console in front of him and began to operate the right-hand lever, the one that retarded progress, until at last all about him lost the ghostly insubstantiality it had hitherto been imbued with and coalesced into solid form. His time machine had stopped; he had arrived at his destination.

Of course, the invasion had been carefully planned. Other time machines that had already traveled here were arrayed about him in a grid, precise rows and columns, with every one of the squat saddle-seated contraptions, puzzles of nickel and ivory and brass and translucent glimmering quartz, packed close to each of its neighbors.

The grid, Grach knew, measured twelve spaces by ten: room for a hundred and twenty time machines, one for each adult member of the Morlock population. It had always seemed unfair that there were ten Eloi for every Morlock, but that was the ratio by which vegetarians typically outnumbered carnivores, by which prey had to accumulate in order to satisfy the appetites of predators.

There were still vacant spots in the grid, scattered here and there, where time machines hadn't yet come forward, or had perhaps overshot their targets slightly and would materialize an hour or two hence.

Grach took a moment to regain his bearings; this hurtling through time was unsettling. And then he dismounted, letting his narrow, curved feet sink into the moist sand of the great beach that spread out in front of him.

A leash of Morlocks shuffled over to greet Grach: it took him a moment in the odd red light to recognize Bilt and Morbon, females both, and the male Nalk.

Grach and his companions walked sideways, making their way out of the maze of time machines, moving out onto the great sandy beach. Grach found himself inhaling deeply; the air was thin. No wind stirred; no waves lapped the shore, although the vast expanse of water did heave slowly up and down, almost like a giant's heart.

And—now that giants were in his mind—Grach thought briefly of the giant who had come to them, apparently from an ancient past. Assuming the counting of years reckoned by the gauges on his machine had started with a "1" near his own departure date, the giant man had come forward some eight thousand centuries. And yet that gulf was tiny compared to the amount Grach and the others had now leapt forward; millions of years separated him from the world of the Eloi and of the white marble sphinx and of the access portals to the Morlock's underground domain, each protected from the elements by a cupola.

Grach's reverie was quickly broken as Morbon shouted, "Look!" She was pointing, her arm appearing nauseatingly pink in the dim, ruddy sun. Grach followed her gaze, and—

There they were.

Three of them, off in the distance.

Three of the giant crablike creatures that by this time had dethroned Morlocks from their dominion over the world.

Three of the enemy they had come to kill.

⧎ ⧎ ⧎

The crabs were each as wide as Grach's armspan, and looked as though they might weigh double what he did. They had massive pincers; supple, whiplike antennae; eyes atop stalks; complex multi-palped mandibles; and corrugated backs partially covered by ugly knobs. Their many legs moved slowly, tentatively, more as if each creature were feeling its way along rather than seeing the ground in front of it.

And they were sentient, these crabs. That hadn't been apparent initially. Drayt, the Morlock who had mounted the first copy of the giant's contraption, who had originally traveled forth to this time, had returned only with wondrous tales of a world in which the surface was perpetually dim, a world in which Morlocks could leave their dismal subterranean existence behind and reclaim the day. Oh, yes, Drayt had seen the crabs, but he'd thought them dumb brutes and suggested that they might provide a superior substitute for the scrawny meat of Eloi haunches that had been the Morlock staple.

Others had come forward, though, and seen the cities of the crabs; their vile, ever-working mouths secreted a compound that caused sand to adhere to itself, forming structures as strong as those of carved stone. They communicated, too, apparently through sounds too high-pitched for Morlocks to hear supplemented by expressive waving of their antennae.

And although they had tolerated the occasional Morlock visitor at first, when Drayt's proposal had been put to the test—when one of the ruddy crustaceans had had its carapace staved, when the white flesh within was sampled and found delicious—the crabs had behaved utterly unlike Eloi, for, unaccountable though it might seem, they *attacked* the Morlocks, decapitating several with neat snaps of their giant claws.

The crabs, then, had to be subdued, just as the Eloi had perhaps been centuries before Grach had been born. They had to learn to accept the honor of being fodder for Morlocks. It was, after all, the natural way of things.

Grach hoped the war would be short. If the crabs were sentient, then they should understand that the Morlocks would never take more than a few of them at a time, that the odds of any particular crab being that day's meal were slim, that there could be a mostly uneventful coexistence between the small population of subjugators and the multitudes of subjugated.

But if the war were long, if they had to slaughter every last crab, well, so be it. Grach and the other Morlocks had no desire to bring Eloi forward; they were tolerable as a foodstuff, but to share a reclaimed surface with those weak, laughing things would be unthinkable. Fortunately, this distant time had other lifeforms that were agreeable to the Morlock palate: Grach had already tried samples of the giant white butterfly-like creatures that occasionally took to the dark skies here, wings beating against attenuated air. And there were other things that swam beneath the sea or made occasional forays onto the beach; many of these had also already been tasted and found most satisfying.

Grach looked behind him. Another time machine was flickering into existence, leaving only two unoccupied spots in the 120-position grid. Soon, the assault would begin.

▥ ▥ ▥

There was little possibility for a sneak attack in this offensive, said Postan, the leader of the Morlocks. Day and night meant nothing here— one hour, or one year, was precisely like the others; there was no cover of total darkness under which to launch themselves against their foes.

And so once all hundred and twenty Morlocks were ready, they simply charged onto the beach, each one brandishing an iron club almost as long as a Morlock body.

The crabs either heard the attackers coming, despite attempts to restrain the normal cooing sounds of Morlock breathing, or else the crabs felt the footfalls conveyed through the moist sand. Either way, the crustaceans—twenty of them were visible, although more could easily be hidden in undulations of the geography—turned as one to face the charging Morlocks.

Grach had known battle once before; he had been part of the group pursuing the time-traveling giant through the woods outside the ancient palace of green porcelain. He remembered the huge fire blazing through the forest—and remembered the excitement, the thrill that went with battle. That night, they had been unsuccessful. But this time, Grach felt sure, they would triumph.

Morlocks learned quickly. They'd never thought of using clubs to attack other life forms; it hadn't been necessary with the Eloi, after all. But that night—a few years ago, now, and a few million—when the Morlocks had fought the ancient giant, they'd seen him use a metal club, a large lever apparently broken off some old machine, to stave in skulls. And so the subterranean workshops weren't only set to the task of duplicating the giant's strange machine, its workings still not fully grasped but its parts easy enough to turn on a lathe or hammer out on an anvil. No, the factories were also set to making sturdy iron rods. Grach held his own rod over his head as he ran, looking forward to hearing the cracking sound of exoskeletons shattering under its impact.

The crabs' claws were each as long as a Morlock's forearm. They snapped open and closed, the sound oddly mechanical in this strange world of the far future. Grach knew to hold his rod out in front of him, and, indeed, it wasn't long before the nearest crab had set upon him. The creature's pincer tried to close tight on the rod, which rang in Grach's hands. But although the claws were strong, they weren't strong enough to cut through iron. Another Morlock, to Grach's right, was waving his own rod, trying to get the crustacean to clamp onto it with its other claw. And a third Morlock—Bilt, it was—had climbed atop the crab from the rear and was now straddling its carapace while pounding down again and again with his own metal rod. The crab's antennae whipped frantically, and Grach caught a glimpse of one of them bringing up a welt as it lashed Bilt's face. But soon Bilt managed a killing blow, a great *crack!* sounding as his rod smashed in the chitinous roof between the thing's two eyestalks. The stalks went absolutely straight for a moment, then collapsed, one atop the other, lying motionless on the broken carapace, liquid from within the animal welling up and washing over them.

The creature's many legs folded up one by one, and its lenticular body collapsed to the sandy beach. Bilt let out a whoop of excitement, and Grach followed suit.

It had been good to aid in the kill—but Grach wanted one of his own. Several of the crabs were scurrying away now, trying to retreat from the onslaught of Morlocks, but Grach set his eyes on a particularly ugly one, its carapace especially rich with the greenish encrustation that marred the shells of some of the others.

Grach wondered if there was another way to defeat a crab. Yes, having his own kill to tell of would be good—but even better would be to have killed one in a way that had occurred to no one else.

There was but a moment to collect his thoughts: fifty or so Morlocks had veered off to pursue retreating crabs; the others were in close combat with the remaining giant crustaceans. But, so far, no one had engaged the crab that had caught Grach's attention.

Grach ran towards his target; there was plenty of noise now to cover his approach—cracking chitin, whooping Morlocks, the harsh screams of the giant white butterfly-like beasts swooping overhead. The crab's rear was to Grach, and it did not turn around as he came closer and closer still.

When at last he'd reached the hideous creature, Grach planted his rod in the moist ground, then reached out with his hands. He got his flat palms underneath the left edge of the crab's carapace. With all the strength he could muster, he lifted the side of the crab.

The segmented legs on that side began to move frantically as they lost contact with the ground. As Grach tipped the creature more and more he could see the complex workings of its underbelly. For its part, the crab couldn't observe what Grach was doing; its eyestalks lacked the reach to see underneath. Still, its claws were snapping in panicky spasms. Grach continued to lift, more, more, more still, until at last the thing's body was vertical rather than horizontal. A final mighty shove toppled the crab over sideways onto its back. Legs worked rapidly, trying to find purchase; the forward claws attempted to right the crab, but they weren't succeeding.

After retrieving his metal rod, Grach jumped onto the thing's under-belly, landing on his knees, the hideous articulations of the limbs shifting and sliding beneath him. He then took his rod in both hands, held it high over his head, and drove it down with all his strength. The rod poked through the creature's underside and soon was slipping easily through its soft innards. Grach felt it resist again as it reached the far side of the shell, but he leaned now with both hands and all of his body's weight on the end of his pole, and at last the exoskeleton gave way. The crab convulsed for a time, but eventually it expired, impaled on the sandy beach.

The battle continued for much of—well, it felt to Grach the length of an afternoon, but there was no way to tell. When it was done, though, a dozen crabs were dead, and the others had fled, abandoning not just the beach but their fused-sand buildings, which were to become the initial sur-face dwellings of the Morlock race.

▦ ▦ ▦

Of course, there had to be *two* great battles. The first—or second; the order of events was so hard to keep straight when time travel was involved—was the one that had already taken place here on the beach. And, naturally, no one would undertake the second battle (or was it the first?) until after the Morlocks had safely secured the far future for themselves.

It had taken Grach and the others quite some time—that word again—to comprehend it all, and perhaps their understanding of such matters was still faulty. But the reasoning they came up with seemed to make sense: first, ensure that the crabs could be routed in the far future, clearing the way for all the Morlocks to travel forward and live again on the surface.

But, with the battle in the future over, the Morlocks couldn't simply leave the Eloi to make their own way in the past. After all, once the Morlocks had traveled forward, the Eloi would venture underground. Oh, surely not at first—months or even years might elapse before the Eloi decided the Morlocks really were gone before any of those timid, frail creatures would dare to climb down the ladders on the inside of the access wells, thereby entering the underworld. But eventually they would—perhaps, Grach thought, led by that bold female who had narrowly survived accompanying the giant during so much of his visit—and just as the Morlocks were now about to regain the surface, so the Eloi would regain what had once been theirs, as well: equipment and tools, technology and power.

Simple experiments with the time machines had proven that changes made in the past would eventually catch up with the future. The time machines, because of their temporal alacrity, allowed one to arrive in the future ahead of the wave of change barreling through the fourth dimension at a less speedy rate. But eventually effect caught up with cause, and the world was remade to conform to its modified past. And so though the beach might now appear as Grach and the others wished it to, there was still a chance that reality would be further modified.

And that could not be allowed; the meek could *not* be permitted to inherit the Earth. For although Morlocks enjoyed violence, Grach and the others couldn't imagine the Eloi ever fighting amongst themselves or with anyone else. No, with all aggression long ago bred out of them, their new technological culture might endure for millions of years—meaning they could still be alive, and hideously advanced, by this time, the time of the beach, the time of the crabs. If the Morlocks didn't take care of that loose end, that dangling thread in the tapestry of time, before permanently moving to the perpetual ruddy twilight of the future, then the Morlocks might find that future becoming a world dominated by Eloi with millions of years of new technology in their hands.

No, now that the crabs were dealt with, it was time to return to the past, time to launch the second offensive of this war.

▮▮ ▮▮ ▮▮

Grach and the other Morlocks returned to the distant past, to the year that, according to the display they'd all seen on the original Time Traveler's machine, had been reckoned by him to be some 800,000 years after his point of origin.

Their fleet of time machines re-appeared whence it had been launched, one after the other flicking into existence inside the giant hollow bronze pedestal of the great marble sphinx, still arrayed in their orderly rows and columns, for although the journey through the fourth dimension had been prodigious, there had been no movement at all in the other three. Of course, there were only 117, instead of 120, machines reappearing. The others were sitting undamaged in the far future, but their riders had been casualties in the battle with the crabs.

There was barely enough room for all the time machines and their passengers within the sphinx's base, but although little air slipped in through the cracks around the upper edges of the vertical door panels, it still seemed richer than the thin atmosphere of the far future.

Naturally, they didn't have to wait until dark. Rather, they had timed their arrival to occur at night. No sooner had the last of the Morlocks returned here than the great bronze panels on either side slid down, opening the interior of the giant pedestal to the elements. The Morlocks spilled out into the night. Grach allowed himself a brief look back over his rounded shoulder; in the starlight he could see the white face of the great sphinx smiling on their venture.

Brandishing clubs, they clambered through the circular portals into the large houses in which the Eloi slept. The Eloi were used to the nighttime raids, to a handful of them being plucked each time to be food for the Morlocks. Those selected did not resist; those not selected did nothing to help the others.

But tonight, the Morlocks didn't want to carry off just a few. Tonight they wished to eradicate the Eloi. The weaklings' skulls yielded juicily to pummeling rods. To that, some Eloi did react, did try to defend themselves or get away—the brighter of these creatures clearly understood that all previous patterns were to be discarded this night.

But even the strongest of the Eloi was no match for the slightest Morlock. Those that had to be chased down were chased down; those that had to be hit with hands were hit with hands; those that had to be strangled had their larynxes crushed.

It didn't take long to dispatch the thousand or so Eloi, and Grach himself happened to be the one to come across that female who had associated herself with the original Time Traveler.

She, at least, had the backbone to look defiant as Grach's rod descended upon her.

▥ ▥ ▥

The return to the far future had gone well. Many Morlocks had clutched infants or children of their kind as they'd ridden forward on the copies of the giant's machine. Others had carried supplies and goods salvaged from the deep prison that bright light had trapped them in.

As time wore on, Grach got used to the thinner air and to the red glow of the now-ancient sun. Mankind, the Morlocks had always known, had started on the surface, and only well into its tenure on Earth had one faction moved underground. Now the Morlocks had reclaimed their birthright, their proper station in the world.

Grach looked out over the beach. Morlocks had feasted on crabs legs and the meat from the invertebrates' rounded bodies. But after that bounty had been exhausted, the broken carapaces were gathered together, making a monument to that glorious battle, and a reminder to any of the crab-beings who might consider reclaiming this beach what fate would await them if they tried.

Of course, Grach knew the world was eventually doomed. He had not made the journey himself, but others had told him of trips to the very end of time, when the sea would freeze and the sun, although bigger even than it was now, would give off almost no light and even less heat.

But that future was far, far beyond even this advanced time. For the remainder of the habitable span of the world, generation after generation of Morlocks would live here. Yes, there might have been an interregnum during which the crabs had been dominant, but that was over now. Morlocks ruled again, and, until the sun's red light finally faded for good, they would continue to do so.

Still, new changes *were* propagating forward. The large white butter-fly-like creatures were now gone. Perhaps, mused Grach, just as the giant's kind had once metamorphosed into Morlocks and Eloi, so the Eloi themselves, flighty creatures at the best of times, had here in the far, far future, literally taken wing. But with no more Eloi in the past, of course no descendants of them could exist. A pity: the flying things had been delicious.

Grach looked out again at the blood-red beach, and he thought about the original Time Traveler, that giant from ages past. Had he found whatever it was he'd been seeking when he came forward from his time? Perhaps not in that year he'd numbered about 800,000. The injustice, after all, of the best of mankind being damned to a subterranean existence surely must have disappointed him. But, Grach thought, if the Time Traveler knew what his machine had ultimately made possible—this wondrous moment, with the very essence of humanity on the surface—surely he would be pleased.

The Eagle Has Landed

Like everyone who loves space travel, I was devastated by the loss on February 1, 2003, of the space shuttle Columbia. *And, as writers always do, I worked out some of my feelings about that on the printed page—in this little piece that appeared in Mike Resnick's anthology* I, Alien.

I freely admit that this isn't my best story—but it is *my favorite one to read aloud. I do impressions of the famous people whose speeches are quoted, and the audiences and I always have a good time. But, still, because of the tragic inspiration that led to me writing it, thinking about this one always leaves me a little sad.*

⊰ ■ ■ ⊱

I've spent a lot of time watching Earth—more than forty of that planet's years. My arrival was in response to the signal from our automated probe, which had detected that the paper-skinned bipedal beings of that world had split the atom. The probe had served well, but there were some things only a living being could do properly, and assessing whether a lifeform should be contacted by the Planetary Commonwealth was one.

It would have been fascinating to have been present for that first fission explosion: it's always a fabulous thing when a new species learns to cleave the atom, the dawn for them of a new and wondrous age. Of course, fission is messy, but one must glide before one can fly; all known species that developed fission soon moved on to the clean energy of controlled fusion, putting an end to need and want, to poverty, to scarcity.

I arrived in the vicinity of Earth some dozen Earth-years after that first fission explosion—but I could not set down upon Earth, for its gravity was five times that of our homeworld. But its moon had a congenial mass; there I would weigh slightly less than I did at home. And, just like our homeworld, which, of course, is itself the moon of a gas-giant world orbiting a double star, Earth's moon was tidally locked, constantly showing the same face to its primary. It was a perfect place for me to land my starbird and observe the goings-on on the blue-and-white-and-infrared world below.

This moon, the sole natural satellite of Earth, was devoid of atmosphere, bereft of water. I imagined our homeworld would be similar if its volatiles weren't constantly replenished by material from Chirp-*cluck*-CHIRP-chirp, the gas-giant planet that so dominated our skies; a naturally occurring, permanent magnetic-flux tube passed a gentle rain of gases onto our world.

The moon that the inhabitants of Earth called "*the* moon" (and "*La* Lune," and a hundred other things) was depressingly desolate. Still, from it I could easily intercept the tens of thousands of audio and audiovisual transmissions spewing out from Earth—and with a time delay of only four wingbeats. My starbird's computer separated the signals one from the other, and I watched and listened.

It took that computer most of a smallyear to decipher all the different languages this species used, but, by the year—being a planet, not a moon, Earth had only one kind of year—the Earth people called 1958, I was able to follow everything that was happening there.

I was at once delighted and disgusted. Delighted, because I'd learned that in the years since that initial atomic test explosion had triggered our probe, the natives of this world had launched their first satellite. And disgusted, because almost immediately after developing fission, they had used those phenomenal energies as weapons against their own kind. Two cities had been destroyed, and bigger and more devastating bombs were still being developed.

Were they insane, I wondered? It had never occurred to me that a whole species could be unbalanced, but the initial fatal bombings, and the endless series of subsequent test explosions of bigger and bigger weapons, were the work not of crazed individuals but of the governments of this world's most powerful nations.

I watched for two more Earth years, and was about to file my report—quarantine this world; avoid all contact—when my computer alerted me to an interesting signal coming from the planet. The leader of the most populous of the nations on the western shore of the world's largest ocean was making a speech: "Now it is time," he was saying, "to take longer strides"—apparently significant imagery for a walking species—"time for a great new American enterprise; time for this nation to take a clearly leading role in space achievement, which in many ways may hold the key to our future on Earth ..."

Yes, I thought. *Yes.* I listened on, fascinated.

"I believe this nation should commit itself to achieving the goal, before this decade"—a cluster of ten Earth years—"is out, of landing a man on the moon and returning him safely to the Earth ..."

Finally, some real progress for this species! I tapped the ERASE node with a talon, deleting my still-unsent report.

At home, these "Americans," as their leader had called them, were struggling with the notion of equality for all citizens, regardless of the color of their skin. I know, I know—to beings such as us, with frayed scales ranging from gold to green to purple to ultraviolet, the idea of one's coloration having any significance seems ridiculous, but for them it had been a major concern. I listened to hateful rhetoric: "Segregation now, segregation tomorrow, segregation forever!" And I listened to wonderful rhetoric: "I have a dream that one day this nation will rise up and live out the true meaning of its creed: 'We hold these truths to be self-evident: that all men are created equal.'" And I watched as public sentiment shifted from supporting the former to supporting the latter, and I confess that my dorsal spines fluttered with emotion as I did so.

Meanwhile, Earth's fledgling space program continued: single-person ships, double-person ships, the first dockings in space, a planned triple-person ship, and then ...

And then there was a fire at the liftoff facility. Three "humans"—one of the countless names this species gave itself—were dead. A tragic mistake: pressurized space vehicles have a tendency to explode in vacuum, of course, so someone had landed on the idea of pressurizing the habitat (the "command module," they called it) at only one-fifth of normal, by eliminating all the gases except oxygen, normally a fifth part of Earth's atmosphere ...

Still, despite the horrible accident, the humans went on. How could they not?

And, soon, they came here, to the moon.

I was present at that first landing, but remained hidden. I watched as a figure in a white suit hopped off the last rung of a ladder and fell at what must have seemed to it a slow rate. The words the human spoke echo with me still: "That's one small step for man, one giant leap for mankind."

And, indeed, it truly was. I could not approach closely, not until they'd departed, but after they had, I walked over—even in my environmental sack, it was easy to walk here on my wingclaws. I examined the lower, foil-wrapped stage of their landing craft, which had been abandoned here. My computer could read the principal languages of this world, having learned to do so with aid of educational broadcasts it had intercepted. It informed me that the plaque on the lander said, "Here men from the planet Earth first set foot upon the moon, July 1969, A.D. We came in peace for all mankind."

My spines rippled. There *was* hope for this race. Indeed, during the time since that speech about longer strides, public opinion had turned overwhelmingly against what seemed to be a long, pointless conflict being fought in a tropical nation. They didn't need quarantining; all they needed, surely, was a little time ...

■ ■ ■

Fickle, fickle species! Their world made only three and half orbits around its solitary sun before what was announced to be the *last* journey here, to the moon, was completed. I was stunned. Never before had I known a race to turn its back on space travel once it had begun; one might as well try to crawl back into the shards of one's egg ...

But, incredibly, these humans did just that. Oh, there were some perfunctory missions to low orbit, but that was all.

Yes, there had been other accidents—one on the way to the moon, although there were no casualties; another, during which three people died when their vessel depressurized on reentry. But those three were from another nation, called "Russia," and that nation continued its space efforts without missing a wingbeat. But soon Russia's economy collapsed—of course! This race *still* hadn't developed controlled fusion; indeed, there was a terrible, terrible accident at a fission power-generating station in that nation shortly before it fell apart.

Still, perhaps the failure of Russia had been a good thing. Not that there was anything inherently evil about it, from what I could tell—indeed, in principle, it espoused the values that all other known civilized races share—but it was the rivalry between it and the nation that had launched the inhabited ships to the moon that had caused an incredible escalation of nuclear-weapons production. Finally, it seemed, they would abandon that madness ... and perhaps if abandoning space exploration was the price to pay for that, maybe, just maybe, it was worth it.

I was in a quandary. I had spent much longer here than I'd planned to—and I'd as yet filed no report. It's not that I was eager to get home—my brood had long since grown up—but I was getting old; my frayed scales were losing their flexibility, and they were tinged now with blue. But I still didn't know what to tell our homeworld.

And so I crawled back into my cryostasis nest. I decided to have the computer awaken me in one of our bigyears, a time approximately equal to a dozen Earth years. I wondered what I would find when I awoke ...

▌▌ ▌▌ ▌▌

What I found was absolute madness. Two neighboring countries threatening each other with nuclear weapons; a third having announced that it, too, had developed such things; a fourth being scrutinized to see if it possessed them; and a fifth—the one that had come to the moon for all mankind—saying it would not rule out first strikes with its nuclear weapons.

No one was using controlled fusion. No one had returned to the moon.

Shortly after I awoke, tragedy struck again: seven humans were aboard an orbital vehicle called *Columbia*—a reused name, a name I'd heard before, the name of the command module that had orbited the moon while the first lander had come down to the surface. *Columbia* broke apart during reentry, scattering debris over a wide area of Earth. My dorsal spines fell flat, and my wing claws curled tightly. I hadn't been so sad since one of my own brood had died falling out of the sky.

Of course, my computer continued to monitor the broadcasts from the planet, and it provided me with digests of the human response.

I was appalled.

The humans were saying that putting people into space was too dangerous, that the cost in lives was too high, that there was nothing of value to be done in space that couldn't be done better by machines.

This from a race that had spread from its equatorial birthplace by walking—*walking!*—to cover most of their world; only recently had mechanical devices given them the ability to fly.

But now they *could* fly. They could soar. They could go to other worlds!

But there was no need, they said, for intelligent judgment out in space, no need to have thinking beings on hand to make decisions, to exalt, to experience directly.

They would continue to build nuclear weapons. But they wouldn't leave their nest. Perhaps because of their messy, wet mode of reproduction, they'd never developed the notion of the stupidity of keeping all one's eggs in a single container ...

▮ ▮ ▮

So, what should I have done? The easiest thing would have been to just fly away, heading back to our homeworld. Indeed, that's what the protocols said: do an evaluation, send in a report, depart.

Yes, that's what I should have done.

That's what a machine *would* have done. A robot probe would have just followed its programming.

But I am not a robot.

This was unprecedented.

It required judgment.

▥ ▥ ▥

I could have done it at any point when the side of the moon facing the planet was in darkness, but I decided to wait until the most dramatic possible moment. With a single sun, and being Earth's sole natural satellite, this world called *the* moon was frequently eclipsed. I decided to wait until the next such event was to occur—a trifling matter to calculate. I hoped that a disproportionately large number of them would be looking up at their moon during such an occurrence.

And so, as the shadow of Earth—the shadow of that crazy planet, with its frustrating people, beings timid when it came to exploration but endlessly belligerent toward each other—moved across the moon's landscape, I prepared. And once the computer told me that the whole of the side of the moon facing Earth was in darkness, I activated my starbird's laser beacons, flashing a ruby light that the humans couldn't possibly miss, on and off, over and over, through the entire period of totality.

They had to wait eight of Earth's days before the part of the moon's face I had signaled them from was naturally in darkness again, but when it was, they flashed a replying beacon up at me. They'd clearly held off until the nearside's night in hopes that I would shine my lasers against the blackness in acknowledgment.

And I did—just that once, so there would be no doubt that I was really there. But although they tried flashing various patterns of laser light back at me—prime numbers, pictograms made of grids of dots—I refused to respond further.

There was no point in making it easy for them. If they wanted to talk further, they would have to come back up here.

Maybe they'd use the same name once again for their ship: *Columbia*.

I crawled back into my cryostasis nest, and told the computer to wake me when humans landed.

"That's not really prudent," said the computer. "You should also specify a date on which I should wake you regardless. After all, they may never come."

"They'll come," I said.

"Perhaps," said the computer. "Still ..."

I lifted my wings, conceding the point. "Very well. Give them ..." And then it came to me, the perfect figure ... "until this decade is out."

After all, that's all it took the last time.

Mikeys

This one is sort of a companion piece to the preceding story, "The Eagle Has Landed," in that it shares a certain wistfulness about the history of manned spaceflight.

I wrote the first draft of this story back in 1978, when I was eighteen, and it was one of the very first that I submitted to magazines. It was quite rightly rejected in its then-current form, but when I was asked by Martin H. Greenberg and John Helfers to contribute to an anthology called Space Stations, *I remembered my old story, dusted it off, and rewrote it, finally—I hope!—making it work.*

"Mikeys" was a finalist for the Aurora Award—Canada's highest honor in SF—for best English story of the year.

◆ ■ ■ ⋊

Damn, but it stuck in Don Lawson's craw—largely because Chuck Zakarian was right. After all, Zakarian was slated for the big Mars surface mission to be launched from Earth next year. He never said it to Don's face, but Don knew that Zakarian and the rest of NASA viewed him and Sasim as Mikeys—the derisive term for those, like *Apollo 11*'s command-module pilot Mike Collins, who got to go *almost* all the way to the target.

Yes, goddamned Zakarian would be remembered along with Armstrong, whom every educated person in the world could still name even today, seventy years after his historic small step. But who the hell remembered Collins, the guy who'd stayed in orbit around the moon while Neil and Buzz had made history on the lunar surface?

Don realized the point couldn't have been driven home more directly than by the view he was now looking at. He was floating in the control room of the *Asaph Hall*, the ship that had brought him and Sasim Remtulla to Martian space from Earth. If he looked left, Don saw Mars, giant, red, beckoning. And if he looked right, he saw—

They called it the Spud. *The Spud,* for Christ's sake!

Looking right, he saw Deimos, the outer of Mars's two tiny moons, a misshapen hunk of dark, dark rock. How Don wanted to go to Mars, to stand on its sandy surface, to see up close its great valleys and volcanoes! But no. As Don's Cockney granddad used to say whenever they passed a fancy house or an expensive car, "Not for the likes of us."

Mars was for Chuck Zakarian and company. The A-team.

Don and Sasim were the B-team, the also-rans. Oh, sure, they had now arrived at the *vicinity* of Mars long before anyone else. And Don supposed there would be *some* cachet in being the first person since *Apollo 17* left the moon in 1972 to set foot on another world—even if that world was just a 15-kilometer-long hunk of rock.

Why build a space station from scratch to orbit Mars, the NASA mission planners had said? Why not simply plant the spaceship you had used to get there on Deimos? For one thing, you'd have the advantage of a little gravity—granted, only 0.0004 of Earth's, but still sufficient to keep things from floating away on their own.

And for another, you could mine Deimos for supplies. Like Mars's other moon Phobos, Deimos was a captured asteroid—specifically, a carbonaceous chondrite, meaning its stony mass contained claylike hydrous silicates from which water could be extracted. More than that, though, Deimos's density was so low that it had long been known that it couldn't be solid rock; much water ice was mixed into its structure.

Deimos and Phobos were both tidally locked, like Earth's moon, with the same side always facing the planet they orbited. But Phobos was just too damn close—a scant 2.8 planetary radii from Mars's center, meaning it was really only good for looking down on the planet's equatorial regions. Deimos, on the other hand, orbited at seven planetary radii, affording an excellent view of most of Mars's surface. In Deimos, Mother Nature had provided a perfect infrastructure for a space station to study Mars. The two

Mikeys would use it to determine the exact landing spot and the itinerary of surface features Zakarian's crew would eventually visit.

"Ready?" said Don, taking his gaze away from the control-room window, from glorious Mars and drab Deimos.

Sasim gave him the traditional thumbs-up. "Ready."

"All right," said Don. "It's time to crash."

▌ ▐ ▌

Deimos's mean orbital velocity was a languorous 1.36 kilometers per second. Don and Sasim matched the *Asaph Hall*'s speed with that of the tiny moon and nudged their spaceship against it. A cloud of dust went up. Phobos had a reasonably dust-free surface, since ejecta thrown up from it was normally captured by Mars. But more-distant Deimos still had lots of dust filling in its craters; whatever was blown off by impacts remained near it, eventually sifting down to blanket the surface. Indeed, although Deimos probably had a similar number of craters to Phobos, which sported dozens, only two on the outer moon were large and distinct enough to merit official International Astronomical Union names: Voltaire and Swift.

The *Asaph Hall* settled without so much as a bang—but it wasn't a landing, not according to the mission planners. No, the ship had *docked* with Deimos: the artificial part of the space station rendezvousing with the natural part.

Apollo flights had been famous for discarding three stages before the tiny CSM/LM combo reached the moon. But *Asaph Hall*, like the *Percival Lowell* that would follow with Zakarian's crew, had retained one of its empty fuel tanks. Each mission would convert its spent cylinder into a habitat module: the *Hall* docked with Deimos in orbit about Mars; the *Lowell* down where the action was, on the Martian surface. There was good precedent, after all. The first space station to orbit Earth, *Skylab*, had been made out of an empty *Saturn* S-IVb booster. And, of course, *Skylab* had been largely crewed by the Mikeys of their day, *Apollo* pass-overs who were not quite good enough to go to the moon.

■ ■ ■

"Mission Control," said Don, "we have completed docking with Deimos."

When Armstrong had said, "Tranquility Base here, the *Eagle* has landed," Houston had immediately replied, "Roger, Tranquility, we copy you on the ground. We've got a bunch of guys here about to turn blue—we're breathing again. Thanks a lot."

But currently, Mars was 77,000,000 kilometers from Earth. That meant it would take four minutes and twenty seconds for Don's words to reach Mission Control, and another four minutes and twenty seconds for whatever reply they might send to start arriving here. He doubted Houston would say anything as emotional as the words beamed back to Tranquility Base; Don would be happy if they just didn't make a crack about Mikeys.

Tranquility Base. That had been *such* a cool name. This place needed a good name, too.

Sasim had evidently been thinking the same thing. "I'm not a fan of 'Mars Landing Precursor Observation Station,'" he said, turning to Don, quoting the official title.

"Maybe we should call it Deimos Station," said Don.

But Sas shook his head. "*Mir* is Russian for 'peace'—that was a good name for a space station. But Deimos is Greek for 'terror.' Not quite correct in these difficult times."

"We'll come up with something," Don said.

■ ■ ■

After the mandatory sleep period, Don and Sasim were ready to venture out onto the surface of Deimos. Although nobody would likely ever quote them back, Don had thought long and hard about what his first words would be when he stepped onto the Martian moon. "We come to the vicinity of the God of War," he said, "in godly peace and friendship."

Sasim followed him out, but evidently felt no one would care what the second person on Deimos had to say for posterity. He simply launched into his report. "The surface, as expected, is covered with dust and regolith ..."

▥ ▥ ▥

Once Sasim was finished, Don looked at him through their polarized faceplates. A big grin broke out on Don's face. He used his chin to tap the control that cut the broadcast back to Earth, while leaving the channel to Sasim open. "All right," he said. "Enough of the formalities. Here's one thing we can do that Zakarian will never be able to."

Don flexed his knees, crouched down, then pushed off the surface, straightening his legs as he did so, and—

Clark Kent had nothing on him!

Up, up, and away!

Higher and higher.

Further and farther.

Closer and closer to Mars itself.

Don looked down. Sasim had dwindled to the size of the proverbial ant, his olive-green space suit just a mote against the dark gray surface of Deimos.

Don continued to rise for a while longer, but at last he felt gentle fingers tugging at him. It took several minutes, but slowly, gradually, *sensually*, he settled to the ground. He'd tried to just go up, but there'd been a slight angle to his flight, and he'd found himself coming down a hundred-odd meters from where he'd started.

"A true giant leap," said Sasim, over the radio. "Beats all heck out of a small step."

Don smiled, although he knew he was too far away for Sasim to see him do that. The jump had been exhilarating. "Maybe this station isn't going to be so bad after all."

▥ ▥ ▥

"I've got an idea," said Sasim, as they continued to work converting the fuel tank into a habitat. "We could call this place Asaph Hall."

"That's the name of our spaceship," said Don, perplexed.

"Well, yes and no. Our ship is called *Asaph Hall*, after the guy who discovered the moons of Mars. And when you refer to a ship, you write the name in italics. But this whole station could be Asaph Hall—'hall,' like in a building, get it?—all in roman type."

"That's a pretty picayune distinction," said Don, unfolding an articulated section divider that had been stored for the outward journey. "It'll get confusing."

Sas frowned. "Maybe you're right."

"Don't worry. We'll think of something."

▮ ▮ ▮ ▮

It took several days to finish the conversion of the empty fuel tank into the habitat, even though all the fixtures were designed for easy assembly. During the process, Don and Sasim had slept in their spaceship's command module, but at last the habitat was ready for them to move in. And although it *was* roomy—bigger than *Skylab* or *Mir*—Don was finally beginning to appreciate the wisdom of making an entire moonlet into a space station. He could see how being confined to just the habitat would have gotten claustrophobic after a while, if he and Sas didn't have the rest of Deimos to roam over.

And roam over it they did. It only took a dozen leaps to circumnavigate their little—well, it wasn't a globe; the technical name for Deimos's shape was a triaxial ellipsoid. It was a lot of fun leaping around Deimos—and, despite the low gravity, it was actually excellent exercise, too. Up, up, up, that brief magical moment during which you felt *suspended*, at one with the cosmos, and then gently, oh so gently, sliding down out of the sky.

Don and Sas were approaching the line that separated Deimos's nearside—the part of the moon that always faced toward Mars—from its farside. Like the blooded horn of some great beast, the now-crescent Mars stretched from Deimos's smooth surface up toward the zenith. One more leap, and—

Yup, there it went: the Red Planet disappearing behind the horizon.

With its glare gone from the sky, Don tried to find Earth. He oriented himself with Ursa Major, found the zodiac, scanned along, and there it was, a brilliant blue point of light, right in the heart of Scorpius, not far from red Antares, the rival of Mars.

Sas, Don had noticed, had a funny habit of bending his knees when he contacted the surface. It wasn't as if there was any real impact to absorb—it was just a bit of theater—and it made Don smile. Don's space suit was a sort of mustard color, a nice contrast with Sas's. The dark ground loomed closer and closer to him, and—

There wasn't enough speed with contact to make any sort of sound that might be conducted through Don's boots. And yet, still, as his soles touched Deimos, something felt strange this time, just different enough from every other landing Don had made so far to pique his curiosity.

He'd raised up a fair bit of dust, and it took him a few seconds to realize exactly what had happened. His foot hadn't hit crumbly regolith. It had hit something unyielding. Something smooth.

Don did a gentle backflip, landing upside down on his gloved hands. He used his right one to brush away dust.

"Sas!" Don called into his helmet mike. "Come here!"

Sasim did a long jump, bringing him close to where Don was. Another small hop brought him right up to Don. "What's up?" asked Sas—perhaps a joking reference to Don's current odd posture.

Don used his fingertips to gently flip himself back into a normal orientation. "Have a look."

Sas tipped over until he was more or less hovering just above the surface. "What the heck is *that?*" he said.

"I'm not sure," said Don. "But it looks like polished metal."

▐▌ ▐▌ ▐▌

Don and Sas brushed dust away for more than an hour, and were still exposing new metal. It was indeed manufactured—it looked to be anodized aluminum. "Maybe it's part of the *Viking* orbiter, or one of those Mars missions like *Mars Polar Lander* that went astray," said Don, sounding dubious even to himself.

"Maybe," said Sas. "But it's awfully big ..."

"Still no sign of an edge," said Don. "Maybe we should try another approach. Let's each go ten meters away, dig down, and see if the sheet is there under the surface. If it is, go on another ten meters, and try again. Keep going until we come to the edge. You go leading; I'll go trailing." On any tidally locked satellite, "leading" was toward the leading hemisphere, the one that faced forward into the direction of orbital motion; trailing was the opposite way.

Sas agreed, and they each set out. Don easily hopped ten meters, and it didn't take more than digging with his boot's toe to uncover more of the metal. He hopped another ten and again easily found metal, although it seemed a little deeper down this time. Ten more; metal again. A further ten and, although he had to dig through about a meter of dust to get to it, he found metal once more. Of course, because of the puny gravity, there was no danger of sinking into the dust, but the stuff that had been disturbed was now hanging in charcoal-black clouds above the surface.

Although it had been Don's plan to go by ten-meter increments, he was starting to think that such trifling hops might result in a lot of wasted time. He gave a more vigorous kick off the ground this time and sailed forward fifty-odd meters. And yet again he found smooth metal, although it was buried even deeper out here, and—

"Don!" Sas's voice, shouting into his speaker. "I've found the edge!"

Don turned around and quickly flew across the 150 or so meters to where Sas was standing. The edge he'd uncovered was perfectly smooth. They both dug down around it with their gloved hands. It turned out the aluminum sheet was quite thin—no more than a centimeter. Don started working along one direction, and Sas along the other. They had to expose several meters of it before they noticed that the edge wasn't straight. Rather, it was gently curved. After a few more minutes, it was apparent that they were working their way along the rim of a disk that was perhaps a kilometer in diameter.

But no—no, it wasn't a disk. It was a *dish*, a great metal bowl, as if an entire crater had been lined with aluminum, and—

"Jesus," said Don.

"What?" replied Sas.

"It's an *antenna* dish."

"Who could have built it?" asked Sas.

Don tipped his head up to look at Mars—but he couldn't see Mars; they were on Deimos's farside.

The farside! Of course!

"Sas—it's a radio telescope!"

"Why would anyone put a radio telescope on the back side of Deimos?" asked Sas. "Unless ... oh, my. Oh, my."

Don was nodding inside his space helmet. "It was built here for the same reason we want to build a radio telescope on the backside of Earth's moon. Luna farside, with all those kilometers of rock between it and Earth, is the one place in the solar system that's shielded from the radio noise coming from human civilization ..."

"And," said Sas, "Deimos farside, with fifteen kilometers of rock between it and Mars, would be shielded from the radio noise coming from ..." His voice actually cracked. "... from Martian civilization."

▌ ▌ ▌

Sas and Don continued to search, hoping there would be more to the installation than just the giant dish, but soon enough Deimos's rapid orbit caused the sun—only half the apparent diameter it was from Earth and giving off just one-quarter the heat—to sink below the horizon. Deimos took 30 hours and 19 minutes to circle Mars; it would be almost fifteen hours before the sun rose on the tiny moon again.

"This is huge," said Sas, when they were back inside the habitat. "This is gigantic."

"A Martian civilization," said Don. He couldn't get enough of the phrase.

"There's no other possibility, is there?"

Don thought about that. There had been a contingency plan for *Apollo 11* in case it found Soviets already on the moon—but NASA was no longer in a space race with anyone. "Well," said Don, "it certainly wasn't built by humans."

"Zakarian and company are going to have a lot to look for on the surface," said Sas.

Don shrugged a bit. "Maybe. Maybe not. There's *weather* on Mars, including sandstorms that last for months. All the large-scale water-erosion features we see on Mars are at least a billion years old, judging by the amount of cratering over top of them. That suggests that whatever Martian civilization might have once existed did so at least that long ago. In a billion years, wind erosion could have destroyed every trace of an ancient civilization down there."

"Ah," said Sas, grinning. "But not here! No air; no erosion to speak of. Just the odd micrometeoroid impact." He paused. "That dish must have been here an awfully long time, to get buried under that much dust."

Don smiled. "You know," he said, "every space station humanity has ever been involved with has been inhabited by successive crews—*Skylab*, *Mir*, *Alpha*. One crew would go down; another would come up."

Sas raised his eyebrows. "But there's never been such a long hiatus between one crew leaving and the next one arriving."

■ ■ ■

When they knew the sun would be up on Deimos farside, Don and Sas headed back to the site of the alien antenna dish. They had almost finished making their way around its perimeter when they found a spoke, projecting outward from the rim of the antenna. They kept digging down, following it away from the dish, until—

"*Allah-o-akbar!*" exclaimed Sasim.

"God Almighty," said Don.

The spoke led to a buried building, and—

Well, its inhabitants *had* been astronomers. It made sense that they'd have a glass roof, a clear ceiling through which they could look up at the stars.

As Don and Sas brushed away more and more dust, they were better able to see in through the roof. There was furniture inside, but none of it designed for human occupants: several bowl-shaped affairs that Don imagined were chairs, and low work tables, covered with square sheets of something that seemed to serve the same purpose as paper. Scattered about were opaque cylindrical units that looked like they might be for storage. And—

Slumped against the wall, at the far end—

It was incredible. Absolutely incredible.

A Martian, perfectly preserved for countless millennia. Either they had no such thing as bacteria leading to decay, or everything had been sterilized before coming to Deimos, or perhaps all the air had leaked out somehow, preserving the being in vacuum.

The former resident of the building was vaguely insectoid, with rusty exoskeletal armor, four arms and two legs. In life, he would have walked proud and upright. His mandible was tripartite; his giant eyes, lidless behind crystal shells, were a soft, kind blue.

"Amazing," said Sas softly. "Amazing."

"There must be a way inside," said Don, looking around. For all they knew from what they'd exposed of the transparent roof so far, the building might be no bigger than a single room. Still, it had been carved into the rocks of Deimos, so the airlock, if there was one, should be somewhere on the roof.

Don and Sas worked at clearing debris, and, after about twenty minutes, Don found what they were looking for. It was a transparent tube, like the one George Jetson shot up through, stretching between the glass roof and the floor. The tube had an opening in its circular walls at ground level, and a hatch up on the roof, forming a chamber that air could be pumped into or out of.

Any space station had lots of electrical parts, but doors were something sane engineers would make purely mechanical. After all, if the power went out, you didn't want to be trapped inside or outside. It took Sas and Don a few minutes to work out the logic of the door mechanism—a central disk in the middle of the roof had to be depressed, then rotated counterclockwise. Once that was done, the rest of the hatch irised open, and the locking disk, attached by what looked like a plastic cord, dangled very loosely at one side.

Don glided down the tube first. He wasn't able to open the inside door until Sas closed the upper lid; a safety interlock apparently prevented anyone from accidentally venting the habitat's air out into space.

Still, it was immediately obvious to Don, once he was out of the airlock tube, that there was no air inside the habitat. The rigidity of his pressure suit didn't change; no condensation appeared on his visor; there was no resistance to waving his arms vigorously. Doubtless there had been some air once, but, despite the safety precautions, it had all leaked out. Perhaps a small meteor had drilled through the roof at some point they hadn't yet uncovered.

Sas came down the airlock tube next—the locking disk could be engaged from either side of the iris. By the time he was down, Don had already made his way over to the dead thing. Its rusty color seemed good confirming evidence that Mars was indeed the being's original home. The creature was about a meter and a half tall, and, if there had been any doubt about its intelligence, that was dispelled now. The Martian wore clothes—apparently not for protection, but rather for convenience; the translucent garment covering part of its abdomen was rich with pockets and pouches. Still, the body showed signs of having suffered a massive decompression; innards had partially burst out through various seams in the exoskeleton.

While Don continued to examine the being—the first alien lifeform ever seen by a human—Sas poked around the room. "Don!" he shouted.

Don reluctantly left the Martian and glided over to Sas, who was pointing through an open archway.

The underground complex went on and on. And Martian bodies were everywhere.

"Wow," said Sas. "Wow."

Don tried to activate the radio circuit to Earth, but he wasn't able to pick up the beacon signal from Mission Control. Of course not: this facility had operated a massive radio telescope; it would be shielded to prevent interference with the antenna. Don and Sas made their way up the airlock tube and out to the surface. There they had no trouble acquiring the beacon.

"Mission Control," said Don. "Tell Chuck Zakarian we hope he has a good time down on Mars's surface—although, given all the wind erosion that goes on there, I doubt he'll find much. But that's okay, Houston; we'll make up for that. You see, it seems we're not the first crew to occupy ..." He paused, the perfect name coming to him at last. "... Mike Collins Station."

The Good
Doctor

There's a tradition in science fiction of short-short stories that build up to a hor-
rendous pun in the last line; the most famous of these are the "Ferdinand
Feghoot" tales by Reginald Bretnor (written under the anagrammatic pen
name Grendel Briarton). In the late 1980s, I perpetrated one of these myself,
and it was published as my third appearance in Amazing Stories, *the world's*
oldest SF magazine, which was founded by Hugo Gernsback, after whom the
Hugo Awards are named.

❧ ■ ■ ❧

"There's a new patient here to see you, Dr. Butcher," said the pleasant con-
tralto over the intercom.

Shaggy eyebrows above craggy countenance lifted in mild irritation.
"Well, what is it? Human? Dolphin? Quint?"

"It's a Kogloo, sir."

"A Kogloo! Send it in." A Kogloo on Earth was about as rare as a current
magazine chip in Butcher's waiting room. The hunched human ushered the
barrel-shaped being into his office. "What can I do for you?"

"Doctor, doctor, I is terrible problem." The words were thick, but, to
its credit, the Kogloo was working without a translator. "I try to writing
Skience Fiction, no?"

"So?"

"So this!" The Kogloo upended a satchel over Butcher's already clut-
tered desk. Countless cards and pieces of paper cascaded out.

"Rejection slips?" Butcher grunted. He had his own collection from
The Lancet. "Unless you've got writer's cramp, I can't help you."

"No, please." The alien's tripartite mandible popped the *P*. "I write good, in mine own language, no?" Butcher had heard that the big four SF chips had Kogloonian editions now. "I send novella to *Amazing*—they love it! They even buy! *Effing SF* is eating out of my foot. *Analog*, the same. But that other one—!" The Kogloo waved its antennae expressively. "Bah, they no want."

"Look," said Butcher, annoyance honing his words. "I'm an M.D., a medical doctor. This is out of—"

"Please! I decide to come to Earth. I want to meet man whose name is in the title, no? But trip out is very, very bad!"

"Now see here!" Dr. Butcher's doctor had warned him to watch his blood pressure. "I'm a busy man—"

"But here is even worse! Flyer, boat, tram, tube train, is all the same."

Butcher exploded. "This is not a travel agency! I'm a doctor, understand. *A doctor!* I treat sickness and injuries. Now, unless you have a medical problem—"

The Kogloo bashed its forehead on the desktop in the traditional gesture of excitement. "Yes! Yes! Every time I get into vehicle, I very uncomfortable. I embarrass myself and anger driver." A sigh. "I afraid I never get to where that title man is."

Butcher's eyes widened in comprehension. "I think I see what's causing your troubles ..."

The Kogloo nodded vigorously. "Doctor, I sick as I move!"

Ineluctable

In November 2000, I was Guest of Honor at Contact 4 Japan, a conference devoted to potential first contact with extraterrestrial life. For that conference, I was asked to devise a role-playing scenario involving the receipt of a series of alien radio messages; teams would try to decode the messages and provide appropriate responses. The conference was one of the most enjoyable events I've ever attended, and it also afforded me an opportunity to meet the staff of Hayakawa, my Japanese publisher.

After the conference, I decided to expand my first-contact scenario into a full-fledged SF story, and sent it off to Stanley Schmidt, the editor of Analog. *Now, by this point, I'd had 300,000 words of fiction in* Analog, *but it had all been in the form of novel serializations:* The Terminal Experiment *(which* Analog *ran under my original title,* Hobson's Choice), Starplex, *and* Hominids. *When Stan bought this story—at 8,800 words, technically a novelette—it became my first short-fiction sale to* Analog. *"Ineluctable" went on to win the Aurora Award for best English story of the year.*

⊰ ◼ ◼ ⊱

What to do? What to do?

Darren Hamasaki blew out air, trying to calm down, but his heart kept pounding, a metronome on amphetamines.

This was big. This was huge.

There *had* to be procedures in place. Surely someone had thought this through, had come up with a—a *protocol*, that was the word.

Darren left the observatory shed in his backyard and trudged through the snow. He stepped up onto the wooden deck and entered his house through the sliding-glass rear doors. He hit the light switch, the halogen glow from the torchiere by the desk stinging his dark-adapted eyes.

Darren took off his boots, gloves, tuque, and parka, then crossed the room, sitting down at his computer. He clicked on the Firefox icon. Of course he had Internet Explorer, too, but Darren always favored the underdog. His search engine of choice was also the current underdog: Yahoo. He logged on to it and stared at the dialog box, trying to think of what keywords to type.

Protocol was indeed appropriate, but as for the rest—

He shrugged a little, conceding the magnitude of what he was about to enter. And then he pecked out three more words: *contact, extraterrestrial,* and *intelligence.*

He'd expected to have to go spelunking, and, indeed, there were over thirteen hundred hits, but the very first one turned out to be what he was looking for: "Declaration of Principles Concerning Activities Following the Detection of Extraterrestrial Intelligence," a document on the SETI League web site. Darren scanned it, his eyes skittering across the screen like a puck across ice. As he did so, he rolled his index finger back and forth on his mouse's knurled wheel.

"We, the institutions and individuals participating in the search for extraterrestrial intelligence ..."

Darren frowned. No one had sought his opinion, but, then again, he hadn't actually been *looking* for aliens.

"... inspired by the profound significance for mankind of detecting evidence ..."

Seemed to Darren that "mankind" was probably a sexist term; just how old was this document?

"The discoverer should seek to verify that the most plausible explanation is the existence of extraterrestrial intelligence rather than some other natural or anthropogenic phenomenon ..."

Well, there was no doubt about it. No natural phenomenon was likely to generate the squares of one, two, three, and four over and over again, and the source was in the direction of Groombridge 1618, a star 15.9 light-years from Earth; Groombridge 1618 was in Ursa Major, nowhere near the plane of the ecliptic into which almost every Earth-made space probe and vessel had been launched. It *had* to be extraterrestrial.

"... *should inform the Secretary General of the United Nations in accordance with Article XI of the Treaty on Principles Governing the Activities of States in the Exploration and Use of Outer Space ...*"

Darren's eyebrows went up. Somehow he doubted that the switchboard at the UN would put his call through to the Secretary-General—was it still Kofi Annan?—if he said he was ringing him up to advise him that contact had been made with aliens. Besides, it was 2:00 a.m. here in Ontario, and UN headquarters were in New York; the same time zone. Surely the Secretary-General would be at home asleep right now anyway.

"*The discoverer should inform observers throughout the world through the Central Bureau for Astronomical Telegrams of the International Astronomical Union ...*"

Good God, is it still possible to send a telegram? Is Western Union even still in business? Surely the submission could be made by E-mail ...

Yahoo quickly yielded the URL for the bureau, which still used the word "telegrams" in its name, but one could indeed fill out an online form on their home page to send a report. Too bad, in a way: Darren had been enjoying composing a telegram in his head, something he'd never done before: "Major news *stop* alien signal received from Groombridge 1618 *stop* ..."

The brief instructions accompanying the form only talked about reporting comets, novae, supernovae, and outbursts of unusual variable stars (and there were warnings not to bother the bureau with trivial matters, such as the sighting of meteors or the discovery of new asteroids). Nary a word about submitting news of the receipt of an alien signal.

Regardless, Darren composed a brief message and sent it. Then he clicked his browser's *back* button several times to return to the *Declaration of Principles*, and skimmed it some more. Ah, now that was more like it: "*The discoverer should have the privilege of making the first public announcement ...*"

Very well, then. Very well.

■ ■ ■

There was nothing to do now but wait and see if the beings living on the third planet were going to reply. Palm-Up-Middle-Fingers-Splayed expected they indeed would, but it would take time: time for the laser flashes to reach their destination, and an equal time for any response the inhabitants of that watery globe might wish to send—plus, of course, whatever time they took deciding whether to answer.

There were many things Palm-Up-Middle-Fingers-Splayed could do to while away the time: read, watch a video, inhale a landscape. And, well, had it been any other time, he probably would have contented himself with one of those. The landscape was particularly appealing: he had a full molecular map of the air in early spring from his world's eastern continent, a heady blending of yellowshoot blossoms, clumpweed pollens, pondskins, skyleaper pheromones, and the tang of ozone from the vernal storms. Nothing relaxed him more.

He'd been afraid at first to access that molecular map, afraid the homesickness would be too much. After all, their ship, the *Ineluctable*, had been traveling for many years now, visiting seven other star systems before coming here. And there were still three more stars—and several years of travel—after this stop before Palm-Up-Middle-Fingers-Splayed would really get to inhale the joyous scents of his homeland again. Fortunately, though, it had turned out that he *could* enjoy the simulation without his tail twitching too much in sadness.

Still, this was not any other time; this was the period when, had they been back home, all three moons would have risen simultaneously, the harmonics of their vastly different orbital radii briefly synchronizing their movements. This was the time when the tides would be at their highest, when the jewelbugs would be taking to the air—and when the females of Palm-Up-Middle-Fingers-Splayed's kind would be in estrus.

Even aboard ship, the estrus cycle continued, never losing track of its schedule. Yes, despite his race's hopes, even shielding females from the light and gravitational effects of the moons did nothing to end the recurring march. The cycle was so ingrained in <hand-sign-naming-his-species>

physiology that it maintained its precision even in the absence of the stimuli that must surely have originally set its cadence.

Palm-Up-Middle-Fingers-Splayed took one last look out his window at the distant yellow star. The planet they'd signaled was invisible without a telescope, although two of the gas giants—the fifth and sixth worlds—shone brightly enough to be seen with naked eyes, despite presenting only crescent faces from this distance.

The ship's computer would flash a signal to alert Palm-Up-Middle-Fingers-Splayed, of course, if any response were received. He set out to find his mate, to find his dear Fist-Held-Sideways.

■ ▥ ▦

Fist-Held-Sideways was in the forward mess hall when Palm-Up-Middle-Fingers-Splayed caught up with her. Now that the *Ineluctable*'s great fusion motors were quiescent, the false sense of gravity had disappeared. Fist-Held-Sideways was floating freely, her gray tail with its blue mottling sticking up above her in a most appealing way.

Palm-Up-Middle-Fingers-Splayed hovered in the doorway, not moving, just watching her as she ate. Her chest opened vertically, revealing the inside of her torso, the polished pointed tips of her ribs moving apart as she split herself wider and wider. Fist-Held-Sideways used the arm coming out of the left side of her head to swat a large melon that had been floating by, directing it into her belly. Palm-Up-Middle-Fingers-Splayed watched as the tips of her ribs came together, crushing the melon, a few spherical drops of juice floating out of Fist-Held-Sideways's torso before she closed the feeding slit. A small mechanical cleaner, moving about the room with the aid of a propeller, sucked the juice out of the air and then demurely retreated.

It wasn't easy getting another <hand-sign-naming-his-species>'s attention in zero gravity. On a planet's surface, one might slap one's tail against the floor hard enough so that the other would feel the vibrations through his or her own tail and feet. But when floating freely, that didn't work; indeed, slapping a tail like that would send you shooting up toward the ceiling, banging your head.

Palm-Up-Middle-Fingers-Splayed used the hand coming out of the right side of his head to push against the doorframe, propelling himself into the mess hall. As soon as he came within Fist-Held-Sideways's field of view, she flared her nasal slits in greeting, welcoming his scent, then used both her hands to make signs. "Palm-Up-Middle-Fingers-Splayed!" she exclaimed, hyperextending her fingers after finishing his namesign to convey her pleasant surprise. "Good to see you! No reply from the aliens yet?"

Palm-Up-Middle-Fingers-Splayed balled his left hand in negation. "It's still much too early. So far, I've just sent them one, four, nine, and sixteen over and over again; sort of a general hello, one sentient race to another. It'll be some time before we receive any response." He paused, seeing if his mate would pick up the hint.

And, of course, she did; Palm-Up-Middle-Fingers-Splayed had heard from Palm-Down-Thumb-Extended, who had been Fist-Held-Sideways's mate last breeding season, that she was wonderfully intuitive and empathetic—unusual, but very desirable, traits in a female. "Your quarters or mine?" signed Fist-Held-Sideways.

"Yours," Palm-Up-Middle-Fingers-Splayed signed back, flexing his wrist wryly. "Too many breakables in mine."

■ ■ ■

The sex, as always, was athletic. Palm-Up-Middle-Fingers-Splayed enjoyed the exercise, enjoyed the tumbling in zero-g, enjoyed the physical contact with Fist-Held-Sideways. But it was the actual consummation, of course, that he was waiting for. Palm-Up-Middle-Fingers-Splayed was a biologist and, although he had indeed repeatedly taught students the precise biochemistry involved, it still fascinated the intellectual part of him every time it happened: when a male's semen finally reached the female's hexagon of egg-cells, a chemical reaction occurred producing a neurotransmitter that brought intense pleasure to both the female and the male, just as—

Yes, yes! Contact! The sensation washed over him, his tail going rigid in excitement, his twin hearts pounding out of synch, his rib points clamping together, as he was overcome by the joy, the joy, *the joy* ...

Palm-Up-Middle-Fingers-Splayed was a considerate enough lover to take additional pleasure from the writhing of Fist-Held-Sideways's body. He squeezed her tighter, and they both relished the simultaneous climax of their intercourse. As they relaxed, floating in the room, the warm afterglow of the neurotransmitter washing over them, Palm-Up-Middle-Fingers-Splayed thought that the Five Gods had indeed been wise. Only together could males and females experience such joy, and—oh, the gods had indeed been brilliant!—it happened *simultaneously*, compounds from his body mixing with chemicals from hers, producing the neurotransmitter. The simultaneity, the shared experience, was wonderful.

Of course, as usual, it would be a problem figuring out what to do with the new children. His race had been saddened indeed when it discovered that any process or barrier that prevented conception also prevented orgasm, and that, because of the neurological interdependence of the fetuses and their host, to terminate a pregnancy would kill the mother.

No, the only method to keep new children from being born was to avoid copulation altogether. And, well, when a female was in estrus, her pheromones—those wonderful, wonderful pheromones—were completely irresistible.

The <hand-sign-naming-his-species> had no choice. With an ever-expanding population, they had to find new worlds to colonize.

▮ ▮ ▮

Darren's next-door neighbor's brother-in-law worked for Newsworld, the CBC's all-news cable channel. He'd met the guy a couple of times at parties at Bernie's place. Darren couldn't recall exactly what the guy did. Director? Switcher? Some behind-the-scenes function, anyway; they'd had a fairly empty conversation last time, with Darren asking him if Wendy Mesley was as cute in real life as she looked on TV. Of course, at this time of night, he didn't want to call Bernie and wake him up—"next door" was a bit of a misnomer; Bernie's place was the better part of a kilometer up the country road.

But at that last party Bernie had held—back in June, it must have been—Bernie's brother-in-law had had to leave early, to get down to Toronto and go to work. So he pulled the night shift at least some of the time, meaning there was a chance he might be at the CBC right now. But what the heck was the guy's name? Carson? Carstone? Carstairs? Something like that ...

Well, nothing to be lost by trying. He got the CBC number from Toronto directory assistance, dialed it, and was greeted by a bilingual computerized receptionist, which gave him the option of spelling out the last name of the person he wanted to speak to on his touch-tone phone. Fortunately, the system recognized the name by the time Darren had pressed the key corresponding to the fourth letter—the last name, as the system informed him, was in fact Carstairs, and the first name was Rory. Darren was transferred to the correct extension and, miracle of miracles, the actual, living Rory Carstairs answered the phone.

"Overnight," said the voice. "Carstairs."

"Hi, Rory. This is Darren Hamasaki—remember me? I live down the street from your brother-in-law Bernie. We met at a couple of his parties." The words of the automated attendant echoed in Darren's mind: *Continue until recognized.* "I've got one of those beards that a lot of people call a goatee, but it's really a Vandyke, and—"

"Oh, sure," said Carstairs. "The space buff, right? You were pointing out constellations to us in Bernie's backyard. Say, nothing's happened to Bernie, has it?"

"No, he's fine—at least, as far as I know. But—but I've got some news to report, and, well, I didn't know who else to call."

"I'm listening," said Carstairs.

▮ ▮ ▮

The carefully devised *Declaration of Principles Concerning Activities Following the Detection of Extraterrestrial Intelligence*, issued by the International Academy of Astronautics in 1989, had been based on the assumption that governments would control access to the alien signals, that giant, multi-million-dollar radio telescopes would be required to pick up the messages.

But the signal Darren had detected was *optical*. Anyone with a decent backyard telescope had been able to pick it out, once he'd made known the celestial coordinates. And in all the places on Earth from which Groombridge 1618 could be seen at night, people were doing just that. Sales of telescopes were at an all-time high, exceeding even the boom during Halley's last visit.

Darren Hamasaki became a media celebrity, interviewed by TV programs from around the world. Of course, all the usual SETI pundits—Seth Shostak and Paul Shuch in the U.S., Robert Garrison in Canada, and Jun Jugaku in Japan—were also constantly being asked for comment. But when the mayor of Las Vegas decided to do something about the alien signal, it was indeed Darren that he called.

Darren had taken to letting his answering machine screen his calls; the phone rang incessantly now. He was leaning back in a leather chair, fingers interlaced behind his head, listening absently to the words coming from the machine's tinny speaker: "Shoot, I'd hoped to catch you in. Mr. Hamasaki, my name is Rodney Rivers, and I'm the mayor of Las Vegas, Nevada. I've got an idea that—"

Intrigued, Darren picked up the phone's handset. "Hello?"

"Mr. Hamasaki, is that you?"

"Speaking."

"Well, looks like I hit the jackpot. Mr. Hamasaki, I'm the mayor of Las Vegas, and I'd like to have you come down here and join us for a little project we got in mind."

"What's that?"

"You ever been to Vegas, son?"

"No."

"Seen pictures?"

"Of course."

"We're one brightly lit city at night, Mr. Hamasaki. So bright, the shuttle astronauts say they can easily see us from orbit. And, well, this is our off-season, you know—the time between Thanksgiving and Christmas. Don't get enough tourist traffic, and it's the tourists that drive our economy, sure enough. So me and some of the boys here, we had an idea."

"Yes?"

"We're goin' to flash the lights of Las Vegas—every dang light in the blessed city—on and off in unison. Send a reply to them there aliens you found."

Darren was momentarily stunned. "Really? Is that—I mean, can you do that? Are you allowed to?"

"This is the U.S. of A., son—freedom of speech and all that. Of course we're allowed to."

"What are you going to say?"

"That's why I'm callin' you, Mr. Hamasaki. We want you to help us work out what the reply should be. Any chance I could entice you down here with a free trip to Vegas? We'll put you up at—"

"At the Hilton. Isn't that the one with *Star Trek: The Experience?*"

The mayor laughed. "If that's what you'd like. How soon could you get down here?"

◼ ◼ ◼

Mayor Rivers was certainly savvy. Over one hundred thousand extra tourists came to Las Vegas to be part of the great signaling event; it was the best early-December business the city had ever had.

Darren Hamasaki's first inclination had been to send a simple message in response. The aliens—whoever they might be—had signaled one flash, four flashes, nine flashes, and sixteen flashes, over and over again; those were the squares of one, two, three, and four. Darren thought the logical reply might be the cubes of the first four integers: one, eight, twenty-seven, and sixty-four. Not only would it make clear that the people of Earth understood the original message—which simply parroting it back wouldn't necessarily have conveyed—but it would also indicate that they were ready for something more complex.

But Las Vegas was a city of spectacles; being that prosaic wouldn't do. Darren spent a week devising a more content-rich message, using the form Frank Drake had worked out for Earth's first attempt at communicating with aliens, back in 1974: an image made of a string of on/off bits, the length of the string being the product of two prime numbers—in this case 59 and 29.

Arranging the bits as a grid of 59 rows each 29 columns wide produced a crude picture. Darren coded in a simple diagram of a human being, and, because ever since he'd read Lilly in college, he'd believed dolphins were intelligent, a simple diagram of a bottle-nosed dolphin, too. He then put binary numbers underneath, expressing the total populations of the two species, and a crude diagram of the western hemisphere of the Earth, showing that the humans lived on the land and the dolphins in the ocean.

Media from all over the world came to cover the event. Mayor Rivers and Darren were invited to the master control room of the Clark County Power Authority. The entire power grid could be controlled from a single computer there. And, at precisely 10:00 p.m., the mayor pushed the key to start the program running. It began—and would end—with one solid minute of darkness, then a solid minute of light, and then another of darkness, to frame the message. Then the glowing marquee at Caesars Palace winked at the night sky, the floodlights at Luxor strobed against the blackness, the neon tubes at the MGM Grand flickered off and on. All along the Las Vegas strip, and in all the surrounding streets, the lights blinked the 1,711 bits of Darren's reply.

Out front of Bally's, surrounded by a huge crowd, a giant grid of lights—specially powered by gas generators—filled in with the pixels of the message, one after the other, line by line, from upper left to lower right, painting it as it was transmitted. The crowd cheered when the human figure was finished, thousands of people raising their right arms in the same salute of greeting portrayed in the message.

After the message had been completed, the mayor took to the podium and addressed the assembled mass, thanking them for their orderly conduct. Then His Honor invited Darren to say a few words.

Darren felt the need to put it all in perspective. "Of course, Groombridge 1618 is almost sixteen light-years from Earth," he said into the mike, his voice reverberating off the canyon of hotels surrounding him. "That means it will take sixteen years for our signal to reach the aliens there, and another sixteen before any reply they might send could be received." This being Las Vegas, there were already betting pools about what date the aliens might reply on, and what the content of their next message might be.

Darren refrained from remarking about how exceedingly unlikely it would be that the aliens would be able to detect one blinking city against the glare of Earth's sun behind it; if humanity ever really wanted to seriously respond, it would likely need to build a massive laser to do so.

"Still," said Darren, summing up, "we've had a lot of fun tonight, and we've certainly made history: humanity's first response to an alien signal. Let's hope that if a reply does come, thirty-odd years from now, we'll have made new friends."

The head of the power authority had the final words for the evening; the crowd was already dispersing by this point—heading back to the casinos, or the hotels, or the late Lance Burton show during which his assistants were topless, or any of the hundreds of other diversions Las Vegas offered at night.

Darren felt a twinge of sadness. He'd enjoyed his fifteen minutes of fame—but now, of course, the story would slip from public consciousness, and he'd go back to his quiet life in rural Ontario.

Or so he'd thought.

▇ ▇ ▇

Palm-Up-Middle-Fingers-Splayed had spent the entire night in Fist-Held-Sideways's quarters but had left by the time ship's morning had rolled around. He was one of ten males aboard the *Ineluctable*, and she, one of ten females. As on the homeworld, though, females were loners, while males—who in ancient times had watched over the clutches of six eggs laid then abandoned by each female—lived communally. The *Ineluctable*'s habitat was shaped like a giant wheel, with ten spokes, each one leading to a different female's lair; the males lived together in the hub.

It was shortly after the fifth daypart when the computer turned on a bright light to get Palm-Up-Middle-Fingers-Splayed's attention. The digitized blue hands on the monitor screen signed the words with precise, unemotional movements. "A response has been received from the third planet."

Palm-Up-Middle-Fingers-Splayed gave himself a three-point launch down the corridor, pushing off the bulkhead with both feet and his broad, flat tail. He barreled into the communications room. Waiting there were three other males, plus one female, Captain Curling-Sixth-Finger herself, who had come into the hub from her command module at the end of spoke one.

"I see we've made contact," signed Palm-Up-Middle-Fingers-Splayed. "Has the reply been deciphered yet?"

"It seems pretty straightforward," said Palm-Down-Thumb-Extended. "It's a standard message grid, just like the ones we were planning to use for our later messages." He made a couple of signs at the camera eye on the computer console, and a screen came to life, showing the message.

"The one on the left is the terrestrial form," continued Palm-Down-Thumb-Extended. "The one on the right, the aquatic form. It was the terrestrial form that sent the message. See those strings beneath the character figures? We think those might be population tallies—meaning there are far, far more of the terrestrial form than of the aquatic one."

"Interesting that a technological race is still subject to heavy predation or infant mortality," signed Palm-Up-Middle-Fingers-Splayed. "But it looks as though only a tiny fraction survive to metamorphose into the adult aquatic form."

"That's my reading of it, too," said Palm-Down-Thumb-Extended. His hands moved delicately, wistfully. There had been a time, of course, when the <hand-sign-naming-his-species> had faced the same sort of thing, when six offspring were needed in every clutch, and a countless clutches were needed in a female's lifetime, just in hopes of getting two children to live to adulthood. So many had fallen prey to gnawbeasts and skyswoopers and bloodvines—

But now—

But now.

Now almost all offspring survived to maturity. There was no choice but to find new worlds on which to live. It was a difficult task: no world was suitable for habitation unless it already had an established biosphere; only the action of life could produce the carbon dioxide and oxygen needed to make a breathable atmosphere. And so the *Ineluctable* traveled from star to star, looking for worlds that were fecund but not yet overcrowded with their own native life forms.

"Maybe they do it on purpose," signed Captain Curling-Sixth-Finger. Palm-Up-Middle-Fingers-Splayed was grateful for the zero gravity; if they'd been on a planet's surface, Curling-Sixth-Finger would have towered over him, just as most adult females towered over most males. But here, with them both floating freely, the difference in size was much less intimidating.

"Do what?" signed Palm-Up-Middle-Fingers-Splayed.

"Maybe they cultivate their own predators," replied Curling-Sixth-Finger, "specifically to keep their population in check. There are—what?" She peered at the binary numbers beneath the blocky drawings. "Six billion of the terrestrial forms? But only a few million of the aquatic adults."

"So it would seem," said Palm-Up-Middle-Fingers-Splayed. "It's interesting that their adult form returns to the water; on the world of that last star we visited, the larvae were aquatic and the adults were land-dwellers." He paused, then pointed at the right-hand figure's horizontally flattened tail. "They resemble the ancestral aquatic forms of our own kind from millions of years ago—even down to the horizontal tail fin."

Curling-Sixth-Finger spread her fingers in agreement. "Interesting. But, enough chat; there are important questions we have to ask these aliens."

❚❚ ❚❚ ❚❚

Darren Hamasaki had just checked in at the Air Canada booth at the Las Vegas airport and was on his way to the Star Alliance lounge—his trip last year to see the eclipse in Europe had got him enough points to earn entry privileges—when Karyn Jones, one of Mayor Rivers's assistants, caught up with him.

"Darren!" she wheezed, touching his arm, and buying herself a few seconds to catch her breath.

"What is it?" said Darren, raising his eyebrows. "Did I forget something?"

"No, no, no," said Karyn, still breathing raggedly. "There's been a *reply*."

"Already?" asked Darren. "But that's not possible. Groombridge 1618 is 4.9 parsecs away."

Karyn looked at him as though he were speaking a foreign language. After a moment, she simply repeated, "There's been a reply."

Darren glanced down at his boarding pass. Karyn must have detected his concern. "Don't worry," she said. "We'll get you another flight." She touched his forearm again. "Come on!"

■ ■ ■

Of course, many observatories now routinely watched Groombridge 1618; it was under twenty-four hour surveillance from ground stations, and was frequently examined by Hubble, as well—not that a reply was expected soon, but there was always the possibility that the aliens would send another message of their own volition, prior to receiving a response from Earth. Even so, few in the astronomical community seriously believed the Groombridgeans would ever see the Las Vegas light show, and the United Nations was still debating whether to build a big laser to send an official reply.

And so, Darren saw the alien's response the same way most of the world did: on CNN.

And a *response* it surely was, for in layout and design it precisely matched the message Mayor Rivers had arranged to be sent. The aliens were bipedal, with broad, flat tails like those of beavers; *Tailiens* was a word the CNN commentator was already using to describe them. Their heads sported V-shaped mouths, and arms projected from either side of the head. There was something strange about their abdomens, though: a single column of zero bits—blank pixels—ran down the length of the chest; what it signified, Darren had no idea.

CNN took away the graphic of the message and replaced it with the anchor's face. "Do you have it on videotape?" asked Darren. "I want to examine the message in detail."

"No," said Karyn. "But it's on the CNN web site." She pointed to an iMac sitting across the room; sure enough, the graphic was displayed on its screen. Darren bounded over to it. He was still trying to take it all in, trying to discern whatever details he could. In the background, he could hear the CNN anchor talking to a female biologist: "As you can see," the scientist said, "the aliens presumably evolved from an aquatic ancestor, not unlike our own fishy forebears. Our limbs are positioned where they are because those were the locations of the pectoral and pelvic fins of the lobe-finned fish we evolved from. This creature's ancestors presumably had its front pair of fins further forward, which is why the arms ended up growing out of the base of the head, instead of the shoulders, and ..."

Darren tried to shut out the chatter. His attention was caught by the string of pixels beneath the alien figure.

The very long string of pixels ...

The crew of the *Ineluctable* hadn't bothered to send an image of a juvenile of their kind alongside the adult; unlike the strange beings they were now communicating with, they had no larval form—babies looked just like miniature adults.

Palm-Up-Middle-Fingers-Splayed and the others didn't wait for another reply from the denizens of the third planet before flashing a series of additional pictures at them. These were standard images, already prepared, showing details of <hand-sign-naming-his-species> physiology at a much higher resolution than that used for the earlier message. The aliens, after all, had seemed willing to reveal their own body form—or forms, given the two lifestages depicted in their first missive. Perhaps they would respond with more details about their own kind.

And then they could determine whether these people and the members of <hand-sign-naming-his-species> would be able to share a world together.

"They're not at Groombridge 1618," Darren said to Mayor Rivers, when His Honor arrived shortly after midnight; the mayor's toupee had been hastily perched and now sat somewhat askew atop his head. "They can't be. Assuming they responded immediately upon receipt of our message, they're only a few light-*hours* away—about the distance Pluto is from the Earth, although, of course, they're well above the plane of the solar system." Darren frowned. "They *must* be in a spaceship, but ... but, no, no, that can't be right. Every observatory on Earth has been taking the spectra of the laser flashes, and they're dead on the D_1 sodium line, which can't be a coincidence. The senders are using a line that's weak in their home star but very strong in our own sun's spectrum to signal us. But, like I said, it's *dead on* that line, meaning there's no Doppler shift. But if the ship was coming towards us, the light from the laser would be blue-shifted, and—"

"And if it were a-flyin' away from us," said Mayor Rivers, "it would be red-shifted."

Darren looked at His Honor, surprised. Rivers lifted his shoulders a bit. "Hey, we're not all hicks down here, you know."

Darren smiled. "But if the light isn't undergoing a Doppler shift, then—"

"Then," said Rivers, "the starship must be holdin' station, somewhere out there near the edge of the solar system."

Darren nodded. "I wonder why they don't come closer?"

▮ ▮ ▮

The next night, Darren found himself flipping channels in his hotel room—they'd put him back in the Hilton. Letterman did a top-ten list of people who would make the best ambassadors to visit the aliens ("Number four: Robert Downey, Jr., because he's been damn near that high already"). And Leno did a "Jay Walking" segment, asking people on the street basic questions about space; Darren was appalled that one person said the sun revolved around the Earth, and that another declared that Mars was "millions of light-years" away.

After that, though, he switched to *Nightline*, which had some more-serious discussion of the aliens. Ted Koppel was interviewing a guy named

Quentin Fawcett, who was billed as an "astrobiologist."

"I've been studying the anatomical charts that the Tailiens sent us," said Fawcett, whose long hair was tied into a ponytail. "I think I've figured out why they don't use radio."

Koppel played the stooge well. "You figured that out from anatomical charts? What's anatomy got to do with it?"

"Can we have the first slide?" asked Fawcett. A graphic appeared on the monitor between Koppel and Fawcett, and, a second later, the image on Hamasaki's hotel-room TV filled with the same image, as the director cut to it. "Look at this," said Fawcett's voice.

"That's the one they're calling three-dash-eleven, isn't it?" said Koppel. "The eleventh picture from the third group of signals the Tailiens sent."

"That's right. Now, what do you see?"

The TV image changed back to a two-shot of Koppel and Fawcett, both looking at their own monitor. "It's the Tailien head," said Koppel. And indeed it was, drawn out like an alligator's.

"Look carefully at the mouth," said Fawcett.

Koppel shook his head. "I'm sorry; I'm not getting it."

"That's not a picture of the head, you know. It's a picture of the Tailien cranium—the skull."

"Yes?"

"It's all one bone," said Fawcett triumphantly. "There's no separate mandible, no movable jaw. The mouth is just a boomerang-shaped opening in a solid head."

Koppel frowned. "So you're saying they couldn't articulate? I guess it *would* be hard to talk without a hinged jaw." He nodded. "No talking, no radio."

"No, it's not the ability to make sounds that depends on the advent of jaws. It's the ability to *hear* sounds, or, at least, to hear them clearly and distinctly."

Koppel waited for Fawcett to go on. "I've got TMJ—temporo-mandibular-joint syndrome," said Fawcett, tapping his temple. "Discomfort where the jaw articulates with the temporal bone; it's pretty common. Well, last winter, I had an infection in my ear canal—'swimmer's ear,' they called it. Except I didn't know it for the longest time; I thought the pain was from my TMJ. Why? Because our ears are located right over our jaw joints—and that's no coincidence. The small bones in our inner ear—the hammer, the anvil, and the stirrup—make our acute hearing possible, and they exist precisely because the skull splits there into the cranium and the jaw. Our earliest vertebrate ancestors were jawless fish—fish with heads very much like the Tailiens still seem to have, consisting of one solid piece of bone."

Koppel was coming up to speed. "So ... so, what? They take in soft food through permanently open mouths? No chewing?"

"Perhaps," said Fawcett. "Or maybe that slit that runs down their torsos is a feeding orifice. But, either way, I'm willing to bet that they don't depend on sound for communication."

∎ ∎ ∎

Darren worked with an illustrator from the Las Vegas *Review-Journal* and a doctor from the UNLV Medical Center coding a series of human-anatomy diagrams, but no one quite knew how to send them. It would take more than a day of flashing the city's lights on and off—the power could only be cycled so quickly—to send even one of these high-resolution images, and the casinos wouldn't stand for it. Every minute the power was off cost them tens of thousands of dollars in betting revenues.

But, before they'd figured out how to reply, a new set of messages—batch number four—arrived from the Tailiens.

∎ ∎ ∎

Palm-Up-Middle-Fingers-Splayed personally supervised the sending of the next messages, since he'd been the one who had coded them. They were designed to convey a series of simple multiple-choice questions. The messages consisted of 23 rows of 79 columns, much smaller than the anatomical charts. Fist-Held-Sideways had opined that bandwidth might be a problem for the third planet in sending similar messages, which was presumably why no response had yet been received.

The top part of each message showed a simple math problem, and the bottom part showed three possible answers, one of which was correct. The boxes containing these answers were labeled, from left to right, with one pixel, two pixels, and three pixels respectively in their upper right-hand corners.

Palm-Up-Middle-Fingers-Splayed, Fist-Held-Sideways, and the rest awaited the answers from the third planet; nothing less than a perfect score on the test would be morally acceptable before they asked the most important question of all.

▮ ▮ ▮

The aliens seemed to have no trouble reading the flashing of Las Vegas's lights, and so the responses to the math problems were sent by that city winking itself on and off. Many of the hundred thousand people who had come to Nevada to be part of the first signaling effort were still in town, thrilled that an actual dialogue between humans and aliens seemed to be opening up.

Fortunately for the croupiers and pit bosses, the math problems only took seconds to reply to; all that had to be sent was the number of the box containing the correct answer: one flash, two flashes, or three flashes.

▮ ▮ ▮

"There's no doubt," signed Palm-Up-Middle-Fingers-Splayed to Captain Curling-Sixth-Finger, "that the aliens understand our syntax. They clearly know how to give the correct response to a multiple-choice question—and they got all the answers right, even the one about division by zero."

"Very well," said Curling-Sixth-Finger, her fingers moving slowly, deliberately. She clearly was steeling herself, in case she had to repeat the action she'd been forced to take at the last star system. "Ask them the big one."

The next message was, in the words of Larry King, who had Darren Hamasaki on his show to talk about it, "a real poser."

"It looks," said King, leaning forward on his desk, his red suspenders straining as he did so, "like they're asking us something about DNA, isn't that right, Mr. Hamasaki?"

"That does seem to be the case," said Darren.

"Now, I don't know much about genetics," said King, and he looked briefly into the camera, as if to make clear that he was speaking on behalf of his viewing audience in confessing this ignorance, "but in *USA Today* this morning there was an article saying that it didn't make sense that the aliens were talking to us about DNA. I mean, DNA is what life on Earth is based on, but it isn't necessarily what alien life will be based on, no? Aren't there other ways to make life?"

"Oh, there might very well indeed be," said Darren, "although, you know, try as we might, no one has come up with a good computer model for any other form of self-replicating biochemistry. But I don't think it matters. Life didn't begin on Earth, after all. It was imported here, and—"

"It *was?*" King's eyebrows shot up toward his widow's peak. "Who says so?"

"Lots of biologists—more and more each day. You know, the initial problem with Darwin's theory of evolution was this: it was clear that the process of natural selection would take a long time to develop complex life forms—but there was no evidence that the Earth was particularly old; we didn't have any proof that it was old until the discovery of radioactivity. Then, when we found that Earth was *billions* of years old, it seemed that there was plenty of time for evolution. But now we've run into another not-enough-time problem: the oldest known fossils are 4.0 billion years old, and they're reasonably complex, which means if life were indigenous to Earth, the first self-replicating molecules would have appeared only a few hundred million years after the solar system was born, 4.5 billion years ago."

"We're going to get letters, I know it," said King, "from people disputing those age claims. But go on."

"Well, that early on, Earth was still being bombarded by meteors and comets; extinction-level events would have been common. Earth simply wouldn't have presented a stable environment for life."

"So you think life came here from outer space?"

"Almost certainly. Some biologists believe that it arose first on Mars—Mars was much drier than Earth, even back then. A comet or asteroid impact has a much greater destabilizing effect on the climate if it hits water than it does if it hits dry land. But the original DNA on Earth could have also come from outside the solar system—meaning, in fact, that these Tailiens might be our distant, distant relatives. All life in this part of the galaxy might share a common ancestor, if you go back far enough."

"Fascinating," said King. "Now, what about this latest message from the Tailiens? Can you take us through that?"

"Well, the top picture shows what looks to be a snippet of DNA, three codons long."

"Codons?"

"Sorry. Words in the DNA language. We read the language a letter at a time: A, C, G, or T. And since A and T always bond together, and G always bonds with C, we can just read the letters off one half of the DNA ladder and know automatically what the letters down the other side will be."

King nodded.

"Well," continued Darren, "each group of three letters—ACG, say, or TAT—is a word specifying one amino acid, and amino acids are the building blocks of life. What we have in the first picture is a snippet of DNA consisting of nine letters, or three words. Next to that, there's space for another snippet of DNA the same length, see? As if you were supposed to place one of the strings from the lower section up here beside this one."

"And how do we choose which one should go there?"

Darren frowned. "That's a very good question, Larry." It was cool getting to call him Larry. He looked at his cheat-sheet on the desktop. "The sequence in the top part of the message is CAC, TCA, and GTC, which codes, at least here on Earth, for the amino acids histidine, serine, and valine."

"Okay," said King.

"And the three possible replies are below. Two of them are strings of DNA. The first one—in answer box one—is a string of DNA very similar to the one above. It reads as CAC—the same as before; TTA—which is one nucleotide different from the string on the top, so it codes for, umm, let me see, for leucine instead of serine; and then there's GTC again, which is valine, just as before."

"So it differs by only one-ninth from the specimen at the top," said Larry. "A close relative, you might say."

Darren nodded. "Exactly. And that brings us to the second possible response. Like the first possible response, it consists of nine codons, but here the codons don't match at all—the sequence is completely different from the one above. And, if you look carefully, you'll see it's not just frameshifted out of synch from the sample above; it really has nothing in common with it. Nor could it be a possible match for the other side of the DNA ladder, because it doesn't have the same pattern of duplicated letters."

"So that second string of DNA represents a distant relative—if it's a relative at all," said King. "Would that be right?"

"It's as good a guess as any," said Darren.

"And the third possible answer?" asked King.

"That's the puzzler," said Darren. "The third answer box is empty; blank. There's nothing in it except three pixels in the upper right, which just indicate that it *is* the third possible answer."

"Have we ever seen an empty box like that before in one of the Tailiens' messages?" asked King.

"Yes," said Darren. "It was in message four-dash-twelve, one of the math problems. They asked us what the correct answer to six divided by zero is. The possible answers they gave us were six, one, and a blank box."

"And—wait a second, wait a second—you can't divide by zero, can you?"

"That's right; it's a meaningless concept: how many times does nothing go into something? So, in that case, we chose the empty box as our answer."

"And what's the correct answer this time?" asked King.

Darren spread his arms, just as he'd seen dozens of other people—including many working scientists, rather than hobbyists like him—do today on other talk shows when asked the same question. "I haven't the slightest idea."

▮ ▮ ▮

Everybody had hoped that other messages would continue to come from the Tailiens. Just as they had gone on to send the math problems after receiving no reply to the anatomy diagrams, humanity hoped that they would continue sending questions or information before a reply was sent.

But the Tailiens didn't. They seemed to be intent on waiting for a response to the DNA puzzle.

And, finally, the United Nations decided that one should indeed be sent. By this point, Darren was pretty much out of the spotlight—and glad of it. The United Nations secretary-general himself was coming to Las Vegas to initiate the blinking of the city's lights. That was fine with Darren; he wasn't sure that the UN scientists had come up with the right answer, and he didn't want sending an incorrect reply to be on his head.

The answer the UN had decided to go with was number one: the DNA that was similar, but not identical, to the sample string. There were various rationales offered for supposing that it was the correct response. Some said it was obvious: the aliens were moving us beyond questions of absolute truth, the kind of clear right or wrong that went with mathematical expressions; this new message was designed to test our ability to think in terms of similarity, of soft relationships. Although none of the three choices matched the sample string, the first one was the most similar.

Another interpretation was that it was a test of our knowledge of evolution. Did new species (the blank space to the right of the sample string) emerge by gradual changes (answer one, with its single nucleotide difference); by complete genetic redesign (answer two, with its totally dissimilar DNA); or out of nothing—that is, through creationist processes?

Some of the fundamentalists at the UN argued that the third answer was therefore the proper one: the aliens were testing our righteousness before deciding whether to admit us to the galactic club. But others argued that everything the aliens had presented so far was scientific—mathematics, anatomical charts, DNA—and that the scientific answer was the only one to give: new species arose by incremental changes from old ones.

Regardless of whether it was a question about inexact relationships or about the principles of evolution, answer one would be the correct response. And so the lights of Las Vegas were turned off one last time in a single, knowing wink at the heavens.

▮ ▮ ▮

Palm-Up-Middle-Fingers-Splayed happened to be in the communications room when the response was received from the third planet. Of course, regardless of what answer they'd chosen, it would begin with one stretch of darkness, so Palm-Up-Middle-Fingers-Splayed waited ... and waited ... and waited for a second and third.

But more darkness never came. Palm-Up-Middle-Fingers-Splayed's tail twitched.

He had to tell Captain Curling-Sixth-Finger, of course; indeed, the computer had probably already informed her that a response was being received, and she was presumably even now making her way down the spoke from her command module, and—

And there she was now: twice Palm-Up-Middle-Fingers-Splayed's size, and capable of the kind of fierceness only a female could muster.

"What is the response?" demanded Curling-Sixth-Finger as she floated into the room.

"One," signed Palm-Up-Middle-Fingers-Splayed with restrained, sad movements. "They chose answer one."

Curling-Sixth-Finger's feeding slit momentarily opened, exposing slick pink tissue within. "So be it," she signed with her left hand, and "So be it" she repeated with her right.

Palm-Up-Middle-Fingers-Splayed whipped his tail back and forth in frustration. It was such a straightforward question: when seeking other life forms to associate with, do you choose (1) the being most closely related to you genetically; (2) the being least related to you genetically; or (3) is it impossible to answer this question based on genetics?

Answer three, of course, was the morally right answer; any advanced being must know that. Oh, it was true that primitive animals sought to protect and favor those with whom they shared many genes, but the very definition of civilization was recognizing that nepotism was not the engine that should drive relationships.

Perhaps, reflected Palm-Up-Middle-Fingers-Splayed, such enlightenment had come more easily to his people, for with partners changing every mating season, genetic relationships were complex and diffuse. The race inhabiting the second planet of the star they had last visited had chosen the wrong answer, too; they'd also picked the first choice.

And they'd paid the price for that.

If nepotism drives you as a species, if protecting those who are most closely related to you is paramount, if forming allegiances based on familial lines is at the core of your society, then how can you ever be trusted in relationships with beings that are alien to you? Yes, it seemed all life, at least in this neighborhood of the galaxy, was based on DNA, and therefore was quite possibly related in its distant, distant past. But, then again, all creatures on any given world also share a common ancestor. And yet—

And yet these benighted souls of the third planet still chose genetic favoritism; indeed, they were so convinced of its righteousness, convinced that it was the proper order of things, that they didn't even attempt to disguise it by giving a false answer. Those poor creatures, prisoners of their own biology ...

Curling-Sixth-Finger was already on the intercom, calling down to the propulsion room, telling Fist-Held-Sideways to engage the fusion motors. Palm-Up-Middle-Fingers-Splayed felt an invisible hand pressing down upon him, driving him to the floor, as the great engines came to life. As he and Curling-Sixth-Finger settled to deck plates, Palm-Up-Middle-Fingers-Splayed looked up at her.

"I've got no choice," she signed. "A species driven by selfish genes is too dangerous to be allowed to live."

Palm-Up-Middle-Fingers-Splayed slowly, sadly spread his fingers in agreement. The *Ineluctable* would dive down into the plane of the solar system, into the cometary belt just past the orbit of the eighth planet, and it would launch a series of comets on trajectories that would send them sailing in for eventual rendezvous with the third planet.

Oh, it would take time—thousands of years—before the impacts. But eventually they *would* strike, and two skyswoopers would be felled with a single rock: the galaxy would have one less selfish species to worry about, and, with most of its native life wiped out, there would be room—a whole new world!—to move billions and billions of members of <hand-sign-naming-his-species> to.

Palm-Up-Middle-Fingers-Splayed was glad that Fist-Held-Sideways and the other females were no longer in estrus. He didn't feel like making love, didn't feel like making babies.

Not now. Not right now.

But, of course, he *would* want to do that again the next time the females came into heat. He, too, he reflected, was a prisoner of biology—and for one brief moment, that shared reality made him feel a bond with the aliens that now, sadly, he would never meet.

The Right's Tough

For some reason, I get asked to write stories for anthologies that are completely contrary to my own personal philosophy and politics: I'm in Future War, *but I'm a pacifist; I'm in the Libertarian anthology* Free Space, *but I'm a Canadian-style socialist; and, with this piece, I appeared in* Visions of Liberty, *an anthology from Baen Books about how the world would be a better place without governments of any kind.*

I finished this story in 2001, ironically on US income-tax day—April 15. The book was to have been published in 2002, but then the September 11 attacks occurred—and suddenly having no government didn't seem quite so palatable an idea. The anthology was held off until July 2004, meaning—again ironically—that it hit the stands in the heat of one of the ugliest presidential elections in US history.

❧ ■ ■ ❧

"The funny thing about this place," said Hauptmann, pointing at the White House as he and Chin walked west on the Mall, "is that the food is actually good."

"What's funny about that?" asked Chin.

"Well, it's a tourist attraction, right? A historic site. People come from all over the world to see where the American government was headquartered, back when there *were* governments. The guys who own it now could serve absolute crap, charge exorbitant prices, and the place would still be packed. But the food really is great. Besides, tomorrow the crowds will arrive; we might as well eat here while we can."

Chin nodded. "All right," he said. "Let's give it a try."

■ ■ ■

The room Hauptmann and Chin were seated in had been the State Dining Room. Its oak-paneled walls sported framed portraits of all sixty-one men and seven women who had served as presidents before the office had been abolished.

"What do you suppose they'll be like?" asked Chin, after they'd placed their orders.

"Who?" said Hauptmann.

"The spacers. The astronauts."

Hauptmann frowned, considering this. "That's a good question. They left on their voyage—what?" He glanced down at his weblink, strapped to his forearm. The device had been following the conversation, of course, and had immediately submitted Hauptmann's query to the web. "Two hundred and ten years ago," Hauptmann said, reading the figure off the ten-by-five centimeter display. He looked up. "Well, what was the *world* like back then? Bureaucracy. Government. Freedoms curtailed." He shook his head. "Our world is going to be like a breath of fresh air for them."

Chin smiled. "After more than a century aboard a starship, fresh air is exactly what they're going to want."

Neither Hauptmann nor his weblink pointed out the obvious: that although a century had passed on Earth since the *Olduvai* started its return voyage from Franklin's World, only a couple of years had passed aboard the ship and, for almost all of that, the crew had been in cryosleep.

The waiter brought their food, a Clinton (pork ribs and mashed potatoes with gravy) for Hauptmann, and a Nosworthy (tofu and eggplant) for Chin. They continued chatting as they ate.

When the bill came, it sat between them for a few moments. Finally, Chin said, "Can you get it? I'll pay you back tomorrow."

Hauptmann's weblink automatically sent out a query when Chin made his request, seeking documents containing Chin's name and phrases such as "overdue personal debt." Hauptmann glanced down at the weblink's screen; it was displaying seven hits. "Actually, old boy," said Hauptmann, "your track record isn't so hot in that area. Why don't *you* pick up the check for both of us, and *I'll* pay you back tomorrow? I'm good for it."

Chin glanced at his own weblink. "So you are," he said, reaching for the bill.

"And don't be stingy with the tip," said Hauptmann, consulting his own display again. "Dave Preston from Peoria posted that you only left five percent when he went out to dinner with you last year."

Chin smiled good-naturedly and reached for his debit card. "You can't get away with anything these day, can you?"

■ ■ ■

The owners of the White House had been brilliant, absolutely brilliant.

The message, received by people all over Earth, had been simple: "This is Captain Joseph Plato of the U.N.S.A. *Olduvai* to Mission Control. Hello, Earth! Long time no see. Our entire crew has been revived from suspended animation, and we will arrive home in twelve days. It's our intention to bring our landing module down at the point from which it was originally launched, the Kennedy Space Center. Please advise if this is acceptable."

And while the rest of the world reacted with surprise—who even remembered that an old space-survey vessel was due to return this year?— the owners of the White House sent a reply. "Hello, *Olduvai*! Glad to hear you're safe and sound. The Kennedy Space Center was shut down over a hundred and fifty years ago. But, tell you what, why don't you land on the White House lawn?"

Of course, that signal was beamed up into space; at the time, no one on Earth knew what had been said. But everyone heard the reply Plato sent back. "We'd be delighted to land at the White House! Expect us to touch down at noon Eastern time on August 14."

When people figured out exactly what had happened, it was generally agreed that the owners of the White House had pulled off one of the greatest publicity coups in post-governmental history.

■ ■ ■

No one had ever managed to rally a million people onto the Mall before. Three centuries previously, Martin Luther King had only drawn 250,000; the four separate events that had called themselves "Million-Man Marches" had attracted maybe 400,000 apiece. And, of course, since there was no longer any government at whom to aim protests, these days the Mall normally only drew history buffs. They would stare at the slick blackness of the Vietnam wall, at the nineteen haunted soldiers of the Korean memorial, at the blood-red spire of the Colombian tower—at the stark reminders of why governments were not good things.

But today, Hauptmann thought, it looked like that magic figure might indeed have been reached: although billions were doubtless watching from their homes through virtual-reality hookups, it did seem as if a million people had come in the flesh to watch the return of the only astronauts Earth had ever sent outside the solar system.

Hauptmann felt perfectly safe standing in the massive crowd. His weblink would notify him if anyone with a trustworthiness rating below 85% got within a dozen meters of him; even those who chose not to wear weblinks could be identified at a distance by their distinctive biometrics. Hauptmann had once seen aerial footage of a would-be pickpocket moving through a crowd. A bubble opened up around the woman as she walked along, people hustling away from her as their weblinks sounded warnings.

"There it is!" shouted Chin, standing next to Hauptmann, pointing up. Breaking through the bottom of the cloud layer was the *Olduvai*'s lander, a silver hemisphere with black legs underneath. The exhaust from its central engine was no worse than that of any VTOL aircraft.

The lander grew ever bigger in Hauptmann's view as it came closer and closer to the ground. Hauptmann applauded along with everyone else as the craft settled onto the lawn of what had in days of yore been the president's residence.

It was an attractive ship—no question—but the technology was clearly old-fashioned: engine cones and parabolic antennas, articulated legs and hinged hatches. And, of course, it was marked with the symbols of the pre-freedom era: five national flags plus logos for various governmental space agencies.

After a short time, a door on the side of the craft swung open and a figure appeared, standing on a platform within. Hauptmann was close enough to see the huge grin on the man's face as he waved wildly at the crowd.

Many of those around Hauptmann waved back, and the man turned around and began descending the ladder. The mothership's entire return voyage had been spent accelerating or decelerating at one *g*, and Franklin's World had a surface gravity twenty percent greater than Earth's. So the man—a glance at Hauptmann's weblink confirmed it was indeed Captain Plato—was perfectly steady on his feet as he stepped off the ladder onto the White House lawn.

Hauptmann hadn't been crazy enough to camp overnight on the Mall in order to be right up by the landing area, but he and Chin did arrive at the crack of dawn, and so were reasonably close to the front. Hauptmann could clearly hear Plato saying, "Hello, everyone! It's nice to be home!"

"Welcome back," shouted some people in the crowd, and "Good to have you home," shouted others. Hauptmann just smiled, but Chin was joining in the hollering.

Of course, Plato wasn't alone. One by one, his two dozen fellow explorers backed down the ladder into the summer heat. The members of the crowd—some of whom, Hauptmann gathered, were actually descendants of these men and women—were shaking the spacers' hands, thumping them on the back, hugging them, and generally having a great time.

At last, though, Captain Plato turned toward the White House; he seemed somewhat startled by the holographic "Great Eats" sign that floated above the Rose Garden. He turned back to the people surrounding him. "I didn't expect such a crowd," he said. "Forgive me for having to ask, but which one of you is the president?"

There was laughter from everyone but the astronauts. Chin prodded Hauptmann in the ribs. "How about that?" Chin said. "He's saying, 'Take me to your leader'!"

"There is no president anymore," said someone near Plato. "No kings, emperors, or prime ministers, either."

Another fellow, who clearly fancied himself a wit, said, "Shakespeare said kill all the lawyers; we didn't do that, but we did get rid of all the politicians ... and the lawyers followed."

Plato blinked more than the noonday sun demanded. "No government of any kind?"

Nods all around; a chorus of "That's right," too.

"Then—then—what are we supposed to do now?" asked the captain.

Hauptmann decided to speak up. "Why, whatever you wish, of course."

▮ ▮ ▮

Hauptmann actually got a chance to talk with Captain Plato later in the day. Although some of the spacers did have relatives who were offering them accommodations in their homes, Plato and most of the others had been greeted by no one from their families.

"I'm not sure where to go," Plato said. "I mean, our salaries were supposed to be invested while we were away, but ..."

Hauptmann nodded. "But the agency that was supposed to do the investing is long since gone, and, besides, government-issued money isn't worth anything anymore; you need corporate points."

Plato shrugged. "And I don't have any of those."

Hauptmann was a bit of a space buff, of course; that's why he'd come into the District to see the landing. To have a chance to talk to the captain in depth would be fabulous. "Would you like to stay with me?" he asked.

Plato looked surprised by the offer, but, well, it was clear that he *did* have to sleep somewhere—unless he planned to return to the orbiting mothership, of course. "Umm, sure," he said, shaking Hauptmann's hand. "Why not?"

Hauptmann's weblink was showing something he'd never seen before: the word "unknown" next to the text, "Trustworthiness rating for Joseph Tyler Plato." But, of course, that was only to be expected.

▮ ▮ ▮

Chin was clearly jealous that Hauptmann had scored a spacer, and so he made an excuse to come over to Hauptmann's house in Takoma Park early the next morning.

Hauptmann and Chin listened spellbound as Plato regaled them with tales of Franklin's World and its four moons, its salmon-colored orbiting rings, its outcrops of giant crystals towering to the sky, and its neon-bright cascades. No life had been found, which was why, of course, no quarantine was necessary. That lack of native organisms had been a huge disappointment, Plato said; he and his crew were still arguing over what mechanism had caused the oxygen signatures detected in Earth-based spectroscopic scans of Franklin's World, but whatever had made them wasn't biological.

"I really am surprised," said Plato, when they took a break for late-morning coffee. "I expected debriefings and, well, frankly, for the government to have been prepared for our return."

Hauptmann nodded sympathetically. "Sorry about that. There are a lot of good things about getting rid of government, but one of the downsides, I guess, is the loss of all those little gnomes in cubicles who used to keep track of everything."

"We do have a lot of scientific data to share," said Plato.

Chin smiled. "If I were you, I'd hold out for the highest bidder. There's got to be some company somewhere that thinks it can make a profit off of what you've collected."

Plato tipped his head. "Well, until then, I, um, I'm going to need some of those corporate points you were talking about."

Hauptmann and Chin each glanced down at their weblinks; it was habit, really, nothing more, but ...

But that nasty "unknown" was showing on the displays again, the devices having divined the implied question. Chin looked at Hauptmann. Hauptmann looked at Chin.

"That *is* a problem," Chin said.

■ ■ ■

The first evidence of real trouble was on the noon newscast. Plato watched aghast with Chin and Hauptmann as the story was reported. Leo Johnstone, one of the *Olduvai*'s crew, had attempted to rape a woman over by the New Watergate towers. The security firm she subscribed to had responded to her weblink's call for help, and Johnstone had been stopped.

"That idiot," Plato said, shaking his head back and forth, as soon as the report had finished. "That bloody idiot." He looked first at Chin and then at Hauptmann, and spread his arms. "Of course, there was a lot of pairing-off during our mission, but Johnstone had been alone. He kept saying he couldn't wait to get back on terra firma. 'We'll all get heroes' welcomes when we return,' he'd say, 'and I'll have as many women as I want.'"

Hauptmann's eyes went wide. "He really thought that?"

"Oh, yes," said Plato. "'We're astronauts,' he kept saying. 'We've got the Right Stuff.'"

Hauptmann glanced down; his weblink was dutifully displaying an explanation of the arcane reference. "Oh," he said.

Plato lifted his eyebrows. "What's going to happen to Johnstone?"

Chin exhaled noisily. "He's finished," he said softly.

"What?" said Plato.

"Finished," agreed Hauptmann. "See, until now he didn't have a trust-worthiness rating." Plato's face conveyed his confusion. "Since the day we were born," continued Hauptmann, "other people have been commenting about us on the web. 'Freddie is a bully,' 'Jimmy stole my lunch,' 'Sally cheated on the test.'"

"But surely no one cares about what you did as a child," said Plato.

"It goes on your whole life," said Chin. "People gossip endlessly about other people on the web, and our weblinks"—he held up his right arm so that Plato could see the device—"search and correlate information about anyone we're dealing with or come physically close to. That's why we don't need governments anymore; governments exist to regulate, and, thanks to the trustworthiness ratings, our society is self-regulating."

"It was inevitable," said Hauptmann. "From the day the web was born, from the day the first search engine was created. All we needed were smarter search agents, greater bandwidth, and everyone being online."

"But you spacers," said Chin, "predate that sort of thing. Oh, you had a crude web, but most of those postings were lost thanks to electromagnetic pulses from the Colombian War. You guys are clean slates. It's not that you have a *zero* trustworthiness rating; rather, you've got *no* trustworthiness ratings at all."

"Except for your man Johnstone," said Hauptmann, sadly. "If it was on the news," and he cocked a thumb at the wall monitor, "then it's on the web, and everyone knows about it. A leper would be more welcome than someone with that kind of talk associated with him."

"So what should he do?" asked Plato. "What should all of us from the *Olduvai* do?"

■ ■ ■

There weren't a million people on the Mall this time. There weren't even a hundred thousand. And the mood wasn't jubilant; rather, a melancholy cloud hung over everyone.

But it *was* the best answer. Everyone could see that. The *Olduvai*'s lander had been refurbished, and crews from Earth's orbiting space stations had visited the mothership, upgrading and refurbishing it, as well.

Captain Plato looked despondent; Johnstone and the several others of the twenty-five who had now publicly contravened acceptable standards of behavior looked embarrassed and contrite.

Hauptmann and Chin had no trouble getting to the front of the crowd this time. They already knew what Plato was going to say, having discussed it with him on the way over. And so they watched the faces in the crowd—still a huge number of people, but seeming positively post-Apocalyptic in comparison to the throng of a few days before.

"People of the Earth," said Plato, addressing his physical and virtual audiences. "We knew we'd come back to a world much changed, an Earth centuries older than the one we'd left behind. We'd hoped—and those of us who pray had prayed—that it would be a better place. And, in many ways, it clearly is.

"We'll find a new home," Plato continued. "Of that I'm sure. And we'll build a new society—one, we hope, that might be as peaceful and efficient as yours. We—all twenty-five of us—have already agreed on one thing that should get us off on the right foot." He looked at the men and women of his crew, then turned and faced the people of the Free Earth for the last time. "When we find a new world to settle, we won't be planting any flags in its soil."

Kata Bindu

Many years ago, with great trepidation, I approached Gregory Benford, the king of hard SF, and asked him to read my novel Starplex, *and, if he liked it, to offer a blurb for the cover. He did so:* "Starplex *is complex but swift, inventive but real-feeling, with ideas coming thick and fast; for big time interstellar adventure, look no farther."*

That was flattering enough, but the best was yet to come: Greg remembered me and, in 2001, when he was putting together an anthology of stories about microcosms, he asked me to contribute. This story is the result of that invitation.

❮ ■ ■ ❯

We sometimes contemplated giving ourselves a name. "Those Who Had Been Flesh" appealed to us. So did "The Collective Consciousness of Earth." And "The Uploaded."

But, to our infinite sadness, there was no need for a name—for there was no one to speak with, no one to proffer an introduction to, no possible confusion about the referents of pronouns. Despite centuries now of scanning the sky for alien radio signals, we'd found nothing.

Because of that, we'd never even had to resolve the question of whether we should refer to ourselves in the singular or the plural. Granted, we had once been ten billion individuals; plurals were no doubt appropriate then. But after almost all members of *Homo sapiens* had taken The Next Step, we had surrendered that individuality, slowly at first, then with abandon—for who would not want to take into themselves the genius of the world's greatest mathematicians, the wit of the cleverest comedians, the virtue of the most altruistic humanitarians, the talent of the most gifted composers, and the tranquility of the most serene contemplatives?

Ah, but it turned out there *were* some who did not want this. Mennonites were long gone; Luddites were likewise a thing of the past. But there was one last group left, in Africa, that still lived by traditional means. They did not want to take The Next Step—and so we instead gave them that famous giant leap: we moved them all to the Moon.

What else could we have done? Although we had been about to become something more than human, we were, and are, still humane: we certainly weren't going to just eliminate them. But we couldn't leave anyone here on Earth, for once we'd uploaded our consciousnesses, once we had merged into the global web, a fanatic could disable the computers, could destroy our helpless, noncorporeal selves.

To send hunter-gatherers to the Moon might seem, well, lunatic: establishing a colony of the least technologically advanced people in a place where technology was the only thing making life possible. But we rationalized that we were actually being beneficent: with their hearts laboring under gentle lunar gravity, they would likely live decades longer, and their elderly—who, on the African veldt, had had no access to artificial hips or even wheelchairs—would be far more mobile than they had been on Earth.

More: we no longer cared what happened to Earth's ecosystem, and, indeed, we knew that the inevitable impact of an asteroid would eventually cause worldwide calamity here. The Last Tribe, of course, could do nothing to avert a meteor strike, and we, no longer physical, could do nothing on their behalf. But now that they were on the airless, waterless moon, only a direct hit to their domed ecosystem would do any real damage. We had likely granted their civilization tens of millions of years of additional life.

Safety for us, and a better life for them.

It should have been a win-win scenario.

■ ■ ■

Prasp fashioned his wings from elephant skin spread between elongated wooden fingers. When Kari, his woman, helped him strap the wings to his arms, they stretched several times as wide as Prasp was tall.

The old stories, handed down now for a thousand generations, told of *wind*, the invisible hand of one of the gods moving through the air, pushing things about. But wind, like the stars of legend, did not exist here; Prasp wondered, despite the spellbinding stories he'd heard, whether it had ever existed even in *Kata Bindu*, the Old Place. Indeed, he wondered whether the Old Place itself was a myth. How could lights—and even orbs, one of fire, another of stone—have moved across the sky? How could people have weighed five or six times as much as they do here? The ancients were said to have been no bulkier, indeed, to have if anything been shorter, than people of today. By what magic could they have acquired additional weight?

Regardless, Prasp was pleased that his weight was what it was. Even with the great wings he'd built, he could barely get aloft. Yes, they did well for gliding from tree to tree—on those rare occasions when he managed to climb a tree without damaging his fragile contraptions. But to take to the air as the birds did still eluded him. Oh, even without the wings, Prasp could jump twice his own body height. But he wanted to go much higher than that.

Prasp wanted to touch the center of the world's roof.

▌▌ ▐▌▌ ▐▌▌

It was easy enough for us, for—The Uploaded; yes, that's what we'll call ourselves—to access information. Indeed, for us, to wonder was to know.

We knew that the refuge for the last primitive humans was in Copernicus, a lunar crater ninety-three kilometers wide. The roof over it consisted in part of two transparent silicone membranes, the outer of which was coated with 2.5 microns of gold. That gold layer was thin enough to screen out UV and other radiation, while still letting most visible light through—sunglasses for the entire sky.

Between those two membranes was a gap twelve meters thick filled with pure water. Transparent gold, transparent membranes, transparent water—the only thing that should have marred the primitives' view upward from the inside of the dome was the crisscrossing network of load-bearing titanium cables, which divided their sky into a multitude of triangles.

If the water only had to shield the habitat from solar radiation, a thickness of 2.5 meters would have been enough. But this multilayered transparent roof—appearing almost flat, but really a section out of a vast sphere—had to contain the habitat's atmosphere, as well. The air inside was almost pure oxygen, but at only 200 millibars: quite breathable, and no more prone to supporting combustion than Earth's own atmosphere, which had a similar partial pressure of O_2.

Still, even that attenuated atmosphere pressed upward with a force of over two tonnes per square meter. So the water shield had been made twelve, rather than two-and-a-half, meters thick; the air pressure helped keep the roof up, and the water's weight eliminated stresses on the inner silicone membrane that would have otherwise been caused by the atmosphere trying to burst out into the vacuum of space.

It was a simple, elegant design—and one that required virtually no maintenance. But there was one more component to the roof, a topmost layer, an icing on the transparent cake. A thin film had been applied overtop of the gold-covered outer membrane, a polarizing layer of liquid crystals that, under computer control, simulated a night of Earthly length by making the dome opaque for eight out of every twenty-four hours during the two-week-long lunar day. It also darkened the sky during the fourteen-day-long lunar night when the Earth was full or nearly full.

And indeed, the sky had blackened just as it should have one evening at 2100 local time, the sun fading and then completely disappearing as the crystals polarized, darkening the re-creation of southern Africa that filled the bottom of Copernicus. The only light came from the lamps located at each crisscrossing of the load-bearing cables; collectively, they providing as much illumination as the full moon did on Earth's surface.

The night had continued on like any other, with beasts prowling, and humans huddling for warmth, and protection, and companionship.

But sometime during that night, the computer controlling that circadian winking, that daily shifting of the sky from opaque to transparent, had crashed. When morning should have come, the polarizing membrane did not clear. The world of the last biological humans was cut off from the rest of the universe by a night that seemed as though it would never end.

▐▌ ▐▌ ▐▌

Prasp ran, each stride taking him two bodylengths farther ahead. He flapped his arms, moving the great wings of skin and sticks, beating them up and down, up and down, as fast as he could, and—

Yes! Yes!

He was rising, lifting, ascending—

Flying!

He was flying!

He rose higher and higher, the ground receding beneath him. He could see the savanah grasses far below, the giant, sprawling Acacia trees diminishing to nothing.

He kept flapping the wings, although he could feel that his face was already slick with sweat and he was gulping in air as fast as he could. His arms were aching, but he continued to move them up and down, his body rising farther and farther. He'd always known the faint lines crisscrossing the dome were actually thick cords, as big around as his own waist, for he had seen them where they touched the mountains that encircled the world. And now he was getting up far enough that he could see that thickness, see the pinpoints of light at each of their intersections resolving themselves into glowing disks, and—

Pain!

A spasm along his right arm.

A great ache in his left wrist.

A seizing of his back muscles, a throbbing in his shoulders.

So near, so close, and yet—

And yet he could go no higher. He wasn't strong enough.

Sadly, Prasp held his arms out straight, keeping the wings flat. He began the slow, long glide down to the grasses, far, far below.

It took a long time for him to come down. As he got closer to the ground, he became aware that a crowd of people had assembled, all of them looking up at him, many of them pointing. As he descended further he could make out their expressions—awe on some the faces; fear on a few of them.

Prasp skidded along the grasses until he was able to stop himself. Kari came running over to him, arriving before the others. She helped him remove the wings, and, once he was free of them, she hugged him tightly. Prasp could feel that her heart was pounding almost as hard as his own; she'd clearly been terrified for him.

Others of the tribe soon arrived. Prasp wasn't sure how they were going to react to his flight; had he committed a sacrilege? Balant, the tribe's greatest hunter, was among those who'd been watching. He looked at Prasp for a time, then held a clenched fist high over his head, and gave a great *whoop*—the tribe's custom when one of its members had made a spectacular kill during the hunt. The others soon followed Balant's lead, whooping with excitement as well.

Prasp was relieved that they'd accepted his flying, but he couldn't join in the shouts of joy.

He had failed.

▥ ▥ ▥

We, The Uploaded, had no way to monitor what was going on beneath the roof over Copernicus, but we could guess. We knew that the artificial lamps on the underside of the roof would have started at low power during that fateful night, collectively providing no more illumination than the full moon as seen from Earth. But we also knew that they were controlled by a separate computer, and so presumably weren't affected by whatever had caused Copernicus's sky to remain perpetually opaque. Those lamps should still flare with light rivaling Sol's own for sixteen hours per Earth-day day during the lunar night. Our simulations of the ecosystem suggested that some of the plant species under the roof would have died off, unable to get used to fourteen Earth-days of dim light, followed by fourteen more of two-thirds bright light and one-third dimness. But many other kinds of plants, most of the animals, and, yes, the humans, should have adapted without too much trouble.

But as to what those humans might be doing, we had no idea.

▌▌ ▐▌ ▐▌

Prasp left his wings near his hut. There were some, he knew, who privately ridiculed his attempts at flying, although none would publicly contradict Balant. And certainly none of them would damage the wings. Prasp was known for his cleverness—and that cleverness often yielded extra meat while hunting, meat he shared freely with others. No one would risk being cut off from Prasp's bounty by wrecking his wings, or allowing their children to do so.

There were people in Prasp's tribe who had run the entire diameter of the circular valley that was their world, staying directly beneath one of the thin lines that crossed through the center of the roof. Although it was easier to run in the cool semi-darkness of night rather than the heat of day, most people had done it during the day, to avoid hyenas and other nocturnal hunters.

But Prasp had to do the run both day and night—he couldn't let fourteen sleeping periods go by without repeating the course, for he wasn't doing this just once to impress a woman or gain status among the men. He wanted to do it over and over and over, back and forth, crossing the valley again and again.

This wasn't a stunt, after all.

This was *training*.

▌▌ ▐▌ ▐▌

One day, as he was about to embark on his run, Prasp found Dalba, one of the tribe's elders, waiting for him—and that was usually a sign of trouble.

"I saw you fly," she said.

Prasp nodded.

"And I hear you intend to fly again."

"Yes."

"But *why?*" asked Dalba. "Why do you fly?"

Prasp looked at her as if he couldn't believe the question. "To find a way out."

"Out? Out to where?"

"To whatever is beyond this valley."

"Do you not know the story of Hoktan?" asked Dalba.

Prasp shook his head.

"Hoktan was a foolish man who lived generations ago. He talked as you are now talking—as if one could leave this place. He tried another method, though: he dug and dug and dug, day after day, trying to make a tunnel out through the mountains that encircle our world."

"And?" said Prasp.

"And one day the gods used *wind* against him, pulling him out through his tunnel."

"Where is this tunnel?" asked Prasp. "I would love to see it!"

"The tunnel collapsed, the wind ceased—and Hoktan was never seen again."

"Well, I do not plan to dig through the roof—but I do hope to find a passage to whatever is beyond it."

Dalba shook her wizened head. "There's *nothing* beyond the roof, child."

"There *must* be. Legend says we came from the Old Place, and—"

Dalba laughed. "Yes, *Kata Bindu*. But it's not somewhere you can go back to. The trip here is a one-way journey."

"Why?" asked Prasp. "Why should it be that way?"

"The name of where we came from," said the elder. "Surely you understand the name?"

Prasp frowned. He'd only ever heard it called *Kata Bindu*, the Old Place; did it have another name? No, no—that was all it was ever called. But ...

"Oh," said Prasp, feeling foolish. He was a hunter, of course, and a gatherer, too—and this place, this territory, this land that his people knew so well, that fed them and sustained them, was *Bindu*, the term in their language for *place*, for territory, for home—but *Bindu* was also the word for *life*, the thing the land gave. *Kata Bindu* wasn't the Old *Place*; it was the Old *Life*.

And this—

"This is heaven," said the Dalba, simply. "You can't go back to the Old Life."

"But if it's heaven," said Prasp, "then where are the Gods?"

"They're here," said the Dalba, tipping her head up at the sky. "They're watching us. Can't you feel that in your heart?"

▥ ▥ ▥

Prasp flew again—but this time he rose farther than he ever had before. His muscles were stronger, his lungs more capacious. All that running had had the desired result.

Prasp was close enough now to the roof to see the circular lights, each wider than his body was long. Of course, it was night now; the lights were glowing dimly. Only a fool would strap on wings and try to fly toward the lights when they were burning with their daytime intensity.

Still, this close, there was enough illumination to make out things he'd never noticed from the ground. He could see that the roof was slightly curved, slightly concave, arching up and away. He continued to fly along, but everything was the same—massive cords, circular lights, and, supporting them, a thick, clear membrane—and beyond that, he couldn't say, for all was dark. The lights all faced down toward the ground, far below.

Prasp thought that if there were an exit anywhere, it might be at the very center of the roof—easy enough to spot, for all the radial cords converged at that point. He knew there was no exit around the edges of the roof, for others had long ago climbed the steep, rocky terraces that surrounded the valley, concentric shelves each wider and higher than the one below it. They'd circumnavigated the world, hiking around its edge, examining the entire seal between the roof and the rocky walls—but there was nothing; no break, no passage, no tunnel.

Finally, Prasp reached the exact center—and there *was* something special there. Prasp's heart began pounding even faster than it already had been. There was a platform hanging from the roof, a wide square, attached at its four corners by cylinders that rose to the sky. The platform was large, and Prasp was able to glide between two of the cylinders, his belly scraping along the platform's inner surface. He skidded along, thinking that the skin on his chest would soon be flayed from his ribs, and—

Gods, no!

There was a giant cube in the middle of the platform, a building of some sort as big as a multifamily hut. Prasp wanted to throw his hands up in front of his face to shield it from the crash, but he couldn't; his arms were strapped to the wings. He continued to skid forward, and he twisted his body sideways, finally slamming into the building.

He lay on the platform, catching his breath, supported from beneath for the first time since he'd taken flight.

Finally, he moved again. The building had a *door* in its side. Prasp had rarely seen doors before; some members of his tribe had tried to make them for their huts—vertical walls of sticks that articulated on gut ties down one side. This one was simpler and more elegant, but it was a door just the same.

Still, there was no way to get through it without shedding his wings— and he *had* to go through that door; he had to see what was on the other side of it. Prasp normally had his woman's help in strapping his wings on before each flight, but surely he'd be able to reattach the wings on his own when it came time to return to the valley. It would be tricky, but he was confident he could do it.

Prasp struggled to divest himself of the great elephant-hide membranes, and at last he was free of them. He rose to his feet and walked toward the door. There was something like a crooked arm attached to it. Prasp grabbed hold of it and pulled, and the door swung open, revealing the inside of the cube.

Prasp's heart immediately sank. There was no other door in the cube, no opening in its roof. He'd thought for sure he'd found the way out, but clearly that was not the case. Still, the room contained *things* the likes of which Prasp had never seen before: angled panels made of something that wasn't wood or stone, with lights glowing upon them. Most were green, but a few were red. He stared at them in wonder.

▮ ▮ ▮

We had access to the plans for the Copernicus refuge, of course. After all, it was we who had built that habitat prior to taking The Next Step. We'd put the computers controlling the habitat high above the ground, hanging from the center of the roof, where the primitives could never reach them. Indeed, from the ground, some 3.8 kilometers below, the computing room and its surrounding platform would be all but invisible.

We'd tried to figure out what exactly had gone wrong. Our best guess was that the computers had failed when February 28, 3000, had rolled around—certainly, the two-week long lunar day that straddled that Earth date had been the one in which the polarizing film had gone dark for the last time. We'd tested the computers for behavior at leap years, but it hadn't occurred to us to check *millennial* years, with their arcane and sometimes conflicting rules about whether the day after February 28 was February 29 or March 1.

We'd called ourselves humane. Every conceivable programming error, every possible bug, every potential infinite loop, had been tracked down in the systems that now hosted us. But somehow the computers that were to look after those not taking The Next Step were given less rigorous testing.

Yes, we'd been humane— and human; all too human, it seemed.

▮ ▮ ▮

In the cubical structure at the roof of the world Prasp found the most remarkable thing: a vertical rectangular panel that had symbols glowing on it, and, resting on a horizontal surface in front of it, a—*something*—that looked like packed animal teeth, white and concave.

Prasp counted them; there were 107, divided into one large cluster and four smaller ones. Most of the teeth had single symbols on them. One whole row of them, plus a few others, had two symbols, one above and one below. A few had strings of symbols. He tried to match the symbols glowing on the panel with those on the teeth. Some of them did have matches; others did not. The glowing strings on the panel made no sense to him, although he looked at each one carefully: "System halted. Press Enter to reinitialize."

On the rack of teeth he could find the *S* symbol—although why the panel showed it in two different sizes, he had no idea. He also found the *P* symbol, and the *E*, and the *z*, and two teeth marked with circles that might be the *o* symbol, and two others marked with vertical lines that might be the *l* symbol. Some of the other symbols had loose counterparts amongst the teeth: the *m* seemed similar to, but less angular, than one of the tooth markings, for instance. But many of the others shown on the panel—*e*, *h*, *a*, *d*, *r*, *n*, and *i*—seemed to have no counterparts among the teeth, and—

"*Enter.*" Right in the middle of the glowing characters was the string "Enter." And that entire string was reproduced on an extra large tooth at the far right of the main collection; that tooth also was marked by a left-pointing arrow with a right-angle bend in its shaft.

Prasp ran his index finger over that large tooth, and was surprised to find it wobbling, almost like a child's tooth about to come out. Very strange. He pressed down on the tooth to see just how much play it had, and it collapsed inward, and then, as soon as Prasp pulled his finger back in disgust, it popped back out again.

But the symbols on the screen disappeared! Whatever Prasp had done clearly had been a mistake; he'd ruined everything.

▦ ▦ ▦

Fourteen sleep periods later, Prasp, his woman Kari, Dalba and the other elders, and the rest of the tribe all watched in awe as something incredible happened. The sky turned *clear*, and high in the sky, there was a giant blue-and-white light, shaped like half a circle, set against a black background.

"What is *that?*" asked Kari, looking at Prasp.

Prasp felt his voice catching in his throat, catching with wonder. "What else could it be?" he said. "The Other Place." He repeated the phrase again, but with a slightly different intonation, emphasizing the double meaning. "The Other Life."

■■ ■■ ■■

Someday, perhaps, the hunter-gatherers of Copernicus will develop a technological civilization. Someday, perhaps, they will even find a way out of their roofed-over crater, a way to move out into the universe, leaving their microcosm behind.

But for us, for Those Who Had Been Flesh, for The Collective Consciousness of Earth, for The Uploaded, there would be no way out. Who'd known that The Next Step would be our last step? Who'd known that the rest of the universe would be barren? Who'd known how lonely it would be to become a single entity—yes, we refer to ourselves in the plural as if that sheer act of linguistic stubbornness could make up for us being a single consciousness now, with no one to converse with.

Maybe, after a thousand years, or a million, the men and women in Copernicus will develop radio, and at last we will have someone else to talk to. Maybe they'll even leave their world and spread out to colonize this empty galaxy.

They might even come here, although few of them will be able to endure Earth's gravity. But if they do come, yes, they might accidentally or deliberately put an end to our existence.

We can only hope.

We are no longer human.

But we *are* humane; we wish them well. *We* are trapped forevermore, but those who are still flesh, and can again see the sky, might yet be free.

We will watch. And wait.

There is nothing more for us to do.

Driving A Bargain

*Although my novels are exclusively hard science fiction, I occasionally write
fantasy or horror at short lengths; indeed, to my delight, I've been nominated
for the Horror Writers Association's Bram Stoker Award.*

*My great friend Edo van Belkom is, without doubt, Canada's top horror
writer (and, just to put me in my place, he's actually won the Stoker). In 2000,
he edited a young-adult anthology called* Be Afraid! *It contained my story
"Last But Not Least," which was reprinted in my collection* Iterations.

Be Afraid! *was a big hit, and so Edo did a sequel anthology,* Be VERY
Afraid! *This story was my contribution to that book.*

⋆ ■ ■ ℛ

Jerry walked to the corner store, a baseball cap and sunglasses shielding him
from the heat beating down from above. He picked up a copy of the
Calgary Sun, walked to the counter, gave the old man a dollar, got his
change, and hurried outside. He didn't want to wait until he got home, so
he went to the nearest bus stop, parked himself on the bench there, and
opened the paper.

Of course, the first thing he checked out was the bikini-clad Sunshine
Girl—what sixteen-year-old boy wouldn't turn to that first? Today's girl
was old—23, it said—but she certainly was pretty, with lots of long blonde
hair.

That ritual completed, Jerry turned to the real reason he'd bought the
paper: the classified ads. He found the used-car listings, and started poring
over them, hoping, as he always did, for a bargain.

Jerry had worked hard all summer on a loading dock. It had been rough work, but, for the first time in his life, he had real muscles. And, even more important, he had some real money.

His parents had promised to pay the insurance if Jerry kept up straight A's all through grade ten, and Jerry had. They weren't going to pay for a car, itself, but Jerry had two grand in his bank account—he liked the sound of that: two grand. Now if he could just find something halfway decent for that price, he'd be driving to school when grade eleven started next week.

Jerry was a realist. He wanted a girlfriend—God, how he wanted one—but he knew his little wispy beard wasn't what was going to impress ... well, he'd been thinking about Ashley Brown all summer. Ashley who, in his eyes at least, put that Sunshine Girl to shame.

But, no, it wasn't the beard he'd managed to grow since June that would impress her. Nor was it his newfound biceps. It would be having his own set of wheels. How sweet that would be!

Jerry continued scanning the ads, skipping over all the makes he knew he could never afford: the Volvos, the Lexuses, the Mercedes, the BMWs.

He read the lines describing a '94 Honda Civic, a '97 Dodge Neon, even a '91 Pontiac Grand Prix. But the prices were out of his reach.

Jerry really didn't care *what* make of car he got; he'd even take a Hyundai. After all, when hardly anyone else his age had a car, *any* car would be a fabulous ticket to freedom, to making out. To use one of his dad's favorite expressions—an expression that he'd never really understood until just now—"In the land of the blind, the one-eyed man is king."

Jerry was going to be royalty.

If, that is, he could find something he could afford. He kept looking, getting more and more depressed. Maybe he'd just—

Jerry felt his eyes go wide. A 1997 Toyota, only twenty thousand miles on it. The asking price: "$3,000, OBO."

Just three thousand! That was awfully cheap for such a car ... And OBO! Or Best Offer. It couldn't hurt to try two thousand dollars. The worst the seller could do was say no. Jerry felt in his pocket for the change he got from buying the paper. There was a phone booth just up the street. He hurried over to it, and called.

"Hello?" said a sad-sounding man's voice at the other end.

Jerry tried to make his own voice sound as deep as he could. "Hello," he said. "I'm calling about the Toyota." He swallowed. "Has it sold yet?"

"No," said the man. "Would you like to come see it?"

Jerry got the man's address—only about two miles away. He glanced up the street, saw the bus coming, and ran back to the stop, grinning to himself. If all went well, this would be the last time he'd have to take the bus anywhere.

███ ███ ███

Jerry walked up to the house. It looked like the kind of place he lived in himself: basketball hoop above the garage; garage door dented from endless games of ball hockey.

Jerry rang the doorbell, and was greeted by a man who looked about the same age as Jerry's father ... a sad-looking man with a face like a basset hound.

"Yes?" said the man.

"I called earlier," said Jerry. "I've come about the car."

The man's eyebrows went up. "How old are you, son?"

"Sixteen."

"Tell me about yourself," said the man.

Jerry couldn't see what difference that would make. But he *did* want to soften the old guy up so that he'd take the lower price. And so: "My name's Jerry Sloane," he said. "I'm a student at Eastern High, just going into grade eleven. I've got my license, and I've been working all summer long on the loading dock down at Macabee's."

The bassett hound's eyebrows went up. "Have you, now?"

"Yes," said Jerry.

"You a good student?"

Jerry was embarrassed to answer; it seemed *so* nerdy to say it, but ... "Straight A's."

The bassett hound nodded. "Good for you! Good for you!" He paused. "Are you a churchgoer, son?"

Jerry was surprised by the question, but he answered truthfully. "Most weeks, with my family. Calgary United."

The man nodded again. "All right, would you like to take the car for a test drive?"

"Sure!"

Jerry got into the driver's seat, and the man got into the passenger seat. Not that it should have mattered to whether the deal got made, but Jerry did the absolute best job he could of backing out of the driveway and turning onto the street. When they arrived at the corner, he came to a proper full stop at the stop sign, making sure the front of his car lifted up a bit before he continued into the empty intersection. That's what they'd taught him in driver's ed: you know you've come to a complete stop when the front of your car lifts up.

At the next intersection, Jerry signaled his turn, even though there was no one around and took a left onto Askwith Street.

The bassett hound nodded, impressed. "You're a very careful driver," he said.

"Thanks."

Jerry was coming to another corner, where Askwith crossed Thurlbeck, and he decided to turn right. He activated the turn signal and—

"No!" shouted the man.

Jerry was startled and looked around, terrified that he'd been about to hit a cat or something. "What?" said Jerry. "What?"

"Don't go down that way," said the man, his voice shaking.

It was the route Jerry would have to take to get to school, but he was in no rush to see that old prison any sooner than he had to. He canceled his turn signal and continued straight through the intersection.

Jerry went along for another mile, then decided he'd better not overdo it and headed back to the man's house.

"So," said the man, "what did you think?"

"It's a great car, but ..."

"Oh, I know it could really use a front-end alignment," said the man, "but it's not that bad, is it?"

Jerry hadn't even noticed, but he was clever enough to seize on the issue. "Well, it *will* need work," he said, trying to sound like an old hand at such matters. "Tell you what—I'll give you two thousand dollars for it."

"*Two* thousand!" said the man. But then he fell silent, saying nothing else.

Jerry wanted to be cool, wanted to be a tough bargainer, but the man had such a sad face. "I'll tell you the truth," he said. "Two thousand is all I've got."

"You worked for it?" asked the man.

Jerry nodded. "Every penny."

The man was quiet for a bit, then he said, "You seem to be a fine young fellow," he said. He extended his right hand across the gearshift to Jerry. "Deal."

▥ ▥ ▥

Today was the day. Today, the first Tuesday in September, would make everything worthwhile. Jerry put on his best—that is, his oldest—pair of jeans and a shirt with the sleeves ripped off. It was the perfect look.

He got in the car—*his* car—and started it, pulling out of the driveway. A left onto Schumann Street, a right onto Vigo. Jerry didn't have any real choice of how to get to school, but was delighted that some of the other kids would see him en route. And if he happened to pass Ashley Brown ... why, he'd pull over and offer her a lift. How sweet would that be?

Jerry came to the intersection with Thurlbeck, where there was a stop sign. But this time he was trying to impress a different audience. He slowed down and, without waiting for the front of the car to bounce up, turned right.

Thurlbeck was the long two-laned street that led straight to Eastern High. Jerry had to pick just the right speed. If he went too fast, none of the kids walking along would have a chance to see that it was him. But he couldn't cruise along slowly, or they'd think he wasn't comfortable driving. Not comfortable! Why, he'd been driving for *months* now. He picked a moderate speed and rolled down the driver's-side window, resting his sleeveless arm on the edge of the opening.

Up ahead, a bunch of kids were walking along the sidewalk.

No ... no, that wasn't quite right. They weren't walking—they were *standing*, all looking and pointing at something. That was perfect: in a moment, they'd all be looking and pointing at *him*.

As he got closer, Jerry slowed the car to a crawl. As much as he wanted to show off, he was curious about what had caught everyone's attention. He remembered a day years ago when everybody had paused on the way to school as they came across a dead dog, one eye half popped out of its skull.

Jerry continued on slowly, hoping people would look over and take notice of him, but no one did. They were all intent on something—he still couldn't make out what—on the side of the road. He thought about honking his horn, but no, he couldn't do that. The whole secret of being cool was to get people to look at you without it seeming like that was what you were trying to do.

Finally, Jerry thought of the perfect solution. As he got closer to the knot of people, he pulled his car over to the side of the road, put on his blinkers, and got out.

"Hey," he said as he closed the distance between himself and the others. "Wassup?"

Darren Chen looked up. "Hey, Jerry," he said.

Jerry had expected Chen's eyes to go wide when he realized that his friend had come out of the car sitting by the curb, but that didn't happen. The other boy just pointed to the side of the road.

Jerry followed the outstretched arm and ...

His heart jumped.

There was a plain white cross on the grassy strip that ran along the far side of the sidewalk. Hanging from it was a wreath. Jerry moved closer and read the words that had been written on the cross in thick black strokes, perhaps with an indelible marker: "Tammy Jameson was killed here by a hit-and-run driver. She will always be remembered." And there was a date from July.

Jerry knew the Jameson name—there'd always been one or another of them going through the local schools. A face came into his mind, but he wasn't even sure if it was Tammy's.

"Wow," said Jerry softly. "Wow."

Chen nodded. "I read about it in the paper. They still haven't caught the person who did it."

■ ■ ■

Jerry finally got what he wanted at the end of the school day. Tons of kids saw him sauntering over to his car, and a few of the boys came up to talk to him about it.

And just before he was about to get in and drive off, he saw Ashley. She was walking with a couple of other girls, books clasped to her chest. She looked up and saw the car sitting there. Then she saw Jerry leaning against it and her eyes—beautiful deep-blue eyes, he knew, although he couldn't really see them at this distance—met his, and she smiled a bit and nodded at him, impressed.

Jerry got in his car and drove home, feeling on top of the world.

■ ■ ■

The next morning, Jerry headed out to school. This time, he thought maybe he'd get the attention he deserved as he came up Thurlbeck Street. After all, even if the cross was still there—and it was; he could just make it out up ahead—the novelty would surely have worn off.

Jerry decided to try a slightly faster speed today, in hopes that more people would look up. But, to his astonishment, he found that the more he pressed his right foot down on the accelerator, the more his car slowed down. He actually craned for a look—it was a beginner's mistake, and a pretty terrifying one too, he remembered, to confuse the accelerator and the brake—but, no, his gray Nike was pressing down on the correct pedal.

And yet still his car was rapidly slowing down. As he came abreast of the crucifix with it wreath, he was moving at no better than walking speed, despite having the pedal all the way to the floor. But once he'd passed the cross, the car started speeding up again, until at last the vehicle was operating normally once more.

Jerry was reasonably philosophical. He knew there *had* to be something wrong with the car for him to have gotten it so cheap. He continued on to the school parking lot. Not even the principal had a reserved spot—it made his car too easy a target for vandals, Jerry guessed. It pleased him greatly to pull in next to old Mr. Walters, who was trying to shift his bulk out of his Ford.

▪ ▪ ▪

Jerry was relieved that his car functioned flawlessly on the way home from school. He still hadn't managed to find the courage to offer Ashley Brown a lift home, but that would come soon, he knew.

The next day, however—crazy though it seemed—his car developed the exact same malfunction, slowing to a crawl at precisely the same point in the road.

Jerry had seen his share of horror movies. It didn't take a Dr. Frankenstein to figure out that it had something to do with the girl who had been killed there. It was as though she was reaching out from the beyond, slowing down cars at that spot to make sure that no other accident ever happened there again. It was scary but exhilarating.

At lunch that day, Jerry headed out to the school's parking lot, all set to hang around his car, showing it off to anyone who cared to have a look. But then he caught sight of Ashley walking out of the school grounds. He could have jumped in his car and driven over to her, but she probably wouldn't get in, even if he offered. No, he needed to talk to her first.

Now or never, Jerry thought. He jogged over to Ashley, catching up with her as she was walking along Thurlbeck Street. "Hey, Ash," he said. "Where're you going?"

Ashley turned around and smiled that radiant smile of hers. "Just down to the store to get some gum."

"Mind if I tag along?"

"If you like," she said, her voice perfectly measured, perfectly noncommittal.

Jerry fell in beside her. He chatted with her—trying to hide his nervousness—about what they'd each done over the summer. She'd spent most of it at her uncle's farm and—

Jerry stopped dead in his tracks.

A car was coming up Thurlbeck Street, heading toward the school. It came abreast of the crucifix but didn't slow down, it just sailed on by.

"What's wrong?" asked Ashley.

"Nothing," said Jerry. A few moments later, another car came along, and it too passed the crucifix without incident.

Of course, Jerry had had no trouble driving home from school, but he'd assumed that that was because he was in the other lane, going in the opposite direction, and that Tammy, wherever she was, didn't care about people going that way.

But ...

But now it looked like it wasn't *every* car that she was slowing down when it passed the spot where she'd—there was no gentle way to phrase it—where she'd been killed.

No, not every car.

Jerry's heart fluttered.

Just my car.

▌▐ ▐▌ ▐▌

The next day, the same thing: Jerry's car slowed down almost to a stop directly opposite where Tammy Jameson had been hit. He tried to ignore it, but then Dickens, one of the kids in his geography class, made a crack about it. "Hey, Sloane," he said, "What are you, chicken? I see you crawling along every morning when you pass the spot where Tammy was killed."

Where Tammy was killed. He said it offhandedly, as if death was a commonplace occurrence for him, as if he was talking about the place where something utterly normal had happened.

But Jerry couldn't take it anymore. He'd been called on it, on what Dickens assumed was his behavior, and he had to either give a good reason for it or stop doing it. That's the way it worked.

But he had no good reason for it, except ...

Except the one he'd been suppressing, the one that kept gnawing at the back of his mind, but that he'd shooed away whenever it had threatened to come to the fore.

Only his car was slowing down.

But it hadn't always been *his* car.

A bargain. Just two grand!

Jerry had assumed that there had to be something wrong with it for him to get it so cheap, but that wasn't it. Not exactly.

Rather, something wrong had been *done* with it.

His car was the one the police were looking for, the one that had been used to strike a young woman dead and then flee the scene.

▉ ▉ ▉

Jerry drove to the house where the man with the basset-hound face lived. He left the car in the driveway, with the driver's door open and the engine still running. He got out, walked up to the door, rang the bell, and waited for the man to appear, which, after a long, long time, he finally did.

"Oh, it's you, son," he said. "What can I do for you?"

Jerry had thought it took all his courage just to speak to Ashley Brown. But he'd been wrong. This took more courage. Way more.

"I know what you did in that car you sold me," he said.

The man's face didn't show any shock, but Jerry realized that wasn't because he wasn't surprised. No, thought Jerry, it was something else—a *deadness*, an inability to feel shock anymore.

"I don't know what you're talking about, son," said the man.

"That car—*my* car—you hit a girl with it. On Thurlbeck Street."

"I swear to you," said the man, still standing in his doorway, "I never did anything like that."

"She went to my school," said Jerry. "Her name was Tammy. Tammy Jameson."

The man closed his eyes, as if he was trying to shut out the world.

"And," said Jerry, his voice quavering, "you killed her."

"No," said the man. "No, I didn't." He paused. "Look, do you want to come in?"

Jerry shook his head. He could outrun the old guy—he was sure of that—and he could make it back to his car in a matter of seconds. But if he went inside ... well, he'd seen *that* in horror movies, too.

The man with the sad face put his hands in his pockets. "What are you going to do?" he said.

"Go to the cops," said Jerry. "Tell them."

The man didn't laugh, although Jerry had expected him to—a derisive, mocking laugh. Instead, he just shook his head.

"You've got no evidence."

"The car slows down on its own every time I pass the spot where the"— he'd been about to say "accident," but that was the wrong word—"where the *crime* occurred."

This time, the man's face did show a reaction, a lifting of his shaggy, graying eyebrows. "Really?" But he composed himself quickly. "The police won't give you the time of day if you come in with a crazy story like that."

"Maybe," said Jerry, trying to sound more confident than he felt. "Maybe not."

"Look, I've been nice to you," said the man. "I gave you a great deal on that car."

"Of course you did!" snapped Jerry. "You wanted to get rid of it! After what you did—"

"I told you, son, I didn't do anything."

"That girl—Tammy—she can't rest, you know. She's reaching out from beyond the grave, trying to stop that car every time it passes that spot. You've got to turn yourself in. You've got to let her rest."

"Get out of here, kid. Leave me alone."

"I can't," said Jerry. "I can't, because it won't leave *her* alone. You have to go to the police and tell them what you did."

"How many times do I have to tell you? I didn't do anything!" The old man turned around for a second, and Jerry thought he was going to disappear into the house. But he didn't; he simply grabbed a hockey stick that must have been leaning against a wall just inside the door. He raised the stick menacingly. "Now, get out of here!" he shouted.

Jerry couldn't believe the man was going to chase him down the street, in full view of his neighbors. "You have to turn yourself in," he said firmly.

The man took a swing at him—high-sticking indeed!—and Jerry started running for his car. The old guy continued after him. Jerry scrambled into the driver's seat and slammed the door behind him. He threw the car into reverse, but not before the man brought the hockey stick down on the front of the hood—somewhere near, Jerry felt sure, the spot where the car had crashed into poor Tammy Jameson.

▥ ▥ ▥

Jerry had no idea what was the right thing to do. He suspected that the bassett hound was correct: the police would laugh him out of the station if he came to them with his story. Of course, if they'd just *try* driving his car along Thurlbeck, they'd see for themselves. But adults were so smug; no matter how much he begged, they'd refuse.

And so Jerry found himself doing something that might have been stupid. He should have been at home studying—or, even better, out on a date with Ashley Brown. Instead, he was parked on the side of the street, a few doors up from the man's house, from the driveway that used to be home to this car. He didn't know exactly what he was doing. Did they call this casing the joint? No, that was when you were planning a robbery. Ah, he had it! A stakeout. Cool.

Jerry waited. It was dark enough to see a few stars—and he hoped that meant it was also dark enough that the old man wouldn't see him, even if he glanced out his front window.

Jerry wasn't even sure what he was waiting for. It was just like Ms. Singh, his chemistry teacher, said: he'd know it when he saw it.

And at last *it* appeared.

Jerry felt like slapping his hand against his forehead, but a theatrical gesture like that was wasted when there was no one around to see it. Still, he wondered how he could be so stupid.

That old man wasn't the one who'd used the hockey stick. Oh, he might have dented Jerry's hood with it, but the dents in the garage door were the work of someone else.

And that someone else was walking up the driveway, hands shoved deep into the pockets of a blue leather jacket, dark-haired head downcast. He looked maybe a year or two older than Jerry.

Of course, it could have been a delivery person or something. But no, Jerry could see the guy take out a set of keys and let himself into the house. And, for one brief moment, he saw the guy's face, a long face, a sad face ... but a young face.

The car hadn't belonged to the old man. It had belonged to his son.

■ ■ ■

There were fifteen hundred kids at Eastern High. No reason Jerry should know them all on sight—especially ones who weren't in his grade. Oh, he knew the names of all the babes in grade twelve—he and the other boys his age fantasized about them often enough—but some long-faced guy with dark hair? Jerry wouldn't have paid any attention to him.

Until now.

It was three days before he caught sight of the guy walking the halls at Eastern. His last name, Jerry knew, was likely Forsythe, since that was the old man's name, the name Jerry had written on the check for the car. It wasn't much longer before he had found where young Forsythe's locker was located. And then Jerry cut his last class—history, which he could easily afford to miss once—and waited in a stairwell, where he could keep an eye on Forsythe's locker.

At about 3:35, Forsythe came up to it, dialed the combo, put some books inside, took out a couple of others, and put on the same blue leather jacket Jerry had seen him in the night of the stakeout. And then he started walking out.

Jerry watched him head out, then he hurried to the parking lot and got into the Toyota.

■ ■ ■

Jerry was crawling along—and this time, it was of his own volition. He didn't want to overtake Forsythe—not yet. But then Forsythe did something completely unexpected. Instead of walking down Thurlbeck, he headed in the opposite direction, away from his own house. Could it be that Jerry was wrong about who this was? After all, he'd seen Forsythe's son only once before, on a dark night, and—

No. It came to him in a flash what Forsythe was doing. He was going to walk the long way around—a full mile out of his way—so that he wouldn't have to go past the spot where he'd hit Tammy Jameson.

Jerry wondered if he'd avoided the spot entirely since hitting her or had got cold feet only once the cross had been erected. He rolled down his window, followed Forsythe, and pulled up next to him, matching his car's velocity to Forsythe's walking speed.

"Hey," said Jerry.

The other guy looked up, and his eyes went wide in recognition—not of Jerry, but of what had once been his car.

"What?" said Forsythe.

"You look like you could use a lift," said Jerry.

"Naw. I live just up there." He waved vaguely ahead of him.

"No, you don't," said Jerry, and he recited the address he'd gone to to buy the car.

"What do you want, man?" said Forsythe.

"Your old man gave me a good deal on this car," said Jerry. "And I figured out why."

Forsythe shook his head. "I don't know what you're talking about."

"Yes, you do. I know you do." He paused. *"She* knows you do."

The guy told Jerry to go ... well, to go do something that was physically impossible. Jerry's heart was racing, but he tried to sound cool. "Sooner or later, you'll want to come clean on this."

Forsythe said nothing.

"Maybe tomorrow," said Jerry, and he drove off.

▮ ▮ ▮

That night, Jerry went to the hardware store to get the stuff he needed. Of course, he couldn't do anything about it early in the day; someone might come along. So he waited until his final period—which today was English—and he cut class again. He then went out to his car, got what he needed from the trunk, and went up Thurlbeck.

When he was done, he returned to the parking lot and waited for Forsythe to head out for home.

▌▌▌ ▌▌▌ ▌▌▌

Jerry finally caught sight of Forsythe. Just as he had the day before, Forsythe walked to the edge of the schoolyard. But there he hesitated for a moment, as if wondering if he dared take the short way home. But he apparently couldn't do that. He took a deep breath and headed up Thurlbeck.

Jerry started his car but lagged behind Forsythe, crawling along, his foot barely touching the accelerator.

There was a large pine tree up ahead. Jerry waited for Forsythe to come abreast of it, and ...

The disadvantage of following Forsythe was that Jerry couldn't see the other kid's face when he caught sight of the new cross Jerry had banged together and sunk into the grass next to the sidewalk. But he saw Forsythe stop dead in his tracks.

Just as *she* had been stopped dead in his tracks.

Jerry saw Forsythe loom in, look at the words written not in black, as on Tammy's cross, but in red—words that said, "Our sins testify against us."

Forsythe began to run ahead, panicking, and Jerry pressed down a little more on the accelerator, keeping up. All those years of Sunday school were coming in handy.

Forsythe came to another tree. In its lee, he surely could see the second wooden cross, with its letters as crimson as blood: "He shall make amends for the harm he hath done."

Forsythe was swinging his head left and right, clearly terrified. But he continued running forward.

A third tree. A third cross. And a third red message, the simplest of all:

"Thou shalt not kill."

Finally, Forsythe turned around and caught sight of Jerry.

Jerry sped up, coming alongside him. Forsythe's face was a mask of terror. Jerry rolled down his window, leaned an elbow out, and said, as nonchalantly as he could manage, "Going my way?"

Forsythe clearly didn't know what to say. He looked up ahead, apparently wondering if there were more crosses to come. Then he turned and looked back the other way, off into the distance.

"There's just one down the other way," said Jerry. "If you'd prefer to walk by it ..."

Forsythe swore at Jerry, but without much force. "What's this to you?" he snapped.

"I want her to let my car go. I worked my tail off for these wheels."

Forsythe stared at him, the way you'd look at somebody who might be crazy.

"So," said Jerry, again trying for an offhand tone, "going my way?"

Forsythe was quiet for a long moment. "Depends where you're going," he said at last.

"Oh, I thought I'd take a swing by the police station," Jerry said.

Forsythe looked up Thurlbeck once more, then down it, then at last back at Jerry. He shrugged, but it wasn't as if he was unsure. Rather, it was as if he were shucking a giant weight from his shoulders.

"Yeah," he said to Jerry. "Yeah, I could use a lift."

Flashes

Lou Anders edits some of the best anthologies out there. He'd invited me to contribute to his Live Without a Net, *but other commitments prevented me from doing so. Undaunted, Lou invited me into his next anthology,* FutureShocks. *This is another of those books that it seems odd for me to be part of: I'm optimistic about "all the bright tomorrows yet to come" (as I once called them in an essay), but Lou wanted downbeat stories about the hidden dark sides of new technologies, discoveries, and breakthroughs. Here's what I came up with ...*

❈ ■ ■ ❧

My heart pounded as I surveyed the scene. It was a horrific, but oddly appropriate, image: a bright light pulsing on and off. The light was the setting sun, visible through the window, and the pulsing was caused by the rhythmic swaying of the corpse, dangling from a makeshift noose, as it passed in front of the blood-red disk.

"Another one, eh, Detective?" said Chiu, the campus security guard, from behind me. His tone was soft.

I looked around the office. The computer monitor was showing a virtual desktop with a panoramic view of a spiral galaxy as the wallpaper; no files were open. Nor was there any sheet of e-paper prominently displayed on the real desktop. The poor bastards didn't even bother to leave suicide notes anymore. There was no point; it had all already been said.

"Yeah," I said quietly, responding to Chiu. "Another one."

The dead man was maybe sixty, scrawny, mostly bald. He was wearing black denim jeans and a black turtleneck sweater, the standard professorial look these days. His noose was fashioned out of fiber-optic cabling, giving it a pearlescent sheen in the sunlight. His eyes had bugged out, and his mouth was hanging open.

"I knew him a bit," said Chiu. "Ethan McCharles. Nice guy—he always remembered my name. So many of the profs, they think they're too important to say hi to a security guard. But not him."

I nodded. It was as good a eulogy as one could hope for—honest, spontaneous, heartfelt.

Chiu went on. "He was married," he said, pointing to the gold band on the corpse's left hand. "I think his wife works here, too."

I felt my stomach tightening, and I let out a sigh. My favorite thing: informing the spouse.

▌▌ ▌▌ ▌▌

Cytosine Methylation: *All lifeforms are based on self-replicating nucleic acids, commonly triphosphoparacarbolicnucleic acid or, less often, deoxyribonucleic acid; in either case, a secondary stream of hereditary information is encoded based on the methylation state of cytosine, allowing acquired characteristics to be passed on to the next generation ...*

▌▌ ▌▌ ▌▌

The departmental secretary confirmed what Chiu had said: Professor Ethan McCharles's wife did indeed also work at the University of Toronto; she was a tenured prof, too, but in a different faculty.

Walking down a corridor, I remembered my own days as a student here. Class of 1998—"9T8," as they styled it on the school jackets. It'd been—what?—seventeen years since I'd graduated, but I still woke up from time to time in a cold sweat, after having one of those recurring student nightmares: the exam I hadn't studied for, the class I'd forgotten I'd enrolled in. Crazy dreams, left over from an age when little bits of human knowledge mattered; when facts and figures we'd discovered made a difference.

I continued along the corridor. One thing *had* changed since my day. Back then, the hallways had been packed between classes. Now, you could actually negotiate your way easily; enrollment was way down. This corridor was long, with fluorescent lights overhead, and was lined with wooden doors that had frosted floor-to-ceiling glass panels next to them.

I shook my head. The halls of academe.

The halls of death.

I finally found Marilyn Maslankowski's classroom; the arcane room-numbering system had come back to me. She'd just finished a lecture, apparently, and was standing next to the lectern, speaking with a redheaded male student; no one else was in the room. I entered.

Marilyn was perhaps ten years younger than her husband had been, and had light brown hair and a round, moonlike face. The student wanted more time to finish an essay on the novels of Robert Charles Wilson; Marilyn capitulated after a few wheedling arguments.

The kid left, and Marilyn turned to me, her smile thanking me for waiting. "The humanities," she said. "Aptly named, no? At least English literature is something that we're the foremost authorities on. It's nice that there are a couple of areas left like that."

"I suppose," I said. I was always after my own son to do his homework on time; didn't teachers know that if they weren't firm in their deadlines they were just making a parent's job more difficult? Ah, well. At least this kid had gone to university; I doubted my boy ever would.

"Are you Professor Marilyn Maslankowski?" I asked.

She nodded. "What can I do for you?"

I didn't extend my hand; we weren't allowed to make any sort of overture to physical contact anymore. "Professor Maslankowski, my name is Andrew Walker. I'm a detective with the Toronto Police." I showed her my badge.

Her brown eyes narrowed. "Yes? What is it?"

I looked behind me to make sure we were still alone. "It's about your husband."

Her voice quavered slightly. "Ethan? My God, has something happened?"

There was never any easy way to do this. I took a deep breath, then: "Professor Maslankowski, your husband is dead."

Her eyes went wide and she staggered back a half-step, bumping up against the smartboard that covered the wall behind her.

"I'm terribly sorry," I said.

"What—what happened?" Marilyn asked at last, her voice reduced to a whisper.

I lifted my shoulders slightly. "He killed himself."

"Killed himself?" repeated Marilyn, as if the words were ones she'd never heard before.

I nodded. "We'll need you to positively identify the body, as next of kin, but the security guard says it's him."

"My God," said Marilyn again. Her eyes were still wide. "My God ..."

"I understand your husband was a physicist," I said.

Marilyn didn't seem to hear. "My poor Ethan ..." she said softly. She looked like she might collapse. If I thought she was actually in danger of hurting herself with a fall, I could surge in and grab her; otherwise, regulations said I had to keep my distance. "My poor, poor Ethan ..."

"Had your husband been showing signs of depression?" I asked.

Suddenly Marilyn's tone was sharp. "Of course he had! Damn it, wouldn't you?"

I didn't say anything. I was used to this by now.

"Those aliens," Marilyn said, closing her eyes. "Those goddamned aliens."

▮▮ ▮▮ ▮▮

Demand-Rebound Equilibrium: *Although countless economic systems have been tried by various cultures, all but one prove inadequate in the face of the essentially limitless material resources made possible through low-cost reconfiguration of subatomic particles. The only successful system, commonly known as Demand-Rebound Equilibrium, although also occasionally called [Untranslatable proper name]'s Forge, after its principal chronicler, works because it responds to market forces that operate independently from individual psychology, thus ...*

▮▮ ▮▮ ▮▮

By the time we returned to Ethan's office, he'd been cut down and laid out on the floor, a sheet the coroner had brought covering his face and body. Marilyn had cried continuously as we'd made our way across the campus. It was early January, but global warming meant that the snowfalls I'd known as a boy didn't occur much in Toronto anymore. Most of the ozone was gone, too, letting ultraviolet pound down. We weren't even shielded against our own sun; how could we expect to be protected from stuff coming from the stars?

I knelt down and pulled back the sheet. Now that the noose was gone, we could see the severe bruising where Ethan's neck had snapped. Marilyn made a sharp intake of breath, brought her hand to her mouth, closed her eyes tightly, and looked away.

"Is that your husband?" I asked, feeling like an ass for even having to pose the question.

She managed a small, almost imperceptible nod.

It was now well into the evening. I could come back tomorrow to ask Ethan McCharles's colleagues the questions I needed answered for my report, but, well, Marilyn was right here, and, even though her field was literature rather than physics, she must have some sense of what her husband had been working on. I repositioned the sheet over his dead face and stood up. "Can you tell me what Ethan's specialty was?"

Marilyn was clearly struggling to keep her composure. Her lower lip was trembling, and I could see by the rising and falling of her blouse—so sharply contrasting with the absolutely still sheet—that she was breathing rapidly. "His—he ... Oh, my poor, poor Ethan ..."

"Professor Maslankowski," I said gently. "Your husband's specialty ...?"

She nodded, acknowledging that she'd heard me, but still unable to focus on answering the question. I let her take her time, and, at last, as if they were curse words, she spat out, "Loop quantum gravity."

"Which is?"

"Which is a model of how subatomic particles are composed." She shook her head. "Ethan spent his whole career trying to prove LQG was correct, and ..."

"And?" I said gently.

"And yesterday they revealed the true nature of the fundamental structure of matter."

"And this—what was it?—this 'loop quantum gravity' wasn't right?"

Marilyn let out a heavy sigh. "Not even close. Not even in the ballpark." She looked down at the covered form of her dead husband, then turned her gaze back to me. "Do you know what it's like, being an academic?"

I actually did have some notion, but that wasn't what she wanted to hear. I shook my head and let her talk.

Marilyn spread her arms. "You stake out your turf early on, and you spend your whole life defending it, trying to prove that your theory, or someone else's theory you're championing, is right. You take on all comers—in journals, at symposia, in the classroom—and if you're lucky, in the end you're vindicated. But if you're unlucky ..."

Her voice choked off, and tears welled in her eyes again as she looked down at the cold corpse lying on the floor.

▌ ▐ ▌ ▐ ▌ ▐

[Untranslatable proper name] Award: *Award given every [roughly 18 Earth years] for the finest musical compositions produced within the Allied Worlds. Although most species begin making music even prior to developing written language, [The same untranslatable proper name] argued that no truly sophisticated composition had ever been produced by a being with a lifespan of less than [roughly 1,100 Earth years], and since such lifespans only become possible with technological maturity, nothing predating a race's overcoming of natural death is of any artistic consequence. Certainly, the winning compositions bear out her position: the work of composers who lived for [roughly 140 Earth years] or less seem little more than atonal noise when compared to ...*

▌ ▐ ▌ ▐ ▌ ▐

It had begun just two years ago. Michael—that's my son; he was thirteen then—and I got a call from a neighbor telling us we just *had* to put on the TV. We did so, and we sat side by side on the couch, watching the news conference taking place in Pasadena, and then the speeches by the U.S. President and the Canadian Prime Minister.

When it was over, I looked at Michael, and he looked at me. He was a good kid, and I loved him very much—and I wanted him to understand how special this all was. "Take note of where you are, Michael," I said. "Take note of what you're wearing, what I'm wearing, what the weather's like outside. For the rest of your life, people will ask you what you were doing when you heard."

He nodded, and I went on. "This is the kind of event that comes along only once in a great while. Each year, the anniversary of it will be marked; it'll be in all the history books. It might even become a holiday. This is a date like ..."

I looked round the living room, helplessly, trying to think of a date that this one was similar to. But I couldn't, at least not from my lifetime, although my dad had talked about July 20, 1969, in much the same way.

"Well," I said at last, "remember when you came home that day when you were little, saying Johnny Stevens had mentioned something called 9/11 to you, and you wanted to know what it was, and I told you, and you cried. This is like that, in that it's significant ... but ... but 9/11 was such a *bad* memory, such an awful thing. And what's happened today—it's ... it's *joyous*, that's what it is. Today, humanity has crossed a threshold. Everybody will be talking about nothing but this in the days and weeks ahead, because, as of right now"—my voice had actually cracked as I said the words—"we are not alone."

▉ ▉ ▉

Cosmic Microwave Background Radiation: *a highly isotropic radiation with an almost perfect blackbody spectrum permeating the entire universe, at a temperature of approximately [2.7 degrees Kelvin]. Although some primitive cultures mistakenly cite this radiation as proof of a commonly found creation myth—specifically, a notion that the universe began as a singularity that burst forth violently—sophisticated races understand that the cosmic microwave background is actually the result of ...*

It didn't help that the same thing was happening elsewhere. It didn't help one damned bit. I'd been called in to U of T seven times over the past two years, and each time someone had killed himself. It wasn't always a prof; time before McCharles, it had been a Ph.D. candidate who'd been just about to defend his thesis on some abstruse aspect of evolutionary theory. Oh, evolution happens, all right—but it turns out the mechanisms are way more complex than the ones the Darwinians have been defending for a century and a half. I tried not to get cynical about all this, but I wondered if, as he slit his wrists before reproducing, that student had thought about the irony of what he was doing.

The source of all his troubles—of so many people's troubles—was a planet orbiting a star called 54 Piscium, some thirty-six light-years away. For two years now, it had been constantly signaling Earth with flashes of intense laser light.

Well, not quite constantly: it signaled for eighteen hours then paused for twenty, and it fell silent once every hundred and twelve days for a period just shy of two weeks. From this, astronomers had worked out what they thought were the lengths of the day and the year of the planet that was signaling us, and the diameter of that planet's sun. But they weren't sure; nobody was sure of anything anymore.

At first, all we knew was that the signals were artificial. The early patterns of flashes were various mathematical chains: successively larger primes, then Fibonacci sequences in base eight, then a series that no one has quite worked out the significance of but that was sent repeatedly.

But then real information started flowing in, in amazing detail. Our telecommunications engineers were astonished that they'd missed a technique as simple as fractal nesting for packing huge amounts of information into a very narrow bandwidth. But that realization was just the first of countless blows to our egos.

There was a clip they kept showing on TV for ages after we'd figured out what we were receiving: an astronomer from the last century with a supercilious manner going on about how contact with aliens might plug us into the *Encyclopedia Galactica*, a repository of the knowledge of beings millions of years ahead of us in science and technology, in philosophy and mathematics. What wonders it would hold! What secrets it would reveal! What mysteries it would solve!

No one was arrogant like that astronomer anymore. No one could be.

Of course, various governments had tried to put the genie back into the bottle, but no nation has a monopoly on signals from the stars. Indeed, anyone with a few hundred dollars worth of equipment could detect the laser flashes. And deciphering the information wasn't hard; the damned encyclopedia was designed to be read by anyone, after all.

And so the entries were made public—placed on the web by individuals, corporations, and those governments that still thought doing so was a public service. Of course, people tried to verify what the entries said; for some, we simply didn't have the technology. For others, though, we could run tests, or make observations—and the entries always turned out to be correct, no matter how outlandish their claims seemed on the surface.

I thought about Ethan McCharles, swinging from his fiber-optic noose. The poor bastard.

It was rumored that one group had sent a reply to the senders, begging them to stop the transmission of the encyclopedia. Maybe that was even true—but it was no quick fix. After all, any signal sent from Earth would take thirty-six years to reach them, and even if they replied—or stopped—immediately upon receipt of our message, it would take another thirty-six years for that to have an impact here.

Until then at least, data would rain down on us, poison from the sky.

▉ ▉ ▉

Life After Death: *A belief, frequently encountered in unenlightened races, that some self-aware aspect of a given individual survives the death of the body. Although such a belief doubtless gives superstitious primitives a measure of comfort, it is easily proven that no such thing exists. The standard proofs are drawn from (1) moral philosophy, (2) quantum information theory, (3) non-[Untranslatable proper name] hyperparallactic phase-shift phenomenology,* *and (4) comprehensive symbolic philosologic. We shall explore each of these proofs in turn …*

■ ■ ■

"Ethan was a good man," said Marilyn Maslankowski. We had left her husband's office—and his corpse—behind. It was getting late, and the campus was mostly empty. Of course, as I'd seen, it was mostly empty earlier, too—who the hell wanted to waste years getting taught things that would soon be proven wrong, or would be rendered hopelessly obsolete?

We'd found a lounge to sit in, filled with vinyl-covered chairs. I bought Marilyn a coffee from a machine; at least I could do that much for her.

"I'm sure he was," I said. They were always good men—or good women. They'd just backed the wrong horse, and—

No. No, that wasn't right. They'd backed a horse when there were other, much faster, totally invisible things racing as well. We knew nothing.

"His work was his life," Marilyn continued. "He was so dedicated. Not just about his research, either, but as a teacher. His students loved him."

"I'm sure they did," I said. However few of them there were. "Um, how did you get to work today?"

"TTC," she replied. Public transit.

"Where abouts do you live?"

"We have a condo near the lake, in Etobicoke."

We. She'd probably say "we" for months to come.

She'd finished her coffee, and I drained mine in a final gulp. "Come on," I said. "I'll give you a lift home."

We headed down some stairs and out to the street. It was dark, and the sky seemed a uniform black: the glare of street lamps banished the stars. If only it were so easy …

We got into my car, and I started driving. Earlier, she'd called her two adult children. One, her daughter, was rushing back to the city from a skiing trip—artificial snow, of course. The other, her son, was in Los Angeles, but was taking the red-eye, and would be here by morning.

"Why are they doing this?" she asked, as we drove along. "Why are the aliens doing this?"

I moved into the left lane and flicked on my turn signal. *Blink, blink, blink.*

Off in the distance we could see the tapered needle of the CN Tower, Toronto's—and, when I was younger—the world's tallest building, stretching over half a kilometer into the air. Lots of radio and television stations broadcast from it, and so I pointed at it. "Presumably they became aware of us through our radio and TV programs—stuff we leaked out into space." I tried to make my tone light. "Right now, they'd be getting our shows from the 1970s—have you ever seen any of that stuff? I suppose they think they're uplifting us. Bringing us out of the dark ages."

Marilyn looked out the passenger window. "There's nothing wrong with darkness," she said. "It's comforting." She didn't say anything further as we continued along. The city was gray and unpleasant. Christmas had come and gone, and—

Funny thing; I hadn't thought about it until just now. Used to be at Christmas, you'd see stars everywhere: on the top of trees, on lampposts, all over the place. After all, a star had supposedly heralded Jesus' birth. But I couldn't recall seeing a single one this past Christmas. Signals from the heavens just didn't have the same appeal anymore ...

Marilyn's condo tower was about twenty stories tall, and some of the windows had tinfoil covering them instead of curtains. It looked like it used to be an upscale building, but so many people had lost their jobs in the past two years. I pulled into the circular driveway. She looked at me, and her eyes were moist. I knew it was going to be very difficult for her to go into her apartment. Doubtless, there'd be countless things of her husband's left in a state that suggested he was going to return. My heart went out to her, but there was nothing I could do, damn it all. They should let us touch them. They should let us hold them. Human contact: it's the only kind that doesn't hurt.

After letting her off, I drove to my house, exhausted emotionally and physically; for most of the trip, the CN Tower was visible in my rearview mirror, as though the city was giving me the finger.

My son Michael was fifteen now, but he wasn't home, apparently. His mother and I had split up more than five years ago, so the house was empty. I sat on the living-room couch and turned on the wall monitor. As always, I wondered how I was going to manage to hold onto this place in my old age. The police pension fund was bankrupt; half the stocks it had invested in were now worthless. Who wanted to own shares in oil companies when an entry might be received showing how to make cold fusion work? Who wanted to own biotechnology stocks when an entry explaining some do-it-yourself gene-resequencing technique might be the very next one to arrive?

The news was on, and, of course, there was the usual report about the encyclopedia entries whose translations had been released today. The entries came in a bizarre order, perhaps reflecting the alphabetical sequence of their names in some alien tongue; we never knew what would be next. There'd be an entry on some aspect of biology, then one on astronomy, then some arcane bit of history of some alien world, then something from a new science that we don't even have a name for. I listened halfheartedly; like most people, I did everything halfheartedly these days.

"One of the latest *Encyclopedia Galactica* entries," said the female reporter, "reveals that our universe is finite in size, measuring some forty-four billion light-years across. Another new entry contains information about a form of combustion based on neon, which our scientist had considered an inert gas. Also, a lengthy article provides a comprehensive explanation of dark matter, the long suspected but never identified source of most of the mass in the universe. It turns out that no such dark matter exists, but rather there's an interrelationship between gravity and tachyons that ..."

Doubtless some people somewhere were happy or intrigued by these revelations. But others were surely devastated, lifetimes of work invalidated. Ah, well. As long as none of them were here in Toronto. Let somebody else, somewhere else, deal with the grieving widows, the orphaned children, the inconsolable boyfriends. I'd had enough. I'd had plenty.

I got up and went to make some coffee. I shouldn't be having caffeine at this hour, but I didn't sleep well these days even when I avoided it. As I stirred whitener into my cup, I could hear the front door opening. "Michael?" I shouted out, as I headed back to the couch.

"Yeah," he called back. A moment later he entered the living room. My son had one side of his head shaved bald, the current street-smart style. Leather jackets, which had been *de rigueur* for tough kids when I'd been Michael's age—not that any tough kid ever said *de rigueur*—were frowned upon now; a synthetic fabric that shone like quicksilver and was as supple as silk was all young people wore these days; of course, the formula to make it had come from an encyclopedia entry.

"It's a school night," I said. "You shouldn't be out so late."

"School." He spat the word. "As if anyone cares. As if any of it matters."

We'd had this argument before; we were just going through the motions. I said what I said because that's what a parent is supposed to say. He said what he said because ...

Because it was the truth.

I nodded, and shut off the TV. Michael headed on down to the basement, and I sat in the dark, staring up at the ceiling.

▮ ▮ ▮

Chronics: *Branch of science that deals with the temporal properties of physical entities. Although most entities in the universe progress through time in an orthrochronic, or forward, fashion, certain objects instead regress in a retrochronic, or backward, fashion. The most common example ...*

▮ ▮ ▮

Yesterday, it turned out, was easy. Yesterday, I only had to deal with *one* dead body.

The explosion happened at 9:42 a.m. I'd been driving down to division headquarters, listening to loud music on the radio with my windows up, and I still heard it. Hell, they probably heard it clear across Lake Ontario, in upstate New York.

I'd been speeding along the Don Valley Parkway when it happened, and had a good view through my windshield toward downtown. Of course, the skyline was dominated by the CN Tower, which—

My God!

—which was now leaning over, maybe twenty degrees off vertical. The radio station I'd been listening to went dead; it had been transmitting from the CN Tower, I supposed. Maybe it was a terrorist attack. Or maybe it was just some bored school kid who'd read the entry on how to produce anti-matter that had been released last week.

There was a seven-story complex of observation decks and restaurants two-thirds of the way up the tower, providing extra weight. It was hard to—

Damn!

My car's brakes had slammed on, under automatic control; I pitched forward, the shoulder belt giving a bit. The car in front of mine had come to a complete stop—as, I could now see, had the car in front of it, and the one in front of that car, too. Nobody wanted to continue driving toward the tower. I undid my seat belt and got out of my car; other motorists were doing the same thing.

The tower was leaning over further now: maybe thirty-five degrees. I assumed the explosion had been somewhere near its base; if it had been antimatter, from what I understood, only a minuscule amount would have been needed.

"There it goes!" shouted someone behind me. I watched, my stomach knotting, as the tower leaned over farther and farther. It would hit other, lesser skyscrapers; there was no way that could be avoided. I was brutally conscious of the fact that hundreds, maybe thousands, of people were about to die.

The tower continued to lean, and then it broke in two, the top half plummeting sideways to the ground. A plume of dust went up into the air, and—

It was like watching a distant electrical storm: the visuals hit you first, well before the sound. And the sound was indeed like thunder, a reverberating, cracking roar.

Screams were going up around me. *"Oh, my God! Oh, my God!"* I felt like I was going to vomit, and I had to hold onto my car's fender for support.

Somebody behind me was shouting, "Damn you, damn you, damn you!" I turned, and saw a man shaking his fist at the sky. I wanted to join him, but there was no point.

This was just the beginning, I knew. People all over the world had read that entry, along with all the others. Antimatter explosions; designer diseases based on new insights into how biology worked; God only knew what else. We needed a firewall for the whole damn planet, and there was no way to erect one.

I abandoned my car and wandered along the highway until I found an off-ramp. I walked for hours, passing people who were crying, people who were screaming, people who, like me, were too shocked, too dazed, to do either of those things.

I wondered if there was an entry in the *Encyclopedia Galactica* about Earth, and, if so, what it said. I thought of Ethan McCharles, swinging back and forth, a flesh pendulum, and I remembered that spontaneous little eulogy Chiu, the security guard, had uttered. Would there be a eulogy for Earth? A few kind words, closing out the entry on us in the next edition of the encyclopedia? I knew what I wanted it to say.

I wanted it to say that we *mattered*, that what we did had worth, that we treated each other well most of the time. But that was wishful thinking, I suppose. All that would probably be in the entry was the date on which our first broadcasts were detected, and the date, only a heartbeat later in cosmic terms, on which they had ceased.

It would take me most of the day to walk home. My son Michael would make his way back there, too, I'm sure, when he heard the news.

And at least we'd be together, as we waited for whatever would come next.

Relativity

Mike Resnick edits a lot of anthologies, and I'm always thrilled when he asks me to contribute to one of them. In 2003, he did a pair of fascinating books for DAW entitled Men Writing Science Fiction as Women *and* Women Writing Science Fiction as Men. *Mike said I could only be in the first, as I was "biologically disqualified" from the second.*

I've always been fascinated by the effect of time dilation on relationships (one of my all-time favorite SF stories is John Varley's "The Pusher"), and so "Relativity" was born.

I'm rather happy with the way the story turned out, but whenever I look at the anthology it originally appeared in, I feel a pang of sadness. One of my best friends, Robyn Herrington, contributed to Women Writing Science Fiction as Men. *She had been mentored through her career by both me and Mike, and we both loved her a lot. Sadly, though, on May 3, 2004, shortly after her story was published, she passed away after a battle with cancer. I'll always miss Robyn, and my latest novel,* Rollback, *is dedicated to her.*

❧ ■ ■ ❧

You can't have brothers without being familiar with *Planet of the Apes*. I'm not talking about the "re-imaging" done by Tim Burton, apparently much ballyhooed in its day, but the Franklin J. Schaffner original—the one that's stood the test of time, the one that, even a hundred years after it was made, boys still watch.

Of course, one of the reasons boys enjoy it is it's very much a guy film. Oh, there had been a female astronaut along for the ride with Chuck Heston, but she died during the long space voyage, leaving just three macho men to meet the simians. The woman ended up a hideous corpse when her suspended-animation chamber failed, and even her name—"Stewart"—served to desexualize her.

Me, I liked the old *Alien* films better. Ellen Ripley was a survivor, a fighter. But, in a way, those movies were a cheat, too. When you got right down to it, Sigourney Weaver was playing a man—and you couldn't even say, as one of my favorite (female) writers does, that she was playing "a man with tits and hips"—'cause ole Sigourney, she really didn't have much of either. Me, I've got not enough of one and too much of the other.

I'd had time to watch all five *Apes* films, all four *Alien* films, and hundreds of other movies during my long voyage out to Athena, and during the year I'd spent exploring that rose-colored world. Never saw an ape, or anything that grabbed onto my face or burst out of my chest—but I did make lots of interesting discoveries that I'm sure I'll be spending the rest of my life telling the people of Earth about.

And now, I had just about finished the long voyage home. Despite what had happened to *Apes*'s Stewart, I envied her her suspended-animation chamber. After all, the voyage back from Athena had taken three long years.

It was an odd thing, being a spacer. My grandfather used to talk about people "going postal" and killing everyone around them. At least the United States Postal Service had lasted long enough to see that term retired, in favor of "going Martian."

That had been an ugly event. The first manned—why isn't there a good non-sexist word for that? Why does "crewed" have to be a homonym for "crude"? Anyway, the first manned mission to Mars had ended up being a bloodbath; the ebook about it—*The Red Planet*—had been the most popular download for over a year.

That little experiment in human psychology finally taught NASA what the reality-television shows of a generation earlier had failed to: that you can't force a bunch of alpha males—or alpha females, for that matter—together, under high-pressure circumstances, and expect everything to go fine. Ever since then, manned—that damn word again—spaceflight had involved only individual astronauts, a single human to watch over the dumb robotic probes and react to unforeseen circumstances.

When I said "single human" a moment ago, maybe you thought I meant "unmarried." Sure, it would seem to make sense that they'd pick a loner for this kind of job, some asocial bookworm—hey, do you remember when books were paper and worms weren't computer viruses?

But that didn't work, either. Those sorts of people finally went stir-crazy in space, mostly because of overwhelming regret. They'd never been married, never had kids. While on Earth, they could always delude themselves into thinking that someday they might do those things, but, when there's not another human being for light-years around, they had to face bitter reality.

And so NASA started sending out—well, color me surprised: more sexism! There's a term "family man" that everyone understands, but there's no corresponding "family woman," or a neutral "family person." But that's what I was: a family woman—a woman with a husband and children, a woman devoted to her family.

And yet ...

And yet my children were grown. Sarah was nineteen when I'd left Earth, and Jacob almost eighteen.

And my husband, Greg? He'd been forty-two, like me. But we'd endured being apart before. Greg was a paleoanthropologist. Three, four months each year, he was in South Africa. I'd gone along once, early in our marriage, but that was before the kids.

Damn ramscoop caused enough radio noise that communication with Earth was impossible. I wondered what kind of greeting I'd get from my family when I finally returned.

▌▐ ▌▐ ▌▐

"You're going *where?*" Greg always did have a flair for the dramatic.

"Athena," I said, watching him pace across our living room. "It's the fourth planet of—"

"I know what it is, for Pete's sake. How long will the trip take?"

"Total, including time on the planet? Seven years. Three out, one exploring, and three back."

"Seven years!"

"Yes," I said. Then, averting my eyes, I added, "From my point of view."

"What do you mean, 'From your point ...?' Oh. Oh, crap. And how long will it be from *my* point of view?"

"Thirty years."

"Thirty! Thirty! Thirty ..."

"Just think of it, honey," I said, getting up from the couch. "When I return, you'll have a trophy wife, twenty-three years your junior."

I'd hoped he would laugh at that. But he didn't. Nor did he waste any time getting to the heart of the matter. "You don't seriously expect me to wait for you, do you?"

I sighed. "I don't expect anything. All I know is that I can't turn this down."

"You've got a family. You've got kids."

"Lots of people go years without seeing their kids. Sarah and Jacob will be fine."

"And what about me?"

I draped my arms around his neck, but his back was as stiff as a rocket. "You'll be fine, too," I said.

▟ ▟ ▟

So am I a bad mother? I certainly wasn't a bad one when I'd been on Earth. I'd been there for every school play, every soccer game. I'd read to Sarah and Jacob, and taught Sarah to cook. Not that she needed to know how: instant food was all most people ever ate. But she *liked* to cook, and I did, too, and to hell with the fact that it was a traditional female thing to do.

The mission planners thought they were good psychologists. They'd taken holograms of Jacob and Sarah just before I'd left, and had computer-aged them three decades, in hopes of preparing me for how they'd look when we were reunited. But I'd only ever seen such things in association with missing children and their abductors, and looking at them—looking at a Sarah who was older now than I myself was, with a lined face and gray in her hair and angle brackets at the corners of her eyes—made me worry about all the things that could have happened to my kids in my absence.

Jacob might have had to go and fight in some goddamned war. Sarah might have, too—they drafted women for all positions, of course, but she was older than Jacob, and the president always sent the youngest children off to die first.

Sarah could have had any number of kids by now. She'd been going to school in Canada when I left, and the ZPG laws—the *zed-pee-gee* laws, as they called them up there—didn't apply in that country. And *those* kids—

Those kids, my grandkids, could be older now than my own kids had been when I'd left them behind. I'd wanted to have it all: husband, kids, career, the stars. And I'd come darn close—but I'd almost certainly missed out on one of the great pleasures of life, playing with and spoiling grandchildren.

Of course, Sarah and Jacob's kids might have had kids of their own by now, which would make me their ...

Oh, my.

Their *great-grandmother*. At a biological age of 49 when I return to Earth, maybe that would qualify me for a listing in *Guinness eBook of Solar System Records*.

Just what I need.

■ ■ ■

There's no actual border to the solar system—it just sort of peters out, maybe a light year from the sun, when you find the last cometary nucleus that's gravitationally bound to Sol. So the official border—the point at which you were considered to be within solar space, for the purpose of Earth's laws—was a distance of 49.7 AU from the sun, the maximal radius of Pluto's orbit. Pluto's orbit was inclined more than 17 degrees to the ecliptic, but I was coming in at an even sharper angle. Still, when the ship's computer informed me that I'd passed that magic figure—that I was now less than 49.7 times the radius of Earth's orbit from the sun—I knew I was in the home stretch.

I'd be a hero, no doubt about that (and, no, not a heroine, thank you very much). I'd be a celebrity. I'd be on TV—or whatever had replaced TV in my absence.

But would I still be a wife? A mother?

I looked at the computer-generated map. Getting closer all the time ...

■ ■ ■

You might think the idea of being an old-fashioned astronaut was an oxymoron. But consider history. John Glenn, he was right out of Norman Rockwell's U. S. of A., and he'd gone into space not once but twice, with a sojourn in Washington in between. As an astronaut, he'd been on the cutting edge. As a man, he was conservative and family-centered; if he'd run for the presidency, he'd probably have won.

Well, I guess I'm an old-fashioned astronaut, too. I mean, sure, Greg had spent months each year away from home, while I raised the kids in Cocoa Beach and worked at the Kennedy Space Center (my whole CV could be reduced to initials: part-time jobs at KFC while going to university, then full-time work at KSC: from finger-lickin' good to giant leaps for ... well, for you know who).

When Greg was in South Africa, he searched for *Australopithecus africanus* and *Homo sterkfonteinensis* fossils. Of course, a succession of comely young coeds (one of my favorite Scrabble words—nobody knew it anymore) had accompanied him there. And Greg would argue that it was just human nature, just his genes, that had led him to bed as many of them as possible. Not that he'd ever confessed. But a woman could tell.

Me, I'd never strayed. Even with all the beefcake at the Cape—my cape, not his—I'd always been faithful to him. And he had to know that I'd been alone these last seven—these last thirty—years.

God, I miss him. I miss everything about him: the smell of his sweat, the roughness of his cheek late in the day, the way his eyes had always watched me when I was undressing.

But did he miss me? Did he even remember me?

The ship was decelerating, of course. That meant that what had been my floor up until the journey's halfway point was now my ceiling—my world turned upside down.

Earth loomed.

■ ■ ■

I wasn't going to dock with any of the space stations orbiting Earth. After all, technology kept advancing, and there was no reason for them to keep thirty-year-old adapter technology around just for the benefit of those of us who'd gone on extrasolar missions. No, my ship, the *Astarte*—"Ah-star-tee," as I kept having to remind Greg, who found it funny to call it the *Ass Tart*—had its own planetary lander, the same one that had taken me down to Athena's surface, four years ago by my calendar.

I'd shut down the ramjet now and had entered radio communication with Houston, although no one was on hand that I knew; they'd all retired. Still, you would have thought someone might have come by especially for this. NASA put Phileas Fogg to shame when it came to keeping on schedule (yeah, I'd had time to read all the classics in addition to watching all those movies). I could have asked about my husband, about my daughter and son, but I didn't. Landing took all my piloting skills, and all my concentration. If they weren't going to be waiting for me at Edwards, I didn't want to know about it until I was safely back on mother Earth.

I fired retros, deorbited, and watched through the lander's sheet-diamond windows as flames flew past. All of California was still there, I was pleased to see; I'd been worried that a big hunk of it might have slid into the Pacific in my absence.

Just like a big hunk of my life might have—

No! Concentrate, Cathy. Concentrate. You can worry about all that later.

And, at last, I touched down vertically, in the center of the long runway that stretched across Roger's Dry Lake.

I had landed.

But was I home?

■ ■ ■

Greg looked *old*.

I couldn't believe it. He'd studied ancient man, and now he'd become one.

Seventy-two.

Some men still looked good at that age: youthful, virile. Others—apparently despite all the medical treatments available in what I realized with a start was now the 22nd century—looked like they had one foot in the grave.

Greg was staring at me, and—God help me—I couldn't meet his eyes. "Welcome back, Cath," he said.

Cath. He always called me that; the robot probes always referred to me as *Cathy.* I hadn't realized how much I'd missed the shorter version.

Greg was no idiot. He was aware that he hadn't aged well, and was looking for a sign from me. But he was still Greg, still putting things front and center, so that we could deal with them however we were going to. "You haven't changed a bit," he said.

That wasn't quite true, but, then again, everything is relative.

Einstein had been a man. I remember being a student, trying to wrap my head around his special theory of relativity, which said there was no privileged frame of reference, and so it was equally true to claim that a spaceship was at rest and Earth was moving away from it as it was to hold the more obvious interpretation, that the ship was moving and Earth was stationary.

But for some reason, time always passed more slowly on the ship, not on Earth.

Einstein had surely assumed it would be the men who would go out into space, and the women who would stay at home, that the men would return hale and youthful, while the women had stooped over and wrinkled up.

Had that been the case, the women would have been tossed aside, just as Einstein had divorced his own first wife, Mileva. She'd been vacationing with their kids—an older girl and a younger boy, just like Greg and I had—in Switzerland when World War I broke out, and had been unable to return to Albert in Berlin. After a few months—only months!—of this forced separation, he divorced her.

But now Greg and my separation was over. And my husband—if indeed he still *was* my husband; he could have gotten a unilateral divorce while I was away—was an old man.

"How are Sarah and Jacob?" I asked.

"They're fine," said Greg. His voice had lost much of its strength. "Sarah—God, there's so much to tell you. She stayed in Canada, and is running a big hypertronics company up there. She's been married, and divorced, and married again. She's got four daughters and two grandsons."

So I *was* a great-grandmother. I swallowed. "And Jacob?"

"Married. Two kids. One granddaughter, another due in April. A professor at Harvard—astronautics, if you can believe that. He used to say he could either follow his dad, looking down, or his mom, looking up." Greg shrugged his bony shoulders. "He chose the latter."

"I wish they were here," I said.

"I asked them to stay away. I wanted to see you first, alone. They'll be here tomorrow." He reached out, as if to take my hand the way he used to, but I didn't respond at once, and his hand, liver-spotted, with translucent skin, fell by his side again. "Let's go somewhere and talk," he said.

▥ ▥ ▥

"You wanted it all," Greg said, sitting opposite me in a little café near Edwards Air Force Base. "The whole shebang." He paused, the first syllable of the word perhaps catching his attention as it had mine. "The whole nine yards."

"So did you," I said. "You wanted your hominids, and you wanted your family." I stopped myself before adding, "And more, besides."

"What do we do now?" Greg asked.

"What did you do while I was gone?" I replied.

Greg looked down, presumably picturing the archeological remains of his own life. "I married again—no one you knew. We were together for fifteen years, and then ..." He shrugged. "And then she died. Another one taken away from me."

It wasn't just in looks that Greg was older; back before I'd gone away, his self-censorship mechanism had been much better. He would have kept that last comment to himself.

"I'm sorry," I said, and then, just so there was no possibility of his misconstruing the comment, I added, "About your other wife dying, I mean."

He nodded a bit, accepting my words. Or maybe he was just old and his head moved of its own accord. "I'm alone now," he said.

I wanted to ask him about his second wife—about whether she'd been younger than him. If she'd been one of those grad students that went over to South Africa with him, the age difference could have been as great as that which now stretched between us. But I refrained. "We'll need time," I said. "Time to figure out what we want to do."

"Time," repeated Greg, as if I'd asked for the impossible, asked for something he could no longer give.

∎ ∎ ∎

So here I am, back on Earth. My ex-husband—he *did* divorce me, after all—is old enough to be my father. But we're taking it one day at a time— equal-length days, days that are synchronized, days in lockstep.

My children are older than I am. And I've got grandchildren. And great-grandchildren, and all of them are wonderful.

And I've been to another world ... although I think I prefer this one.

Yes, it seems you *can* have it all.

Just not all at once.

But, then again, as Einstein would have said, there's no such thing as "all at once."

Everything is relative. Old Albert knew that cold. But I know something better.

Relatives are everything.

And I was back home with mine.

Biding Time

After winning the Hugo Award for Best Novel of the Year late in 2003 (for my novel Hominids, *first volume of my "Neanderthal Parallax" trilogy), I found myself much in demand for public speaking, teaching, scriptwriting, and so on, plus I was also busy editing my own science-fiction line, the Robert J. Sawyer Books imprint published by Fitzhenry & Whiteside.*

I very much enjoyed doing all those things, but the net effect was that by the summer of 2004, I was way behind on my seventeenth novel, which was under contract to Tor Books. And so I made a resolution, after finishing the novella "Identity Theft" on July 14, 2004: I was going to give up writing short fiction. After all, I find writing short stories enormously hard work; I'm much more at home at novel-length. Also, the sad reality is that short fiction pays an order of magnitude less well per word than do my novels.

I dutifully turned down various commissions for the next four months, but in November 2004, I was Guest of Honor at WindyCon 31, a large science-fiction convention in Chicago. Two things happened there that at least temporarily broke my resolve. First, a limited-edition hardcover collection by me called Relativity *was published by WindyCon's sponsoring organization, ISFiC, and I was enormously pleased with how that book turned out. It contained eight short stories (four of which appeared in my previous collection,* Iterations, *and four more of which also appear here in* Identity Theft), *plus almost 60,000 words of my nonfiction: essays, articles, and speeches by me about SF. I decided I liked having collections to put on my brag shelf—but I didn't quite have enough words yet for a third one.*

Second, on the Saturday night of the convention, Carolyn and I had dinner with editor John Helfers, who works for Martin Harry Greenberg's company Tekno-Books, and John's wife Kerrie, plus editor Bill Fawcett and writer Jody-Lynn Nye. We had a terrific time, and a fabulous meal, at Harry Caray's steakhouse, a Chicago institution. I was in a mellow mood, and when John asked me to contribute to an anthology of cross-genre SF stories—tales that combined science fiction and any other category—I found myself saying yes.

Of course, saying yes is the easy part. Coming up with the story is the hard part—normally. But not this time. I had already built a cross-genre world for my novella "Identity Theft," and I had a motive for a murder already in mind. I'd devised it originally for my novel Mindscan, *but then cut the subplot that used it from the final version of the book. I married that salvaged idea to the world of Martian private eye Alex Lomax, and this story was born. I'm now back on my "no more short fiction" kick, and so "Biding Time" may in fact be the last short story I will ever write.*

But I'm pleased to be going out with a bang: just as I was putting the finishing touches on this book, I got word that renowned mystery writer Peter Robinson had selected "Biding Time" for The Penguin Book of Crime Stories *(and for a bigger reprint fee than I got for writing the story in the first place!). And on top of that, as I was proofreading the galleys for this collection, "Biding Time" won the Aurora Award for best English-language short story of the year.*

Like its prequel, "Identity Theft," this story is set in New Klondike on Mars. And on the day after I sent this book manuscript off to the publisher, I headed off for the old Klondike, *here on Earth, for a three-month-long writing retreat at the childhood home in Dawson City of famed Canadian nonfiction writer Pierre Berton. And although I have a specific novel to be working on there—the first volume of my upcoming* WWW *trilogy—I'm sure the surroundings will keep me thinking about the Great Martian Fossil Rush.*

⚜ ■ ■ ⚜

Ernie Gargalian was fat—"Gargantuan Gargalian," some called him. Fortunately, like me, he lived on Mars; it was a lot easier to carry extra weight here. He must have massed a hundred and fifty kilos, but it felt like a third of what it would have on Earth.

Ironically, Gargalian was one of the few people on Mars wealthy enough to fly back to Earth as often as he wanted to, but he never did; I don't think he planned to ever set foot on the mother planet again, even though it was where all his rich clients were. Gargalian was a dealer in Martian fossils: he brokered the transactions between those lucky prospectors who found good specimens and wealthy collectors back on Earth, taking the same oversize slice of the financial pie as he would have of a real one.

His shop was in the innermost circle—appropriately; he knew *everyone*. The main door was transparent alloquartz with his business name and trading hours laser-etched into it; not quite carved in stone, but still a degree of permanence suitable to a dealer in prehistoric relics. The business's name was Ye Olde Fossil Shoppe—as if there were any other kind.

The shoppe's ye olde door slid aside as I approached—somewhat noisily, I thought. Well, Martian dust gets everywhere, even inside our protective dome; some of it was probably gumming up the works.

Gargalian, seated by a long worktable covered with hunks of rock, was in the middle of a transaction. A prospector—grizzled, with a deeply lined face; he could have been sent over from Central Casting—was standing next to Gargantuan (okay, I was one of those who called him that, too). Both of them were looking at a monitor, showing a close-up of a rhizomorph fossil. "*Aresthera weingartenii*," Gargalian said, with satisfaction; he had a clipped Lebanese accent and a deep, booming voice. "A juvenile, too—we don't see many at this particular stage of development. And see that rainbow sheen? Lovely. It's been permineralized with silicates. This will fetch a nice price—a nice price indeed."

The prospector's voice was rough. Those of us who passed most of our time under the dome had enough troubles with dry air; those who spent half their lives in surface suits, breathing bottled atmosphere, sounded particularly raspy. "How nice?" he said, his eyes narrowing.

Gargantuan frowned while he considered. "I can sell this quickly for perhaps eleven million ... or, if you give me longer, I can probably get thirteen. I have some clients who specialize in *A. weingartenii* who will pay top coin, but they are slow in making up their minds."

"I want the money fast," said the prospector. "This old body of mine might not hold out much longer."

Gargalian turned his gaze from the monitor to appraise the prospector, and he caught sight of me as he did so. He nodded in my direction, and raised a single finger—the finger that indicated "one minute," not the other finger, although I got that often enough when I entered places, too. He nodded at the prospector, apparently agreeing that the guy wasn't long for this or any other world, and said, "A speedy resolution, then. Let me give you a receipt for the fossil ..."

I waited for Gargalian to finish his business, and then he came over to where I was standing. "Hey, Ernie," I said.

"Mr. Double-X himself!" declared Gargalian, bushy eyebrows rising above his round, flabby face. He liked to call me that because both my first and last names—Alex Lomax—ended in that letter.

I pulled my datapad out of my pocket and showed him a picture of a seventy-year-old woman, with gray hair cut in sensible bangs above a crabapple visage. "Recognize her?"

Gargantuan nodded, and his jowls shook as he did so. "Sure. Megan Delacourt, Delany, something like that, right?"

"Delahunt," I said.

"Right. What's up? She your client?"

"She's *nobody's* client," I said. "The old dear is pushing up daisies."

I saw Gargalian narrow his eyes for a second. Knowing him, he was trying to calculate whether he'd owed her money or she'd owed him money. "Sorry to hear that," he said with the kind of regret that was merely polite, presumably meaning that at least he hadn't lost anything. "She was pretty old."

"'Was' is the operative word," I said. "She'd transferred."

He nodded, not surprised. "Just like that old guy wants to." He indicated the door the prospector had now exited through. It was a common-enough scenario. People come to Mars in their youth, looking to make their fortunes by finding fossils here. The lucky ones stumble across a valuable specimen early on; the unlucky ones keep on searching and searching, getting older in the process. If they ever do find a decent specimen, first thing they do is transfer before it's too late. "So, what is it?" asked Gargalian. "A product-liability case? Next of kin suing NewYou?"

I shook my head. "Nah, the transfer went fine. But somebody killed the uploaded version shortly after the transfer was completed."

Gargalian's bushy eyebrows went up. "Can you do that? I thought transfers were immortal."

I knew from bitter recent experience that a transfer could be killed with equipment specifically designed for that purpose, but the only broadband disrupter here on Mars was safely in the hands of the New Klondike constabulary. Still, I'd seen the most amazing suicide a while ago, committed by a transfer.

But this time the death had been simple. "She was lured down to the shipyards, or so it appears, and ended up standing between the engine cone of a big rocketship, which was lying on its belly, and a brick wall. Someone fired the engine, and she did a Margaret Hamilton."

Gargalian shared my fondness for old films; he got the reference and winced. "Still, there's your answer, no? It must have been one of the rocket's crew—someone who had access to the engine controls."

I shook my head. "No. The cockpit was broken into."

Ernie frowned. "Well, maybe it was one of the crew, trying to make it look like it *wasn't* one of the crew."

God save me from amateur detectives. "I checked. They all had alibis—and none of them had a motive, of course."

Gargantuan made a harrumphing sound. "What about the original version of Megan?" he asked.

"Already gone. They normally euthanize the biological original immediately after making the copy; can't have two versions of the same person running around, after all."

"Why would anyone kill someone after they transferred?" asked Gargalian. "I mean, if you wanted the person dead, it's got to be easier to off them when they're still biological, no?"

"I imagine so."

"And it's still murder, killing a transfer, right? I mean, I can't recall it ever happening, but that's the way the law reads, isn't it?"

"Yeah, it's still murder," I said. "The penalty is life imprisonment—down on Earth, of course." With any sentence longer than two mears—two Mars years—it was cheaper to ship the criminal down to Earth, where air is free, than to incarcerate him or her here.

Gargantuan shook his head, and his jowls, again. "She seemed a nice old lady," he said. "Can't imagine why someone would want her dead."

"The 'why' is bugging me, too," I said. "I know she came in here a couple of weeks ago with some fossil specimens to sell; I found a receipt recorded in her datapad."

Gargalian motioned toward his desktop computer, and we walked over to it. He spoke to the machine, and some pictures of fossils appeared on the same monitor he'd been looking at earlier. "She brought me three pentapeds. One was junk, but the other two were very nice specimens."

"You sold them?"

"That's what I do."

"And gave her her share of the proceeds?"

"Yes."

"How much did it come to?"

He spoke to the computer again, and pointed at the displayed figure. "Total, nine million solars."

I frowned. "NewYou charges 7.5 million for their basic service. There can't have been enough cash left over after she transferred to be worth killing her for, unless ..." I peered at the images of the fossils she'd brought in, but I was hardly a great judge of quality. "You said two of the specimens were really nice." 'Nice' was Gargantuan's favorite adjective; he'd apparently never taken a creative-writing course.

He nodded.

"*How* nice?"

He laughed, getting my point at once. "You think she'd found the alpha?"

I lifted my shoulders a bit. "Why not? If she knew where it was, that'd be worth killing her for."

The alpha deposit was where Simon Weingarten and Denny O'Reilly—the two private explorers who first found fossils on Mars—had collected their original specimens. That discovery had brought all the other fortune-seekers from Earth. Weingarten and O'Reilly had died twenty mears ago—their heat shield had torn off while re-entering Earth's atmosphere after their third trip here—and the location of the alpha died with them. All anyone knew was that it was somewhere here in the Isidis Planitia basin; whoever found it would be rich beyond even Gargantuan Gargalian's dreams.

"I told you, one of the specimens was junk," said Ernie. "No way it came from the alpha. The rocks of the alpha are extremely fine-grained—the preservation quality is as good as that from Earth's Burgess Shale."

"And the other two?" I said.

He frowned, then replied almost grudgingly, "They were good."

"Alpha good?"

His eyes narrowed. "Maybe."

"She could have thrown in the junk piece just to disguise where the others had come from," I said.

"Well, even junk fossils are hard to come by."

That much was true. In my own desultory collecting days, I'd never found so much as a fragment. Still, there had to be a reason why someone would kill an old woman just after she'd transferred her consciousness into an artificial body.

And if I could find that reason, I'd be able to find her killer.

❚❚❚ ❚❚❚ ❚❚❚

My client was Megan Delahunt's ex-husband—and he'd been ex for a dozen mears, not just since Megan had died. Jersey Delahunt had come into my little office at about half-past ten that morning. He was shrunken with age, but looked as though he'd been broad-shouldered in his day. A few wisps of white hair were all that was left on his liver-spotted head. "Megan struck it rich," he'd told me.

I'd regarded him from my swivel chair, hands interlocked behind my head, feet up on my battered desk. "And you couldn't be happier for her."

"You're being sarcastic, Mr. Lomax," he said, but his tone wasn't bitter. "I don't blame you. Sure, I'd been hunting fossils for thirty-six Earth years, too. Megan and me, we'd come here to Mars together, right at the beginning of the rush, hoping to make our fortunes. It hadn't lasted though—our marriage, I mean; the dream of getting rich lasted, of course."

"Of course," I said. "Are you still named in her will?"

Jersey's old, rheumy eyes regarded me. "Suspicious, too, aren't you?"

"That's what they pay me the medium-sized bucks for."

He had a small mouth, surrounded by wrinkles; it did the best it could to work up a smile. "The answer is no, I'm not in her will. She left everything to our son Ralph. Not that there was much left over after she spent the money to upload, but whatever there was, he got—or will get, once her will is probated."

"And how old is Ralph?"

"Thirty-four." Age was always expressed in Earth years.

"So he was born after you came to Mars? Does he still live here?"

"Yes. Always has."

"Is he a prospector, too?"

"No. He's an engineer. Works for the water-recycling authority."

I nodded. Not rich, then. "And Megan's money is still there, in her bank account?"

"So says the lawyer, yes."

"If all the money is going to Ralph, what's your interest in the matter?"

"My interest, Mr. Lomax, is that I once loved this woman very much. I left Earth to come here to Mars because it's what she wanted to do. We lived together for ten mears, had children together, and—"

"Children," I repeated. "But you said all the money was left to your *child*, singular, this Ralph."

"My daughter is dead," Jersey said, his voice soft.

It was hard to sound contrite in my current posture—I was still leaning back with feet up on the desk. But I tried. "Oh. Um. I'm ... ah ..."

"You're sorry, Mr. Lomax. Everybody is. I've heard it a million times. But it wasn't your fault. It wasn't anyone's fault, although ..."

"Yes?"

"Although Megan blamed herself, of course. What mother wouldn't?"

"I'm not following."

"Our daughter JoBeth died thirty years ago, when she was two months old." Jersey was staring out my office's single window, at one of the arches supporting the habitat dome. "She smothered in her sleep." He turned to look at me, and his eyes were red as Martian sand. "The doctor said that sort of thing happens sometimes—not often, but from time to time." His face was almost unbearably sad. "Right up till the end, Megan would cry whenever she thought of JoBeth. It was heartbreaking. She couldn't get over it."

I nodded, because that was all I could think of to do. Jersey didn't seem inclined to say anything else, so, after a moment, I went on. "Surely the police have investigated your ex-wife's death."

"Yes, of course," Jersey replied. "But I'm not satisfied that they tried hard enough."

This was a story I'd heard often. I nodded again, and he continued to speak: "I mean, the detective I talked to said the killer was probably off-planet now, headed to Earth."

"That *is* possible, you know," I replied. "Well, at least it is if a ship has left here in the interim."

"Two have," said Jersey, "or so the detective told me."

"Including the one whose firing engine, ah, did the deed?"

"No, that one's still there. *Lennick's Folly*, it's called. It was supposed to head back to Earth, but it's been impounded."

"Because of Megan's death?"

"No. Something to do with unpaid taxes."

I nodded. With NewYou's consciousness-uploading technology, not even death was certain anymore—but taxes were. "Which detective were you dealing with?"

"Some Scottish guy."

"Dougal McCrae," I said. Mac wasn't the laziest man I'd ever met— and he'd saved my life recently when another case had gone bad, so I tried not to think uncharitable thoughts about him. But if there was a poster boy for complacent policing, well, Mac wouldn't be it; he wouldn't bother to get out from behind his desk to show up for the photo shoot. "All right," I said. "I'll take the case."

"Thank you," said Jersey. "I brought along Megan's datapad; the police gave it back to me after copying its contents." He handed me the little tablet. "It's got her appointment schedule and her address book. I thought maybe it would help you find the killer."

I motioned for him to put the device on my desk. "It probably will, at that. Now, about my fee ..."

■ ■ ■

Since Mars no longer had seas, it was all one landmass: you could literally walk anywhere on the planet. Still, on this whole rotten globe, there was only one settlement—our domed city of New Klondike, three kilometers in diameter. The city had a circular layout: nine concentric rings of buildings, cut into blocks by twelve radial roadways. The NewYou franchise—the only place you could go for uploading on Mars—was just off Third Avenue in the Fifth Ring. According to her datapad, Megan Delahunt's last appointment at NewYou had been three days ago, when her transfer had actually been done. I headed there after leaving Ye Olde Fossil Shoppe.

The NewYou franchise was under new management since the last time I'd visited. The rather tacky showroom was at ground level; the brain-scanning equipment was on the second floor. The basement—quite rare on Mars, since the permafrost was so hard to dig through—was mostly used for storage.

"Mr. Lomax!" declared Horatio Fernandez, an employee held over from the previous ownership. Fernandez was a beefy guy—arms as big around as Gargalian's, but his bulk was all muscle.

"Hello," I said. "Sorry to bother you, but—"

"Let me guess," said Fernandez. "The Megan Delahunt murder."

"Bingo."

He shook his head. "She was really pleasant."

"So people keep telling me."

"It's true. She was a real lady, that one. Cultured, you know? Lots of people here, spending their lives splitting rocks, they get a rough edge. But not her; she was all 'please' and 'thank you.' Of course, she was pretty long in the tooth ..."

"Did she have any special transfer requests?" I asked.

"Nah. Just wanted her new body to look the way she had fifty Earth years ago, when she was twenty—which was easy enough."

"What about mods for outside work?" Lots of transfers had special equipment installed in their new bodies so that they could operate more easily on the surface of Mars.

"Nah, nothing. She said her fossil-hunting days were over. She was looking forward to a nice long future, reading all the great books she'd never had time for before."

If she'd found the alpha, she'd probably have wanted to work it herself, at least for a while—if you're planning on living forever, and you had a way to become super-rich, you'd take advantage of it. "Hmmph," I said. "Did she mention any titles?"

"Yeah," said Fernandez. "She said she was going to start with *Remembrance of Things Past*."

I nodded, impressed at her ambition. "Anybody else come by to ask about her since she was killed?"

"Well, Detective McCrae called."

"Mac came here?"

"No, he *called*. On the phone."

I smiled. "That's Mac."

▦ ▦ ▦

I headed over to Gully's Gym, since it was on the way to my next stop, and did my daily workout—treadmill, bench press, and so on. I worked up quite a sweat, but a sonic shower cleaned me up. Then it was off to the shipyards. Mostly, this dingy area between the eighth and ninth circles was a grave for abandoned ships, left over from the early fossil-rush days when people were coming to Mars in droves. Now only a small amount of maintenance work was done here. My last visit to the shipyards had been quite unpleasant—but I suppose it hadn't been as bad as Megan Delahunt's last visit.

I found *Lennick's Folly* easily enough. It was a tapered spindle, maybe a hundred meters long, lying on its side. The bow had a couple of square windows, and the stern had a giant engine cone attached. There was a gap of only a few meters between the cone and a brick firewall, which was now covered with soot. Whatever had been left of Megan's shiny new body had already been removed.

The lock on the cockpit door hadn't been repaired, so I had no trouble getting in. Once inside the cramped space, I got to work.

There were times when a private detective could accomplish things a public one couldn't. Mac had to worry about privacy laws, which were as tight here on Mars as they were back down on Earth—and a good thing, too, for those, like me, who had come here to escape our pasts. Oh, Mac doubtless had collected DNA samples here—gathering them at a crime scene was legal—but he couldn't take DNA from a suspect to match against specimens from here without a court order, and to get that, he'd have to show good reason up front for why the suspect might be guilty—which, of course, was a catch-22. Fortunately, the only catch-22 I had to deal with was the safety on my trusty old Smith & Wesson .22.

I used a GeneSeq 109, about the size of a hockey puck. It collected even small fragments of DNA in a nanotrap, and could easily compare sequences from any number of sources. I did a particularly thorough collecting job on the control panel that operated the engine. Of course, I looked for fingerprints, too, but there weren't any recent ones, and the older ones had been smudged either by someone operating the controls with gloved hands, which is what I suspected, or, I suppose, by artificial hands—a transfer offing a transfer; that'd be a first.

Of course, Mac knew as well as I did that family members commit most murders. I'd surreptitiously taken a sample from Jersey Delahunt when he'd visited my office; I sample everyone who comes there. But my GeneSeq reported that the DNA collected here didn't match Jersey's. That wasn't too surprising: I'd been hired by guilty parties before, but it was hardly the norm—or, at least, the kind of people who hired me usually weren't guilty of the particular crime they wanted me to investigate.

And so I headed off to find the one surviving child of Megan and Jersey Delahunt.

Jersey had said his son Ralph had been born shortly after he and Megan had come to Mars thirty-six Earth years ago. Ralph certainly showed all the signs of having been born here: he was 210 centimeters if he was an inch; growing up in Mars's low gravity had that effect. And he was a skinny thing, with rubbery, tubular limbs—Gumby in an olive-green business suit. Most of us here had been born on Earth, and it still showed in our musculature, but Ralph was Martian, through and through.

His office at the water works was much bigger than mine, but, then, he didn't personally pay the rent on it. I had a DNA collector in my palm when I shook his hand, and while he was getting us both coffee from a maker on his credenza, I transferred the sample to the GeneSeq, and set it to comparing his genetic code to the samples from the rocket's cockpit.

"I want to thank you, Mr. Lomax," Ralph said, handing me a steaming mug. "My father called to say he'd hired you. I'm delighted. Absolutely delighted." He had a thin, reedy voice, matching his thin, reedy body. "How anyone could do such a thing to my mother ..."

I smiled, sat down, and took a sip. "I understand she was a sweet old lady."

"That she was," said Ralph, taking his own seat on the other side of a glass-and-steel desk. "That she was."

The GeneSeq bleeped softly three times, each bleep higher pitched than the one before—the signal for a match. "Then why did you kill her?" I said.

He had his coffee cup halfway to his lips, but suddenly he slammed it down, splashing double-double, which fell to the glass desktop in Martian slo-mo. "Mr. Lomax, if that's your idea of a joke, it's in very poor taste. The funeral service for my mother is tomorrow, and—"

"And you'll be there, putting on an act, just like the one you're putting on now."

"Have you no decency, sir? My mother ..."

"Was killed. By someone she trusted—someone who she would follow to the shipyards, someone who told her to wait in a specific spot while he—

what? Nipped off to have a private word with a ship's pilot? Went into the shadows to take a leak? Of course, a professional engineer could get the manual for a spaceship's controls easily enough, and understand it well enough to figure out how to fire the engine."

Ralph's flimsy form was quaking with rage, or a good simulation of it. "Get out. Get out now. I think I speak for my father when I say, you're fired."

I didn't get up. "It was damn-near a perfect crime," I said my voice rock-steady. "*Lennick's Folly* should have headed back to Earth, taking any evidence of who'd been in its cockpit with her; indeed, you probably hoped it'd be gone long before the melted lump that once was your mother was found. But you can't fire engines under the dome without consuming a lot of oxygen—and somebody has to pay for that. It doesn't grow on trees, you know—well, down on Earth it does, sort of. But not here. And so the ship is hanging around, like the tell-tale heart, like an albatross, like"—I sought a third allusion, just for style's sake, and one came to me: "like the sword of Damocles."

Ralph looked left and right. There was no way out, of course; I was seated between him and the door, and my Smith & Wesson was now in my hand. He might have done a sloppy job, but I never do. "I ... I don't know what you're talking about," he said.

I made what I hoped was an ironic smile. "Guess that's another advantage of uploading, no? No more DNA being left behind. It's almost impossible to tell if a specific transfer has been in a specific room, but it's child's play to determine what biologicals have gone in and out of somewhere. Did you know that cells slough off the alveoli of your lungs and are exhaled with each breath? Oh, only two or three—but today's scanners have no trouble finding them, and reading the DNA in them. No, it's open-and-shut that you were the murderer: you were in the cockpit of *Lennick's Folly*, you touched the engine controls. Yeah, you were bright enough to wear gloves—but not bright enough to hold your breath."

He got to his feet, and started to come around from behind his funky desk. I undid the safety on my gun, and he froze.

"I frown on murder," I said, "but I'm all for killing in self-defense—so

I'd advise you to stand perfectly still." I waited to make sure he was doing just that, then went on. "I know *that* you did it, but I still don't know why. And I'm an old-fashioned guy—grew up reading Agatha Christie and Peter Robinson. In the good old days, before DNA and all that, detectives wanted three things to make a case: method, motive, and opportunity. The method is obvious, and you clearly had opportunity. But I'm still in the dark on the motive, and, for my own interest, I'd like to know what it was."

"You can't prove any of this," sneered Ralph. "Even if you have a DNA match, it's inadmissible."

"Dougal McCrae is lazy, but he's not stupid. If I tip him off that you definitely did it, he'll find a way to get the warrant. Your only chance now is to tell me *why* you did it. Hell, I'm a reasonable man. If your justification was good enough, well, I've turned a blind eye before. So, tell me: why wait until your mother uploaded to kill her? If you had some beef with her, why didn't you off her earlier?" I narrowed my eyes. "Or had she done something recently? She'd struck it rich, and that sometimes changes people—but ..." I paused, and after a few moments, I found myself nodding. "Ah, of course. She struck it rich, and she was old. You'd thought, hey, she's going to drop off soon, and you'll inherit her newfound fortune. But when she squandered it on herself, spending most of it on uploading, you were furious." I shook my head in disgust. "Greed. Oldest motivation there is."

"You really are a smug bastard, Lomax," said Ralph. "And you don't know *anything* about me. Do you think I care about money?" He snorted. "I've never wanted money—as long as I've got enough to pay my life-support tax, I'm content."

"People who are indifferent to thousands often change their ways when millions are at stake."

"Oh, now you're a philosopher, too, eh? I was born here on Mars, Lomax. My whole life I've been surrounded by people who spend all their time looking for paleontological pay dirt. My parents both did that. It was bad enough that I had to compete with things that have been dead for hundreds of millions of years, but ..."

I narrowed my eyes. "But what?"

He shook his head. "Nothing. You wouldn't understand."

"No? Why not?"

He paused, then: "You got brothers? Sisters?"

"A sister," I said. "Back on Earth."

"Older or younger?"

"Older, by two years."

"No," he said. "You couldn't possibly understand."

"Why not? What's that got—" And then it hit me. I'd encountered lots of scum in my life: crooks, swindlers, people who'd killed for a twenty-solar coin. But nothing like this. That Ralph had a scarecrow's form was obvious, but, unlike the one from Oz, he clearly *did* have a brain. And although his mother had been the tin man, so to speak, after she'd uploaded, I now knew it was Ralph who'd been lacking a heart.

"JoBeth," I said softly.

Ralph staggered backward as if I'd hit him. His eyes, defiant till now, could no longer meet my own. "Christ," I said. "How could you? How could anyone ..."

"It's not like that," he said, spreading his arms like a praying mantis. "I was four years old, for God's sake. I—I didn't mean—"

"You killed your own baby sister."

He looked at the carpeted office floor. "My parents had little enough time for me as it was, what with spending twelve hours a day looking for the goddamned alpha."

I nodded. "And when JoBeth came along, suddenly you were getting no attention at all. And so you smothered her in her sleep."

"You can't prove that. Nobody can."

"Maybe. Maybe not."

"She was cremated, and her ashes were scattered outside the dome thirty years ago. The doctor said she died of natural causes, and you can't prove otherwise."

I shook my head, still trying to fathom it all. "You didn't count on how much it would hurt your mother—or that the hurt would go on and on, mear after mear."

He said nothing, and that was as damning as any words could be.

"She couldn't get over it, of course," I said. "But you thought, you know, eventually ..."

He nodded, almost imperceptibly—perhaps he wasn't even aware that he'd done so. I went on, "You thought eventually she would die, and then you wouldn't have to face her anymore. At some point, she'd be gone, and her pain would be over, and you could finally be free of the guilt. You were biding your time, waiting for her to pass on."

He was still looking at the carpet, so I couldn't see his face. But his narrow shoulders were quivering. I continued. "You're still young— thirty-four, isn't it? Oh, sure, your mother might have been good for another ten or twenty years, but *eventually* ..."

Acid was crawling its way up my throat. I swallowed hard, fighting it down. "Eventually," I continued, "you would be free—or so you thought. But then your mother struck it rich, and uploaded her consciousness, and was going to live for centuries if not forever, and you couldn't take that, could you? You couldn't take her always being around, always crying over something that you had done so long ago." I lifted my eyebrows, and made no effort to keep the contempt out of my voice. "Well, they say the first murder is the hardest."

"You can't prove any of this. Even if you have DNA specimens from the cockpit, the police still don't have any probable cause to justify taking a specimen from me."

"They'll find it. Dougal McCrae is lazy—but he's also a father, with a baby girl of his own. He'll dig into this like a bulldog, and won't let go until he's got what he needs to nail you, you—"

I stopped. I wanted to call him a son of a bitch—but he wasn't; he was the son of a gentle, loving woman who had deserved so much better. "One way or another, you're going down," I said. And then it hit me, and I started to feel that maybe there was a little justice in the universe after all. "And that's exactly right: you're going down, to Earth."

Ralph at last did look up, and his thin face was ashen. *"What?"*

"That's what they do with anyone whose jail sentence is longer than two mears. It's too expensive in terms of life-support costs to house criminals here for years on end."

"I—I can't go to Earth."

"You won't have any choice."

"But—but I was *born* here. I'm Martian, born and raised. On Earth, I'd weigh ... what? Twice what I'm used to ..."

"Three times, actually. A stick-insect like you, you'll hardly be able to walk there. You should have been doing what I do. Every morning, I work out at Gully's Gym, over by the shipyards. But you ..."

"My ... my heart ..."

"Yeah, it'll be quite a strain, won't it? Too bad ..."

His voice was soft and small. "It'll kill me, all that gravity."

"It might at that," I said, smiling mirthlessly. "At the very least, you'll be bed-ridden until the end of your sorry days—helpless as a baby in a crib."

Despite my vow to give up short fiction, some offers really are *too good to refuse. In October 2007, I was contacted by Carol Toller, an editor at* Report on Business Magazine, *one of Canada's top glossy magazines (and one that I had written for occasionally in my freelance-journalist days; my last article for them had been in 1992). For their January 2008 issue, the magazine was preparing a look at the business environment a decade down the road. They wanted me to contribute a creative piece, and offered $1.50 a word (by comparison, a really good rate for an SF story from a science-fiction publication is eight cents a word). How could I say no?*

For the record, my real agent is the wonderful Ralph Vicinanza, who also represents Stephen King, the estate of Isaac Asimov, and most of the major SF writers working today—and, no, he's never once called me "baby."

▐█▌ ▐█▌ ▐█▌

MS GoogleHoo E-Mail

INBOX

To: Robert J. Sawyer
From: Big Name Author Multimedia Agency
Date: February 14, 2018, 9:31 a.m. EST
Subject: Going, going ... gone!

Rob, baby, Happy Valentine's Day! Oh, wait—got that dang wavy purple underline in Word: intellectual-property problem. Let me correct that:

Happy FedEx Valentine's Day—when your love absolutely, positively has to be there overnight, heh heh.

Seriously, speaking of sponsorship, we're closing the bidding in two hours on the beverage product placements in your next novel. Please don't give me a hassle this time, okay, Rob? That "I'm an artiste" stuff is *so* last millennium; I don't care if the character is the kind of guy who'd only drink fine wine ... if *you* want to drink anything that isn't rotgut, you'll do it my way!

I'm pretty sure Coke is going to take the Canadian rights, but Pepsi in the U.S. is hot on science fiction right now, what with their billboard on the side of the International Space Station, so I suspect they'll be the high bidder here. And just be happy that Coke and Pepsi haven't merged yet—monopolies mean only one bid!

And, yeah, I know Pepsi pays in U.S. dollars, but, hey, those are still worth something down here even if they don't go very far up in Toronto, and, believe me, I'm barely keeping body and soul together with the paltry 40% commission I'm charging you. What's the greenback worth now? Forty-five cents Canadian? I swear, someday we'll be out of this Iraq quagmire! And don't even get me started on what we're doing in Colombia ...

Anyway, keep that BlackBerry implant of yours turned on, baby! I'll have more news soon.

Your pal in the Big Apple™ (all rights reserved),
Jock

"Intellectual property has the shelf life of a banana."—Bill Gates

To: Robert J. Sawyer
From: Big Name Author Multimedia Agency
Date: February 14, 2018, 11:42 a.m. EST
Subject: Your book is all wet ...

Color me surprised! (Or maybe that should be *colour*—you guys still doing that "u" thing? You *do* know the NorAm Economic Union is going to standardize spellings soon, right?) Anyway, Ontario Clean Water Inc. outbid Pepsi—for the *U.S.* rights. All the characters in your next novel are going to be kicking back cool, clear Canadian H_2O—the best that money can buy (as we New Yorkers well know)!

Hey, speaking of Canada, I wish I'd bought Canadian biotech stocks ten years ago—you guys are going through the roof! Who'd've thunk that the United States would fall so far? But I guess when you stop teaching evolution in the schools, you end up with no competent life scientists. And when you ban stem-cell research and all that, well, it's no surprise that someone else is picking up the slack.

And, on the topic of Canuck ingenuity, man, I love that lawsuit you guys have brought in the World Court! Seeking a royalty on compasses because the magnetic north pole is in Canada—doing that takes Timbits! Still, I guess if it's possible to claim ownership of parts of the human genome—and all sorts of companies do!—you should be able to do the same with other natural phenomena, no? I suppose I'm not the first to suggest that if you win the case, the royalty will come to be known as the pole tax ... :)

Your taxing representation,
Jock

"Software licenses are perhaps the only product besides half-eaten food, underwear and toothbrushes, which can't be resold."—Computer scientist Jordan Pollack

■ ■ ■

To: Robert J. Sawyer
From: Big Name Author Multimedia Agency
Date: February 14, 2018, 12:02 p.m. EST
Subject: And speaking of taxes ...

I always forget about taxes when thinking about life up there in the Great Green-Now-In-Lots-of-Places North. I saw that piece on the *GlobeSunStar* site (hey, remember printed newspapers—man, I'm showing my age!) about your tax-freedom day now coming so late in the year that it coincides with your Thanksgiving. Guess that finally gives you guys a real reason to celebrate that holiday, you Pilgrimless plagiarists, you. Hey, maybe *we* should launch an intellectual property suit over that! I mean, maybe McWendy's should—it's their holiday now.

Yours in literature,
Jock

P.S.: By the way, did I ever tell you how much I love the new novel? Man, if it were still possible to get people to actually buy intellectual property, instead of copying it for free, I bet we could have sold a ton. Ah, well, at least you've got the Canada Council for the Arts up there, until it gets outlawed as an unfair subsidy, and I know its juries love science fiction ... don't they? Hey, shouldn't I be getting a cut of your grants? No, no, Rob, put that meat cleaver down ... :)

"If you cannot protect what you own, you don't own anything." —Jack Valenti, President of the (defunct) Motion Picture Association of America

Robert J. Sawyer is one of only seven writers in history to win all three of the world's top awards for best science fiction novel of the year: the Hugo (which he won for *Hominids*), the Nebula (which he won for *The Terminal Experiment*), and the John W. Campbell Memorial Award (which he won for *Mindscan*); the other winners of all three are David Brin, Arthur C. Clarke, Joe Haldeman, Frederik Pohl, Kim Stanley Robinson, and Connie Willis.

In total, Rob has won forty-one national and international awards for his fiction, including ten Canadian Science Fiction and Fantasy Awards ("Auroras"), three Japanese *Seiun* awards for Best Foreign Novel of the Year, and the *Premio UPC de Ciencia Ficción*, the world's largest cash prize for SF, which he's also won three times. In addition, Rob has won the *Science Fiction Chronicle* Reader Award, the Analytical Laboratory award from *Analog Science Fiction and Fact* magazine, and the Crime Writers of Canada's Arthur Ellis Award, all for Best Short Story of the Year. He's also won the Collectors Award for Most Collectable Author of the Year, as selected by the clientele of Barry R. Levin Science Fiction & Fantasy Literature, the world's leading SF rare-book dealer, and the Galaxy Award—China's top honor in SF—for Most Popular Foreign Author. In addition, he's received an honorary doctorate from Laurentian University and the Alumni Award of Distinction from Ryerson University.

Rob's books are top-ten national mainstream bestsellers in Canada, and have hit number one on the bestsellers' list published by *Locus*, the American trade journal of the SF field. He edits the acclaimed Robert J. Sawyer Books science-fiction imprint for Fitzhenry & Whiteside; is a frequent TV guest, with over two hundred appearances to his credit; and has been keynote speaker at many science, technology, and business conferences.

Rob, who lives in Mississauga, Ontario, with his wife Carolyn, was the first SF author to have a web site, and that site has now grown to contain more than a million words of text. Please visit it at **sfwriter.com**.

ROBERT J. SAWYER BOOKS

Rob Sawyer edits the Robert J. Sawyer Books imprint for Fitzhenry & Whiteside, a line of cutting-edge, thematically rich science-fiction books, including:

Letters from the Flesh by Marcos Donnelly
Getting Near the End by Andrew Weiner
Rogue Harvest by Danita Maslan
The Engine of Recall by Karl Schroeder
Sailing Time's Ocean by Terence M. Green
A Small and Remarkable Life by Nick DiChario
Birthstones by Phyllis Gotlieb
The Commons by Matthew Hughes
Valley of Day-Glo by Nick DiChario
The Savage Humanists edited by Fiona Kelleghan

For more information, see **robertjsawyerbooks.com**.

Copyright for Individual Stories

Introduction copyright 2008 by Robert Charles Wilson.
Individual story introductions copyright 2008 by Robert J. Sawyer.
"Identity Theft," copyright 2005 by Robert J. Sawyer. First published in *Down These Dark Spaceways*, edited by Mike Resnick, Science Fiction Book Club, New York, May 2005.
"Come All Ye Faithful," copyright 2003 by Robert J. Sawyer. First published in *Space Inc.*, edited by Julie E. Czerneda, DAW Books, New York, July 2003.
"Immortality," copyright 2003 by Robert J. Sawyer. First published in *Janis Ian's Stars*, edited by Janis Ian and Mike Resnick, DAW Books, New York, August 2003.
"Ineluctable," copyright 2002 by Robert J. Sawyer. First published in *Analog Science Fiction and Fact*, November 2002.
"Shed Skin," copyright 2002 by Robert J. Sawyer. First published in *The Bakka Anthology*, edited by Kristen Pederson Chew, The Bakka Collection, Toronto, December 2002; first U.S. publication in *Analog Science Fiction and Fact*, January-February 2004.
"The Stanley Cup Caper," copyright 2003 by Robert J. Sawyer. First published in *The Toronto Star*, Sunday, August 24, 2003.
"On The Surface," copyright 2003 by Robert J. Sawyer. First published in *Future Wars*, edited by Martin H. Greenberg and Larry Segriff, DAW Books, New York, April 2003.
"The Eagle Has Landed," copyright 2005 by Robert J. Sawyer. First published in *I, Alien*, edited by Mike Resnick, DAW Books, New York, April 2005.
"Mikeys," copyright 2004 by Robert J. Sawyer. First published in *Space Stations*, edited by Martin H. Greenberg and John Helfers, DAW Books, New York, March 2004.
"The Good Doctor," copyright 1989 by Robert J. Sawyer. First published in *Amazing Stories*, January 1989.
"The Right's Tough," copyright 2004 by Robert J. Sawyer. First published in *Visions of Liberty*, edited by Mark Tier and Martin H. Greenberg, DAW Books, New York, July 2004.
"Kata Bindu," copyright 2004 by Robert J. Sawyer. First published in *Microcosms*, edited by Gregory Benford, DAW Books, New York, January 2004.
"Driving A Bargain," copyright 2002 by Robert J. Sawyer. First published in *Be VERY Afraid!: More Tales of Horror*, edited by Edo van Belkom, Tundra Books, Toronto, 2002.
"Flashes," copyright 2006 by Robert J. Sawyer. First published in *FutureShocks*, edited by Lou Anders, Roc Books, New York, January 2006.
"Relativity," copyright 2003 by Robert J. Sawyer. First published in *Men Writing Science Fiction as Women*, edited by Mike Resnick, DAW Books, New York, November 2003.
"Biding Time," copyright 2006 by Robert J. Sawyer. First published in *Slipstreams*, edited by Martin H. Greenberg and John Helfers, DAW Books, New York, May 2006.
"E-Mails from the Future," copyright 2008 by Robert J. Sawyer. First published in *The Globe and Mail's Report on Business Magazine*, Toronto, January 2008.